Lifelong romance addi... break from her career ... a family and found her ... author instead. She now lives in New Zealand and finds that writing feeds her very real obsession with happy endings and the endorphin rush they create. You can follow her at jcharroway.com, and on Facebook, X and Instagram.

Annie O'Neil spent most of her childhood with her leg draped over the family rocking chair and a book in her hand. Novels, baking and writing too much teenage angst poetry ate up most of her youth. Now Annie splits her time between corralling her husband into helping her with their cows, baking, reading, barrel racing (not really!) and spending some very happy hours at her computer, writing.

MISTLETOE BABY MIX-UP

JC HARROWAY

THEIR CHRISTMAS PREGNANCY SHOCK

ANNIE O'NEIL

MILLS & BOON

First published in Great Britain 2025
by Mills & Boon, an imprint of HarperCollins*Publishers* Ltd,
1 London Bridge Street, London, SE1 9GF

www.harpercollins.co.uk

HarperCollins*Publishers* Macken House, 39/40 Mayor Street Upper,
Dublin 1, D01 C9W8, Ireland

Mistletoe Baby Mix-Up © 2025 JC Harroway

Their Christmas Pregnancy Shock © 2025 Annie O'Neil

ISBN: 978-0-263-32521-8

10/25

This book contains FSC™ certified paper
and other controlled sources to ensure responsible forest management.

For more information visit www.harpercollins.co.uk/green.

Printed and Bound in the UK using 100% Renewable Electricity
at CPI Group (UK) Ltd, Croydon, CR0 4YY

MISTLETOE BABY MIX-UP

JC HARROWAY

MILLS & BOON

To Mum. Thanks for all the Christmas magic.

CHAPTER ONE

Four weeks to Christmas

SPINAL SURGEON CONNIE DUBOIS tucked a stray lock of hair under her surgical hat as she left the theatre changing rooms, energised to be back at work after two days of absence. As she sailed along the corridor, smiling at passing colleagues, she hugged her precious secret to her like a warm, cosy blanket. She'd finally taken control of her personal life and all that was left to do was simply wait and wonder if the intrauterine insemination procedure she'd undergone two days ago might have worked. She could be pregnant right now, not that a pregnancy test would turn positive for a week or more.

Connie headed for her designated operating room for her full day of surgeries ahead. When her phone rang with a call from her best friend, Tristan, she picked up.

'How did it go?' he asked, his voice full of cautious optimism. Wonderful Tris had offered to be her sperm donor so she could have a child all by herself.

'Good. But I'm glad to be back at work.' She rested a hand on her flat stomach and inhaled through the flutter of premature excitement and anticipation.

She'd always wanted a child. Of course, she'd assumed that by the age of thirty-five she might have found the love of her life with whom to have a baby, but that hadn't panned out. Her former fiancé had proved himself a liar and a cheat. The only other man with potential, Tristan's brother Théo... Well, he'd been another massive mistake she regretted.

'Any second thoughts?' Tris asked hesitantly.

'No regrets,' she said, decisively. She didn't need a man in her life. Or love, or even sex. She was a determined and capable professional woman who could and would do this alone.

'How about you and Victor?' she asked about Tristan's soon-to-be husband. Neither he nor Victor wanted children of their own. But all three of them had done their homework and brainstormed the pros and cons of their unconventional decision before proceeding.

'No regrets here either,' Tris said. 'I'm just glad the procedure wasn't too awful for you. Listen, Con... I, um, have something to tell you...'

In that moment, Connie arrived at the theatre reception desk and handed over her pager so it could be answered while she was operating.

'Okay.' Connie glanced at the clock on the wall and winced. 'I'll call you later though, after my surgery. I'm about to scrub in and I'm running late.' Knowing Tristan, who was also a doctor at the same hospital, would understand that patients always came first, she disconnected the call and gave the receptionist instructions to field any urgent enquiries to Connie's registrar, Jules.

In theatre ten's scrub room, she reached for a mask from a box on the wall, her mind turning to the busy day of spinal surgeries ahead. Fortunately she loved her job, so wasn't daunted by the prospect of the long and complex surgery she was about to perform with a colleague.

And her patient, sixteen-year-old Elodie, had been prey-ing on Connie's mind. The young woman's severe scolio-sis had begun to impinge on her breathing. She deserved a life free of pain and physical limitation.

Connie had just raised the mask to her face when the door squeaked open at her back. Expecting it to be Dr Bedeau, the surgical colleague assisting her with this morning's surgery, she turned to greet the man with a warm smile.

Shock snatched at her breath. Her arms fell limply to her sides as she took in the surgeon who'd arrived instead: Théo Augustin, Tristan's older brother.

'What on earth are you doing here?' she asked, stunned and more than a little embarrassed to see the man she disliked almost as much as her ex-fiancé at *her* hospital. And how dared he be just as sexy as when she'd last seen him three years ago?

Tall, broad-shouldered, with untamed dark brown hair and coffee-coloured eyes, he oozed sex appeal and con-fidence, flooding Connie's body with heat and hormones and inconvenient memories of the night she'd stupidly let down her guard and slept with him after too much champagne. It had been lust at first sight when they'd met at *le réveillon de Noël*, the Christmas Eve party at his Paris apartment. Every time she'd sought him out with her eyes that evening, he'd been looking at her, the sexual tension building to frantic levels. When Tristan had headed to bed after the guests had left, she'd offered to load the glasses into the dishwasher and she and Théo had kissed before tearing into each other's clothes, right there in the kitchen.

But they'd both instantly regretted that one night of rebound sex—well, in Connie's case, *almost* instantly. It had taken the humiliation of overhearing Théo express his regrets the next morning to shunt Connie from post-best-sex-of-her-life dream state to one-night-stand remorse.

'Dr Dubois,' he said, his bold stare sweeping over her and his sexy deep voice buzzing at her eardrums like the irritating drone of a chainsaw. 'Good to see you again.'

With her body on fire from humiliation and rejecting his easy-going smile that stretched his sexy mouth and flashed his straight white teeth, Connie watched in horror as he joined her at the sinks without further explanation. He reached for his own mask, confidently tying it on as if he were about to scrub in. On *her* surgery.

'This is *my* OR,' Connie pointed out, still gaping at him in disbelief. 'You must be in the wrong place, the wrong hospital even.'

Had he hit his head and suffered memory loss? He worked at Paris University Hospital, not here at St Raphaël. And despite that one foolish mistake they'd made three years ago, despite Connie's close relationship with Tris, she'd deliberately gone out of her way to avoid this man. But now he was in her face, too close, too hot, too…utterly infuriating even though he'd only spoken a handful of words.

'Haven't you heard?' he asked, shooting her a quizzical look before starting the flow of water to commence his hand-washing routine. As if he were the surgeon in charge. 'I'm assisting you today. The Elodie Verdier case.' Théo shrugged and Connie caught a whiff of his delicious cologne.

'Elodie Verdier is *my* patient,' she snapped, quickly tying on her mask to block out the sexy scent of him, which only flooded her brain with more erotic memories.

'Right,' he said, unfazed, opening a fresh scrubber and lathering up his strong muscular forearms with iodine suds, his movements automatic. 'Sixteen-year-old with a fifty-three-degree thoracic scoliosis, shortness of breath and impaired lung functions tests. I'm up to speed on the case. I met the patient yesterday and reviewed the scans while you were absent.'

Despite the mask covering most of his face, she could tell he was smiling that sexy and charming smile of his. She might still find him attractive, but she'd changed in the past three years. When they'd met her confidence had been at an all-time low after she'd dumped her cheating ex, Guy, six months before.

'But you don't work here,' she pointed out, icy panic sliding through her veins.

'I do as of today,' he said, calmly. 'I've been head-hunted to lead spinal surgery at St Raphaël. We'll be working together from now on. Didn't Chief of Surgery let you know?'

'No…' she muttered, in shock. She couldn't deny that he was a good surgeon, or so she'd heard. But working together?

Théo frowned as if frustrated. 'I was aware my acceptance of the role might cause some…awkwardness, given we slept together,' he said, his stare lingering for a fraction too long, as if he too was remembering that passionate night. 'But the promotion was too good an opportunity to pass up, I'm afraid. Besides, we're both professional adults. I assumed we could leave the past behind.' He worked the scrubber over his hands and under his nails as he spoke. 'If the positions were reversed, I'd hope you wouldn't overlook a promotion simply to avoid me.'

'I can't believe this…' Connie muttered, her doubts building as she processed his words. 'Why didn't Tris warn me about you?'

Unless this had been what her friend had wanted to tell her earlier when she'd been in a hurry and preoccupied with the possible pregnancy.

'That's my fault,' he said with regret. 'I asked Tris to hold off telling you until I knew for sure I wanted to accept the position, which was yesterday. Then it all happened so quickly. They asked me to start right away and I had some annual leave accrued at my former position so I could.'

'But…where's Dr Bedeau?' Connie asked in desperation, determined to be immune to Théo's charms as she fumbled over opening her own scrub brush and tossed the packaging in the bin. This was why she struggled to take time off work. It was easy to lose touch with the goings-on at the hospital and clearly something monumental had occurred while she'd been absent. Théo Augustin had happened!

But she didn't want to operate with Théo Augustin. She didn't want to look at him, talk to him or even think about him. She certainly didn't want to recall that amazing night and the resulting humiliation of the morning after when she'd overheard him voice his regrets they'd slept together to Tristan. Him casting her aside after rebound sex had brought up all the freshly scabbed-over pain of Guy's betrayal and rejection.

Of course, smarting from what her ex had done—lied, cheated and impregnated the other woman—Connie should have known better than to expect anything else from a man…

'Dr Bedeau had some scheduling conflicts today,'

Théo said reasonably. 'When he found out I would be leading the team, he asked me to step in for him. I am quite good at this surgery stuff, you know. No need to look so horrified.'

Connie looked away from his smiling eyes and waved her hand at the sensor to activate the flow of water from her tap, unready to accept his attempts to lighten the mood. 'Don't you think, as a courtesy, consultant to consultant, you should have let me know you'd be assisting with my patient?'

She scrubbed at her nails, desperate now to claw back control of her surgery. 'When it comes to my professional life,' she added, 'I'm afraid I demand honesty and full transparency. So if you plan on working with me, that's something to bear in mind.'

'I did try,' he said, glancing her way with a frown. 'I didn't know you'd be absent. I spoke with Jules, your junior, yesterday on the ward. Didn't he tell you?'

'No.' Connie lathered up her arms and hands, scrubbing so vigorously her skin tingled.

She hadn't had chance to catch up with her registrar yet this morning. And the date for the insemination procedure had been last minute and unplanned to coincide with ovulation.

But why was this happening to her? She'd arrived at work earlier, cradling the possibility of a pregnancy, glad to be back and eager to perform Elodie's surgery. But now she needed to contend with the resurfaced humiliation of that night, her stubborn sexual attraction to the man and awkwardness of having him as a colleague.

'By the way,' he said. 'I'm always honest and transparent.'

Connie gaped under her mask. Him, always honest?

Not in her experience, but then now wasn't the time for personal conversations.

'Is there some unfinished business between us that I'm unaware of?' he continued in that reasonable tone that only wound her tighter. 'I assumed not, given the way things ended.'

'None whatsoever,' she lied, because he was the last person to whom she wanted to show any hint of vulnerability, especially at work. 'As far as I'm concerned, you and I never happened. It was so forgettable.'

He nodded, his stare disbelieving and his eyes crinkling in the corners as he smiled under the mask. 'Yes, you made your regret pretty clear the next morning. Fleeing without so much as a goodbye and ignoring me ever since.'

Connie scrubbed her hands harder. 'The past is the past.' She was focussed on the future. *Her* future, motherhood, a baby.

'All I care about,' she continued, aware of his eyes on her, 'is that you're muscling in on my surgery. This is my patient and I never asked for your help.'

'Some would consider my help and experience invaluable, Connie,' he scoffed, then stepped back from the sink and held his dripping-wet arms before him, his handwashing complete. 'Why don't we, as you suggest, put the past behind us and find some way of working together?'

Connie bit her tongue. He was the more experienced surgeon. His expertise was a good thing for Elodie. She could swallow down her pride and dislike and behave professionally at work for the sake of her patients. And if he'd been invited to take the surgical lead in her department, she'd have no choice but to interact with him. That didn't mean she and Théo Augustin would be having any sort of personal relationship. Not even friends.

'Fine,' she said finally, caught between a rock and a hard place. 'I'll tolerate your assistance on this one occasion.' With Dr Bedeau absent, she unfortunately needed Théo's help. She could definitely use her distrust to counter the fact that she still fancied him. 'But don't make a habit of sneaking into my surgeries without first speaking to me,' she warned.

'Noted,' he said with a nod. After a moment's rapt fascination, where he stared as if he had more to say, he pushed at the door with his back and entered the operating room to gown up.

Connie slowly exhaled, her adrenaline fading. Trying to shove Théo and the memories he ignited from her mind, she focussed on cleaning her hands, her joyously optimistic and potentially life-changing morning washed away like suds down the drain.

CHAPTER TWO

GOWNED UP AND revved up, Théo held his sterile gloved hands in front of him, waiting for Connie to appear in the operating room. These past three years since they slept together, he'd only seen her in photographs with Tristan. But in person, she looked good. *Really* good. Of course, she was also still eager to avoid him. Still cryptic and unfriendly. Still way too sexy...

But trying to pretend as if that night hadn't happened? Was she kidding? Théo had done his best over the years to forget, but no matter how deep his own regrets over the poor timing—he'd slept with Connie Dubois when he was still grieving the death of his brief and tumultuous marriage—forgetting about that night and sex that hot would be a struggle.

Théo sighed. Clearly whatever regrets she'd had after sleeping with him were still very much alive. He'd feared as much, the reason he'd hesitated over taking the job at St Raphaël. But his career had become the second most important thing in his life after Tris. And he truly hoped he and Connie could lay the past to rest.

She appeared from the scrub room, slipping into sterile gown and gloves with the assistance of a scrub nurse. Before he could speak to her again, to try and smooth things over because he could appreciate her dislike of being caught off guard by his sudden appearance, the anaesthetised patient was wheeled in.

While the patient was draped in sterile sheets and attached to the various machines the anaesthetist would use to monitor her, Théo once more tried to make peace.

'Look, I'm sorry that you weren't expecting me,' he said, frustrated that his attraction to her hadn't diminished in the slightest, despite her reception being as frosty as the cold and empty bed he'd returned to that morning three years ago. 'Maybe I should have warned you sooner. But we're about to spend the next few hours operating together.'

Other apologies formed on his tongue as he observed her rigid posture and haughty silence. He should never have slept with her so soon after his divorce. Should never have slept with anyone, least of all a good friend of his brother's. He'd still been emotionally reeling from the failure of his marriage and the dashed hopes of having a family of his own. Of course, the moment he'd met Connie, he'd reeled for a whole other reason—instant, intense and unexpected attraction. The next morning, despite a great night, he'd realised he still wasn't ready for any sort of relationship, which was exactly what he'd planned to tell Connie. Only he'd never had the chance to explain himself or ask her what she expected or let her down gently. She'd left his place without saying goodbye to him or Tris, who'd brought her along to the party, and ignored Théo's texts. Théo had tried to summon up relief that she'd left before they'd had a chance to talk, but for some reason all he'd felt was hollow and guilty.

'Which is why I think it's best if we leave our personal stuff at the door, don't you?' Connie said, stiffly, as if it were anything but fine.

'I agree,' he said, wondering again what she'd meant by all that cloak and dagger stuff about honesty and transparency.

'Good. Let's start, shall we?' Connie said as the theatre technicians manipulated the unconscious patient into the correct position, lying on her side.

As they began the surgery, Théo was eager to discover what kind of surgeon Connie was. 'Are you tethering over spinal fusion?' he asked about the possible corrective procedure for scoliosis that involved a chain of screws placed into the individual vertebrae, which were then connected by a wire under tension that helped to realign the abnormal curvature.

'Yes,' she said, casting him another wary look. 'Why? What would you do?'

Théo stifled a sigh at her defensiveness. 'I'd do the same in this case. It wasn't a trick question, Connie. Have you seen the cutting-edge approaches to scoliosis surgery coming out of Denmark?'

'I've read a few papers on the Holm technique,' she said, casting him a dismissive look as she readied the surgical instruments she'd need.

Théo nodded, impressed that she was across the emerging surgical approaches. 'I've performed it a couple of times,' he said. 'I'd be happy to lead you through it some time.' But his offer was met only with a terse and dismissive nod.

For the next thirty minutes, they worked together in near silence. Considering Connie hadn't been expecting him, nor was he her favourite person, Théo was impressed by how readily they set aside their personal issues and collaborated. With the patient on single lung ventilation—a technique that intentionally collapsed one lung to facilitate visibility of the thoracic spine—they readied the thoracoscope, a camera they could pass into the chest through a small incision between the ribs to visualise the misaligned thoracic vertebrae. The minimally invasive technique was often better for the patient, but required more than two hands.

'Can you please hold the thoracoscope?' Connie asked him once they'd established clear visibility to the severely curved spine.

While Théo held the camera in place, Connie made another small incision between the ribs and passed a further scope inside the chest. The images from the camera were displayed real time onto monitors so the surgeons could accurately guide their instruments to the correct place. With the first few screws successfully placed into the misaligned vertebrae, suddenly the operative field became obscured by blood.

'Suction,' Connie said, quickly switching instruments.

'Let me,' Théo said, taking the suction from her. 'You get ready to cauterise the bleeder.' Théo held the thoracoscope steady in order to maintain visibility and directed the suction while Connie hurriedly manipulated the diathermy probe. It took some coordinated repositioning of the various instruments, but after a few tense moments of cooperation, anticipating what the other person might need, Connie successfully identified the bleeding capillary and quickly sealed it off.

Théo sighed with relief, seeing the same emotion in Connie's eyes as she briefly looked up at him.

'How are things looking there?' she asked the anaesthetist, who monitored Elodie's vital signs: pulse, blood pressure, respiration and blood oxygenation.

'Stable,' he confirmed.

Connie appeared to take a deep breath, carefully checking for further bleeding before she was happy to proceed. Then she looked down from the monitors, her eyes meeting Théo's.

'Thank you,' she said, curtly.

'No problem,' he replied, feeling as if he'd won a major victory not just a simple word of thanks. But as the operation resumed, time passing without further incident, Théo feared things between him and Connie as colleagues would be anything but straightforward. For one thing, he hadn't expected his attraction to her to be as intense as before. Not, it seemed, that he'd need to worry about there being a repeat of that night or starting relationship with a colleague. Connie was a focussed and intuitive surgeon, but, on a personal level, she obviously didn't like or trust him one bit.

St Raphaël Hospital was located in the medieval Latin Quarter of Paris, a short walk from the River Seine. Later that evening, Connie wrapped her woolly scarf around her neck as she left the hospital and crossed the road towards a cobbled square where one of the city's famous Christmas markets was in full swing. After a long day at work, Connie allowed herself to be lured by the magic. Twinkling lights were suspended overhead, strung from every building, lamp post and plane tree around the square. An ice-skating rink occupied the centre, encircled with numerous vendor stalls selling everything from Eiffel Tower Christmas decorations to *vin chaud* or mulled wine and every conceivable type of street food.

Desperately trying to block out Théo's unexpected and inconvenient appearance at St Raphaël, Connie mingled through the crowds of families and tourists, her mind stubbornly contemplating her first day of working with Théo.

After picking up her scalpel, she'd completely ignored their past and focussed on the case. To Connie's annoyance, Théo had seemed to anticipate her every move, instinctively clearing the operative field for better visibility and helpfully passing her instruments just when she needed them. He hadn't once tried to take over or dominate the operation, and by the time they'd sewn Elodie's wounds up, Connie had felt a begrudging gratitude that he'd been there, given his experience and the extra pair of hands. It was no surprise they were more able to effectively communicate about surgery than their personal issues. But rather than stay and chat after, she'd made some excuse and quickly left Theatre.

Now, Connie expelled a sigh. If he was going to be leading spinal surgery at St Raphaël, she would need to find some way to ignore him and all the memories he stirred. But with a possible pregnancy on which to focus, her obstinate attraction to a man from her past was the least of her concerns.

A young couple walking ahead of Connie stopped to kiss under a large, strategically placed bunch of mistletoe. Connie smiled, her heart thudding anew as she remembered the last man she'd kissed with that kind of passion had been Théo. Her handful of tame dates these past three years hadn't progressed beyond a chaste peck on the cheek. To her utter dismay, Théo was still infuriatingly sexy in the same way that had appealed to her the first time they'd met. Driven, intelligent and comfortable in his own skin, he had a way of looking at you as if you were the only person in the room.

Appalled that he could still affect her that way, that she

still fancied him rotten, Connie ambled on through the market, which was crowded and lively with Christmas cheer. Surrounded by so many delicious cooking aromas, her stomach growled. After her long day of surgeries and the adrenaline of working with Théo, she was too tired to contemplate the idea of cooking when she arrived home. Instead, she headed for a stall selling hot *soupe à l'oignon* topped with crusty bread and melted Gruyère cheese. Hopefully the soup would still be warm by the time she arrived at her apartment, two *Métro* stops away.

'I had the same idea,' a deep voice at her side said.

Connie looked up to find Théo smiling broadly. She was caught once more off guard by his stunning sex appeal, her pulse racing fast enough to leave her speechless. Wearing a smart woollen coat and a chic plaid scarf, his cheeks slightly ruddy from the cold, Théo looked ridiculously effortless Parisian chic. And despite the cool reception she'd given him that morning, he peered down at her with his signature confident smile and a glint of the heat it seemed impossible to ignore since they'd been intimate.

Connie smiled tightly, glancing away from that glint in his eyes. Her cheeks warmed with excitement even as she held herself rigid, annoyed by the physical attraction, which came so effortlessly.

'Lunch feels like a long time ago,' she muttered, watching the vendor spoon ladles of steaming soup into a takeaway container before sliding the cheese-topped toasted bread into a separate paper bag. Hoping to avoid the sexy scent of his cologne and the warmth from his body, she took a small step sideways.

'I agree. It does,' Théo said, placing some money on the counter for his own order. 'Can I buy you a *vin chaud*?'

he asked Connie. 'To make up for my unexpected appearance this morning.'

Connie stiffened, shunted off balance by her body's violent responses to his smile and exhilarating eye contact. She didn't want to be rude, but nor could she handle any more of his distracting company. After all, she'd worked valiantly to avoid any mention of him these past three years while she'd put the hurt of that night behind her.

'No, thank you,' Connie replied primly, watching in horror as the stallholder packed both her and Théo's food into side-by-side bags as if they were one of the loved-up couples milling around the market, while another ladled Théo's mulled wine into a takeaway cup.

'Shame,' Théo said in the same playful tone after taking a sip. 'It's delicious.'

Connie pressed her lips together and looked away from his sexy mouth, disgusted with herself. Maybe if he hadn't been so supportive and instructive in Theatre, she might have found him easier to dismiss now. But they weren't friends. She had no intention of confiding her precious secret to him of all people—that she might be carrying his brother's baby.

'Well, I'm heading home,' Connie said, scooping up her dinner and offering Théo a polite smile. 'Goodnight.'

She turned away. Better he understood that she had no personal interest in him whatsoever. She had no interest in any man, especially not one who'd essentially kicked her when she was down. It had taken months after discovering Guy's horrible deception for Connie to even face socialising. Then, when she'd finally accepted one of Tris's many invitations, to his brother's Christmas *réveillon*, she'd foolishly slept with Théo and lived to regret it. She should have known her judgement had still been flawed. But trusting Guy, who she'd believed to be the one, only to find out he'd been living a lie, had left her riddled with self-doubt.

'Hold on.' Théo strode after her, easily catching up. 'Are you heading for the *Métro*?'

'Yes.' Without breaking her stride—no easy feat given the slowly ambling crowds—she tried to put some distance between her and Théo.

'Me too,' he said, still on her tail. 'I'll walk with you.'

Connie paused to shoot him a horrified look. 'Haven't we spent long enough in each other's company today? Why can't you simply ignore me the way we've been ignoring each other for the past three years?'

Bad enough that she'd been forced to set aside how he'd hurt her and watch him work today, to witness how impressive a surgeon he was. Meticulous and diligent and clearly dedicated to his career. There'd been no sign of that arrogance she'd detected when she'd overheard him tell Tris that by sleeping with her he'd been on the rebound and made a mistake.

'I hoped we could talk,' he said, reasonably, 'away from work.' Distracted by a couple of excited children tottering towards the ice rink on their skates, he smiled down at them then glanced back at Connie.

Connie shuddered as her hormones surged. Why did he have to be so good at everything? So sexy and likeable and charming? But his façade couldn't be trusted and she'd been a fool to think he'd be any different from her ex, Guy. After all, they'd been engaged and living together. After four years together, she'd made plans for a future—marriage, a family—that Guy had rewritten with someone else. He'd deceived her and had a child with another woman. She'd felt stupid that she hadn't seen through him. Of course, he'd taken advantage of the fact her career often involved long and unpredictable hours in order to conduct his affair.

'I was actually hoping to invite you out for a drink some time,' Théo went on, smiling, unaware that Connie felt suddenly nauseous with humiliation and rejection. 'After all, we're hardly strangers. And it's Christmas.'

'I thought we said everything we needed to this morning,' she threw out dismissively, heading for the nearest exit from the square, desperate to get away from him and the inconvenient memories he stirred up, both the thrill of that night in his bed and her raw vulnerability when the hurt Guy had caused came rushing back the next morning.

And go for a drink…? Was he serious? She was doing her best to forget that he'd come back into her life, today of all days. All she really wanted to do was go home and dream about her optimistic future and motherhood and the life that might, right now, be growing inside her.

'I have questions,' he said, stepping aside for a pregnant woman pushing a toddler in a buggy.

'About work?' she asked, pausing at the exit. Maybe if she answered his query quickly, he'd leave her alone.

'No,' he said as they fell into step once more. 'About what you said in Theatre, about honesty and transparency. I know you have trust issues when it comes to relationships…' he added quietly.

Connie winced. That night, she'd told him she'd recently gone through a bad break-up. Likewise, Théo had confided in her about his mutual-consent divorce, something Tris had mentioned in passing. She'd found their similar experiences comforting, foolishly assuming they had more in common than their careers and Tris. But soon realised she didn't know this man.

'But have I done something to offend you,' he went on, 'aside from taking the job at St Raphaël, that is?' His good-natured smile and his enquiry left her itching with frustration.

'Really,' Connie said, her stomach twisting with discomfort. 'You want to do this here? Now?'

She glanced pointedly at the cheerful crowds milling around them. The last thing she wanted was to relive that humiliating morning when, for a moment after waking up, she'd felt desirable again after Guy's betrayal and hopeful that she might be ready to move on.

'Do what?' He frowned, as if he had no idea what he'd said that morning. 'I'm trying to clear the air, Connie. We have Tris and Victor's wedding coming up soon and we have to work together, after all.'

'That's down to you,' Connie muttered, wishing she'd confronted him three years ago rather than sneaking out of his apartment with her tail between her legs. But she'd still been wounded from the way hateful Guy had decimated her confidence with his deception and cruelty. She hadn't been able to face another confrontation back then. But she was harder now. Less gullible.

A steely glint entered his stare. 'You're right. I made a judgement call based on a career-topping job,' Théo said with a sigh. 'I assumed that you and I could work out what went wrong three years ago and be civil. But if I've done something to upset you, tell me and I'll apologise. Besides,' he added, stepping closer and lowering his head, his stare dipping to her mouth and inconveniently heating her blood, 'I've only ignored you because I thought that was what *you* wanted. You're the one who sneaked out without a word that Christmas.'

She stepped closer too, the fact that she still found him

wildly attractive fuelling her indignation. 'Are you saying you wanted me to stay for breakfast? Because that wasn't the impression you gave.'

His frown deepened. 'You never gave me a chance to say anything. You just left and then ignored my texts.'

Connie inhaled a deep breath, the humiliation extinguishing the sparks being this close to him ignited. 'I heard you, Théo. Heard you telling Tristan that we'd slept together and how much you regretted it. *That's* why I left that morning. I'd heard enough to realise that what I thought we'd shared didn't mean anything to you.'

Wishing she could stalk off as fast as her sloshing soup and comfy boots could carry her, she paused at the flicker of shame and hesitation in his eyes.

'I'm sorry,' he said quietly, his strong brow dipping in a frown. 'Obviously I didn't know that you'd overheard our conversation. But that's not true.' He stepped closer and dropped his voice further. 'It did mean something, Connie. Did you tell Tris you'd overheard?'

His voice was full of apology, but Connie shook the knowledge of his regret from her head. It would be easier to work with him and ignore their chemistry if she clung to her dislike and distrust. This was exactly why she preferred to be alone. Even now, three and a half years since she'd discovered Guy's deception after overhearing him on the phone to his lover, she still had to maintain her guard against the pain.

'No. I told him you and I wouldn't be happening again,' she said, raising her chin. 'That the subject was closed.'

She glanced across the street longingly. The *Métro* station and escape were just in sight.

'Obviously it's not closed,' he said reasonably, his voice

that same low murmur that had groaned sexy things that night, 'if you're still upset with me.'

'I'm not upset. I told you, for me the sex was instantly forgettable.' Connie kept her voice calm as she lied. 'I only left without confronting you that morning because I was angry. You acted as if I expected some grand commitment from you, which was ridiculous.' Of course, he'd acted so carefree and unemotional that night she'd assumed he was well and truly over his marriage and ready to move on. A part of her had even wondered if that night might have been the start of something between them, more fool her.

'We had ill-judged sex that we both regretted after too much wine at a Christmas party,' she continued, trying to conceal how hurt she'd been to hear him dismiss what for her had been an amazing night. 'But you told your brother, my best friend, that you didn't want to see me again. What makes you so certain that I would have wanted to see *you* again?' She pointed her finger at the centre of his chest, finally losing the threads of her composure.

A few of the people enjoying the market cast them amused looks as if they were in the middle of a lovers' tiff. When one man glanced pointedly at Théo and then raised his gaze skywards, Connie, too, looked up.

Théo and she stood underneath an archway strung with twinkling lights from which was suspended another large bunch of mistletoe tied with a red velvet ribbon.

Connie's cheeks flamed with embarrassment. Only Théo could make her argue in a public place with an audience. She met his stare once more, furious. But further admonishment was trapped in her throat by the seductive look in his eyes and the answering shudder it sent through her body. Infuriatingly, in spite of everything, she still fancied him.

'Shame to pass up on an opportunity,' Théo said, a suggestive smile tugging at his lips. He tilted his head cheekily and raised one eyebrow as if in invitation, obviously suggesting they simply kiss and make up.

'You have got to be kidding me?' Connie scoffed and spluttered, her pulse racing at the memory of that last time they'd locked lips and the speed at which that late-night Christmas kiss had escalated to a night of intense and unforgettable passion. Théo was an amazing kisser. But did he really think he could kiss his way into her good books after his past indiscretion and gatecrashing her surgery?

He shrugged. 'When I knew I was definitely joining St Raphaël, I was curious to see if our chemistry was still alive.' His dark eyes bored into hers. 'Now I know that it is.'

'It's also irrelevant,' Connie said, impressed with the coolness of her voice given the way her entire body seemed about to melt. 'I don't trust you and I'm happily single. I've moved on.' To the next chapter in her life. Having the child she'd always wanted. Taking life into her own hands and abandoning the search for love and commitment from untrustworthy men. 'I'm sorry for you if you haven't,' she finished, an annoying niggle of compassion for him blooming in her chest.

Now she understood that when they'd hooked up, she too had been on the rebound. Vulnerable and needy. She'd slept with Théo that night partly to prove she could still be attractive to the opposite sex, despite Guy's cheating. But she refused to feel ashamed for that, especially when Théo had clearly had his own agenda that night.

'And I'm sorry for being indiscreet that morning. You're absolutely right. I should have spoken to you first, not Tris,' he said, regret wiping the flirtatious smile from his face.

Regret that they were arguing in public or that she'd turned down the opportunity of a kiss?

'Tris and I are very close. I admitted to him that I shouldn't have seduced you because I probably wasn't ready to move on, which wasn't fair to you. My divorce made me feel like a failure and the night we met I was still a bit of a mess...'

'Maybe I seduced you,' she interrupted, deaf to his explanations because all day she'd been telling herself it was easier to lump him in with her devious, self-serving ex as just another man she couldn't trust. 'Maybe I was on the rebound, too,' she said defensively.

He stepped closer and dropped his voice, his glittering stare turning darkly intense. 'I think we seduced each other, Connie.' His gaze skittered over her mouth as if he desperately wanted that kiss. As if he saw through her bravado. Saw how much she still fancied him and how hard she was trying to forget.

Connie's pulse throbbed in her fingertips, danger signs flashing in her head. He was right about chemistry. She had no idea who'd touched who that night, but with the first touch they'd burst into flames as if doused in petrol. Even now, her entire body flushed hot from delicious memories. 'It makes no difference now.' She dragged in a frigid breath, her insides trembling with adrenaline and the need to get away from him. 'You've apologised for talking about me behind my back with my best friend, making out I wanted a ring after one night. After misguidedly trusting my cheating ex, I should have known better. It was a mistake we both regret. Let's just leave it there.'

She tried to step away but the flash of anger in his stare stalled her departure.

'Hold on,' he said, inching closer so Connie grew more aware of his imposing height, strong build and broad-chested manliness, which only reminded her of how it had felt to be in his arms. 'I might have expressed doubts that I was ready for more than one night to my brother, something I'd planned to say to you when you woke that morning, by the way, but that's the extent of my wrong-doing. I'm no cheat, Connie. My marriage ended for other reasons. Mutual reasons. And I'd been divorced three months the night we met. I think you're overreacting here. Transferring your anger at the man who hurt you onto me. Maybe I shouldn't have slept with you that night. I regret the timing, but I don't for one second regret what happened between us.'

Connie spluttered, confused by his openness and far more excited than she should be by his sexy admission.

'Well, I do,' she lied, still clinging to her indignation. She would never know if she still would have regretted sleeping with him if she hadn't overheard his conversation that morning. But she hated the idea that she'd been so vulnerable and easily hurt so soon after Guy.

Desperate to flee the way Théo was making her question certainties—that he couldn't be trusted, that she didn't need sex, that she was done with relationships—she fisted her hand on her hip. 'I understand that we have to work together, and I'm glad we've finally cleared the air. But unless we're collaborating on a patient, there really is nothing more to say.'

She was going to have a baby. Another man's baby.

Even if she could forgive Théo, even if she wanted another night of mindless passion with him, she now had other priorities.

'Okay,' he said quietly and stepped back, a determined mask falling over his expression. 'If that's how you want to leave things.'

'It is,' Connie said, her adrenaline draining to leave a vague sense of what felt like disappointment. But that was silly and probably just a reaction to her fatigue, to all the Christmas cheer around them, to having finally had the confrontation she'd put off for three years while she'd recovered her decimated self-esteem.

With her pulse bounding and her throat aching, as if she were close to tears, she stepped away from him and offered a tight smile. 'Enjoy your soup.'

Then she crossed the road and ducked into the *Métro* station and headed for her train, replaying every word of their conversation over and over until nothing made sense, least of all the confusing swirl of her emotions.

CHAPTER THREE

STILL RELIVING HIS frustrating interaction with Connie the night before, Théo arrived at the hospital from his early morning session at the gym determined to do as she'd asked and ignore every infuriating, gorgeous inch of her. It certainly wasn't how he'd imagined their reunion would play out. Secretly, part of him had hoped that if they'd successfully cleared the air that spark might still be there, which of course it was. Only more of a raging inferno than a spark.

But if she could ignore the obvious chemistry between them, he would too. Because Connie was the kind of distraction he in no way needed. His life was finally in a good place. Both he and Tris had fulfilling careers they loved. His brother was about to be married, having found the love of his life in Victor. And Théo had spent most of his adult life convinced that if Tris was happy, he could be too.

Not to mention it was Christmas soon. Théo's favourite time of year: a precious time to be with friends and loved ones and make family memories. And, of course, he looked forward to his annual Christmas *réveillon*.

He'd just sat at his desk to check his work emails when his younger brother appeared in the doorway.

'Very nice,' Tris said, about Théo's office, which was

small, but had a view of the Seine from the window. 'Settling in all right?'

'Come in and close the door,' Théo said, standing to briefly embrace Tris, who worked as a renal physician at St Raphaël and had been in Connie's year at medical school, which was where they'd become firm friends.

'What's up?' Tris asked, taking a seat and resting one ankle on the opposite knee.

'I was hoping you might help me answer that question,' Théo replied, observing Tris, who appeared a little distracted. Perhaps, like Théo, he had a busy day ahead.

'Oh? In what way? You're being very cryptic,' his brother pointed out with a mocking smile.

Théo dragged in a breath and exhaled. 'It's about Connie. I spoke to her yesterday.' And it had cost him dearly: a restless night of erotic dreams and waking fantasies where, instead of dismissing his apology, she forgave him and they'd utilised that convenient bunch of mistletoe.

Tris winced. 'I tried to warn her about you yesterday. Maybe if you'd allowed me to tell her sooner…'

'I thought I was doing the right thing,' Théo said. 'There seemed no point upsetting her until it was confirmed and I'd actually signed the contract. And I didn't know they'd want me to start right away or that she'd booked time off.'

'Still, you knew your paths would cross,' Tris said, brushing a speck of lint from his immaculate trousers and avoiding Théo's stare.

'Of course,' Théo said, seeking patience. 'We work in the same speciality and now the same department. I hoped we could clear the air and move on. What I didn't expect was that she'd still be upset with me over something that happened three years ago. I…hurt her. Did you know about that?' Of course, he'd been horrified that she'd overheard that conversation, but he was genuinely sorry.

Tristan shook his head, clearly clueless. 'Know about what?' he asked, frowning warily. 'What did you do?' As a loyal friend, Tris rarely talked to Théo about Connie.

Théo sighed, certain there would be more sleepless nights thinking about her in his future. 'Did you know that she overheard us talking the morning after the Christmas party where she and I…met?' Met? Insert *had a night of wild sex*.

'Of course not,' Tris said, appearing genuinely shocked. 'She never said a word to me but that explains a lot.'

'What *did* she say?' Théo pushed, still embarrassed that he'd been so indiscreet. He'd awoken before dawn, left her asleep in his bed, gone to make coffee and found Tris in the kitchen doing the same. The minute Tris had seen the two cups of coffee and guessed that he'd slept with Connie, he'd reeled off a string of warnings about how badly she'd been hurt by her ex. Théo had reassured Tris that he wasn't ready for more than casual sex anyway, unaware that Connie had overheard him express regret for the timing.

Tris shrugged. 'She didn't really want to talk about you at all. I assumed she'd had an…underwhelming night.'

Théo scoffed and tilted his head. 'She had a great night, trust me.' They'd had sex three times. He'd dragged orgasm after orgasm from her. They'd acted like insatiable teenagers.

Tris held up his hands. 'Okay, I believe you. But I didn't want the details. She's my friend and you're my brother.' He gave a small shudder. 'Anyway, when I asked her why she left without telling me she said she was embarrassed that she'd slept with you and asked if we could never talk about it again. I'm a good friend, so I agreed. I assumed it was bad timing for her given what Guy had put her through. He really hurt her. She hadn't recovered enough to start dating, which was why I was so surprised to learn the two of you had…hit it off. After you'd confided in me that you weren't ready for anything serious either, I thought the subject was closed and we could all move on, no harm done.'

'Except there was harm done.' Théo impatiently tapped at the desk with his index finger as he recalled Connie's hurt expression from the night before and the wash of shame he'd felt. 'I obviously hurt her, because she hates my guts now, which is very inconvenient because I actually like and respect her as a colleague and we have to work together.' Not to mention she was still as sexy as sin… Another thing he'd need to ignore.

'Do you want me to talk to her and explain?' Tris asked, looking a little uncomfortable at the prospect of doing Théo's dirty work. 'I need to apologise to her anyway. I should have warned her sooner that you might be joining the team.'

'No, I'll clean up my own mess,' he said. 'I just wondered if you had any extra insights, that's all.'

Tris shook his head thoughtfully. 'I took her at her word. Assumed she regretted sleeping with you.'

Théo pressed his lips together in frustration. 'Oh, she regrets it all right… But I take full responsibility.' Because hot on the heels of her ex, Théo too had let Connie down and inadvertently hurt her. Maybe Anaïs, his ex-wife, was right. Maybe he was too emotionally distant. Marriage between him and Anaïs had been fine for a couple of years when they'd seemed to want the same things. But she'd kept putting off the family they'd discussed, blaming him for the something that was missing from their relationship and stating a baby wouldn't fix it. So when she'd announced, after that final row, it was over, he'd felt devastating guilt along with a depressing sense of inevitability.

'Don't worry,' he reassured Tris, who wore a concerned frown. 'I'll sort things out with Connie.'

He would apologise again and move on because, since his divorce, Théo avoided complicated in favour of casual. In his experience, relationships weren't worth all the heartache and loss. So what if his family consisted only of him, Tris and Tris's partner, Victor? Quality was better than quantity any day.

'Why did you come to see me anyway?' he asked Tris, shoving Connie from his mind once more.

Tris winced, glancing away. 'I um… I have something to tell you. Funny story, in fact, because it also involves Connie.'

'Okay…' He stiffened. 'Let's hear it, then.'

'Well,' Tris began hesitantly, 'you know that Victor and I definitely don't want children, right?'

Théo nodded and Tris went on. 'I mean, we knew that when we met and neither of us is likely to change our mind.'

'Okay…' Théo nodded, aware that he needed to be on the ward in five minutes to review Elodie Verdier. If Tris didn't get to the point soon, they'd have to reschedule this conversation.

'Well, Connie's always wanted a family,' Tris explained, growing cagier, 'and she's given up on finding Mr Right. She has understandable trust issues when it comes to dating, so she decided to go it alone and I um…'

Braced for bad news, Théo shook his head, interrupting. 'Please don't tell me what I think you're going to tell me.'

Tris shrugged, his cheeks flushing. 'I just wanted you to know. Victor agreed and Connie and I discussed all the pros and cons. I said I'd be her sperm donor.'

Théo stared in shock as if he'd been punched. One, Connie had given up on men at the age of thirty-five? Two, just because Tris and Victor were about to become happily married didn't mean there wouldn't be emotional implications if Tris was to father a child. And three, what right did Théo have to utter one single word of caution when he himself, years before as a cash-strapped medical student, had donated his sperm to one of the city's fertility clinics?

'This way,' Tris continued, unaware of Théo's turmoil, 'she has the child she wants and I'll always be there as Uncle Tris because of our friendship. I guess that will make you Uncle Théo.' He laughed nervously, but Théo couldn't join in.

Uncle Théo? He closed his eyes and sighed under his breath. Growing up without a father, and ever since their mother and then grandmother died and they'd been placed into foster care aged twelve and nine, Théo had been looking out for Tristan. As an adult, he'd desperately tried to be a male role model for his brother and to recreate the family stability they'd missed out on as boys. He was proud of the kind, intelligent man his brother had become. It warmed Théo to know that, while their family had been snatched away from them and while his own marriage had failed, Tris was in a loving and committed relationship.

But a sperm donor…? Connie potentially having Théo's

niece or nephew. When she could hardly stand him. When he knew exactly what it was like to grow up thinking your father didn't love you enough to stick around.

'Are you sure this is a good idea after everything we've been through?' Théo asked cautiously. 'Even if you won't be raising it, a baby is a serious emotional consideration. We know from our upbringing that family is everything. A child needs to know both its parents, to know it's loved. And aside from that, my main concern is that you'll somehow be hurt.'

Could Tris really be in Connie's life, see his biological child all the time and not yearn for more contact? Théo wouldn't be able to be an absent father. And what if Tris and Connie's friendship broke down? What then? Would he and Tris lose another family member they loved?

Tris shook his head, adamant. 'Connie is my best friend. We're always going to be a part of each other's lives anyway, and she was heartbroken when Guy cheated and got the other woman pregnant.'

Théo gaped, stunned by this new detail and horrified for Connie. 'I know…' he said, his mind whirring through all the potential pitfalls for his brother. 'But there are clinics. She could have a child with an anonymous donor. Hell, some crazy people buy sperm on the Internet. Just think about it,' he urged. 'A child is a big commitment, even if you won't be raising it. And what happens if you sign away your parental rights and one day Connie denies you access to your child?'

Tris's expression turned guilty. 'Thanks for the words of warning. I know you're always looking out for me, and I appreciate how much you care. But it's kind of too late for the pep talk. Connie underwent the procedure earlier this week. She could already be pregnant for all we know.'

'What? Are you serious?' Théo's blood drained from his body, head to toe. Was Connie already carrying his brother's baby? What would that mean for her and Théo's relationship? Not that there was going to be a relationship beyond a professional one, but their chemistry didn't seem to care. And what about this innocent baby that might grow up desperate for its father's love?

'Yes,' Tris said. 'That's why I'm coming to you now. I thought you should know that Connie might be having your niece or nephew. And I'm happy to hand over my parental rights, otherwise I'd never have offered.'

'Which is why you maybe should have come to me sooner so we could discuss this,' Théo gritted out in frustration, his past colliding with the present. He himself had always wanted a family, which was why it had been so devastating that Anaïs had changed her mind about having a family with him.

But just because Tris felt comfortable fathering Connie's child, didn't mean that Théo would feel comfortable having a niece or nephew he never saw. He'd spent most of his life craving the perfect family. Would he be able to ignore a child he was related to just because Connie had given up on men and found a way to have a baby alone? But given her dislike of him, Connie was unlikely to allow him to have any contact with the child, anyway. He'd be in a horrible position with no rights…

Just then Tris's pager sounded and he stood, silencing it. 'Sorry, I need to go. My clinic is about to begin.'

Théo reeled. Talk about dropping a bombshell…

'Wait,' he said as Tris headed for the door. 'Does Connie know that you planned to tell me?' He didn't want any further misunderstandings between them, not when he somehow needed to wriggle his way back into her good books for multiple reasons.

'She gave me permission to tell whoever I saw fit,' Tris said. 'It's in the contract we had drawn up.'

'How very efficient of you both,' Théo muttered darkly, not sure if he wanted to hug or berate his brother. But neither was necessary. Tris wasn't a child. If he and Connie thought this was a sensible plan, who was Théo to argue? Only losing their caregivers at a young age, growing up without a proper family, had made Théo determined to give Tris as close to a traditional family as he could manage. This foolproof plan of theirs made him very nervous indeed.

'When you see her,' Tris said, hesitating in the doorway, 'just go easy on her, yeah?'

'Me go easy on *her*?' Théo laughed, recalling his hostile reception from Connie the day before and the dressing-down she'd given him under the mistletoe.

'She's been pretty hormonal lately, what with the ovulation shots, and I guess it's only going to get worse if the procedure worked and she is pregnant.' Tris shrugged. 'I don't know. Just be nice.'

Be nice? Théo sighed. He could try, but then Connie had made it clear she wanted absolutely nothing from him. He didn't think him playing *nice* would make one bit of difference.

CHAPTER FOUR

LATER THAT AFTERNOON, after successfully avoiding Théo all day, Connie took an urgent call from the neurology registrar, who had a patient in A & E for her to review.

'I'll be right there,' she said, hanging up the phone.

She left her office and rushed to the emergency department, her mind snagged, as it had been for most of the past twenty-four hours since he'd joined the team at St Raphaël, on Théo.

As she'd feared, he'd dominated her thoughts for most of the previous evening after their confrontation. She'd been forced to admit that when he'd accused her of taking out her Guy-directed hurt and anger on him, he might have had a point. When she'd closed her eyes for sleep, all she could see were his regrets and that sexy seductive look in his eyes as they'd stood underneath the mistletoe at the Christmas market. All she'd heard over the hum of the city noise outside, which normally lulled her into unconsciousness, was him admitting that their chemistry was still alive.

On reviewing the conversation she'd overheard three years ago in light of Théo's explanation, Connie found there'd been a ring of truth to his apologies. The night she'd slept with him, she'd assumed he was moving on after his divorce because he hadn't seemed cut up. But she more than anyone knew how the effects of a bad break-up could be long lasting.

Maybe that night had simply been bad timing for both him and Connie.

But his shocking revelations changed nothing. She was focussed on becoming a mother and didn't need a man. Her trust had, she suspected, been irreparably damaged by Guy's deceit. She never wanted to feel that vulnerable again. It just wasn't worth the risk. Not even if it meant going without sex as hot as she'd shared with Théo.

Feeling a momentary twinge of regret, she sighed as she entered the emergency department wondering if taking Théo at his word made her a trusting fool. It certainly didn't help her to dismiss and ignore him...

Glad to have work on which to focus, Connie marched up to the neuro registrar, who stood at a computer terminal looking harassed. Before Connie could take a look at the notes or hear the other doctor's history of the patient, she spied Théo striding their way, his handsome face wearing a frown of concern.

'What do we have?' he asked as he joined them, flicking Connie an inscrutable look that made her rapid pulse surge faster.

'Fifty-four-year-old male with lower back pain,' the registrar said, addressing them both. 'He gives a classic history of cauda equina syndrome—bladder dysfunction in the form of urinary retention, pain radiating down the back of his legs, numbness of the buttocks and weakness of both feet.'

'Any history of trauma?' Connie asked, glancing at Théo to see from his expression that he shared Connie's clinical concern for the patient. Cauda equina syndrome was a rare but serious spinal emergency usually caused by a herniated lumbar disc.

'None,' the registrar said.

'When did the symptoms begin?' Théo asked the very question that Connie was thinking, proving how professionally attuned they were.

'Yesterday,' the registrar said. 'He thought it was sciatica and would resolve, but the symptoms are worsening.'

'So we're against the clock,' Connie confirmed, catching Théo's eye. They both knew that if left untreated the nerve compression could lead to permanent leg paralysis, bladder and bowel issues and sexual dysfunction. Which was why the emergency treatment of choice was a surgical decompression of the ruptured disc.

'The MRI results should be back now,' the registrar said, logging into the computer. She opened the radiology report and all three of them scanned the results and the relevant scan images and X-rays.

'There, between L4 and L5,' Théo said, pointing out the obvious disc herniation between the lowest two lumbar vertebrae.

'Thanks.' Connie reached for the notes the registrar had taken. 'Dr Augustin and I will examine him and consent him for an emergency microdiscectomy. If you could make sure he's ready for a general anaesthetic with all relevant blood work and call the anaesthetist.'

While the neurology registrar rushed off to organise blood tests, Connie scanned the patient's medical history before passing the tablet to Théo.

'Do you want me to take this case?' she asked, uncertain of him after their talk the night before and the way she'd behaved so defensively. But they were each professional enough to set aside their personal issues and focus on work.

'I'm still getting used to the theatre protocols here,' he said, wearing a small frown of concern. 'So if you can tolerate my presence, I'd welcome the opportunity to assist.'

'Of course.' Connie nodded, her concern for the patient outweighing the need to keep Théo and his insistent attractiveness at arm's length.

She might be having his brother's baby. There was no space in her life for romance, flirtation or casual sex, least of all with Théo.

'I like to try the endoscopic approach first,' he said, glancing her way as if seeking her opinion on the best course of action in this case.

'Even with herniations of this size?' she asked, surprised. 'My first inclination was a tubular microdiscectomy.' The procedure she favoured was slightly more invasive for the patient, but visibility was improved, leading to shorter duration under anaesthetic.

'Why don't we examine him, review the scans again and then decide?' Théo diplomatically suggested, clearly trying to make amends for the past and his first day.

Connie nodded, unable to argue with his reasonable suggestion. 'Sounds like a plan,' she said, heading off to find the patient, aware of Théo behind as if the air between them were electrically charged.

For the time being, it seemed there would be little escape from his distracting presence, from the sexy memories, or the way, despite it all, working with him was easy. All she could hope for was that her hormones would soon tire of constantly lusting after him and give up the ghost. And if that failed, she'd simply wait it out until she became too heavily pregnant to do anything about their chemistry. Easy.

* * *

After the emergency micro-endoscopic discectomy on their cauda equina syndrome patient, Théo was just about to leave the hospital for the night when he spied Connie emerging from the theatre changing rooms up ahead.

He hesitated, his heart pounding with trepidation and the ever-present flicker of excitement the sight of her induced. Connie was the sort of woman who appealed to him on every level. Whether she was dressed in scrubs or the smartest suit, her glossy brown hair tied up and tamed, she always looked elegant and sophisticated and yet feminine. Smart, driven and with a strength of character he couldn't help but admire. He found her company both addictive and intriguing.

Of course, now that she might be pregnant with his niece or nephew, there were bigger fish to fry than their attraction. Tris's news about being her donor had left him unsettled, probably because he had no memories of his own father, who'd left when Théo was two and before Tris was born. If Théo and Connie were going to be a permanent fixture in each other's lives, connected by her and Tris's child, they should at least try to get along. For Tris's sake and for the sake of the child. Who knew, maybe the pregnancy and the family connection would kill their chemistry for good? He could only hope that would be the case, because nothing else seemed to be working.

'Connie,' he called out, torn between ignoring her as promised, and keeping his word to Tris by playing nice. But loyalty to his brother won. Théo didn't want bad blood between him and Connie to sour things for Tris's relationship with his child. Not when the situation they'd engineered between them was already so unconventional.

Connie turned, pulling on her coat. 'I'm heading home,' she said, eyeing him warily but less frostily than before. Was she thawing towards him now that he'd had a chance to apologise for his slip-up three years ago?

'I won't hold you up.' He caught up to her, catching the scent of her perfume and concealing a wince. That floral scent was so distracting. She'd left it on his sheets and pillow three years ago and his body remembered, his blood pumping harder. 'I just wanted you to know that Tristan confided in me about your um…arrangement.'

'Oh.' She quickly recovered from her surprise and tilted up her chin, her guard obviously rising as if she expected Théo's disapproval. 'And?'

'And nothing,' he said, swallowing down most of his reservations for fear of causing offence. 'I'm simply being transparent, as requested. I'm sure the two of you know what you're doing. It's no one else's business, mine included.'

'I agree,' she said, and rolled her gorgeous amber-flecked eyes. 'But I sense a but all the same.'

Théo took her mocking smile as a win. At least she wasn't stomping off angrily. But he had so many buts he didn't know where to begin.

'Obviously,' he said, quietly, emotion tightening his throat, 'I have concerns for Tris. I'm protective of my brother. I'd be letting him down if I wasn't uneasy that he might somehow have future regrets if there is a baby. Tris never knew our father and I don't really have any memories of him either.' He swallowed, the deeply ingrained feelings of loss and rejection stinging like a reopened wound. 'Tris has a big heart, which can leave him exposed to being hurt.'

'He's also a grown man capable of making his own decisions,' she countered, but a small frown tightened her lips, as if Tris had never really talked about their father, which was unsurprising to Théo.

He shrugged. 'I know. But after losing our mother and then our grandmother when we were boys, and growing up in care, you can understand how family means a lot to us.' Obviously more so to Théo than Tris. With the exception of that desperate sperm donation in his early twenties, Théo could never do what Tris had signed up for. He couldn't live knowing he'd fathered a child with someone he knew. A child he might see but not help to raise, or, if the worst happened, a child he loved but, because of circumstances, rarely saw. He'd never understood how his own father could make two sons and just walk away without ever reaching out. He and Tris had talked about it over the years and neither of them was interested in finding or knowing the man. It was enough that they had each other and the memories of the years they'd spent with their two maternal figures.

'I'm just concerned that when the baby arrives,' he continued, 'Tris might regret signing away his parental rights.' He allowed his voice to harden slightly. 'I don't want him to be hurt or lose any more family than he already has.'

As if it were *his* hypothetical baby they were discussing, Théo's throat turned dry with fear. In Théo's experience, people who should have cared for him disappeared and people he loved and cared about tended to be snatched away. He just wanted to protect Tris, and even his and Connie's child, from more heartache. All kids deserved to know both their parents.

Connie swallowed, her expression turning serious and

a little guilty. 'I don't want him to be hurt either. He's my best friend. I care about him as much as you.'

She blinked up at him and, for the first time since they'd come back into each other's lives, Théo saw the unguarded Connie. His heart lurched with compassion. She'd been badly hurt too.

'I know you do.' He tried to smile, but his protective urges wouldn't be silenced. A part of him still felt uncomfortable by Tris and Connie's clinical arrangement, despite their reassurances. 'It heartens me that you care about Tris's feelings. I guess not wanting him to be hurt is the one thing on which you and I can agree.'

Connie gave him a small nod, assessing him with those big brown eyes. For a second, it was as if they were back in his kitchen, moments before they kissed. That unfathomable connection between them powerful.

'I'd never stop Tris seeing the baby if that's what he wanted,' she said, quietly, as if she felt the electricity too and was scared to move.

'I'm not suggesting you would,' Théo said, concealing a sigh because the effect she had on him was beyond irrelevant. 'But you must agree your arrangement has the potential to create…emotional complications.'

Flushing slightly, she raised her chin. 'I think Tris and I have it under control.' She buttoned up her coat, clearly preparing to walk away. 'But thanks for letting me know that he's confided in you. Now I don't need to worry about keeping it a secret.'

Because he wasn't wholly comforted, and, maybe because he wasn't ready for her to walk away, Théo stepped closer and dropped his voice. 'Listen, I think you and I should try to get along, don't you? I know we got off to a bad start yesterday. I know I behaved indiscreetly three years ago. But I've sincerely apologised, and, if we take our sexual chemistry off the table, surely we can get along for Tris's sake. Especially if there is a baby.'

As if she was made uncomfortable by his closeness and his mention of their attraction, her pupils dilated, her cheeks flushed and her breaths gusted excitedly. But she didn't move away or even argue the presence of their chemistry.

'It's Tris and Victor's wedding soon,' Théo went on, pushing his rationale. 'I'm best man and you're maid of honour. And if you're having my brother's baby, we're about to become family.'

'I wouldn't say that,' she said, her wariness back.

Clearly it would take a lot for him to win back her trust.

'One of the most attractive things about having a child this way,' she said, 'is that the baby will be *all* mine. I'm happy doing this alone. I don't need anyone else.'

Théo nodded placatingly even as his skin began to crawl. Depressingly, uncles had no legal parental rights. 'But technically,' he said, needing to defend both his and Tris's agenda all the same, 'I'll be the baby's uncle. That's important to me, Connie. Family is important, don't you think?'

'I guess. Sometimes…' She shrugged, clearly dubious about allowing Théo into her circle of trust. 'Sometimes family can be overwhelming, noisy and opinionated. My brothers drive me mad whenever we're all together. Most families aren't perfect.'

Théo tilted his head in challenge. 'I'm afraid I wouldn't really know. My family is Tris. Look,' he said, inhaling a deep breath for patience, 'I'm having my annual Christmas Eve party in Provence this year. It will be a small gathering—Tris, Victor and some close friends—and I'd love for you to be there, too, as would Tris, I'm sure.'

'Provence?' she asked, her eyebrows raised in curiosity as her stare shifted over his face.

Théo shrugged, equally curious about how she normally spent Christmas. 'I inherited a home there a few years ago, from an old professor who mentored me at medical school.'

'Wow. Impressive,' she muttered and glanced at her feet, her cheeks colouring.

Was she, like him, remembering the previous Christmas party she'd attended, the night they'd spent together, barely sleeping, having sex over and over until they were both exhausted?

While his pulse surged, he inched closer and dropped his voice, hoping humour might win her over. 'I promise not to seduce you this time.'

'Very funny.' She laughed ironically then snagged her bottom lip with her teeth as she looked up at him with something akin to uncertainty.

'You don't have to decide now,' he said, sensing her imminent refusal. 'I just thought, as we work together and we both love Tris and if you have his baby, that will make us all family, you and I should try to put the past behind us and get along.'

Aware of his emotional manipulation tactics, she narrowed her eyes. 'I don't really do big family parties, especially at Christmas,' she said, that thread of steel in her voice. 'In fact, I usually work over the holidays. In my experience Christmas is an excuse for people to drink too much and behave badly.'

Was she talking about them sleeping together again? Beating him over the head with her regrets, which, he was aware, she hadn't recanted in light of his explanation and apology?

'My siblings all have children,' she added with a sigh, 'so it's always noisy chaos. My uncles, aunts and cousins congregate at my parents' house. There are usually at least two family members who have a disagreement and fall out. I prefer to avoid all the drama.'

'That doesn't sound very festive of you,' he teased with a smile. 'Where's your Christmas spirit? I always make the most of family moments, even if it's just for me and Tris and now Victor. And if your plan works, next year you'll have a child of your own.'

Théo's heart thumped harder, the urge to win just a sliver of her trust a personal challenge. Now that Tris had volunteered to father Connie's child, it seemed more important than ever before to make the most of family get-togethers. So that Connie and Tris's baby knew its father's side of the family. Tris might be happy to have a casual relationship with Connie's child, but Théo would want to be a close uncle. To be there for anything the kid might need. To shower it with love and attention and gifts so it grew up in no doubt it was safe, loved and accepted.

'Sounds like you have enough Christmas spirit for both of us,' she said dryly but smiled begrudgingly so he sensed the smallest of thaws.

Théo grinned. She had a great sense of humour. 'Since I changed the venue to Château Bijou,' he explained, eager to keep her talking, 'it's kind of become a whole-day event.'

'Sounds very…debauched,' she said with mocking raised eyebrows. But there was a flicker of excitement and curiosity in her stare and she wasn't walking away.

'Not really,' he said, with a smile. 'I was approached

by a local special needs school looking for a venue to host their Christmas grotto. I was happy to help, giving them access to the old converted stables. There are stalls and games and a sensory experience and, of course, Père Noël pays a visit. Last year, I even donned the red suit and beard myself when our Santa double-booked himself.'

Connie's eyes widened with surprise as if he'd given her a debauched version of events.

'Then in the evening I host the traditional Christmas *réveillon*,' he went on, addicted to how they could challenge each other and the resultant sparks. 'Lots of delicious food and good company. Tris usually organises games and dancing. I think he'd love to have you there this year, if you can bring yourself to attend. And it goes without saying that there's enough guest rooms at the *château* for you to stay the night if you want.'

His heart thumped at the idea of having her in his home. A chance for a fresh start. He brushed his excitement aside, telling himself he was simply laying the foundations for future years when Connie might bring the baby.

'So you're basically running Christmas HQ now?' she said teasingly, her eyes bright with mirth. 'Sprinkling magic and good cheer wherever you go.'

'Not really.' His heart thudded that he'd managed to draw out her playful side. 'But I do enjoy seeing everyone have a good time. And this year will be special as Théo and Victor will have tied the knot by then. Their first Christmas as a married couple.'

Deciding he'd pleaded his case as well as he could, he held up his hands and stepped back. 'Just think about it. I'll email through the invitation. It should be a magical night and who knows? By then, you might have some baby news to celebrate.'

He glanced down to her stomach. When he looked back up she was staring again, her eyes shining and her lips parted. His attention lingered on their glossy curves, the fullness and softness he could almost taste. A moment of silent understanding seemed to pass between them, that nagging pull of attraction as if they were each aware that before things had gone wrong, they'd sparked off each other like a lit box of fireworks.

'Well, goodnight, Connie. See you tomorrow.' He forced himself to move away, clinging to the relief that they might find a way to finally put their misunderstandings and animosity behind them and one day be friends.

As he headed down the corridor towards the exit, telling himself to proceed with caution because there was more at stake now than simple sexual tension, she called after him.

'Night, Théo.'

Théo waved over his shoulder but kept his eyes front and centre, the slight hesitation he'd heard in her voice and the feel of her eyes on him making him wonder if they'd ever be able to set aside their chemistry.

CHAPTER FIVE

Three weeks to Christmas

FOR THE PAST week Connie had hardly seen Théo at the hospital beyond catching sight of him on the surgical ward or in the theatre staffroom grabbing a coffee between operations. Rather than feel comforted from having time to put all of their conversations into perspective, she'd reluctantly needed to reassess most of her impressions of the man, an inconvenient state of affairs that left her mildly Théo-obsessed.

His honesty about their attraction, his protectiveness for Tris, his openness about his heartbreaking childhood. Tris never talked to Connie about their father. The one time Connie had asked, he'd said he had no interest in looking for a man who'd walked out on his beloved Maman before he was even born. But, of course, Tris had grown up with Théo as protector and male role model, whereas Théo, it seemed, had had no one, a thought that left Connie desperate to learn more about the man she couldn't seem to brush from her mind.

Now, having just finished seeing her final outpatient of the morning, she was heading for her office to grab a quick bite of lunch when her phone rang. Without checking the caller ID, she answered.

'Connie Dubois,' she said, leaving the outpatient department and taking the stairs to the floor above.

'Dr Dubois, this is Marcel Roulet from Fertility First.'

'Hello.' Connie paused midway up the first flight of stairs, her mind calculating the dates. Maybe this was the follow-up call she'd been expecting from the clinic, not that she'd had time to take the pregnancy test yet. She'd planned to do it first thing tomorrow morning.

'I'm um…calling with an apology,' Roulet said, his voice high pitched with worrying tension. 'I'm afraid there was an incident last week at the clinic on the day you attended for your procedure.'

'Okay…' Connie glanced at her watch, aware she had only a ten-minute window to grab some lunch before she needed to meet her registrar, Jules, for a ward round.

'Yes, there was a clerical error, I'm afraid.'

'I'm sorry, Mr Roulet,' Connie said, retaking the stairs, 'I'm at work at the moment. Could you perhaps pop your reason for calling into an email and I'll look at it when I can?'

'Oh, no, I can't do that,' the man said, the urgency in his voice rising. 'You see, I'm actually calling to inform you that, due to a mistake at our end, I'm afraid you were given the wrong deposit during your insemination procedure.'

Connie froze and gripped the stair rail, light-headed with shock. 'What?' Had she heard him correctly? Had he really just dropped that bombshell as casually as saying *we gave you the wrong appointment time*?

'I know, it's most irregular,' Roulet added in total understatement. 'I can only apologise profusely and reassure you that we are looking into how this mistake happened.' She heard him swallow. 'I wondered if you'd had chance to confirm a pregnancy or not yet?'

Connie snorted in angry disbelief. She could almost hear his mind working. If she wasn't pregnant, their *mistake* wouldn't matter. They'd be in the clear.

'No,' she said, tightly. 'I was planning on taking a test tomorrow. After day ten, you said.' She dragged in a calming breath, her mind racing as she tried to make sense of his call. 'So I didn't get my friend's sperm. Is that what you're telling me?'

Her heart banged from adrenaline. How could this have happened? What would she tell Tris? Although from a selfish perspective, while regrettable, for Connie it wouldn't be the end of the world. Before Tris had volunteered to be her donor, she'd considered using one of the clinic's anonymous donors instead.

'No, I'm afraid not,' Roulet confirmed flatly.

'So whose sperm did I receive?' she snapped, before chewing at her lip as she considered all the implications. Tris was unlikely to be devastated given he didn't want a family of his own. But it was still an embarrassing and inconvenient situation. Having Tris's baby had felt safe. They were best friends. There was less risk of misaligned expectations. She'd even imagined that one day, when the child was old enough to understand, she would tell her little one that dear Uncle Tris was its father.

'I'm afraid,' Roulet said, 'that due to Fertility First's privacy policy, I can't disclose that information until I've spoken to the donor.'

Connie wanted to laugh. But there was nothing funny about this situation.

'So now you're dotting the i's and crossing the t's,' she said drolly. 'Why didn't you speak to him first, before calling me with such…inconvenient news?'

She understood that mistakes happened, although she'd

never imagined they'd happen at a fertility clinic of all places, but she was losing her patience with this man.

'I haven't been able to get hold of the donor concerned yet,' he said, 'but as soon as I have his consent to disclose his identity, I'll be back in touch.'

'Great,' Connie said dryly. 'Presumably if the procedure wasn't successful and I'm not pregnant, you're off the hook.'

There was a squeak of nervous laughter. 'I really am terribly sorry, Dr Dubois. Needless to say, we have launched a full review of all our procedures and safeguards so we can identify how this error was made and avoid a recurrence in the future. I'll call you back soon, unless you have any other questions for me at this stage.'

'None that would be helpful,' Connie said tightly, her jaw clenched.

'In that case, good day.'

After washing up following a long morning of routine surgeries, Théo collected his phone from Reception and left Theatres. Six missed calls from an external number. Strange. Someone really wanted to get hold of him.

On his way upstairs to his office, he dialled the number to return the call. Théo had taken the two flights of stairs when the call connected and a man answered.

'This is Théo Augustin returning your calls.' Théo pushed through the doors at the top of the stairs, turned left towards his office.

'Mr Augustin,' the man said, his voice carrying a sense of urgency and relief. 'I'm so glad to finally get hold of you.'

'It's Dr Augustin,' Théo said. 'What can I do for you?'

'My name is Marcel Roulet, Clinical Director of the Fertility First clinic.'

Théo smiled. 'I'm a spinal surgeon, Mr Roulet. I think you might have the wrong number.' Wait…fertility clinic. Maybe the guy was after Tris.

'No, I definitely need to speak to you,' Roulet said, sounding increasingly flustered.

'Are you sure you don't want Dr Tristan Augustin? He's a doctor here at St Raphaël Hospital, too.'

There was a beat of silence that made the hairs stand on the back of Théo's neck with foreboding.

'You donated a sample some years ago,' Roulet said hesitantly.

That caught Théo's attention. He froze outside his office, unease coiling in his stomach. 'I did. Many years ago, but I assumed you'd thrown it out. You never contacted me to confirm it had been used.'

Was this guy calling to tell him his sperm had finally been defrosted, after all this time?

'I'm afraid I need to inform you of a procedural error here at the clinic, sir. You see, we had two donors with very similar names…'

Théo's head began to buzz with the sound of white noise. He braced his hand on the door jamb and locked his knees, trying to remain upright while half listening to the man drone on about his regrets and apologies and reassurances that *this kind of mix-up would never happen again*.

Théo closed his eyes, the implications of this call hitting him like a shock wave following an explosion. He knew what was coming next. What were the chances that his sperm had been mixed up with another man's the week that Tris, whose name was similar to Théo's, had donated so that independent, go-it-alone Connie could have a child?

Just then, with Roulet still nervously prattling in his ear, clearly building up to the big reveal, Théo became aware of movement nearby. He glanced up. Connie left the ladies' room and crossed the corridor, heading for her office a few doors down from his.

She spied him. Their eyes met. A polite but hesitant smile tugged at her lovely lips. That surge of connection that always came struck him in the solar plexus and he almost laughed at its utter irrelevance. How ironic that as they finally seemed to have brokered a truce and agreed to put their sexual chemistry behind them and get along for Tris's sake, fate had thrown them a monumental cock-up.

Seeing him frozen in place with the phone to his ear, Connie ducked into her office and quietly closed the door.

Dread settled in the pit of Théo's stomach as he tuned back into Roulet's apologies and excuses.

'Enough,' he said, reeling. He had questions for the man. Lots of questions. And a bad feeling that he wouldn't like any of the answers. And nor would Connie.

CHAPTER SIX

HAVING RETURNED FROM the bathroom to her office, Connie stared down at the test on her desk, her eyes stinging with happy tears. It was positive. It had worked. She was going to have a baby.

Covering her mouth with her hand, she smothered a delighted giggle. After everything she'd been through in her personal life with Guy and then Théo, finally something was going her way. Automatically, she picked up her phone to text Tris the news, but then remembered the baby wasn't his and hesitated, her joy diminished.

Would her friend be upset that he wasn't the father after all? She hoped not, given he'd decided against raising children of his own, but she chewed at her lip worriedly all the same. Tris's friendship had seen Connie through some tough times in the past. They were always there for each other, through heartache and work dilemmas and for the good times. All she could do was tell him about the mix-up and hope he would continue to support her the way he always had.

Before she could call him to explain the bizarre turn of events and the news she'd received from the clinic, there was a knock at the door. Connie stood and pulled it open, surprised to see Théo standing there wearing a dark and worrying frown.

'What's wrong?' she asked, her heart thudding at both his proximity and his ashen complexion. He'd obviously been in the middle of a serious-looking phone call just now. 'Is it a patient?'

He shook his head and stepped into her office. 'I need to talk to you.'

Slightly miffed by his abruptness, Connie closed the door. Her office seemed too small with him in it. His big sexy body encroaching on her personal space and making her all too aware she was a woman who hadn't had sex for almost three years. She brushed that thought aside and turned to face him. He was staring at the pregnancy test on the desk.

Connie flushed, embarrassed, and stepped in front of her desk, blocking the test from his sight. She should have thought to hide it before answering the door. But Théo already knew she might be having Tristan's baby.

'Is it positive?' he asked darkly, his glittering stare locked to hers and his body emanating a kind of coiled energy as if he was still looking out for his brother's welfare and convinced Connie would somehow hurt Tris. And maybe now, through no fault of her own, she might.

Defensive, Connie raised her chin. 'Yes. Not that it's really any of your business. So you can put away the scowl.' Because of the mistake at the clinic, the baby was wholly Connie's. He wouldn't be Uncle Théo. He wouldn't need to worry about Tris's parental rights.

'I disagree,' he said, inching closer so her heart leapt excitedly and her body temperature spiked.

Still, Connie rolled her eyes in exasperation. 'Don't start all that Uncle Théo stuff again...'

While the possessive glint in his eyes thrilled the part of her still desperately attracted to him, she knew she should tell him that he wouldn't in fact be related to her child. But she owed it to her friend to speak to Tris first. She didn't want him finding out from anyone else but her.

'Tell me,' Théo said, shoving his hands into his trouser pockets as he pinned her with his intense, impassioned stare, 'does the name Marcel Roulet mean anything to you?'

While his voice was calm, steely determination shone in his eyes as he inched closer, watching her mouth, waiting for her answer.

More heat flamed in Connie's cheeks at his line of questioning. Had Tris already been contacted about the mix-up at the clinic? Did Théo already know Connie seemed to have chosen the world's most incompetent fertility clinic for her procedure? Was he here to berate her for messing Tris around? And why, when this had turned into some sort of farce, when she had her ward round to get to, was she still exquisitely aware of Théo's manliness and raw sex appeal?

'I know him,' she admitted carefully, blaming her hormones. 'But I told you last night, this is between me and Tris. When are you going to stop parenting him? He's a grown man. He's about to be married. He has his life far better sorted than either you or I,' she scoffed.

'Tris is my brother,' Théo said, his eyes narrowing. 'The only family I have.'

'I know...' Connie winced, compassion for him coming unbidden and once more sending her off balance.

'I'll never stop looking out for his welfare and happiness,' he went on, in that same eerily calm voice. 'But that's beside the point. Are you expecting a call from this Marcel Roulet by any chance?'

Connie huffed, embracing her anger at his intrusive

questions over the irrelevant lust she couldn't seem to escape when he was around. 'Again, none of your business.' But how did Théo know that?

'Unless it *is* my business.' He moved closer, into her personal space, his stare shifting over her face, once more dropping to her mouth where she was slack-jawed in disbelief at his effrontery.

Stunned by the giddy tingle in her lips, as if he'd done more than stare, she glared back. 'And why would it be anything to do with you?' She fisted her hands on her hips, her annoyance finally piqued even as her pulse flew at his closeness and the wild, protective look in his eyes. It made her shudder deliciously, the way she had when she'd climaxed crushed in his strong arms that night. She had the highly inappropriate and thrilling thought that he might touch her or kiss her again. But she couldn't possibly actually want that, could she? She was having a baby. Another man's baby. This…*thing* with Théo, whatever it was, should be the last thing on her mind.

Théo smiled but there was no warmth in the expression. Only determination and that heated kind of hunger she wasn't sure was real or a figment of her hormonal imagination.

'Because I too spoke to Mr Roulet this morning,' he said, glancing down at her stomach.

Ridiculously, Connie placed her hand there to shield the baby from his possessive gaze.

'And from what he said,' Théo went on, his cool tone in stark contrast to the flames in his eyes, 'I'm almost one hundred per cent certain that your baby is also mine.'

Connie gaped, too stunned to laugh in his face at the absurdity of his outlandish claim. 'Don't be ridiculous,' she muttered finally, Marcel Roulet's words trickling through her panicked mind.

...a clerical error...the wrong deposit...can't disclose that information until I've spoken to the donor.

'No...no,' Connie whispered, slumping into a chair before she lost all strength in her legs. 'You're crazy. Why would it be your baby?' It didn't make sense.

She looked to Théo in desperation, willing him to laugh and say it was all a prank, willing him to say there was no way it could be his child because he'd never visited a fertility clinic. But instead his face hardened.

'Because I sold my sperm, years ago when I was an impoverished medical student,' he confirmed. 'They mixed up the samples. Clearly having two *T Augustins* on the books was too much for the clinic's primitive filing system.' He snorted and shook his head in disgust.

Was it true? Why would he lie? He would never play a trick this cruel on Tris.

'This isn't funny,' Connie said automatically, clinging to the hope that she'd received another donor's sperm and not Théo's. The last thing she wanted was to have *his* baby, especially given their past animosity and current pretty rampant sexual tension. She could just about tolerate working with him. How on earth would she survive raising a child with him and not go mad?

Because where Tris had been happy to take a back seat in the baby's life and watch from afar, she had a bad feeling that perfect-family-obsessed Théo would want to be intimately involved in his child's upbringing. Which meant also being involved in Connie's life.

'At last we agree,' he said, his tone sarcastic but his expression serious. 'It's not funny at all, Connie.'

'Maybe...it wasn't your sperm,' she reasoned hopefully, clinging to any hope she could muster. She didn't want to do this with him. She'd planned to do it alone.

Théo shot her a pitying look. 'We'll soon see. But if this baby is mine, that changes everything.' He leaned closer so she saw predatory sparks in his impassioned eyes. 'You can forget your plan to raise my child alone.'

'*Our* child,' Connie pointed out automatically. Her breathing sped up excitedly as she watched him inch closer, his stare bouncing between hers and her mouth so her lips tingled harder and her breath gusted and she felt certain he was about to kiss her.

'I'm not my brother,' he continued, resting his hands on the arms of her chair, looming over her so she had to crane her neck to keep eye contact, 'happy for you to raise our baby by yourself. I'm going to want more. To be a real father to our child as it deserves. To be there for every birthday, every Christmas, every school play and parents' evening. You're going to see a whole lot more of me than you want and you'll just have to get used to that.'

Connie opened her mouth to deny him but she was too shocked to speak. Ludicrously, with total disregard for timing or relevance, her body was achingly turned on. By him!

'No. This can't be happening,' she muttered when he moved away. 'It must be a mistake. It wasn't supposed to be this way. It wasn't supposed to involve you.' He must be deluded or misinformed.

Théo cast her a withering, slightly pitying look as if he'd somehow slotted all the pieces of this mix-up together long before Connie.

Then, with impeccable timing that made Connie feel as insignificant as a pawn on a giant cosmic chessboard being manoeuvred by malicious higher forces, her phone rang and her stomach dropped like a stone.

* * *

Connie hung up the call, which had obviously been from the fertility clinic, the pallor of her skin confirming Théo's worst suspicions. Earlier, he'd given Marcel Roulet permission to inform the recipient of his identity. One look at Connie's devastation told him that she finally believed what Théo had already guessed.

The clinic had switched Tris's specimen for his. Connie was carrying Théo's baby.

'I can't believe this,' she whispered, staring at him accusingly as if he'd deliberately tricked her or telepathically impregnated her or somehow engineered the specimen switch.

'My entire reason for doing it this way,' she went on angrily, 'was because I'm not interested in dealing with all that relationship stuff but I wanted a child. But now there's you to deal with.' She shot him an accusing look, as if he and the man who'd hurt and betrayed her were one and the same.

'Maybe it's a lesson for us both,' he muttered darkly, aware she was simply lashing out. 'We have the consequences without having experienced the joy of the conception. Maybe babies should be made the old-fashioned way...'

But a part of him experienced the first trembles of excitement that he was actually, finally going to be a father. After all the heartache with Anaïs, who'd changed her mind about having a child with him, after his own abandonment and tumultuous childhood, here was a chance for a fresh start. Only hot on the heels of that thought, protective urges surged inside him like tidal waves. For Tris, whose role in all this had now been discarded. For the baby, who, like Théo and Tris, would grow up in a fractured family. Even for Connie herself, who looked pale with shock.

Once she'd processed his offhand comment, her wounded gaze flew to his. 'The old-fashioned way didn't work out for me. Despite the plans and promises we made, my ex-fiancé preferred to impregnate one of his office colleagues while I pursued my surgical career. This way, I could have a family to my own timeline and without having to trust someone unworthy. Without getting my heart broken in the process. But it wasn't supposed to involve anyone else, least of all you.'

Théo winced as fear replaced the compassion he felt for Connie. When he'd sold his specimen all those years ago, he'd signed a waiver renouncing his legal responsibilities for any child conceived. But if Connie decided to exclude him, he would fight to be a part of their child's life, knowing as he did what it was like to grow up without a father.

As they locked stares, each processing the news and battling their own doubts, that damned connection of theirs crackled, drawing them together as if they were puppets and fate were laughing while pulling their strings.

'And yet here we are,' he said, desperately clinging to his composure. 'Ironic considering you wanted nothing to do with me.' Of course, he could understand she'd been hurt and deceived in the past, but Théo wasn't that man.

Dragging in a deep breath, he tried to apply logic to the situation. 'But whatever you planned, however much you wished to ignore me, all that is irrelevant now.'

'What does that mean?' she asked, clearly still stunned by the news and emotionally guarded.

'It means,' he said, his heart pounding with fear that she had all the power here, 'that family is everything to me, as I told you. I'm not going to lose out on a relationship with my child just because you can't forgive me and planned to do this alone. A child needs to know its father, so don't go thinking you can dismiss me or sweep my feelings aside or conveniently cut me out of the picture.'

She gripped the arms of the chair and leaned forward. 'Do *you* even want a baby?' she asked with a frown. 'You're almost forty and single. Are you sure you want to go down this track?'

Théo gaped in disbelief. 'I assume by *down this track* you mean being a parent to my own child. I've always wanted a family of my own. One of the reasons my marriage ended was because Anaïs changed her mind. I never imagined it would happen this way or with you, but I fully intend to father our child. You might take your big boisterous family for granted, but you know my past, know that I never knew my own father. All children should know they are loved and accepted by both parents.'

'You're right. I'm sorry...' She deflated and looked away, blinking rapidly as if she might cry. 'I would never stop you having a relationship with the baby, just like I'd never have stopped Tris.'

Her voice broke and compassion swamped him. He stepped closer, took another deep breath and softened his tone. 'Look, I might have...overreacted just now... marching in here. This has been a terrible shock for us both. But I should have got a hold of my composure first or let you discover the news from Roulet.'

He could admit he was highly sensitive to any perceived threat to those he loved. The minute he'd put all of the pieces together, his first thought, after concern that Tris might be upset that he wasn't the father after all, was that Connie hated him and he was about to lose his child even before it was born.

She sniffed and nodded but wouldn't look at him.

Théo sought the calm he used in the operating room. 'If we're mature and respectful of each other,' he went on, trying to hide the desperation from his voice, 'we can figure this out together. At least the procedure worked and you got what you wanted: a baby.'

'Yes…' She kept her gaze down, still appearing dazed and numb.

Théo poured her a glass of water and set it on the desk. 'Drink this for the shock. Doctor's orders.'

When she smiled thinly and meekly obeyed he went on, soothingly. 'I know you think it's easier to do this alone after the hurt and betrayal you've been through, but I'm not that man, Connie.' He wasn't asking for her trust, just a chance to be involved. 'Surely when it comes to parenting, two heads are better than one.'

She sipped, silently nodding, albeit reluctantly.

Because his legs felt weak, he pulled up a seat opposite hers. 'How are you feeling, physically?' he asked, cautiously, trying to put himself in her shoes. He'd not only hurt her in the past, he'd also stormed back into her life and discovered that the baby she'd thought she'd be raising alone was his, not Tris's.

'Fine.' She sipped the water, her hand trembling, peering at him with lingering doubt. 'Absolutely fine.'

'Now that the question of the paternity is resolved,' he said, trying on a half-smile to make light of the crazy situation none of them could have foreseen, 'I think congratulations are in order.' He jerked his chin towards the pregnancy test on the desk and reached for her hand, ignoring the thud of his heart at the contact and how a part of him wanted to hold her, to reassure her everything would work out, to make her see that he wouldn't let her or their child down. Ever.

'Thanks,' she muttered, swallowing hard, the tiniest of smiles tugging at her lips. 'You too, I guess.'

'Look, just because neither of us planned this,' he said quietly, staring into her deep brown intelligent eyes, 'doesn't mean we can't make it work for everyone.' Connie was a caring compassionate woman. If he looked past his own fear, he felt confident she would do the right thing and put the baby's needs first. 'The most important person to consider is the one you're now carrying. That's all that matters, don't you agree?'

'I do.' She nodded, seeming to pull herself together as she looked up.

For a few seconds, while his pulse buzzed in his ears, Théo sat trapped in the moment. Her hand was warm and soft in his. Her big eyes swam with emotion behind their long lashes. Her mouth, only inches away from his, parted as her breaths gusted in rapid little pants he just couldn't ignore.

'I need to get back to work,' she whispered, not pulling her hand away.

Théo nodded. 'Me too.'

What was he thinking? Just because he had all these protective urges, didn't mean he could indulge his attraction to Connie. It was still irrelevant, maybe even more so now that she was having his baby. She didn't trust him and he would do anything to safeguard his relationship with his child, and, by extension, Connie.

Reluctantly, he let go of her hand and pushed back his chair to give her some space. He stood, planning to leave her to mull things over in private while he did the same, but her phone rang again.

She snatched it up and answered, slipping on her work persona before his eyes. 'Okay. Yes.' She glanced his way meaningfully, a small frown tugging at her lips. 'I'll be right there.'

When she'd hung up, she stood and reached for her stethoscope. 'Elodie Verdier's condition is deteriorating. My registrar thinks she might have sepsis.'

'Then let's go see her together,' he said, grateful to have something to think about beyond the fact that, astonishingly, he and Connie were having a baby together when they'd only had sex that one time three years ago.

They rushed to the post-op ward where they met Connie's registrar, Jules.

'Elodie Verdier spiked a fever during the night and was commenced on antibiotics,' Jules said, speaking rapidly. 'I organised a repeat X-ray and scan this morning, but she's been deteriorating throughout the day. Her blood pressure is low, the fever is high, her urine output is reduced and she's showing signs of delirium.'

Théo and Connie hurried to the patient's bedside while the registrar continued to relay blood-test results. Since they'd reviewed the patient the day before, she'd clearly deteriorated rapidly. Now her skin was grey, her breathing rapid behind an oxygen mask and she seemed confused, unaware of who they were or where she was.

'Roll her, please,' Connie asked the nursing staff, who rolled Elodie onto her side so she could listen to her lungs.

Théo took her pulse and auscultated her heart from the front, then checking the wounds for signs of infection.

'Have you taken blood for culture?' he asked Jules. If they knew what pathogen they were dealing with, they'd have a better chance of treating the infection.

The registrar nodded. 'The doctor who started the antibiotics took them overnight, and I've repeated them this morning. No results back yet.'

When Connie finished her examination, they left the room to discuss their findings.

'The heart sounds are normal,' Théo said, looking to Connie.

'And the chest is clear,' Connie added, frowning with concern. 'But she's clearly in septic shock. We should transfer her to Intensive Care.'

Jules nodded, making notes.

'The scan should show us if there's a collection or haematoma internally,' Théo said, impressed that he and Connie could set aside their shocking revelations of the morning and collaborate so effectively.

'Again, I'm waiting for those results,' Jules said.

'We could head down to Radiology,' Connie suggested, looking to Théo for his nod of agreement. 'Speak to the radiologist and try to expedite the results.'

'Yes. Let's do that.' He addressed Jules once more. 'You speak to ICU. Insert a central line and start some vasopressin for her hypotension. We need to get her stabilised in case we need to take her back to Theatre.'

Then, without further mention of the momentous events that had transpired in their personal lives, he and Connie hurried to the radiology department, once more a team of sorts.

CHAPTER SEVEN

LATER THAT EVENING, having checked up on Elodie on ICU and found her patient in a stable condition, Connie left the surgical floor and headed for the hospital's rear staff exit. After an unbelievable and emotional day, she was mentally and physically exhausted and looking forward to sleep to reset her brain. In true denial, she couldn't even contemplate thinking about Théo and the implications of the baby being his until she'd eaten dinner, taken a long soak in the bath and had a full night's sleep.

Maybe tomorrow, everything would once more make sense… With any luck, she'd wake up to find it had all been a bad dream.

The lift doors opened on the ground floor. On autopilot, Connie stepped out and found herself greeted with the enchanting sound of a choir singing at the entrance to the children's ward. A crowd of patients, staff and visitors had gathered to listen to the beautiful harmonised singing.

Smiling, Connie joined the crowd, taking comfort from the well-known children's songs about wintertime, Christmas trees and Papa Noël. Her troubled mind eased as the familiar melodies reminded her that Christmas was right around the corner. This time next year, she'd have a baby and all the excitement and wonder of its first Christmas to celebrate. But it was also Théo's baby. He would want to be involved and she couldn't for one second deny him, regardless of their messy past and her reasons for choosing to do this alone, just as she wouldn't have denied Tris a relationship with his son or daughter. He'd been through enough heartache and uncertainty with his childhood and his divorce. When he'd talked about a child needing its father, Connie's heart had almost split in two. She'd never really considered the full impact of Tris and Théo's upbringing from Théo's perspective.

And Théo wasn't her ex. He was a decent man who cared deeply about people: his patients and Tris especially. And after everything he'd lost—his father, his mother and grandmother and his marriage and hopes of children—he deserved family. He was certainly right about a child deserving to know they were safe and loved and cherished by both parents.

Overwhelmed once more, Connie sighed. Everything was such a mess. Earlier, within the space of minutes, she'd gone from delight that she was having the baby she'd wanted, to having to share it with Théo of all people. But surely if she and Théo could trust each other in the operating room and when it came to the patients in their care, they could come to some sort of suitable co-parenting arrangement that would satisfy them both.

As if he'd heard her thoughts, Théo materialised at her side. Dressed in St Raphaël navy-blue scrubs, he too appeared a little fatigued, his dark hair a little ruffled, presumably from wearing a surgical hat.

'Hi,' she whispered, getting lost in his eyes and the intense way he looked at her, as if to him she were a fascinating stranger who happened to be carrying his baby.

And in many ways they were strangers. They might have intimate knowledge of each other's bodies, but, up to now, she'd deliberately avoided getting to know him better. Suddenly, the shocking events of the day meant she had questions. Lots of questions. About his foster parents, his marriage breakdown and his world view, which was likely different from Tris's given Théo was older and had always tried to protect Tris. But who had been looking out for Théo?

'Hi.' He smiled, his stare clouded by uncertainty as if he too had more he wanted to say. Then, taking her by surprise, Théo joined in with the choir and the crowd, singing along to the well-known songs in a deep baritone while flicking her the kind of playful smile that made her breath catch.

Connie chuckled to herself when he sang with even greater enthusiasm, grinning her way unselfconsciously. But that was Théo. A man comfortable enough in his own skin that there was no pretence. He could admit his mistakes and apologise. He fought fiercely and passionately for those he loved. All admirable qualities.

As the festive music swirled around them, things seemed surmountable once more. Connie surrendered and sang along too, grateful for the few moments of joyous distraction from what had been an overwhelming day.

When the song came to an end, she and Théo stepped aside. 'I've been in Theatre all afternoon and I'm on call tonight,' he said quietly as, together, they walked towards the exit. 'Have you managed to review our ICU patient?'

Connie nodded, aware that his concern for Elodie matched her own. Connie brought him up to speed on Elodie's progress as they left the hospital and paused outside. 'Her blood pressure has stabilised. Test results show it's an atypical bacterial infection.' The scans had shown a small paraspinal collection of fluid, which for now didn't seem to be compressing any nerves and might resolve on its own. 'I suggest we watch and wait.'

She moved just beyond the exit, away from the busy comings and goings through the electronic doors. Connie glanced down at her feet, her emotions all over the place once more. As Elodie's lead surgeon, she couldn't help but feel responsible for the post-op infection.

'Don't blame yourself,' Théo said, somehow sensing her feelings. 'Infection is always a risk with any surgery. We were both responsible for Elodie, and we did everything right.'

Connie nodded, grateful for his words of comfort. 'I know.'

'I'll look in on her later,' Théo said, his breath forming a cloud in the frigid winter air. 'Look, I know we have other things to discuss, but you should go home,' he added, his stare softening with compassion. 'Get some sleep. You look tired and it's been an emotional roller coaster of a day that neither of us were expecting.'

Choked by his understanding and ashamed by her earlier overreaction and by all the things she'd said to him since he'd started working at St Raphaël, Connie nodded. 'You're right. It has.' A patient unwell enough to need ICU, the fertility clinic mix-up, discovering Théo not Tris was the father of her baby...

'I'm sorry...for earlier,' she said, forcing herself to meet his warm stare. 'For the way I acted. I was knocked sideways with shock. I said things...'

As she looked up at him, a flood of questions rushed her mind. How on earth would they make this work? What were his expectations when it came to the baby?

And perhaps most pressing—how could she switch off this insistent thrill of attraction, when she had way bigger issues on which to focus?

As if he could read her mind, Théo's expression softened further. 'It's all going to be okay, Connie. I promise.' He stepped closer and rested his hand on her shoulder so familiar heat spread through her veins. 'We'll figure it out together.'

'I hope so.' Connie glanced at her feet and nodded, even though she didn't fully share his confidence. The last time she'd trusted a man's promise, it had been one of Guy's and it had broken as easily as a bird's egg. But Théo's touch was comforting and she didn't need to trust him with her emotions. Just her baby. *Their* baby.

'Thanks,' she said, blinking up at him as her heart fluttered. 'For saying the right things today and for your apology last week. It means a lot. I should have confronted you about what I'd overheard that morning sooner. Cleared the air. I just...' She looked down again, ashamed. 'Well, my trust had been badly damaged and I was a mess too. But you were right. I did overreact, back then and on your first day. I'm sorry.'

'It's okay,' he said, his hand gently squeezing her shoulder. 'I understand what you've been through. Look, if you're free tomorrow, we could talk then, away from here.' He dropped his hand and Connie reeled, instantly missing his touch. 'About the baby and how we're going to do this. It might be wise to speak before we get caught up in Tris and Victor's wedding the weekend after.'

'Okay. That sounds sensible,' she said, aware that it was cold and, unlike her, he wasn't wearing a coat. 'I need to figure out how I'm going to tell Tris that the baby isn't his.'

But maybe because they'd had such an emotional

day, maybe because she was having his baby, maybe because she was in no rush to be alone with her tumultuous thoughts and she'd seen a more human side to him this evening—a man singing rousing Christmas songs for sick kids—she couldn't make her feet move.

She didn't need to rely on anyone. But if she had to, a man like Théo—responsible, moral and selfless—would be her man of choice.

'We can figure out how to tell Tris tomorrow too if you like. Do you want me to call you a ride?' he said, unmoving.

Connie shook her head, her confusion building. 'I'm happy on the *Métro*.' So why was she lingering, her body still abuzz from his touch? Why were those stubborn memories of how electrifying their first kiss had been spinning in her head? Why was her body inching towards his as if she was about to do something reckless?

'Goodnight, then,' he said finally, his hand returning to her shoulder as he swooped in to press his lips first to one cheek, then the other in the French way.

The gesture was almost automatic, but as he lingered in her personal space as if he couldn't bear to step back, Connie's breathing stalled. The warmth and scent of him that close made her heart race with longing. Before she knew what she was doing, she turned her face to his and their lips grazed in the barest of tentative kisses.

Thrilling excitement slammed through her. For a loaded-with-possibility second, Théo stilled apart from his fingers, which curled around her shoulder possessively. His heated stare, locked to hers, darkened and made Connie feel naked. That connection she'd been fighting since he'd walked back into her life, there between them since the first time they met, built stronger than ever and harder to deny because now they would always be connected through the life growing inside Connie.

Tired of fighting her attraction to him and because she knew from past experience how good it would feel, Connie surged up on her tiptoes as Théo swooped in to capture her lips with his. Desperate to switch off her mind's incessant questioning, Connie pressed her cold lips to his warm ones, losing herself in the kick of safe physical desire.

It felt so good to surrender, to feel desired by someone she knew wasn't looking for a relationship. Someone who knew her history, understood her priorities were the pregnancy and the baby. Someone with whom she was safe to just be a woman attracted to a man without agenda.

Adrenaline surged through her system, shunting her heart rate higher as Théo held her close. His kiss turned quickly bold and commanding, his lips moving against hers as if he'd been dreaming of doing this for days. As if he too were powerless.

Dangerously, Connie slid her hands around the back of his neck, her fingertips grazing his hairline, and parted her lips against his, a tiny moan escaping her throat as the kiss deepened in an erotic tangle of lips and tongues and panted breath. Théo's arms hauled her closer so her body was pressed to his hard chest, hard thighs, the start of an erection grazing her hip.

A moment's doubt rushed her mind. She shouldn't be doing this. Kissing him in the hospital car park, making herself more turned on than she'd felt in three years. It wasn't fair to send him mixed messages. But she had mixed emotions. It was as Théo had said earlier—they had the consequences of a baby without having experienced the thrill of making it. And it would have been thrilling. Sexually, she and Théo just clicked.

In that second, with their lips still locked and their hearts racing side by side, the nearby hospital doors slid open and the sound of the choir singing *'Vive le Vent'*, the French version of 'Jingle Bells' grew louder, the upbeat catchy tune drifting out to break the spell. Snapped from the madness of practically making out with Théo in the hospital car park, Connie pulled back, her heart racing erratically and her regrets warming her cheeks.

Théo looked as dazed as she felt, his fierce expression in stark contrast to the jolly Christmas song, which told the story of the winter wind and an old man walking in the snow. Their eyes met as they each caught their frosty breaths. The absurdity of the moment struck Connie and she laughed, giggling harder when Théo joined in, pressing his lips swiftly to her forehead and then sliding his hands from her waist and stepping back.

With the tension snapped and the moment broken, Connie ran a hand through her hair, trying to pull herself together. 'I think you're right. I should go home and get some sleep. I'm acting emotionally. That probably wasn't a good idea.'

Although for some reason, maybe because they'd slept together before and neither of them was denying their attraction no matter how badly it complicated things, she couldn't bring herself to apologise for the kiss. She didn't regret it. It had happened in the moment. Call it Christmas madness. A response to fatigue and worry and the romance of the silly season, just like the last time she'd behaved recklessly and slept with him.

'I'll see you tomorrow,' he said, a ghost of that gorgeous smile on his lips and unmistakeable hunger and disappointment in his eyes.

Connie turned away before she could once more succumb to temptation, casually waving over her shoulder. But as she crossed the car park, her senses were on high alert as if he was watching her retreat. At the last minute, before she left the hospital grounds, she glanced back.

He was where she'd left him, still observing with an inscrutable expression. Still handsome and vulnerable and looking as confused as Connie felt. Still making her blood hot as if she had her own portable central heating system under her coat.

CHAPTER EIGHT

THE NEXT DAY was Saturday. Despite being on call, and after the shocking revelations and that incendiary kiss in the car park, Théo had somehow managed to get a few hours' sleep. Eager to capitalise on their tentative truce and discuss how they would work as parents, he'd arranged to meet Connie, at Rue de Rivoli. She was wrapped up against the cold, her green scarf making her eyes seem brighter and her cautious smile resurfacing all those protective urges of his, and he had pressed a restrained kiss to her cheek and forced himself to behave.

Wanting her physically had become way more complicated. Now there was too much at stake for him to focus solely on their attraction, no matter how rampant. And he couldn't afford to mess this up.

As they walked the city, chatting about inconsequential things and admiring how every street seemed to sparkle with twinkling lights, every historic square boasted a towering Christmas tree and every shop window glittered with magical Christmas displays, they'd each cautiously acknowledged that they were still reeling from the turn of events and their respective calls from the clinic.

Hoping to explore trickier subjects than Tris's wedding the following weekend and the upcoming Christmas festivities, Théo took Connie to one of his favourite cafés for hot chocolate and pastries. Café Solène was located down a cobbled street, well away from the main tourist areas, so they easily found a table in the window and ordered *chocolat chaud* and croissant.

'So,' he said when the waitress departed, resisting the temptation to touch her hand across the table, 'should we talk about that unexpected and incredibly hot kiss last night?' He softened his bold question with a playful smile.

He wasn't naive. He knew it meant nothing. They'd had a highly emotional and shocking day yesterday. But that reckless moment served as an acknowledgement that, regardless of what else was going on between them, if you scratched beneath the surface, their fierce sexual attraction was undeniable.

'I'd rather talk about the baby,' she said, shooting him a good-natured smile. Then her expression became serious.

'Okay,' Théo conceded, surprised that she'd chosen to broach the main topic on his mind. 'Do you want to start?'

Connie hesitantly looked up from the small Christmas tree at the centre of their table. 'First, I'm curious,' she said, watching him with obvious interest. 'What made you donate all those years ago, when you've clearly always wanted a family of your own?'

Théo dragged in a breath. He rarely looked back, preferring to focus on creating a stable and hopeful future. But for Connie, he would make an exception.

'It was Tris, actually,' Théo said with a shrug, continuing when she frowned in confusion. 'He was about to turn eighteen. Money was tight as we were both in full-time education, him still at school and me at medical school. But he was desperate for the same gaming console all his school friends had.'

As he recalled those difficult years when the weight of responsibility had sometimes felt overwhelming and only highlighted his sense of anger at the father who'd rejected them, his heart thudded. 'And it was worth it. You should have seen his face when he opened my gift. Of course, I never told him how I'd got the money.'

'Wow, Théo…' she said, looking at him with awe as if he'd done something truly special.

'What about you?' Théo asked, changing the subject. 'What made you go down the donor route? Have you really abandoned the search for a committed relationship? You're only thirty-five.'

When she pressed her lips together, her eyes darting away, he quickly added, 'I'm not judging. I understand how devastating it can be when someone you love lets you down. When you had a plan to spend for ever with someone and the other person changed their mind. But you're a smart, attractive woman, Connie. You have an awful lot going for you.' Did she really want to be alone for the rest of her life?

Connie sighed, the stare she levelled on him defiant so he saw the depth of her past hurt and betrayal. 'I told you about my fiancé, Guy,' she said, idly twirling the miniature Christmas tree as if it were part of a wind-up music box. 'What he did—the lies, the double life, taking advantage of my long hours at the hospital—it really damaged my ability to trust.'

'He sounds despicable,' Théo said, furious that anyone would treat caring, gorgeous Connie with such little respect and consideration.

'Yes. But the worst part was that I doubted myself. My instincts. I felt stupid, as if I should have somehow known what was going on if only I'd opened my eyes wider.'

'That's understandable,' he said as soon as the waitress who'd delivered their drinks and croissants departed. 'Everyone would react that way.' He wouldn't patronise her. Connie was an intelligent woman. She would know what her ex had done said nothing about her and everything about his inadequacies.

'With the exception of a drunken rebound one-night stand one Christmas eve,' she added, flicking him a knowing look that heated his blood, 'it took me a long time to date again. Then, when I did pluck up the courage, I just never seemed able to get past a second or third date before seeing all these red flags,' she admitted quietly, stirring her hot chocolate thoughtfully.

'I'm sorry,' he said, fighting the growing urge to touch her. 'My careless comments that morning probably added to your poor impression of men in general.'

She watched him carefully, an insightful gleam in her eyes. 'At least you and I had chemistry,' she said. 'Other men I dated looked great on paper, but when we met in person there was just no spark at all.'

Théo nodded, thinking their sparks could probably ignite the earth's atmosphere.

'Suddenly I was thirty-five and happy to be single,' she went on, when he stayed quiet, absorbing every word as a detective stored away clues. 'I love my job. I have a great apartment, lots of friends, an active social life.'

'But you still wanted a family,' he said, able to empathise. He'd always hoped to have children one day. When Anaïs had left, his dreams of a child of his own had been pushed back, then he'd grown busy with his career and spending time with Tris and Victor and trying to create some semblance of family from the rubble left from his past losses and failed marriage.

Connie nodded, seeming to relax further. 'My friend Chloe, who's a couple of years older than me, had just been diagnosed with lupus and was advised to delay starting a family until it was under control. She'd just got married and had been looking forward to having a baby. I suddenly thought, why am I putting this off? I've reached the top of the career ladder. I'm on my way to forty. None of us knows what is around the corner health-wise... I just felt that it was now or never and I didn't want to find myself in my forties with regrets. Then I talked to Tris about it and he didn't laugh or call me crazy. Instead he offered to be my donor and... Well, you know the rest. Here we are.'

She took a sip of hot chocolate and licked her lips, distracting Théo from his next question with memories of the passion behind their kiss the night before, the urge to kiss her again obliterating all the reasons he shouldn't indulge.

'What about you?' she asked, turning the questions his way. 'What happened with Anaïs?'

'The divorce was by mutual consent,' he began cagily, because opening up wasn't something that came naturally. 'We of course talked about having a family when we first got together. But after we married, Anaïs kept putting it off. We were both busy with work, as you can imagine. You know how demanding surgery can be. On calls, late nights, working the holidays. Anaïs often complained that I was hardly ever there, even when I was home. But she too was chasing promotions and building her real-estate career.'

Connie nodded encouragingly.

'Towards the end, it seemed that every time I raised starting a family, she shut the topic down. It was as if she'd actually decided she didn't want children after all without telling me. Finally, she admitted that she had changed her mind. That she was enjoying her career too much and no longer wanted a family. Not with me. She said I constantly held back from her emotionally.'

'Was she right?' Connie asked, observing him carefully.

'Maybe she had a point.' He shrugged, his barriers rising because he didn't often discuss his feelings, preferring to leave the past behind. 'I didn't see it at the time, but I guess I can be…emotionally cautious, shall we say?'

Maybe he'd overprotected himself from being hurt again after losing his family. But then again, maybe he'd been right to keep those barriers up. His marriage had failed after all, although he'd largely blamed himself.

'Can't we all?' Connie scoffed, flicking him a sympathetic smile. 'And in your case I can kind of understand why, after what you and Tris went through growing up. Tris doesn't talk about it much, but I suspect you each have a different take on your childhood anyway, from what you've told me. At least Tris had you.'

Théo swallowed, finding Connie easy to talk to but eager to avoid discussing the rejection and losses of his painful past. 'I guess the deal-breaker for Anaïs was my failure to be present in my relationship, for which I take responsibility.'

'And for you it was the issue of children,' she said.

He nodded, relieved he was finally having a child, just not in the traditional way.

'Clearly you and Anaïs wanted different things,' Connie said. 'You can't take all the blame for the relationship ending if she changed her mind about family but kept you dangling.'

'I guess not,' Théo admitted, feeling way too exposed.

'I'm really sorry that it didn't work out for you,' she said, tilting her head in empathy. 'So you haven't been tempted to try to find love again?'

Théo dodged the question. 'I guess we're both quite similar, you and I.' He shrugged, the conversation skating close to his comfort level. 'With the exception of personal relationships, our lives are good. It would take something really special to make us want to take the risk again, don't you agree? And now…well, the baby takes precedence.'

His pulse lurched as she nodded thoughtfully and stared the way she had the night before, just before they'd kissed, as if she saw him more clearly. Théo's temperature soared, that urge to touch her returning.

'What?' he asked finally, licking his top lip, wondering if he had a chocolate moustache.

'Nothing.' She shook her head, but continued to stare enigmatically. 'I'm just…learning new things about you.'

'Is that why you kissed me?' he challenged playfully, trying to lighten the mood and address the other hot topic. 'Because you realised I'm actually a nice guy?' Although trying to win her over or thinking about that kiss was trivial. They were going to be parents. That was the most important thing.

She shook her head and scoffed. 'We'll come to the kiss,' she said, deflecting. 'Let's get back to talking about the baby.'

'Right. So what are you going to say to Tris?' he asked. 'About the baby being mine and not his.'

Théo hated keeping secrets from his brother, but he'd been at the hospital until after midnight last night and Tris and Victor were busy today with last-minute wedding preparations. Plus it was Connie's place to tell him.

Connie shrugged and frowned. 'Just the truth, I guess.

I'm seeing him tonight. I thought it would be better to tell him in person so I can see if he's truly upset.' She nibbled at her lip. 'Do you think he will be?'

Before he'd even registered he'd moved he touched the back of her hand, drew her fingers through his. Her skin was warm and soft and he felt instantly closer to her, as if they would figure out this parenting journey together. 'I hope not. He was happy to help you out without wanting any parental responsibilities,' he reasoned. 'He must have prepared himself for the possibility that the procedure might not have worked. And it's not like there's ever been anything romantic between you two.'

'No,' Connie said, worry tightening her mouth as her fingers flexed against his. 'I just hope he isn't…disappointed.'

'I'll call him this evening to see how he feels,' Théo said, squeezing her hand. 'I'm sure he'll be happy for you and invested in last-minute wedding plans. Don't worry. We're in this together and we've already established that we both love Tris to bits.'

Connie's smile widened and lit her eyes. That zing of awareness arced between them once more. She didn't pull her hand away, so he stroked his fingertips over her skin. 'Is there anything you need from me?' he asked quietly. 'With regards to the baby and the pregnancy?'

He didn't want to crowd her, but he wanted her to know that he'd be there if she needed him.

'I don't think so.' She smiled. 'I've seen my family doctor and I'm booked in for a scan after Christmas. I can let you know the time and date if you'd like to attend.'

'Yes, I'll be there. Thank you.' He waited until she looked up then added, 'I realise this wasn't how you planned it and that it might seem that I'm muscling in on your pregnancy, the way I muscled in on your surgery that first day. But I don't want to take over. I just want to help and to have a chance at a relationship with our little one.'

She nodded, her eyes shining. 'Of course, Théo. You're its father.'

Relief washed through him. Until that moment he hadn't been certain that Connie would allow him access to their baby. But as a few beats of charged silence passed, a new kind of relentlessness built. Just because they were having a baby together hadn't diminished their chemistry. Not even the possibility that she would have Tris's baby had achieved that.

As if she too was aware of it, and wanted to take a step back, Connie slid her hand from his and picked up her mug, taking a sip.

Théo swallowed down the surge of panic and physical desire, the confusing feelings drowning out the urge to get to know Connie better, because she was going to be the mother of his child. They needed to stay on talking terms. There'd be plenty of time over the next nine months to get to know each other beyond what they knew from briefly being past lovers. Théo couldn't risk failing at another relationship and missing out on contact with his child. Anaïs and he had each played their part in the breakdown of the marriage and lack of clear communication, but Théo could admit his failings.

'So, about that kiss,' she said, when she placed her mug back down on the table. 'I've never denied our chemistry, but I was obviously feeling emotional last night. And it's Christmas…' She raised one shoulder in a shrug. 'I told you it makes people behave badly.'

There was mirth in her eyes, a small smile tugging

at her lovely lips, so Théo smiled back, letting her off the hook.

'Right,' he said, slowly nodding. He understood why she would back-pedal. Things were complicated enough between them without adding sex to the mix, no matter how desperately and inconveniently tempting.

'I mean, clearly we're still attracted to each other,' she went on conversationally, as if they were discussing Christmas gift ideas. 'But we'd be foolish to do anything about it, don't you agree? It's like you said, the baby is the important thing.'

Unsure who she was trying to convince, him or herself, he nodded. 'You're right—there are other priorities now.' But before yesterday, before he'd discovered Connie's baby was also his, he'd fantasised over and over about sleeping with her again, perhaps going on a few dates to see if there could be anything there worth pursuing now they were both in a better place emotionally.

She nodded, taking her cue from him. 'It's like you said, I've more or less written off dating anyway. And you've been through enough drama with your divorce. It's family that's important now. Creating one that meets everyone's needs.'

'I can't argue with any of that,' he said wistfully. The last thing he wanted to do was recklessly indulge his desires and risk upsetting or hurting Connie, given things were already so precariously balanced. He couldn't survive losing another person he loved and, even though his baby was little more than a ball of cells, he'd discovered that parental love was pretty much instantaneous.

'Of course,' she said carefully, glancing down at the table, 'I'm in no position to have sex with anyone else at the moment either. I mean, I'm having a baby. *Your* baby.'

'I'm aware of that,' he said, his stare holding hers as possessive feelings conjured up hypothetical men she might have otherwise slept with. But was she saying she'd thought about sleeping with him again too? That she'd been open to exploring their chemistry before the fateful call from the clinic had changed everything? That certainly explained the passion of last night's kiss.

Théo's heart thudded with pointless excitement. 'If it helps,' he said, his tone playful, 'I'm willing to abstain from sex until after the baby is born to keep you company.' With his head full of Connie and the baby, he'd have no appetite for dating let alone sleeping with anyone else anyway.

She laughed. 'Thanks. I appreciate the offer. I'll let you know if your sacrifice is necessary.'

Théo grinned, glad they were able to tease each other, given the tension of the past few days. 'So we just ignore the kiss? Ignore our chemistry?' he asked, certain that he could try but would probably fail. Hopefully focussing on Connie's pregnancy and the baby would help strengthen his resolve just enough.

She nodded. 'We just ignore it. I promise not to kiss you again.' She smiled, apology and a mischievous glint in her eye. 'Just don't go standing near any mistletoe.'

'Okay,' he said, laughing it off. 'Good decision.'

Although in reality there was no decision to make. The needs of baby trumped their own physical needs. As Anaïs had accused, Théo had a tendency to hold back emotionally. And Connie had some pretty big trust issues. They needed all their energy to ensure they could get along as parents.

'Friends, then,' he said, holding up his mug of hot chocolate in a toast, somewhat reassured that this was for the best. He would make it work.

'*Santé,*' she said with a smile and clinked her mug to his.

But something about the way she looked at him as she sipped heated his blood and left him hungry for more, complications or not.

CHAPTER NINE

AFTER TRAIPSING THE streets of Paris's sixth arrondisse-
ment with Théo, and after their heartfelt talk over hot
chocolate, all Connie truly wanted was to go home and
process her up-and-down feelings. But she had another
emotional conversation to get through. She needed to tell
Tris the outcome of their botched plan.

Curled into her friend's comfy sofa, nursing a mug of
steaming tea, Connie brushed aside the memory of Théo's
exhilarating farewell embrace as he'd wished her luck
and told her to call him any time if she needed to talk.
Stalling for time, she glanced around Tris and Victor's
cosy and chic apartment. It was decorated for Christmas
with a stunning real pine tree in the window, garlands of
fresh spruce, cedar and holly draped on the mantel and
clusters of lit pillar candles nestled here and there to create a cosy ambience of flickering light.

'It's so stylish in here,' Connie said, unable to fight the
magic of Christmas, despite her nerves and worries that
Tris would be upset by her news. 'Can I borrow Victor
to decorate my apartment?' she asked playfully of Tris's
partner, who was one of Paris's most sought-after interior designers. 'I haven't put up a single decoration yet.'

'Of course you can,' Tris said, placing his drink on
the coffee table. 'He'd jump at the chance.' He took a

seat next to her wearing an encouraging smile. 'So tell me. Any news?'

His stare sparkled with hopeful excitement and Connie swallowed and set her tea aside, terrified to hurt his feelings. Part of her wished she'd brought Théo along for moral support.

Pulling herself together, she reached for his hand and nodded bravely. 'It worked, Tris. I'm pregnant.' Tears stung her eyes as he beamed and squeezed her fingers.

'Congratulations. I'm so happy for you, Con.' He dragged her into a comforting hug but she pulled back.

'Thanks.' She sniffed, her joy dampened by the clinic's mistake. 'But there's more. Please don't be upset.' She gripped his hand tighter, begging him with her eyes.

'Okay,' he said with a small frown that made Connie feel sick.

She took a deep breath. 'I found out yesterday that there was a mix-up at the clinic. I'm really sorry, Tris, but it turns out I wasn't actually given your specimen during the insemination procedure.'

'What? That's crazy.' His frown deepened. 'So whose specimen were you given?'

Connie swallowed, her throat dry. There was no way to sugar-coat it. 'Théo's.'

Tristan's mouth gaped in shock. 'My Théo?' he asked and Connie nodded in confirmation, her treacherous emotions forcing images of what a great father family-obsessed Théo would likely be into her mind.

'I don't understand…' Tris said, frowning. 'Why did they have Théo's sperm at the clinic?'

'Apparently it was an old sample,' Connie explained. 'He donated for money when he was a medical student.

He said it was to buy you a gaming console for your eighteenth birthday.'

'Wow,' said Tris, looking stunned. 'I never knew that.'

'Are you disappointed? Angry?' she asked cautiously after a moment of searching his expression. 'It's okay if you are. I was. So was Théo.'

Tris shook his head. 'I'm surprised. I'm not sure how else I feel, but it's kind of irrelevant anyway. The deed is done. You're pregnant.'

'I'm sorry,' she said, gripping his hand tighter. 'It wasn't supposed to happen this way. You made a selfless gesture to help me and it all went wrong. I still feel frustrated with the clinic.' And confused for herself.

And for Théo…? She had too many feelings to untangle. She knew being his friend was for the best, but she wasn't sure how she would find the strength to resist temptation. Just spending time with him made her feel…alive.

Tris squeezed her fingers. 'Don't be sorry. The main reason I offered to donate was because I don't want children of my own. But I'm thrilled for you that it worked. That you're going to have the baby you wanted. What does Théo think about it all? He must be overjoyed. He's always wanted kids.'

Connie inhaled a shaky breath, recalling Théo's thrilling possessiveness, his offers of help and his eagerness to attend the antenatal scan. 'He was shocked too at first, obviously. But he says he wants to be involved so I'm just getting used to that idea.'

Tris tilted his head in understanding. 'Yes, I'm afraid he will want to be as hands-on as possible. He's always dreamed of having a family but after his marriage to Anaïs failed I guess he's really only dated casually since.

How do you feel about sharing the baby when that wasn't part of your plan?'

Connie blinked away the sting in her eyes, grateful that, after the initial shock had worn off, Théo had been wonderfully supportive, saying all the right things. 'I was stunned and angry about the mix-up at first, obviously. I mean, I wouldn't have chosen to do it this way or with Théo.' She looked down at her lap, ashamed of her disloyalty and eager not to criticise Théo in front of Tris. 'But after time to get used to the idea, I think we can find a way to make it work. We have to.' Teamwork didn't seem so bad after all with a man like Théo.

Tris nodded and smiled. 'I think you can too. So does this mean you've decided to forgive him?'

'Of course. It was just a misunderstanding,' she said, embarrassed by her part in it. 'We rushed into sleeping together three years ago when neither of us was ready.'

Tris nodded and reached for her other hand. 'I know he hurt you back then, but Théo is an honourable guy. A great guy. You could do a lot worse for a baby daddy.'

Connie laughed then groaned, burying her face in her hands. 'Oh, Tris… What a mess. Part of me still can't believe it's all happening.'

Tris rubbed her back soothingly. 'At least you're still keeping it in the family. I'll still be Uncle Tris, although please never ask me to change a nappy. That might push our friendship a step too far.'

Connie looked up, her throat aching as she tried to smile through the sting of tears. 'You're really okay with this?'

'I'm really okay. I promise. But…what about you and Théo and your, um, history?' Tris picked up his drink, sipped and settled back into the sofa.

'There is no me and Théo,' she said. But even as she denied it, she recalled how exhilarating it had felt when he'd touched her hand in the café earlier. Recalled that reckless, seriously sexy kiss outside the hospital that she'd started.

She parted her tingling lips, abuzz from just the memory of how much that kiss had turned her on at the time. If they'd been in a different location, if he hadn't been on call, would she have stopped at a kiss? Or would she have been swept up in their chemistry and slept with him again? Because despite what she'd said to him about ignoring their chemistry, she'd had to constantly stop herself from touching or kissing him again as they'd traipsed around the city.

'Really?' Tris pushed with a narrowed stare, perhaps sensing her fickle train of thought. 'Because I know that cagey look on your face.'

Afraid to answer Tris's question, she looked down at her lap. Now she and Théo had talked, they had their polite and mature guarantee to fall back on: to focus on being friends and parents. Surely that was enough incentive to keep temptation at bay.

'You're right,' she said finally, sighing. Who was she trying to kid? She needed to talk to someone. 'It's not going to be that cut and dried, because I kissed him last night outside the hospital when I was feeling emotionally overwhelmed.'

And what was more, despite her promises, she couldn't one hundred per cent swear that she wouldn't do it again. It was just so...tempting. And good. And now she'd added fresh memories to those of the past.

'Okay...' Tris held up his hand. 'No judgement here.

I mean, you're obviously still hot for each other in spite of everything.'

Connie nodded, tired of denying it and secretly thrilled that Théo might be struggling too. They *were* crazy hot for each other. 'But we've talked about it,' she said, trying to convince herself that ignoring their chemistry was for the best, 'and we both agree to forget about that and focus on the baby. That's all that matters now, right?'

Not sure if she wanted Tris to agree with her or point out the glaringly obvious flaw in their plan, she looked up expectantly.

'Right,' Tris said, nodding, his expression full of worrying doubt. 'I mean, of course, there are other ways to deal with chemistry,' he went on, his stare suggestive. 'It's not like you haven't done it before. And neither of you is looking for a relationship.'

As if highly infectious, Tris's doubts made Connie's multiply. How would she see Théo every day, share her pregnancy with him and eventually her baby and not want him with the same mindless preoccupation? When she wasn't working, Théo, his heart-stopping smile, his mad sexual skills and how awesome that kiss had been were all she could think about.

'Are you encouraging me to have a fling with your brother?' she asked, her pulse leaping at the intoxicating idea. After all, they were adults. She wasn't interested in dating other men, given she was pregnant. Nor was it fair that they'd made a baby without any physical contact when they'd previously been great together in that department…

'Do you want to have a fling with my brother?' Tris asked, looking mildly uncomfortable but also daring her to be honest.

She might…

'Does he want to have one with you?' Tris continued when she didn't respond. 'I mean, you're both adults. Théo doesn't date much these days. And personally, I'm not sure how in the hell you've managed to last three years without sex.'

Connie playfully smacked his arm and dramatically flopped back against the cushions. 'I'm so confused. And hormonal. You have to help me figure this out. You're my friend.'

'No way.' Tris shook his head and scooted down the sofa, literally distancing himself. 'You're on your own with this decision. He's my brother.' He took a sip of his tea, then gave her the side eye and a cheeky wink.

They both cracked up and the conversation shifted to the wedding plans. But try as she might to force Théo from her mind, Connie found herself picking at the scab of the sensible, restrained decision they'd made over hot chocolate for the rest of the night.

CHAPTER TEN

Two weeks to Christmas

A WEEK LATER, Connie stood on the balcony of the Hôtel Marquis alongside the rest of the wedding guests, beaming at the camera. The boutique hotel in the heart of Paris where Tris and Victor had tied the knot boasted stunning views of the Eiffel Tower. As the wedding party posed for another group photo, Connie beamed, her cheeks aching because she'd smiled so much already. Tristan and Victor's winter wedding had been small, intimate and breathtakingly romantic. She'd shed more than one tear throughout the ceremony, her gaze repeatedly drawn to the man at Tristan's side, his handsome best man, Théo.

While the photographer adjusted his camera settings, Connie glanced over at her friend, who looked gorgeous in his royal-blue suit and so happy he wore a permanent smile. Théo, at his side, beamed with pride, his unwavering love and support of Tris almost bringing fresh tears to Connie's eyes.

Three years ago when they'd first met, she hadn't truly appreciated everything Théo must have done for his brother over the years. But seeing them together on this special day, knowing how Théo felt about family, highlighted the strength of their sibling bond. Théo was completely invested in Tris's happiness, as if it represented a safeguard from everything they'd been through growing up, losing not one but two maternal figures in short succession and never knowing their father. No wonder Théo was obsessed with the perfect family. No wonder he'd avoided the risk of falling in love and losing yet another person from his life after his marriage had failed. But he had so many great qualities, it hurt Connie's heart to think of him alone out of fear to be hurt again.

Blaming her hormones for the rush of longing and compassion she felt for the man she was learning something new about every day, Connie slapped on another smile as the camera clicked once more.

Leaving Tris and Victor to have couple shots, Connie stepped inside with the other guests, grateful to be out of the chill. Théo materialised before her with a glass of bubbles he assured her were zero alcohol. In a room full of other people, they were still drawn to each other.

'You look beautiful,' he said, passing her the glass, his stare brimming with admiration and heat as it passed over her body.

'Thanks,' she croaked, her skin tingling everywhere his stare rested so her breasts ached and heat pooled in her belly. 'So do you.'

Understatement of the century. Théo wore a tailored suit as an acrobat wore a full Lycra body leotard. The cut showed off his tall muscular physique, broad shoulders and confident grace. The dress shirt and tie gave him an additional air of authority he in no way needed and when he removed the jacket his backside in the dress trousers made her want to bite her own hand to hold in a lusty groan.

For the past week at work, they'd dodged all talk of the

elephant in the room: their stifling chemistry, that crazy hot kiss and their plan to ignore both and just be friends. But escaping Théo seemed impossible. If anything, the decision to be friends had made her longing and obsession much worse. The urgency to feel something, anything, beyond this constant desire was overwhelming. She needed either to run away from Paris and her life to avoid him or stop denying herself and rip off his clothes.

She swallowed, covering the nervous gesture with a sip of virgin fizz, hoping to successfully dodge the near constant pull of his forcefield for a few more hours until she could escape.

'You look like a proud father,' she teased as they both watched the newly-weds pose for joyful photos backdropped by Paris's iconic landmark. Any subject was better than trying to untangle her conflicted feelings, how, ever since that night of the kiss, she'd thought about him as a dieter dreamed of chocolate cake.

And he hadn't made it easy on her. He'd sent her messages about antenatal classes and well-respected obstetricians. They had discussed Tris and his reaction to the news of the mix-up. And every time their eyes had met over a patient or the operating table, she'd felt it: a thrilling certainty that, whatever had happened in the past, this man cared about her. And it had been so long since she'd felt cared for.

'I am proud,' he said about Tris, his gorgeous eyes shining with the kind of emotion that made Connie choked. 'My brother is an incredible man and he deserves to be happy.'

'I can't argue with you there.' Connie nodded vigorously, certain she could say the same about Théo. 'As you know, I love him to bits.'

Théo smiled and Connie caught her breath, her next question slipping past her guard. 'What does happiness look like for you?'

Théo frowned at her directness. 'I guess it's this,' he said, glancing at Tris then back at Connie. 'Tris and Victor happily married and you and I raising our baby.'

Connie nodded, mildly disappointed by his answer. But of course, like Connie, Théo wasn't looking for love and she understood why. Except he too had so much more to give.

She glanced around the room, aware that most of the family members in attendance belonged to Victor's side of the family. 'So you and Tris were never tempted to find your father?' she asked hesitantly, desperate to talk about anything other than how much she wanted him, despite her denials, the complications and how dangerous it felt. 'Tris doesn't like to talk about it.'

'No,' Théo confirmed, looking down at his feet as if he too was reluctant. 'I have no real memories of him. Just a photograph of him holding me as a baby. He left when I was two, before Tristan was born.'

'Why do you think he left?'

Théo shrugged, his obvious discomfort building. 'Maman always used to say that he loved us but had no fixed abode when she'd met him, and he struggled with settling in Paris. That he needed to be free. I have no idea if that's true and somewhere in my angry teens, I stopped waiting for him to come and find us and rescue us from care. Instead, I tried to be the kind of big brother Tris could look up to'

'Théo…' Connie whispered, her heart aching for him so she touched his arm and squeezed.

'It's fine,' he said, brushing his moment of vulnerability aside. 'As youngsters we never felt like we missed out. We were raised by our wonderful *maman* and grandmother and had all the love and happiness a kid could need.'

He looked up and locked eyes with Connie. 'That's why I want our baby to feel the love of family, yours and mine, all around them.'

Connie nodded, momentarily too choked to speak.

Whenever he discussed his past, she'd noticed he focussed on the positives and on Tris. But now that she'd pushed him, Connie couldn't help but wonder if minimising his own grief and confusion was a defence mechanism. Drawn to him, and to his past heartache, Connie stepped closer and lowered her voice. 'Tris once told me your mother died in a car accident.'

Théo nodded, looking uncomfortable. 'I was eight and Tris was five,' he said hesitantly.

'What was your grandmother like?' she gently pushed, desperate to understand what was holding him back, sabotaging his marriage and stopping him from taking another chance on a relationship.

The intense look on his face, the few seconds of silence before he answered, wrapped them in a bubble of privacy. The noise of chatter and laughter and glassware clinking dimmed.

'Mémé was wonderful. Caring and fun. We lived with her until she got too sick to care for us,' he said unemotionally. 'She died of breast cancer four years after we lost Maman.' His voice was matter-of-fact but Connie felt every emotion and fear he must have felt back then as a scared twelve-year-old trying to put on a brave face for his little brother.

'I'm so sorry that happened to you.' She stepped closer

and touched his arm again so her heart fluttered erratically and all she could think about was holding him, letting him know that he was no longer alone.

'Don't be,' he said, shrugging it off in a way that appeared well practised. 'Tris and I were two of the fortunate ones. We had each other. We were placed in the same foster home and always managed to stay together. Not every sibling in care is as lucky.'

Connie nodded, aware he was minimising his grief, which would have been every bit as confusing and terrifying as Tristan's, despite their three-year age gap. Twelve was no age to throw off childhood to care for the emotional well-being of a younger sibling.

'Tris said you became his guardian at eighteen,' she said, coaxing him to continue because she needed to understand him better. For herself and for their baby. 'That was a big responsibility to take on.'

No wonder Théo felt so protective of and paternal towards Tris, given his life experience. It explained the emotional caution he'd admitted had contributed to the breakdown of his marriage. Explained why he avoided the possible rejection and loss of serious relationships now. It was as he'd hinted that day over hot chocolate— love just wasn't worth the risk.

'Well, there was no way I intended to leave him after I'd aged out of the system.' He shrugged, once more glancing Tris's way. 'He'd lost enough people in his young life.'

Connie stilled, her breathing tight. Couldn't he see that he'd lost just as much as Tris, if not more because Tris at least had had a wonderful male role model in Théo?

'So had you,' she said carefully, cautious of digging too deeply but seeing through his nonchalance.

Three years ago, when she'd acted on lust and slept with him, she had been too wrapped up in her own feelings of hurt and betrayal to look beyond what she'd overheard that fateful morning. Now that they'd made a baby, they were bound together for life and she couldn't help but see the real man beneath the façade.

'He was a pretty good kid,' Théo said, staring outside where Tris and Victor still posed for photographs. 'I enrolled in university, got a part-time job and he was busy with school.' The quick flash of vulnerability on Théo's face as he shrugged made her throat tight. 'We made it work.'

Connie nodded, the hollow ache of longing inside her expanding as she saw him more clearly than ever. How many other young adults would be compelled to raise a teenaged brother? Théo was an exceptional man. Trustworthy, generous and inspiring. He would be a great father to their baby. Tris was right. Their child was incredibly lucky. Why did that make him even more dangerously attractive in her eyes? The man had been hard enough to resist when they were resentful past lovers.

'Have you told your family about the baby?' he asked, changing the subject, his eyes once more sliding down her body so she shuddered under a wave of spreading tingles.

Connie shook her head. 'Not yet. I wanted to wait until the second trimester before I tell them.'

He nodded. 'That makes sense.'

They stared at each other in loaded silence for a few seconds. Feeling closer to him than ever, Connie kept her feet glued to the floor, even though every bone in her body clamoured to step closer. 'How's your best man speech coming along?' she finally asked.

She too needed to change the subject before she threw

herself into his arms and begged him to put her out of her self-induced misery with another passionate kiss.

'Good. I have plenty of funny anecdotes stored up here.' He tapped his temple and grinned. 'And I'm not sure Tris has ever met a person who doesn't instantly adore him. My audience are primed. Piece of cake.' He shrugged, playfully confident.

Connie joined him in laughing but inside her insides twisted in yearning. Both Augustin brothers were kind of irresistible, charismatic and charming. But there was only one who made Connie ache and burn, fearful for her sanity and ready to throw caution to the wind for one more dangerously reckless kiss.

As the evening party hit its stride, Théo looked up from his current conversation with a group of wedding guests, his eyes, as they'd been for most of the endless-seeming day, drawn to Connie across the room.

She looked achingly beautiful. Her navy-blue halter dress caressed her figure in way that tortured him with memories of her gorgeous body. Her long, tumbling dark hair kissed bare freckled shoulders every time she moved. Théo's lips tingled, desperate to brush over her skin, to taste her, lingering, savouring, drawing out that passion he recalled from three years ago as if it were yesterday.

He mentally snorted. So much for friends…

While he ignored the conversation swirling around him and stared like a fanatic, Connie laughed at something Victor said, swinging her hair over one bare shoulder and exposing her neck.

Still unsettled from the way she'd drawn him out earlier when she'd asked about his upbringing, and tightly wound with sexual frustration, Théo groaned silently and momentarily closed his eyes. He needed a distraction from this lust spiral and fast. Disgusted by his weakness for her, he took one last look. Then he would stop staring for the rest of the night, have a cold shower and try to ignore how every passing day deepened the torture.

In that very moment, she turned her head and glanced his way. Their gazes locked with searing eye contact the way they had all day through what felt like a million accidental looks. But they hadn't been accidental. And they were both kidding themselves if they thought they could simply ignore this preoccupation.

They stared for a few seconds as if daring the other to look away first. With his heart thumping and telling himself he shouldn't want her after they'd agreed to try friendship, Théo conceded and dropped his gaze, pretending to rejoin the group conversation.

Why was he fighting so hard to deny himself? As soon as he'd recovered from the shock that she was having his baby, he'd vowed he wouldn't hurt her. Vowed to protect their relationship as parents as fiercely as he would protect their child. But they were both adults. They understood that neither of them wanted a long-term romantic relationship. If they surrendered to what was becoming an untenable temptation, they could dispose with all this…pining and move on, this time without the misunderstanding of before.

Leaving the group conversation he'd half-heartedly participated in while simultaneously watching Connie like a hawk, he crossed the room in her direction. He'd deliberately forced himself to give her space to talk to other guests this evening, but he was done deluding himself.

'Want to dance?' he asked when he reached her and she and Victor looked his way.

She hesitated for the merest fraction of a second, then smiled up at him and held out her hand. 'Sure.'

Théo took her hand and led her to the dance floor, where other couples were slow-dancing as the band sang covers of popular love songs. He held her close, placed his other hand in the small of her back and moved them to the music, entranced by the scent of her perfume, the length of her eyelashes and her gloss-slicked lips as she smiled.

'Are you having a good time?' he asked, his pulse going crazy as if he were a teenager on a first date. But she felt way too good in his arms, her breasts brushing his shirt, her stare wide and vulnerable, her breath shallow as if she felt it too. This incessant need.

She nodded and sighed happily. 'It's been such a lovely wedding. Tris is so happy. I'm having a great time. How about you?'

'It's been magical,' he agreed. 'But I have to be honest, I haven't been able to take my eyes off you, as hard as I've tried.'

Maybe because he knew she was carrying his child, she'd never looked more radiant. Her lips parted in a soft gasp, excitement glowing in her eyes.

'Théo…' she whispered imploringly but she didn't look away and her pulse fluttered excitedly in her neck as she pressed her body a little closer.

'I know we're supposed to be ignoring the way we make each other feel,' he said, unable to deny his feelings. 'But I wanted you to know that, for me, it's a constant struggle.'

She looked down, a flush to her cheeks. 'For me too,' she admitted softly, glancing back up so their eyes met once more and energising euphoria pounded through his system.

Théo slid his hand a fraction higher, his fingertips grazing the mink-soft bare skin between her shoulder blades. 'Are you staying at the hotel tonight?'

She looked up from his mouth and need all but choked him. Surely she felt this fever raging in him, felt the connection they had little hope of denying. The last thing he wanted to do was complicate things further or hurt Connie. But they were already pretty complicated as it was, and this infatuation seemed to be going nowhere. He would never hurt her and it was just sex, something they already knew they were good at.

'Yes.' Her fingers curved over his shoulder, gliding around the back of his neck where her fingertips brushed his skin. Her lips parted invitingly. 'You?'

Théo nodded, his gaze drawn to her mouth, his instincts demanding he kiss her and finish what they'd started that night at the hospital.

'I'm in room twenty-eight,' he said quietly. 'You could come to me or I'll come to you, when the party is over.' His heart thudded against his ribs, his muscles tense. But he was beyond caring that she might sense how badly he wanted her. The time for pretence was over.

The song came to an end too soon. Théo reluctantly released her, trying to dampen down the flare of desire making his mouth dry and his body tense.

'My room,' she said quietly as she dropped her hand from his shoulder, her palm skimming his chest, which was rising and falling with his rapid breaths. 'Room number sixteen.'

She held his stare for a moment then, with the barest hint of seductive knowing smile, she left the dance floor and sought out Tris, leaving Théo to count the minutes until the party and his best-man duties were over.

CHAPTER ELEVEN

DRESSED IN THE hotel's robe after a shower, Connie sat on the edge of the bed, her stomach knotted in a ball of nerves. She glanced at her phone to check the time, her eyes darting to the stubbornly silent door. She stood. Paced. Chewed at her lip. Her mind veered back and forth between flickers of doubt and raging impatience.

Where was he? Maybe this was a mistake. Maybe she should text him and tell him she'd changed her mind. Only that would be a lie. She knew that come Monday morning when she saw him at work, she would want him still. Perhaps this way, there on neutral territory, they could get this…obsession out of their systems and move on. She trusted Théo. Not with her heart, but enough to sleep with him again. Enough to know that neither of them would allow sex to get in the way of raising their child.

A quiet tap at the door sent her pulse soaring. She hurried to open it and quickly dragged Théo inside.

'I thought you'd changed your mind,' she said, frantically taking in his appearance. He'd removed his tie and suit jacket, but still wore his white dress shirt and suit trousers. With his top few shirt buttons undone to reveal a glimpse of dark chest hair, he looked so sexy she almost sobbed.

'No.' Théo cupped her face and tilted up her chin, his stare boring into hers. 'Have you changed yours?'

Too turned on to speak, Connie shook her head as his breath gusted over her tingling lips. If he didn't kiss her soon she was going to explode or melt. 'But I think we should establish some ground rules,' she croaked, finding some hidden reserves of strength to shield her battle-scarred heart.

'Okay.' He nodded, his fingers restlessly sliding into her hair and his stare caressing her mouth with hunger. 'I'm listening.'

'It's just sex,' she said, sliding her hands around his waist because he was too far away. 'We're not stupid. We both know what we want and it's not a relationship. We've agreed to focus on the baby. And this time, we have a very good reason to stay friends after it's over.'

Impressed with her mental restraint, she dragged in a shuddering breath.

'I agree and feel the same.' He nodded, his thumb tracing her lower lip so she sighed and parted her lips, the tip of her tongue brushing the pad of his thumb. 'I'm ashamed of how miserably I failed to ignore this.'

'I know, me too.' Connie sighed as his hands slid to her shoulders and down her arms. 'I blame my hormones,' she said, tilting her head back to give him access when he leaned in and kissed her neck, groaning as he inhaled deeply and slid his mouth to the sensitive place just below her earlobe.

'I have no such excuse,' he murmured, Connie's body temperature soaring with every delicious glide of his lips.

She slid her hands up his muscular back and pressed her body to his until her breasts brushed his hard chest and her knees almost buckled with lust.

Pulling back, he tightened his arms around her waist.

'I just want you and I'm tired of denying it. But I promise, I won't hurt you.'

'I want you too,' she said, her breath panting as she looked up at him and processed his words, her heart stalling as they prodded at her deepest fear. 'Kiss me, Théo.'

Instead of immediately obliging, Théo slowly slipped the belt of the robe free and slid it from her shoulders, staring at her nakedness, his eyes dark with desire and determination.

'I wish I could say I'd forgotten how beautiful you are,' he said, his voice a husky croak as his stare shifted over her body, prolonging the anticipation so Connie ached for him from head to toe. 'But I haven't.'

His hand caressed her throat, her chest, unhurriedly cupping one breast and zinging the nipple erect with a brush of his thumb.

'I want to see you too,' she said, impatiently reaching up to undo the buttons of his shirt, but before she was even halfway down he dragged her body flush with his, wrapped one arm around her waist, cupped her face with the other hand and slowly, intently, lowered his mouth to hers.

A groan rumbled in his chest as he slid his lips over hers, finally giving her what she craved. But unlike the kiss outside the hospital, which had been a cautious reaction to an emotional day, this was passion unleashed, pure and simple. And Théo took control.

Connie moaned too as he parted her lips and their tongues surged together, sliding and tasting, the euphoria sweeping her entire body up into a storm of sensation. Her pulse raged and she forgot to breathe. Tongues tangled, lips clung, teeth bumped and moans were swallowed as they fought to stay connected amidst the firestorm.

Connie tried to undress him but the minute she exposed another inch of warm tanned skin, she couldn't stop herself from caressing, from pressing her naked body close so his scent was left behind on her skin.

'Take your clothes off,' she demanded when he finally let her up for air. She tugged his shirt free of his waistband and undid his belt, eager to get her hands on the body that was hard and straining towards hers as if any distance was too great.

Within seconds he was naked too. They stood facing each other, panting hard, their eyes and hands roaming each other's bodies as they re-learned contours and dips and sensitive spots. But unlike three years ago, Connie was pretty certain they were both stone-cold sober and desperate to savour every second of the night.

Théo scooped his arm around her waist and ducked his head, laving his moist tongue over her nipple. 'Are you too sensitive?'

'No.' Connie moaned as he sucked a little harder, her knees buckling. Sliding her hand around his erection to stroke him in return, she smiled when he growled and backed her up towards the bed.

This time when they parted for breath, there was a new urgency in his expression. He pulled Connie down to lie at his side, his mouth returning to hers and his hand caressing her breast, her waist, her hip and finally between her legs where she burned for his touch.

'I fought it as long as I could,' he admitted, sighing over her parted lips as he stared down at her, his fingers sliding over her clit.

'Me too,' she said, gasping and parting her thighs as he stroked her faster and she stared into his dark eyes swimming with desire. 'If you hadn't cracked tonight, I would have.'

Rather than smile, he dipped his head and captured her nipple in his mouth. Connie moaned and writhed against him, needing him closer. 'Théo…'

'Do you want me to use a condom?' he asked, brushing his lips over hers as if he couldn't keep his hands and mouth off her. As if he ached and burned every bit as much as Connie.

She shook her head, certain that Théo was responsible and into safe sex. 'I haven't slept with anyone else since you,' she whispered, swallowing that vulnerable feeling when he looked down at her in surprise.

But then his expression turned possessive, his hand still working between her legs as he watched her submit to pleasure. Because his fingers were gliding in a rhythm that made her moan and writhe under him, she dragged his lips back to hers and kissed him deeply, pressing her tongue against his, her wild kisses taking him from carefully in control to untamed and determined.

'Connie,' he groaned as she hooked one thigh over his hip and dragged him on top of her so his erection was crushed against her stomach and not at all where she wanted him.

But rather than rush ahead, Théo found some hidden depths of restraint. He shifted, held his weight on his braced arms and kissed a slow tortuous path over her chest, her abdomen, her inner thighs and finally her sex.

'Théo,' she gasped as he went down on her, his tongue wreaking havoc as effortlessly as his fingers had done.

He positioned her thighs over his shoulders and Connie gripped his hair as delicious electrifying sensation uncurled from her pelvis to every part of her body. Close to orgasm, she cried his name, then moaned louder in protest as he reared above her, leaning over her to kiss her once more. She clung to his lips with hers, gripped his shoulders, his hips and buttocks, parting her thighs to urge him inside her.

'Why did we fight this for so long?' he asked, finally joining them, skin to skin, his heart thundering against hers.

'I don't know,' she wailed, biting her lip against the pleasure of his possession and the reverent way his gaze shifted over her face and down her body to where they were joined.

Connie smiled and moaned, her heart beating so fast she felt dizzy as she wrapped her legs around his hips and he sank lower, his face fierce with the desire she remembered from before.

But she knew him so much better now. Knew he was a good man with a massive heart. Knew that he cared fiercely about the people in his life and that he would value Connie, as the mother of his child, no matter what.

'You feel so good,' he said, cupping her face to drag her mouth up to his as he moved his hips, making her gasp.

'So do you.' She panted, her hips jerking to meet his as he began to thrust faster, quickly shoving them into a tangle of sweaty limbs and grasping hands, of pants and moans and the safety net of their connection past and present.

'Come for me,' he said, his hand delving between their bodies to stroke her clit as his hips powered harder.

Connie nodded, her stare locked to his so she saw the moment he shrugged off the shackles of restraint and acted purely on animal instinct, his wildness for her matching the fire burning her up.

'Théo,' she cried as he dived to capture her nipple in his mouth.

He groaned, crushing her body in his arms as her orgasm stole her breath and strength and even her mind so all she could do was cling to him and ride through the scorching inferno to the other side.

Moments later, as they lay panting and staring at the ceiling, catching their breath, Connie rested her hand on his sweaty, hair-dusted chest.

'Is my memory playing tricks on me, or was that better than three years ago?' She smiled, her heart pounding, endorphins draining as the first flutters of doubt burned in her chest. How would she give up sex that good? How would she give up a physical relationship with Théo when there would be no escaping their connection? How would she see him every day, watch him love their child, and not want him still?

Théo placed his hand over hers, raising it to his mouth to press a kiss there. 'Do you know, I think it might have been.' Dragging her close so her head rested on his chest, he pressed a kiss to her forehead.

'What is it about Christmas?' she chuckled, trying to dismiss the trickle of anxiety chilling her blood.

'Blame it on the silly season, why don't you?' he said, his voice light and teasing.

Connie smiled but, inside, that growing sense of foreboding unfurled. She should make him leave, erect those *just sex* boundaries, even though she wasn't ready for the night to be over, having denied this for so long.

Focussed on his promise not to hurt her and her certainty that this fling was as safe as it could be, given their stance on relationships and what was at stake, Connie tangled her fingers with his when he reached for her hand and brushed aside her fears.

CHAPTER TWELVE

THE NEXT MORNING after a scant hour of sleep, Théo stumbled down to the hotel's dining room for breakfast with the newly-weds, his gut a restless ball of exhilaration and apprehension as he scanned the room for Connie.

He'd spent most of the night in her bed. The first time had seeped into a second and then a third and he just hadn't been able to bring himself to leave, despite the feeling that he should in order to stick to the rules. But he couldn't seem to get enough of her, having denied himself for weeks. Just before dawn, she'd roused him from an exhausted nap and kicked him out of her hotel room, sending him off with a kiss that left them both impressively breathless considering the orgasm count.

But once he was alone under the shower spray, away from the physical temptation of Connie, his mind had finally found space for doubts. Not regrets as such, just the niggle of fear that, by further complicating an already entangled situation, he was essentially operating blind. Never a good thing for a surgeon.

Now, reassured that he and Connie were smart enough to stick to the ground rules they'd voiced last night and put the baby first, he spied Tris and Victor and Victor's parents and joined them at their table.

'Morning, everyone,' he said, taking a seat at Tris's side and signalling the waiter to order strong black coffee.

'How are you feeling?' he asked the couple as Victor's parents went up to the breakfast buffet. 'Any hangovers to report?'

'I haven't danced so much in years,' Victor said, shooting Tris an indulgent loved-up smile that made Théo mildly envious.

'You disappeared right on the dot of midnight,' Tris said, watching Théo shrewdly as Victor joined his parents at the breakfast buffet. 'Like Cinderella worried her coach was about to become a pumpkin.'

'Sorry. Us old guys need our beauty sleep,' Théo said evasively. 'But I had a great night. Are you happy to be a married man?'

His stomach pinched with another twinge of envy. He'd once been in Tris's shoes, blissfully in love, certain that life was about to begin, eager to embrace his future as a husband and father, unaware of the heartache and disappointment ahead.

But weddings were always romantic. Théo wasn't really eager to have what Tris and Victor had, knowing as he did how things could go so very wrong. Especially now there was Connie and their child on which to focus. Only, having spent the night with Connie, waking up with her naked and wrapped around him like a vine, knowing that as he held her, he also held their baby… It had left him unsettled, as if what he'd once craved—the love of his life, a family of his own, belonging—was once more within grasping distance. The last two out of those three things were, he guessed. And the first… Was that worth the risk now there was a good relationship with Connie and his child at stake?

'Of course.' Tris beamed. 'I'm ecstatic. I can't wait for our few days in Geneva.' He glanced over at Victor longingly. 'But don't worry. We wouldn't miss Christmas Eve.'

'Has Connie been down?' Théo asked, accepting his coffee from the staff member and talking a scalding sip to cover the yearning in his voice.

'Not yet,' Tris said. 'Oh, here she comes now.'

Théo turned to see Connie enter the dining room and spy their table. Wearing a pair of black jeans and a red sweater, she looked utterly breathtaking, her skin glowing, eyes bright and her hair swept up into a messy topknot so her neck was on display. Memories of kissing her there swamped him—the softness of her skin, the scent of her perfume, the way she'd moaned in delight and clung to him harder.

'Morning.' She leaned down and pressed her mouth to Tris's cheek then took the seat opposite Théo. Her face wore a bright smile, her gaze landing anywhere but on him, and those possessive urges he'd experienced since discovering she was having his baby resurfaced. Théo realised with a dry swallow of fear that he wanted her again.

Under the table, he slid his feet forward until their toes touched and she looked up.

'Morning, Théo,' she said politely, a split second of vulnerability in her stare before she turned to Tris. 'What a fabulous wedding. I still have a romance hangover.'

Tris smiled and reached across the table for Connie's hand. 'Well, so far,' Tris said smugly, 'I can highly recommend getting married.' He smiled softly at Connie, whose cheeks flushed. 'Don't write it off completely, will you? You never know who is just around the corner.'

Théo winced, jealousy a jab between his ribs and compassion for Connie, who'd once been engaged, a burn in his throat. He looked down at the table, unable to witness her discomfort at Tris's throwaway words. His brother was just happy and wanted to see his best friend the same. He wasn't being flippant and obviously had no idea that Théo and Connie had restarted their physical relationship last night. But the idea of Connie one day moving on, of her maybe falling in love, of another man raising his child…completely decimated his appetite.

'Tea, please,' Connie said to the server during the tense moment that followed. Her stare avoided Théo as she added, 'I'm starving. Think I'll help myself to breakfast.' She stood and approached the buffet.

Tris turned accusing eyes on Théo. 'You slept with her again, didn't you?' he whispered harshly.

'Shh,' Théo urged. 'None of your business.' He pushed back his chair and stood but Tris gripped his arm.

'Be careful,' his brother urged, wearing a frown. 'Don't hurt her.'

Théo nodded, suddenly desperate to speak to Connie alone. 'I'm going to get some breakfast.'

At the omelette station, where the chef was busy cracking eggs for her order, Théo grabbed a plate and sidled close to Connie's side. Tris's words rang in his head. But hurting Connie was the last thing he wanted to do.

'How are you feeling?' he asked, carefully, after her abrupt departure from the table.

'Fine,' she said automatically, looking up at him with vulnerable eyes bearing a flicker of hurt. 'Did you tell Tris…? About last night? About us?'

'Of course not.' Théo frowned, horrified and a little depressed that she'd needed to ask. She clearly still had trust issues with him in spite of how close they'd grown this past couple of weeks.

With frustration coiling in his belly like an angry snake, he inched closer, wishing they were somewhere private so he could kiss her and hold her and reassure her that nothing had changed. 'It's our business, Connie. Tris is just on a high after yesterday and thinks everyone should be as in love as he is.'

'Thank you.' Connie nodded, looking both relieved and uncomfortable at the same time. 'Perhaps we just keep it to ourselves. Things are…complicated enough as it is. And it doesn't mean anything. We don't want Tris getting the wrong idea.'

'Of course not,' Théo said, a pinch of disappointment stealing his breath for a second. She was right about the complications. Last night he'd hoped that sleeping with her again would relieve the tension and allow him to think about something else, but he already knew that he wanted another night, and another… Dangerous wants he would need to contain.

Weighed down by apprehension, he dropped his voice. 'Are you having regrets?'

His pulse buzzed in his fingertips as if he'd stuck them into an electrical socket. He'd be lying if he said he hadn't had one or two doubts himself since leaving her room. But it was nothing he couldn't handle and set aside. He'd thought it all through in the shower. He would stick to the rules, enjoy a passionate fling with Connie until it had run its course, then he would make the switch to a friend, cherish her as a co-parent and do his best to never let her or their baby down.

Connie shook her head, a small frown tugging down her mouth. 'I mean, I think we need to be careful,' she said, glancing over her shoulder to the rest of the wedding party, who were tucking into their breakfasts and talking animatedly. 'But we're responsible adults. We went in with our eyes open.'

Théo nodded, desperate to touch her again. 'I was thinking the same thing,' he said trying to reassure her and himself. 'We can't afford to mess this up or mess each other around. There's more at stake this time than just the two us.' He glanced down at her stomach, knowing she would understand that his priorities matched hers.

'I agree,' she said quietly, a cautious smile spreading.

'That being said—' He inched closer still because he couldn't help himself, breathing in her subtle scent as visions of her naked and plastered against him surfaced. 'I wondered if you had plans later. I could make you dinner.' Cooking her meal could be classified as simply caring for her during the pregnancy so wasn't technically breaking any rules.

She inhaled a shaky breath but grinned wider. 'Because we don't see enough of each other every day at work?'

Théo shrugged and smiled back, his heart leaping with anticipation as the chef slid Connie's mushroom omelette onto her plate and added a sprinkle of chives with a flourish.

'I need to do some Christmas shopping later,' she said, talking her plate. 'I haven't even begun yet and it's less than two weeks until Christmas.'

Théo grinned. 'I could go shopping. It's a well-known fact that I am the official Christmas gift master. Just ask Tris.'

Connie chuckled and gave him a playful shove. 'The gift master? Self-proclaimed, I take it.'

Glad he could make her smile after that bumpy moment, Théo shrugged. 'Just think, next year, I can really go to town. Our little one's first Christmas is going to be so special.'

As if he'd dropped to one knee and proposed or announced to the entire room that they were a couple, the atmosphere chilled as Connie smiled thinly then looked away.

'Can I let you know about the shopping expedition? I might be too tired, although I really need to get it done.'

'Of course,' he said with a guilty wince. He was getting ahead of himself, dreaming of next Christmas when this one was yet to come. And Connie had planned to raise their baby alone. With them sleeping together again she probably thought he was rushing ahead.

'Either way,' he said, 'the offer of dinner still stands.'

'I'll text you later.' With a small enigmatic smile, she took her breakfast back to their table, leaving Théo unnerved and in no way hungry for food.

He needed to be careful and temper his excitement for the baby. Ensure that his feelings about the pregnancy didn't spill over into his relationship with Connie. He didn't want to scare her off or further complicate their situation or break the rules. Nor could he make her any promises and risk another failure. Already the line he would need to walk seemed incredibly fine, as if one wrong move could ruin everything.

CHAPTER THIRTEEN

GALERIES LAFAYETTE, PARIS'S LARGEST department store, stocked everything on Connie's gift list. As she waited outside for Théo later that afternoon, memories of the night before pushed insistently at her mind.

If she'd thought she and Théo had been sexually attuned three years ago, the intervening time had only stoked the fire. A big part of her hadn't wanted the night to end. But the minute she'd closed the door on him that morning, her reservations had grown, stumbling over each other to make themselves known.

If they'd met years earlier, before his divorce and Guy's betrayal, Théo might have been the perfect man. He was everything she'd once thought she wanted in a partner: kind, dependable, honest and principled, with a great career. But he was also uninterested in giving love a second chance and she understood his reasons why. She even shared his reservations.

The horrified look on his face when Tris had recommended marriage haunted her still. But she shouldn't have been surprised by his reaction and, no matter how right she'd felt in his arms, she was in no way ready for feelings or to be that vulnerable with another man. It wasn't worth the risk to her heart, especially when she and Théo had to work together and raise a child together, and he clearly felt the same.

Wishing she'd been able to refuse when he'd suggested shopping and dinner, she glanced up in time to see him appear from around the corner and cross the street. His smiling gaze caught hers, sending her blood pressure through the roof with dizzying excitement. So much for playing it cool and being careful.

He kissed both her cheeks in greeting then reached for her hand as they entered the store. Connie shuddered ridiculously at the intimacy of holding his hand. The man had kissed and tongued every inch of her body last night, possessing her until she'd sobbed his name, over and over again. She could still feel him between her legs when she walked.

But whereas Théo might be able to detach physical intimacy from emotional intimacy, Connie considered holding hands something that couples did.

'Did the newly-weds get off on their honeymoon okay?' she asked, because Théo was looking at her as though he wanted to devour her. *Again.* And she needed to think about something else.

'They did. I dropped them at the airport. They're excited to go skiing and visit the ice caves.'

Connie smiled. Tris's happiness was infectious and the wedding had certainly stirred up emotions for Connie. She couldn't help but wonder how different her life might have been if Guy had stayed faithful. But then she was also increasingly relieved that she was having Théo's baby, because she had no doubt he'd be a wonderfully dedicated father.

'Right, let's get this over with,' Connie said, sliding her hand from his and ambling towards the menswear department, determined to set aside the turmoil the events of yesterday had aroused.

While she considered a green cashmere sweater that Tris would love, Théo cautiously asked, 'You seem distracted. Are you upset…? About what Tris said earlier? You know he adores you and didn't mean anything by his comments about marriage. He just wants you to be happy.'

'I know,' Connie said, pretending to consider the same jumper in blue to hide her eyes from him. 'Don't worry. He's listened to me rant often enough to know that I won't be following him down the aisle any time soon. I think the green for Tris, don't you?' she asked, holding up both choices although she'd already decided.

Théo nodded, his frown deepening. 'Not all men are the same,' he said quietly, forcing Connie into a defensive position.

'I know.' She still felt a little guilty for asking Théo if he'd told Tris they'd slept together again. But for Connie it was a sign that, no matter how amazing last night had been, she clearly wasn't ready to fully trust someone else.

'Do you think one day you'll be ready to move on?' Théo asked, casually, as if he weren't really interested in the answer.

'I don't know.' Connie replaced the blue sweater and tossed the green one into her basket, her guard rising. 'But it's like Tris said, never say never.'

Théo swallowed and hesitated as if considering his response while also debating dropping the subject. Connie wished he would, but then maybe it was better that he understood her standpoint. Just because they'd slept together, nothing had changed.

'I think Tris probably worries that you're missing out

on the potential of something good because of your past,' he went on, looking increasingly uncomfortable.

'So are you,' she pointed out, turning the tables. 'You're just as reluctant to risk another failed relationship. We're both scared and with good reason, I think.'

Théo glanced down at the ground. 'You're right. It does feel safer to hold back. Having messed up before, I'm not sure I'm fit for romantic relationships.'

'And I'm not sure I can be that vulnerable again,' she said boldly, meeting his cagey stare. 'I'm certainly not interested in ever being as gullible as I once was. The way I look at it, I've had my one lucky escape.'

His dark eyes turned stormy as if he were jealous. 'Believe me, I'm not encouraging you to rush out and date other men. We're both committed to focussing on the baby for now.'

'Exactly,' Connie said, triumphantly, trying to rein in her touchiness and the hollow feeling of doubt that took her by surprise. He wasn't jealous, he was thinking about their child.

'I just want you to be happy,' he said, adding to Connie's doubts. He wanted her to be happy, just not with him.

Hardening her resolve to protect herself, she said, 'Rest assured that for the foreseeable future, you will be the only man in our baby's life.'

Tris was right. She needed to keep an open mind. Maybe one day she would be ready to find love again.

Leaving him at the sweaters, she shifted to a display of silk ties. Her heart pounded with adrenaline as she focussed on the selection and tried to block out his confusing words. He was obviously worried about his place in their child's life. And Connie could understand. She wouldn't want to miss a Christmas or birthday either.

Immediately spotting a tie that would suit Théo, she forced herself to ignore that one and chose another for Tris, adding it to her basket.

As she tried to calm down, she considered that she shouldn't have slept with him again. In indulging her desires, she'd opened herself up to doubts, second-guessing the decision and every word he said. She knew with absolute certainty that she would make the same choice to sleep with him again, but she was scared to trust her instincts. Hoping she was simply having a fatigue-induced wobble after a romantic weekend, she took some deep breaths.

Her skin prickled as Théo once more stepped close to her side, warming her with his body heat and turning her on with the scent of his cologne.

'This one is nice,' he said, reaching for her hand again and fingering the very tie she'd have chosen for him were she buying him a gift.

She hadn't planned on that. But maybe she should get him something, especially if she intended to attend his Christmas Eve party.

She plastered on a carefree smile and they moved on to the gift department, where Connie chose an interior design book for Victor and gifts for both her brothers and sisters-in-law. Finally, as they ended up in the children's department, she consulted her list.

'I have a horde of nieces and nephews to buy for,' she said, wandering over to a rack of toddler clothes, the cute little outfits building her excitement to meet their baby.

'What about this teddy bear?' Théo suggested, holding it up and waving its paw at Connie. 'Every kid needs a bear to love.'

Connie looked up and wrinkled her nose, her pulse flying at how sexy he was. 'Nolan is eight months old.

I think his parents would appreciate a more useful gift.'
She waggled a jumper-and-jeans set his way.

Théo gasped in mock horror and covered the ears of the
teddy bear. 'She doesn't mean that,' he stage-whispered
to the cuddly toy. 'She thinks you're very handsome and
loveable.' Then to Connie he added, 'Look, he even has
a festive bow tie. Take it from the gift master, we can't
possibly leave him behind.'

Desperate to kiss him, Connie instead heaved an exag-
gerated sigh. 'Fine. But I'm getting the outfit too.'

Théo smugly tossed the bear into the basket and they
moved on to boardgames for her older nieces and nephews.

'Are you going to be like this with our child?' Connie
asked, distractedly, to take her mind off how badly she
wanted him and how careful she needed to be, given he
was so practised at holding back emotionally. 'Spoiling
it to death.' She shot him a censorious look and then pe-
rused the selection of games lining one wall.

When he'd mentioned buying gifts for their child earlier that morning, she'd had a moment's panic. She understood and loved Théo's enthusiasm of fatherhood, but
she simply couldn't think that far ahead, not now that
she'd surrendered to temptation and slept with him again.
Not when her feelings were so volatile and couldn't be
trusted. It all felt too…permanent, which she guessed it
was. She and Théo would always have a relationship as
parents, just not a romantic one.

While her heart raced and her stomach pinched with
fear that she might not be able to stick to the rules, Théo
leaned down to press a kiss to her temple. 'Can you really spoil a child?' he said quietly, falling serious. 'Don't
they simply need as much love and support and reassurance as you're able to give?'

Connie swallowed, her heart in her throat as she looked up at his earnest expression. He was going to be such an amazing father. And as he'd never known his own, as he'd lost both his female caregivers at a young age, Connie knew she would never be able to deny him a single indulgence. Even if it meant tolerating his extravagances and spending every Christmas with him and their child.

'I suppose you're right,' she croaked through her fear.

How would she spend so much time with him and still switch off this longing? How would she see him be the wonderful father she knew he would be and not want him for herself, for the connection that at times last night had felt so effortless and uplifting and right?

'Okay,' she said, swallowing down the hot ache in her throat that came whenever she imagined a young Théo trying to make sense of the loved ones he'd lost. 'I'm getting these two.' She pulled the boardgames from the shelf and placed them in the basket. 'I think we're done.'

They headed for the sales desk, where Théo insisted on paying for the Christmas bear he christened Claude. As she watched him charm the sales clerk with his handsome smile and good manners, Connie sighed with a confusing mix of unease and longing.

Maybe he was right. Maybe, one day, she might be ready to fall in love again. Maybe she'd find another man as wonderful and sexy and unselfish as Théo. Or maybe he was one of a kind and Connie would simply need to find a way to live with her regrets that she just couldn't have it all.

After an afternoon of shopping, they took a taxi back to Théo's apartment. Théo set the oven timer and put dinner in to warm and then carried in a tray of no-alcohol mulled wine to the coffee table before the fire, where Connie sat placing her purchases in the stylish, reusable fabric gift bags she'd bought at Galeries Lafayette.

'I love your tree,' Connie said, tucking her legs up beside her on the sofa, looking more relaxed than earlier, when she'd seemed distant and cagey as if, despite her reassurances, she did regret the night before.

Théo tried to calm himself, his sense of foreboding building. On the one hand, as he'd stated earlier, he too wanted Connie to be happy. He wanted her to let go of the past, to open her heart and stop punishing herself for what her ex had done. But on the other hand, he selfishly wanted her for himself. He certainly wanted to be the only important man in his child's life. And Connie's vagueness over the baby was making him feel paranoid.

But she was right. They were both messed up, both scared to take another risk when it came to relationships. And while she was content to mess around with him, at least he could feel secure that their priorities were aligned: work, each other, the baby.

That had to be enough.

'Victor helped me decorate it,' he said about the tree, sliding in next to her and resting his arm along the back of the sofa, because it had been too long since he'd touched her and his doubts were back. The worst one that, one day, Connie would move on and another man might help raise his child.

Brushing aside that terrifying thought, Théo focussed on keeping Connie relaxed. 'He and Tris have decided to go to Château Bijou a few days early,' he said, panic an acidic burn in his throat. 'To decorate the house for Christmas, for which I'm very grateful.'

'How many people have you invited to the *réveillon*?'

she asked taking a sip of the warm spicy drink and sighing contentedly.

'Around ten. Just close friends and partners. Plus me, Tris and Victor and you if you decide to join us. Maybe next year you can decide whether we host here in Paris or at the *château*. Will you…bring the baby?' he asked, hesitant to upset her again as he slid his fingers to the nape of her neck to stroke her skin.

Her earlier reaction to his mention of the baby's first Christmas had plagued him all day. Yes, she'd originally planned to raise a child independently, but her evasiveness was worrying, fuelling his paranoia that he would mess things up between them and lose the most amazing gift he'd ever been granted.

'I…um… I guess so,' she said, staring at the fire. 'Although I'm pretty sure that babies aren't that into parties.' She glanced down at her lap and a disheartened burn began in his chest.

'Then I won't organise a party next year,' he said, resolute, trying to show her that she and their child were his priority. 'I'll just spend Christmas with you and our little one. Unless you have other plans, of course…'

The desperation in his voice scared him as much as the strength of his apprehension. He understood her emotional caution because he shared it. Yes, they'd complicated things by sleeping together again, but there was no way Théo would allow that, or anything else for that matter, to interfere with their role as parents.

'We can decide nearer the time,' Connie said, but wouldn't look at him.

Théo cupped her face and turned her eyes to his. 'Am I going too fast?' he asked quietly, the anxiety-driven burn behind his sternum spreading so he almost couldn't breathe.

'A little,' she said, smiling guiltily.

'I'm sorry,' he whispered, feeling as if he'd just stepped onto paper-thin ice covering the deepest part of the ocean. 'What I'm actually trying to say is that I don't care about parties. This relationship—you and me as parents—is the most important one of my life. And with the scan booked, I guess I'm feeling a bit overexcited about the baby.'

She smiled indulgently, resting her cheek on his arm and looking at him through her lashes. 'Me too. I just haven't really given solo parenthood a lot of thought yet. I'm not even sure how it's all going to work out. Shared custody, working, childcare… I guess by next Christmas I'll likely still be on maternity leave though.'

Théo held his breath, his heart racing with panic because he felt as if she was slipping away. 'I know this wasn't how you planned parenthood,' he said carefully. 'You thought you'd be doing it alone. But I want to be involved, Connie. I want to help if you need it and spend time with you and the baby. I think we can figure out all the details together. Just know that I'm here and willing.'

'I know and I appreciate that,' she said, her eyes shining as they moved over his face. 'I understand. Family *is* important. And you're right. Together we'll make our unconventional little family, just the three of us, work.'

Looking at him as if he were made of glass, she put down her glass and slid closer into his arms. Sagging with relief, he held her close, breathing through her hair as she rested her cheek over the thump of his nervously pounding heart. When she was in his arms like this, he felt invincible. But then the moment he tried to figure out the future, to plan and dream and visualise them being just friends, it all seemed insurmountable. After all, he'd failed to hold onto Anaïs and they'd been husband and wife. What if he somehow failed Connie and lost her and his baby too? He couldn't allow that to happen.

'Was it truly awful?' she whispered after a moment, looking up at him with shining eyes. 'I keep picturing you and Tris as scared little boys living with strangers and my heart breaks for you.'

Théo swallowed down the surge of desire for her as he registered her abrupt change of subject. Confused and reluctant to look back to the worst time of his life, he shook his head.

'No. Not awful at all,' he said, slipping straight into his favourite coping mechanism: denial. 'I don't really like to think about it. To talk about it. But we always had food and warmth and a safe place to sleep,' he went on, trying not to think about the nights he'd spent lying awake with tears soaking into his pillow. 'Just not a lot of love. At least not the kind of love we'd been used to.'

'I'm so sorry, Théo.' She pressed her lips to his as if she could kiss away his pain and grief. She pulled back, her stare searching his as if she easily saw the truth: that of course he'd been lonely and terrified and had needed to grow up pretty quickly to put on a brave face for Tris.

'It's fine,' he said, trying to smile while the past and his present desire for her collided in a sickening mass of renewed doubt. 'Our foster parents were good people but we weren't their real kids.'

Connie tilted her head with compassion. 'And you were old enough to know the difference, to remember your mother's and grandmother's love,' she said, intuitively understanding because she was a wonderfully caring woman. 'Tris was so lucky to have you.'

Théo's hands gripped hers tighter. He shrugged, his throat choked by fear. Fear that she would see how broken he was. That she too would reject and leave him, because his best wasn't good enough. That he'd be alone once more.

Connie cupped his face and peered into his eyes intently. 'But you were loved, Théo. By Tris, by your mother and grandmother. Even by your professor mentor, the one who left you the *château*. You had so much love, despite how much you lost, and because of the man you are, you still do.'

Because her words felt dangerous, painful, he wrapped his arms around her waist and dragged her close, kissing her until she moaned and twisted free, panting.

'Connie,' he said in warning, scared that she would demand he face all the feelings he'd buried all those years ago.

She gripped his face and forced him to meet her stare. 'Just like you want me to be happy, I want the same for you. Don't shut yourself off because a part of you maybe didn't process your childhood grief at the time. I know it's scary to put yourself out there, but maybe we both need to risk it again. One day, I mean.'

He frowned in denial, his heart racing because she saw something in him no one else ever had.

'I'm trying,' he said in desperation. 'Which is why I'm so excited about the baby. You don't understand what an amazing gift this is for me. If you let me, I'll cherish the two of you, always.' And part of him, that selfish part that wanted Connie for himself, would hate to see her happy with another man.

Connie blinked rapidly as if she might cry. 'I know you will. And what's more our baby is going to adore you and not because you're the gift master. But because you're its father and you're going to be so amazing.'

Overcome with feelings too big for his body, Théo crushed her in his arms. Her fingers glided through his hair as she held his face and kissed him with the same passion and need as the night before.

Théo groaned, not certain how he could want her again with the same urgency, as if last night hadn't happened. But with his emotions too convoluted to untangle, he was done questioning this.

Connie pulled back, then straddled his lap, shifting her hips forward until his erection was bathed in the heat between her legs as she kissed his lips, his face, the side of his neck. Théo slid his hands along her thighs, caressed her waist, her back, her shoulders, cupping her face to hold her lips to his as, finally, his panic that he might lose her receded.

'I want you,' she said, tugging at his sweater, pulling it over his head then tossing it to slide her hands over his bare chest while she trailed her lips down the side of his neck.

Drunk with desire, he pulled back to stare into her beautiful eyes. 'You have to promise me that we won't allow anything or anyone to threaten our family,' he croaked, choked once more by fear that everything he had might be snatched away.

Deep down, he knew the biggest threat to his happiness was himself. He was terrified that he'd mess up again, let Connie and the baby down or somehow lose them for ever.

Connie shook her head, brushing her lips over his. 'I promise,' she said, impassioned. 'We are going to raise our baby together. You and me.'

He nodded, part appeased, part sensing that she was still holding back. And he couldn't blame her. They were both damaged, both navigating an unplanned situation, both desperate not to hurt each other.

As he crushed her close, his paranoia rose up. He needed her to understand that he was trying his best. 'You can trust me, Connie. I want you to know that. I won't let you down.'

'I do trust you and I know.' She nodded so he was engulfed by relief, relief that was then dampened when she added, 'But, please…don't ever make me a promise that you can't deliver.'

Théo stared deep into her eyes, his confusion once more building at her warning. But she was right to be cautious. Better to value what they already had than to try for something more and fail.

'I won't.' Théo swore, determined to double down on his efforts to focus on the baby and on not hurting Connie. All that mattered were the promises they'd made and how she made him feel in that moment.

As she trailed her mouth over his chest, scooting back on his lap, his mind all but blanked as arousal overwhelmed him. Chasing the same blind desire they'd surrendered to last night, Théo kissed her, pausing only to remove her sweater and pop her bra clasp while she attacked the fly of his jeans. In seconds they were naked, their caresses, kisses and groans finally shoving his doubts aside.

As he buried himself inside her and drove them towards climax, he renewed his vows to take extreme care, to shut down any dangerous flights of fancy about having more of her than this, and to simply value what he'd always craved and what was tantalisingly tangible: family.

CHAPTER FOURTEEN

It was the Wednesday after Tris and Victor's wedding before Connie and Théo were back in Theatre together again. Since that endlessly romantic weekend, they'd seen each other every day. Snatching a coffee together during the work day, speaking on the phone, knocking on each other's apartment doors late at night for the wild, uninhibited sex neither of them seemed able to do without.

Despite the promises they'd whispered to each other Sunday evening on the sofa before the fire in Théo's apartment, with every passing day, Connie grew increasingly aware of two things: One, she was scarily addicted to Théo, and two, he still seemed intent on emotionally distancing himself. He was playful and attentive, as crazy for their intimacies as her and said all the right things. But whenever the conversation steered anywhere near his past or his feelings, he subtly changed the subject. Connie couldn't blame him. Of course, she was trying to do the same thing, reluctant to trust what was going on inside her head and heart.

Meeting up with him in the anaesthetic room off theatre three, Connie smiled politely his way while her heart raced, just from his friendly glance.

'Good morning, Mrs Pascal,' Connie said to their

seventy-seven-year-old patient. 'Are you ready to be a new woman?'

Marjorie Pascal had presented with slowly progressive weakness of her legs, an unsteady gait and back pain. The diagnosis—a spinal meningioma—was a benign tumour of the membrane covering the spinal cord. Hopefully removing it would alleviate all her symptoms.

'I'm in good hands with you two,' Marjorie said, fondly reaching for Théo's hand and gazing up at him with adoration.

Connie smiled and concealed a shudder. Sadly, she shared Marjorie's adoration. But the emotional turmoil raging inside her contrasted harshly with the warning bells that had been going off in her head for days. If Théo was guarding his emotions the way he'd always done, she needed to do the same or she might end up hurt.

'We'll see you when it's all over,' she told the elderly woman who was the main carer for her husband who suffered from dementia. Marjorie had confided in Connie that they were about to celebrate their fiftieth wedding anniversary. Some people really did find their soul mate and spend their lives together.

She tugged her mask over her face, and Théo joined her in the scrub room, the sense of déjà vu stifling. Was it only a few short weeks ago that he'd joined the team at St Raphaël? Then they'd been hostile strangers and now they were having a baby and a physical relationship, sharing every aspect of their lives together as if making a lifelong commitment to each other.

As they scrubbed up side by side, they discussed the technical aspects of the surgery, which involved removing the spinous processes of two of the vertebrae to access the tumour, resection of the mass, followed by closure of the defect in the dura, the membrane covering the spinal cord, with a synthetic patch. At a pause in the conversation, Connie's mind turned to Christmas.

'I meant to say,' she added as they each scrubbed their hands, 'I will join you for Christmas Eve if the invitation still stands.'

Although part of her was dreading spending Christmas in Provence. No matter how often she chastised herself to be careful or reminded herself that Théo wasn't interested in a real relationship and she was still terrified to be hurt again, she couldn't seem to get enough of him, craving his company and his touch, as if she were already falling helplessly in love.

But she couldn't go there. Yes, she'd come to trust him to some degree. But how could she give him her heart when they were both scared to take that final leap of faith? When he wasn't sure he could make another romantic relationship work and she was scared to trust her instincts and confess that she was developing feelings. When there was one very good reason to be cautious and hold back: the baby.

'That's great,' he said, smiling her way. 'Tris will be delighted and so am I. We can take the train down to Marseilles together on the twenty-fourth if you like.'

Connie nodded, desperate not to interpret his excitement as anything more than his desire to play festive happy families. They stepped into the operating room to gown up and soon the surgery was under way and all thoughts of Christmas and their relationship were sidelined.

The slow, cautious surgery was almost complete, when the cardiac-monitor alarms sounded and the anaesthetist shot to his feet.

'She's in ventricular tachycardia,' he said. 'Blood pressure falling.'

Connie and Théo and the anaesthetist all felt for a pulse.

'Nothing,' Connie said, glancing up at Théo, who also shook his head.

Abandoning the surgery, Théo commenced cardiac compressions on Marjorie while Connie readied the defibrillator to shock the heart back into a regular rhythm and the anaesthetist stuck gel pads onto the patient's chest.

With the first shock administered, all eyes glued to the cardiac monitor, a collective sigh of frustration seeming to sound as the heart showed zero response.

'Still no pulse. Administering adrenaline,' the anaesthetist said as Théo recommenced chest compressions.

They repeated the defibrillation-CPR cycle three more times, growing increasingly desperate with each cycle as the patient remained stubbornly in cardiac arrest.

'Keep going,' Connie pleaded, her stare clinging to Théo's as if he could miraculously fix this.

Connie couldn't bear to consider the consequences of losing this patient, who until this surgery for a debilitating but otherwise benign condition was fit and healthy.

'She takes care of her husband,' Théo explained to the anaesthetist and theatre nurses, who were looking increasingly pessimistic as time went on. 'They're about to celebrate fifty years together.'

Connie swallowed, sharing Théo's desperation and loving that he too knew these relevant facts about Marjorie. Losing a patient was always hard. Losing one after what should have been a straightforward surgery the week before Christmas would be devastating.

Seeing that Théo shared her determination, Connie recharged the defibrillator paddles, ready to deliver the next shock.

'Clear,' Théo said, holding up his hands, his shocked, grave stare urging Connie to proceed.

This time with the shock delivered, the heart rhythm returned to normal. Shaking from adrenaline and relief, Connie felt for a pulse, nodding as the artery beat steadily at her fingertips.

'Blood pressure climbing,' the anaesthetist said.

But Connie could only look to Théo, her heart in her throat with gratitude and euphoria that together they'd managed to revive their patient.

As the anaesthetist drew Marjorie's blood for testing and handed it to a theatre technician, Connie focussed on completing the surgery and sewing up the patient's wounds. It was only later, after de-gowning and washing up, that she allowed herself to be comforted by Théo.

As they left their operating room together, he drew her into a deserted storage room and closed the door, dragging her into a tight embrace. 'Are you okay? None of us was expecting that.'

Connie nodded, her throat tight but her eyes dry as Théo's reassuring heartbeat pulsed under her cheek. 'Yes. Like you, I kept thinking about her husband, their anniversary, how they depended on each other and what would become of him if we lost her.'

And she couldn't help but compare herself to Marjorie Pascal, who'd spent at least fifty years with the love of her life.

'I know,' he said, stroking her back, his lips pressed to her forehead. 'I know.'

Connie buried her face against his neck for a few more indulgent seconds, willing herself to step away because she was scared to rely on him so deeply.

'I'll be okay,' she said finally, looking up at his worried frown. 'There's never a good time to lose a patient, but it seems even more unfair at Christmas.'

Théo nodded, his hands sliding from her shoulders, down her arms until he wrapped his fingers around hers. 'Well, she's on her way to Cardiac Intensive Care now. Let's hope she recovers in time to be discharged so she can spend Christmas with her family where she belongs.'

He pressed his lips to hers in a restrained kiss, but let them sit there for a few seconds as if he needed the comfort of her touch just as much. But all Connie could think about was where she belonged. Since discovering the baby was Théo's, she would no longer be parenting alone. But would she only be included in Théo's family plans until the baby become old enough to be separated from Connie? Would she then be once more cast aside the way she'd been with her ex? Would Théo eventually move on and meet someone he wanted to invite into his life?

'Can I see you tonight?' he asked in a low voice when he pulled back.

With panic making her heart race, Connie stared into his troubled eyes, wondering if, like her, he felt they were playing fast and loose with fire. Or maybe, for Théo, everything was working out perfectly. He would have the family he'd always craved without the risk of a relationship, keeping his feelings secure. Whereas Connie… Sometimes she felt completely composed of feelings and she was terrified to examine them too closely.

'Maybe we should have a night to ourselves,' she said, suggesting the opposite of what she wanted just to prove she could go without him, that like him she too could still create some emotional distance. 'I've been a bit more tired this week.'

Only momentarily disappointed, he smiled and nodded. 'Okay. Another time, then. You sure you're okay?'

'Just shaken up,' she said, telling a partial truth as she swallowed down the lump in her throat. 'But I'll be fine.'

'I'm going to get some lunch before our next surgery,' he said, reaching for the door handle. 'Want to join me?'

Again Connie shook her head. 'I'm not really hungry. Think I might have a bit of morning sickness. And I need to speak to Jules about an admission. You go grab some lunch and I'll see you later.'

Hesitating for a second, he pulled open the door so they could once more step out of their bubble of comfort and intimacy and back into the real world.

But as she watched him walk away, her stomach twisted with fear. Bubbles were a fleeting illusion, there one minute, gone the next. Maybe Connie's feelings were out of sync with Théo's and couldn't be trusted in case they once more let her down.

The day after Marjorie Pascal's cardiac arrest, Connie was on call at the hospital. Théo knew from speaking to her that morning that she'd admitted a young man with spinal trauma following a fall and had spent half the night in Theatre performing an emergency decompression and stabilisation surgery.

Missing her and concerned that the pregnancy was beginning to take its toll on her energy levels, Théo had texted ahead then called at her apartment, his arms full of groceries.

Connie opened the door and smiled tiredly. 'Hi. Come in.'

'Let me make you dinner,' he said, placing the bags on the kitchen counter and handing her the flowers he'd also grabbed on a whim.

'Thank you,' she said, taking them in one hand and wrapping her other arm around his neck so she could kiss him. 'I was just about to take a soak in the bath. Want to join me?'

Théo smiled, his arms tightening around her waist. 'I'd love to.' He brushed his lips over hers for an indulgent second before he reined in his ever-present desire for her. 'But I'm here to take care of you, not seduce you. Let me run you a bath.'

Connie sighed and stepped back. 'Shame,' she said, her voice playful. 'I'll just put these in water.'

In the bathroom, Théo turned on the bath taps and poured some scented oil into the water. Then, spying a box of matches on the shelf, he lit the candles in the corner of the bath and turned out the lights.

'Oh, I could get used to this,' Connie said moments later. She untied her robe and stepped into the bath, her gorgeous naked body sliding under the water.

'How's the morning sickness?' he asked to take his mind off how badly he wanted her and how his doubts seemed to be growing with each passing day.

'I think it's more fatigue than anything else at the moment.' She swirled her hands through the water, drawing his attention to her breasts, not that he needed any encouragement to stare.

'I checked on Elodie Verdier before I left the hospital,' he said. 'She's being discharged tomorrow.'

'And Marjorie Pascal is off the coronary care ward. Good news all round.' Her relieved smile made his heart beat harder. She was such an amazing woman. Caring and fiercely loyal.

'I'll just put dinner in the oven to warm,' he said, turning to leave the room before he forgot why he'd come over.

As he passed her, Connie reached for his hand. 'Come back and talk to me while I wallow.'

In the kitchen, Théo mastered his desires. Slicing a pomegranate in half to remove the seeds, he made a virgin punch and carried a tall glass back to Connie.

'So, tell me about your friends,' she said, taking a sip and moaning. 'The ones coming to the Christmas *réveillon*.'

Théo perched on the side of the bath and reached for a bar of handmade soap to wash her back, encouraging her to lean forward. 'Two are friends from university and their wives,' he said, sliding the bar over her skin, wishing it were his lips. 'Victor's sister and her husband—you met them at the wedding. And some couple friends of Tristan's that I've only met a few times but they're good company.' He set the soap aside and used his hand to scoop water over her shoulders and back, rinsing away the suds. 'I've ordered way too much food, but it wouldn't be Christmas otherwise, would·it?'

She smiled and leaned back in the bath. 'So everyone else but us will be in a couple?' she asked, her voice seeming relaxed. But she kept her eyes downcast as if fascinated by her toes peeking from the water.

'Yes,' he croaked. 'Is that…okay?'

'Of course.' She reached for his hand. 'Don't worry. I'm used to flying solo. Hopefully your and Tris's friends will be a little more tactful than my family, who always grill me about my love life or lack of one over dinner. When I split from my ex,' she said, smiling, her tone light but something vulnerable in her stare, 'I'm not sure who was more disappointed that there wouldn't be a wedding: me or my mother.'

She smiled wider but Théo's responding gesture felt half-hearted as his unease grew. He'd always assumed that Connie was still happy to be alone. But it couldn't be easy attending family gatherings solo when everyone else was married with kids and also knew her history.

'Are you…nervous to meet my friends?' he asked cautiously. 'I promise they're all lovely.'

'No,' she said, seeming more relaxed. 'I'll be fine. Do…any of them know about the baby?'

Théo slid his fingers between hers, his gaze on their hands. 'Only Tris and Victor.'

She nodded. 'Perhaps we don't tell anyone else until after the scan. I don't want to spend Christmas Eve answering awkward questions about the unusual conception and the status of our…relationship.'

'Of course,' he said, pricks of apprehension climbing his spine. 'I want you to be comfortable, Connie. I want you to have fun.' But it hadn't for one second occurred to him that others might ask his intentions towards Connie and wasn't sure how he would respond beyond *it's complicated.*

'I will. I'm looking forward to it,' she said. 'And I can't wait to see this *château* I've heard so much about.' She leaned forward, seeking a kiss. He obliged, bending down to press his mouth to hers, careful to keep it restrained.

'I'll go check on dinner,' he said, reluctantly rising to

his feet. Part of him wished he'd climbed into the bath with her, but he could tell she was tired.

Later, after Connie invited him to stay the night, he lay awake long after she'd fallen asleep in his arms, his wants at war with his doubts. Could he and Connie have more than just sex? Could he take that risk and would she be ready for more? One thing was certain—he wasn't ready for this to be over yet. In fact every time he pictured the future, pictured himself and Connie nothing more than friends and parents, the crushing sense of panic he was trying to keep contained only flared anew.

CHAPTER FIFTEEN

One week to Christmas

THÉO SPENT THE week leading up to Christmas in a frenzy of last-minute activity. At work, he, Connie and the rest of the spinal surgery team tried to get through as many surgeries as possible before Christmas. He and Connie spent nearly every evening together, eating out or attending movies or classical music concerts, before stumbling back to either his or her apartment for sex that felt both increasingly vital and terrifyingly desperate, as if they knew this honeymoon period couldn't last.

Secretly, that was how Théo wanted to spend that night too. But instead, he'd arranged to meet Tris after work.

'How was Geneva?' he asked, embracing his brother then setting off for the *Métro* station near the hospital.

'Perfect,' Tris said, smiling happily. 'You must visit some time. So what's up?' Tris asked, flicking Théo an inquisitive look. Since Victor had come into Tris's life, they spent less time together, not that Théo minded in the slightest.

'I need your advice,' Théo said, still debating his plan. 'I...want to get a Christmas gift for Connie.'

Tris paused, surprised, then continued walking. 'So

it's getting serious, then, is it?' he asked cautiously, his loyalties clearly torn.

Théo winced. He'd been worried about his gesture arousing Tris's suspicion. But if anyone knew what Connie might appreciate as a gift, it was his brother. And he was happy for Connie that she had such a devoted and loyal friend.

'Um… I wouldn't say serious,' he replied cagily, stepping into the nearest train carriage with Tris at his side. The doors closed and the train set off.

'But you're still seeing her?' Tris asked, wearing a small frown of concern as he clung to a vertical rail. 'Outside work?'

'Yes.' He wanted his brother's help. It seemed answering his questions was the price Théo had to pay. 'But it's fine. We've talked a lot. I'm not going to hurt her. You know me.' He glanced down at his feet. 'I don't want to repeat the mistakes of the past and, despite being married to Anaïs, there's more at stake this time with Connie.'

Tris's silence was ominous. 'And how does Connie feel? I mean, she's working with you, sleeping with you, having your baby. Are you sure you have this under control?'

'Why?' Théo asked, his paranoia finding an outlet because he wished he had it fully under control. 'Has she… said anything to you?' If Connie had reservations, she would confide in Tris.

With every passing day, Théo felt more unstable, reliving and analysing every conversation they had, uncertain of how Connie felt, despite what she said.

'No,' Tris confirmed, looking uncomfortable. 'I haven't seen her since I got back from Geneva.'

'Sorry.' Théo sighed. 'That was unfair of me to ask.

Look, she's told me she isn't ready to risk her heart for another relationship right now. But, believe me, I want her to be happy as much as you do.'

Tris's frown deepened. 'But you're not looking for a relationship either, are you?'

Théo shook his head, a part of him wishing it were that simple. Given the intensity of his and Connie's relationship, he was starting to wonder if he might be ready to take things to the next level. He just needed to be careful he didn't rush too far ahead and freak her out. But then, on the other hand, he couldn't seem to get enough of her.

'We've been honest with each other from the start,' he said, hoping to appease Tris's concerns. 'If you're that worried that I'm leading her on, then speak to her yourself. I'm not buying her a ring or anything…extravagant. It's just a Christmas gift. A gesture.' Although he had considered buying her a necklace but only if Tris thought it was appropriate. 'I want to give her something on Christmas Eve. So will you help me, or not?'

'Of course I'll help you,' Tris said after a beat, still looking worried, but this time Théo suspected it was for him and not Connie.

And when it came to his own feelings, and his fear of doing or saying the wrong thing and putting the wonderful gift he'd been given under threat, Théo could offer neither his brother nor himself any such reassurance.

Christmas Eve

The weekend of the Christmas Eve party arrived in all its wintry glory. After a three-hour train journey to Marseilles followed by a short drive into the forest and vineyard-clad hills, they arrived at Château Bijou. Located outside the medieval village of Chauvel, the modest *château* nestled at the bottom of a gravel driveway and guarded by tall wrought-iron gates was a charming terracotta-roofed, ivy-draped country house made from Provence's iconic white limestone.

'Oh, Théo, it's stunning,' Connie said, admiring the green shutters framing the windows and imposing front door complete with brass knocker.

She wanted to say more, but the minute she'd met Théo at Paris's Gare du Nord to board the Marseilles-bound train, a sense of foreboding had washed over her. Dressed casually and carrying a stylish leather weekend bag, his dark eyes bright with excitement, he'd pulled her close for a kiss that had left her breathless. She'd been quiet on the journey, terrified to blurt out the questions filling her head in case she didn't like the answers. And more than that, she was scared to examine her own feelings in case, as she feared, they were at complete odds with Théo's.

Théo collected their bags from the boot of the taxi and as they approached the front door, Tris flung it open to welcome them with outstretched arms.

'Perfect timing,' he said, pressing kisses to their cheeks. 'We've just finished putting up the decorations.'

Inside, the elegant old *château* was a little more ramshackle. The floors were uneven, the boards under the carpets creaking with age. The ceiling beams were weathered and the ancient glass in the windows was warped in places. But the furnishings and decor were warm and cosy, there was a roaring fire in the grate of the salon and Tris and Victor had done themselves proud with the decorations. Both the hall and salon boasted stunning Christmas trees and every horizontal surface a pine garland and clusters of fat, flickering pillar candles so it even smelled like Christmas.

'I've made tea,' Tris said, taking Connie's coat and scarf before ushering her to sit before the fire.

'I'll take your bag upstairs,' Théo said, hesitating in the doorway. 'I've put you in the green room, which has its own en suite and the best view.'

'Thank you,' she said, smiling but for some unknown reason feeling unsure of him all of a sudden.

'Victor has gone to change,' Tris said. 'But he'll be down soon. Then, after tea, we can all go the children's grotto if you like.'

'Sounds lovely.' Connie laughed, caught up in the excitement.

As soon as Théo departed, Tris poured the tea. 'Is everything okay?' he asked, handing Connie a cup. 'You seem…subdued.'

Connie swallowed, her carefree smile wobbling. She was torn between needing her friend's counsel and not wanting to put him in the middle because Théo was his brother.

'I'm just a little tired,' she said eventually, evading the truth. 'I don't know about you renal physicians, but for us surgeons it's been a crazy week. Everyone wants their operation before Christmas so they can recuperate with their family.'

Unconvinced, Tris eyed her suspiciously as he reached for her hand. 'I know we haven't talked much recently, what with the wedding and honeymoon and Christmas plans, but I'm still here for you, Con. You know that, right? I love my brother, but I love you too.'

Connie nodded, trying desperately not to cry. She

wanted to talk about her relationship with Théo, of course she did. But she couldn't do that to Tris. It wasn't fair.

'It's a bit awkward, isn't it?' she said, trying to make light of things. 'Normally we'd gossip about our conquests, but this time is different. Besides, you're happily married now. I'll have to tell my single friends about my relationship dramas from here on.' She smiled, hoping to reassure him, hoping he'd change the subject, especially as Théo was upstairs.

'You've got feelings for him, haven't you?' Tris whispered instead, glancing at the stairs as if watching for Théo's return.

'Of course, I have.' Connie kept her voice light and breezy and her smile in place. 'We're going to be raising a child together. I care about him. We care about each other.' But she couldn't admit that sometimes, like when she fell asleep in his arms, a part of her wondered if that longing in her chest meant more than contentment.

'Okay…' Tris said, still frowning suspiciously.

'Look. You don't have to worry, okay.' She squeezed his hand. 'We're not a couple. I'm just here this weekend as a friend.'

Of course, it was way more complex than that, and Connie wasn't sure she could ever be Théo's friend. But she could keep her fears and feelings inside for a couple of days and pretend. 'Let's just have a lovely Christmas *réveillon* together.'

Just then, they were joined by Victor, who kissed Connie hello and sat on the floor beside Tris, lovingly plucking an unnoticed pine needle from his sweater.

Connie glanced away from their happiness, part of her desperate to have what her friend had found, to be part of a couple with a person who just understood her. Who was crazy about her and loved her. But she'd been there before and didn't want to be hurt again, especially now that she was having a baby. And Théo… He might understand her, he might want her physically. But beyond that, he wasn't that man.

CHAPTER SIXTEEN

LATER THAT EVENING, when Connie came down the stairs wearing a sparkly little black dress that shimmered in the twinkling lights Tris and Victor had strung in every room, Théo's mouth turned dry with lust, longing and the rumbling dread that the more he tried to hold on, the more he feared he might be losing her. He couldn't put his finger on what was different about Connie, but ever since they'd almost lost Marjorie Pascal, he'd sensed her growing distance.

She smiled and he held out his hand for hers, praying that he was wrong, that he could keep a firm hold of what they'd found.

'You look beautiful,' he said, drawing her close to brush his lips over her smiling mouth, then resting his forehead against hers and breathing in the scent of her perfume and the sheer decadence that she was there, in his home for Christmas, about to meet the friends he cared about most.

Her lovely smile widened. 'Thank you. I like this colour on you.' She brushed her palm over his chest, admiring his favourite cashmere sweater.

Théo took her hand and led her into the salon, where a roaring fire crackled in the hearth, the scent of pine permeated the air and candles flickered around the room.

'An aperitif before the others arrive,' he said, pouring chilled non-alcoholic champagne into two flutes and handing her one. *'Santé!'* He touched his glass to hers, then, when they'd each sipped, swooped in and tasted her lips once more, lingering over the kiss as if it might be their last, but that was simply nerves.

Today, as he'd watched Connie's delight as they'd looked at the grotto, he'd come to a pretty momentous decision.

'I have something for you,' he said, leading Connie to the sofa, where he took a seat at her side.

'I thought we were doing gifts after dinner,' she said, her wary dark eyes reflecting the room's many flickering lights. 'I left yours upstairs.'

'We are,' he said, raising her hand to his lips because he was fully addicted to touching her. 'This is just a teaser. I wanted you to have it before we get carried away with good food, good company and lively conversation. Tris is threatening after-dinner games and has even created a playlist for anyone who wants to dance.'

Théo sat beside her on the sofa, his excitement building in spite of his reservations that Connie seemed distant. He reached for the small wrapped box he'd left on the side table. Connie took it hesitantly, a small frown pinching her eyebrows together. She squeezed the edges of the cylindrical box together and it popped open. She tipped the contents into her palm, her eyes widening in surprise. 'A key...'

'Yes.' He'd put the key on a wooden keyring in the shape of a mistletoe sprig that he'd bought earlier from one of the stalls at the children's Christmas grotto.

'It's to my apartment.' Théo brushed a lock of hair back from her cheek, eager to see her reaction. 'I know it's sudden, but I want you to move in with me, Connie.'

His heart pounded with anticipation and fear. But every time he thought about the future, this move was the only thing that made any sense.

She blinked down at the key on her palm, her frown deepening. 'Théo... I...'

Théo clasped her hand and she looked up. 'Hear me out, okay. I've thought it all through and it makes so much sense. We've proved that we get along, at work and in our personal lives, that we can compromise and respect each other. If we live together, we can actually raise our baby together, without always shipping it back and forth.'

Connie swallowed, something evasive shifting over her expression. 'Yes, but—'

'Look,' he interrupted, 'I don't know about you, but I hate the idea of missing out on any of the baby's milestones. First smile, first steps, first birthday. And if we keep two separate homes, one of us will always end up missing out. I don't want a broken family for us or for our little one.' He didn't want to be an absent father. And, selfishly, he wanted Connie too, even though he might never be able to offer her everything she deserved. But then after what she'd been through, she perhaps didn't want the promise of love and marriage.

'So we'll be roommates?' she asked, once more staring at the key with uncertainty.

'No...' Théo winced. He was messing this up. 'That's not what I mean.' He hadn't imagined she'd want to label them and hadn't actually thought that far ahead. 'I just... I figured that as we're both in the same place when it comes to relationships but want to raise the baby together, this makes the most sense. I want to be there for you and the baby. And I can't come up with a single reason as to why this couldn't work and be the best thing for us all.'

'So would we be a couple?' she pushed, her expression guarded so he had no idea how she felt either way. 'Would we still sleep together, for example?'

Théo shrugged, his gut twisting with doubt that she wasn't as excited about this as him. 'I mean, we can be whatever you want. Friends, lovers, all of the above. We're definitely going to be parents. And given that we made our baby in an unconventional way, we can raise it that way too. We can make our own family unit, just like you said. We could at least give it a try.'

Connie swallowed, gave a small nod and glanced down.

Desperate, Théo cupped her face, bringing her eyes back to his. 'You don't have to answer now. Just think about it.' He curled her fingers around the key. 'If you decide you want to keep your own place, then that's fine. You can keep the key anyway. If we're going to be family, I want you to come and go as you please. My homes are yours and the baby's.'

Connie nodded thoughtfully. 'Okay, I'll think about it.'

Théo smiled and pressed his lips to hers. Short of her instant, delighted yes, this was the next best thing.

Just then, Tris bounded down the stairs excitedly. 'They're here,' he called, flinging open the front door to greet the first carload of guests.

Théo pulled Connie to her feet and brushed her lips with his. 'Let's enjoy *le réveillon de Noël*. I want to introduce you to my friends.'

Connie nodded and followed him into the hall. But as the festivities began, the drinks began to flow and laughter and conversation filled the *château*, Théo couldn't help but feel there was something a little forced about Connie's smile.

* * *

In the typical way of a traditional French Christmas Eve celebration, dinner went on for hours. One course of delicious delicacies followed another and then another, until the dining table groaned under the weight of so much sumptuous food, local wine and the elbows of Tris and Théo's friends, who were locked in various animated conversations.

Connie, her stomach hollow with heartache and doubt, had barely eaten a thing. Oh, she'd smiled and chatted and pretended her heart wasn't slowly withering, but inside she grew more and more desolate.

Théo's gift, the key to his Paris apartment, felt like a poisoned chalice. On the surface, moving in together was a logical next step. She could understand why he'd asked. He was desperate for a family of his own and didn't want to miss out on time with the baby. But here, surrounded by couples in love, Connie couldn't muster one single scrap of excitement for the idea.

How could she work with him, live with him and raise a child with him while still protecting her heart? Because she'd known, the minute that piece of cool metal and warm wood had slipped onto her palm earlier, that somewhere along the line she'd fallen desperately in love with Théo Augustin.

Not that she knew what to do about it. She certainly couldn't tell him her feelings this weekend. What if he was horrified and she ruined Christmas? But staying silent also carried a price to pay. She kept going around in sickening circles.

'Bring out the *bûche de Noël*,' Tris, who was a little tipsy, called suddenly to a round of applause, dragging Connie from her depressing thoughts.

While Victor stood to fetch the traditional yule-log dessert, at her side, Théo dipped his head, his warm breath sliding down her neck.

'Come with me,' he whispered, reaching for her hand under the table.

People had been leaving the dining room all evening— to dance, to admire the trees, or fetch more wine from the cellar—so no one paid them any attention as they stood. Connie clutched his hand and followed him down a hall-way to a room he'd decorated as a library and home of-fice, one wall lined with oak bookshelves complete with a rolling library ladder.

'What is it?' he asked, gently closing the door as if Con-nie were made of glass and one violent disruption of the air currents might cause her to shatter. 'Do you feel unwell?'

He slid his hands up her bare arms to rest on her shoul-ders, his expression concerned.

Connie shook her head, terrified to tell him the truth, but knowing she could never live with him the way he'd proposed—a clinical practical solution to ensure neither of them missed out on parenting their child. It would de-stroy her.

'We should go back,' Connie pleaded, taking the cow-ard's way out. 'You're the host.'

'Connie,' he said, his frown deepening. 'Talk to me. Please. Don't…shut me out.'

Because she couldn't trust herself to be honest while also craving his touch, she turned away. 'I'm fine, Théo. I just…'

'It's the key, isn't it?' he said, his voice flat. 'I've freaked you out. I'm sorry. You don't have to accept it.'

Connie shook her head. 'It's not the key.'

Whether she accepted the key or not was irrelevant.

That his only concern was that he might have moved too fast only added to her certainty that when it came to feelings, she and Théo weren't even close to being on the same page. But his gift had made her realise how badly she wanted him, wanted a proper, committed relationship. She was ready to trust him with her heart, to put everything on the line and aim for all she'd ever wanted: a loving relationship, the baby, a real family. As she looked at him now, seeing his confusion and hope, her throat ached with longing.

As if unable to stay away, he strode closer and pulled her into his arms. 'I'm sorry. My timing was off. I just… I want you, Connie. I want us to build our little family of three together. I want to take care of you and laugh with you and share all those beautiful moments in our future with you and our baby.'

Connie nodded, her eyes stinging because his words had sounded like a declaration so close to her heart's desire she almost buckled and acquiesced. 'I want that too.'

'Connie,' he said, reaching for her, pressing a desperate kiss to her lips, wrapping her in his strong arms as if he could simply hold on tight and never let her go.

Connie kissed him back, awash with all the feelings she'd been denying for days. She loved him. Was utterly head over heels. She wanted everything he wanted and more. But now wasn't the time to tell him how she truly felt. She needed to pretend for a while longer, until they were alone.

'Théo,' she whispered as his lips slid down her neck and his hand caressed her breast through her dress, 'I'm scared.' She gave him half the story.

'Me too,' he said, pressing frantic kisses over her face, tangling his fingers in her hair, sliding his mouth over hers to swallow her moans as his hands roamed her body and set her alight. 'We can be scared together. It could be perfect, Connie. You, me, the baby. We can make it work.'

Losing herself in his intoxicating words and in his kiss, Connie clung to the last thread of denial and hope that maybe, just maybe, Théo was right. It could work. They had more reasons than most to make it a success. Maybe she could give moving in with him the serious consideration it deserved before she rushed into any drastic declarations or decisions. Maybe it would help her to come to terms with her feelings and judge how Théo felt in return.

Aching for him, Connie slid her hands under his sweater and caressed his smooth, warm skin. Her tongue surged against his and her desire for this man overwhelmed her. Hadn't he proved her wrong time and time again, showing her that he was different? Hadn't he shown her what was lacking from her life, what she was denying herself because of one bad experience? Maybe it was time for Connie to be brave and trust her instincts again.

'Théo,' she moaned as he rubbed his thumb over her nipple, slipping his other hand under her dress to stroke between her legs through her underwear.

'Connie, I can't get enough of you,' he said on a strangled groan as he pressed his erection into her hip. 'I'm crazy with wanting you. It never lessens. I want to sleep beside you and wake up with you every day. I want to take care of you and run you a bath and comfort you after a bad day. I want so many things it scares me too.'

He slid his hand inside her underwear and her knees almost gave out as his kisses and his touch and his words turned her on until all she cared about was him. This. Them.

'Hurry,' she said between kisses, grappling with his

belt and the fly of his trousers. This had always made sense. Surely he felt the same deep connection she felt when they were together. Surely this could be trusted, could grow into more.

She shimmied out of her underwear, backed up against the edge of the desk and shoved the hem of his sweater up until he removed it and tossed it aside.

Then he was back in her arms, his warm skin burning against hers as she spread her thighs and he leaned, reaching for her lips as she pushed his trousers and boxers over his hips.

'Connie…' He groaned, bracing one hand on the desk beside her and circling her hips with the other as he kissed her deeply, over and over until she was drunk with need and unable to think straight.

Then he was pushing inside her, filling her up, making her gasp with delight as she stared into his deep brown eyes, every part of her his.

As he crushed her in his arms, Théo's heart banged against hers. She wrapped her legs around him and dropped back her head, exposing her neck to his kisses.

'Don't leave me,' he whispered into her hair as his hips bucked and he thrust into her, his fingers stroking her nipple through her dress so she lost her mind and simply clung to him for dear life.

She loved him. She could never hurt him.

'I won't,' she cried, holding him, kissing him, staring into his eyes until they were both groaning and gasping in their search for release.

But even as she lost herself to pleasure, as they came together in a crescendo of mingled cries, of crushed-together mouths and bodies moving as one, prickles of trepidation tingled down her spine.

Panting hard, his face buried against her neck, Théo held her still as if scared to move and break the spell. Still joined as they caught their breath, Connie pulled back to look into his eyes, certain she could no longer pretend.

'I love you, Théo,' she whispered, the relief of finally admitting it euphoric.

Théo froze, his heart racing underneath her palm. Connie looked away from the confusion in his stare, pushing at his chest so he slowly withdrew and released her so she could slide from the desk.

'Connie… I…' Clearly stunned, he pulled up his underwear and jeans.

'Don't,' she said, scooping up her own underwear from the floor. 'Don't say something you don't mean. Don't patronise me. You said you wouldn't make promises you couldn't keep and I can see from your face that you're horrified.'

He reached for her arm and forced her to look at him. 'I'm not horrified or patronising you. I meant every word I've ever said to you, Connie. Why do you think I gave you the key? I want us to live together. I want us to raise our baby together. And maybe…see where this could go.'

'See where it can go?' she asked, tears stinging the backs of her eyes because she loved him, was having his baby and he was still hedging his bets. 'I know exactly where it will go, Théo. I want more than a key. More than some friends-with-benefits cohabitation. I want it all. I want you.'

'You want marriage?' he said, his expression crestfallen, as if she'd asked for the moon.

'No. Yes. Maybe.' Connie swallowed hard, humiliation clogging her throat. 'I don't know.'

How could she have been so stupid? How could she

have judged this so wrong? Again. Part of her had hoped he might love her back, but he didn't, and she'd ignored the warning signs.

'But I definitely want you to have feelings for me,' she said. 'And not simply because you want the baby, because you want this figment of a perfect family, whatever that is. But because you can't live without me. Can't sleep unless I'm beside you. Can't breathe unless we're together this Christmas and every one after.'

'Connie… I do have feelings for you. I care about you. I—' His face twisted in agony, his genuine regret obvious. 'But I don't know if I even want to be married again. But I don't want to hurt you. I don't want to lose you. I can't. I can't take that risk.'

'Forget marriage,' she said, certain now that he could never love her back. 'I'm talking about for ever. You and me.' Desperately in love… How could she have been so naive? How could she have ignored the warning signs? He'd made it clear his main interest was in the baby. She'd been carried away by Christmas and his stunning *château* and the time they'd spent together.

'I…' He gripped his hair and stared pleadingly. 'I'm trying my best, Connie. I'm trying to do the right thing for us all. I'm trying not to hurt you. Not to let you down and lose you, because I've been there before. I'm partly responsible for my divorce. I thought I'd found someone I could build a family with, but I failed. I tried to be a good husband but it wasn't enough.' He stepped close and gently gripped her upper arms. 'Let's just live together and see what happens.'

Connie twisted away, unable to tolerate the burn of his touch now that her dreams were crumbling. 'That's not the same,' she said flatly, sickened by how badly she'd judged his feelings. 'Don't you understand that if I move in with you all I'll feel is resentment? I'll get hurt again. I'll be destroyed, because I can see how much you have to give, if only you weren't so scared to risk it, scared of losing it all. Don't you see?' she continued, because he was staring mutely. 'A part of you is still that terrified, grieving little boy.'

'A part of me always will be that terrified little boy,' he said, his voice dead as if she'd wounded him.

'And I want all the parts of you,' she said, defeated. 'But I can't move in with you just for the baby. I can't share my entire life and my job and my whole heart with you, knowing you're stuck in the past, holding something back, just in case.' She wanted him to want her with the same desperation.

His expression hardened. 'The past can't be changed. No matter how badly we wish it could.'

'I know,' she said, crestfallen as just how at odds their feelings were was confirmed. 'But it can be acknowledged. Feelings admitted. Isn't that the first step to learning from the past so it doesn't taint our future?'

Just then, as he stared at her dumbfounded and clueless, a raucous swell of laughter reached them from the dining room followed by Tris bellowing Théo's name.

Connie dropped her hands to her sides in defeat. She was selfishly hogging him at his own party. Throwing love bombs when it was explicitly against the rules they'd vowed. Expecting him to change the habits of a lifetime for her because she'd changed and now wanted something more.

Théo gripped her elbows before she could step back. 'I need to see what he wants. Can we talk about this later when we're alone? I've heard everything you said, and I want to make this work. I promise you.' His stare shifted frantically between her eyes and she nodded sadly.

'Of course. You're the host,' Connie said. 'It's okay.' Stooping to pick it up from the floor, she handed him his sweater. 'You go back to the others. I might just take a moment to freshen up before I rejoin you.'

Nausea swirled in her stomach, the idea of going back to the party and pretending too much to bear.

After a beat of hesitation, Théo donned the sweater, then wrapped his arms around her shoulders and fiercely kissed the top of her head. 'Connie... I'll be back soon. Just...let me find out what Tris wants.'

With her head on his chest, she nodded but winced, knowing he couldn't see. It was obvious he was lost. She'd judged it completely wrong. Her feelings were so out of line with his: he wanted to safeguard his place in their child's life and she wanted it all.

With her heart breaking, she looked up at him. 'Go. We can talk later.' Fighting tears, she watched him hesitate then leave, her heart finally free to break in two.

CHAPTER SEVENTEEN

CREEPING DOWN THE stairs minutes later clutching her overnight bag, Connie placed her gift and card for Théo on the hall table and quietly let herself out of the house. The minute she'd been alone in her room, she'd broken down. Despite what she'd promised him, she couldn't stay a minute longer in his beautiful home, not when she'd finally given him all of her heart and he was only prepared to offer her a consolation prize in return.

Sliding into the back seat of the taxi she'd called, Connie tried to compose a message to Théo. She didn't want him to worry when he discovered her gone, but nor had she been able to face him knowing that he couldn't love her back. Not now and perhaps not ever.

After much typing and deleting, she sent a brief text.

Need some space. Gone back to Paris. Let's talk after Christmas.

With the message sent, she stared out of the window at the inky blackness of the passing countryside, every mile taking her further from Théo, further from what she'd hoped might be possible, that he'd be ready to love again. Ready to love Connie. Not just the baby. But just because he wanted to play an equal role in the raising of their child wasn't reason enough for Connie to deny how she felt and pretend.

Later, as she sat on the pretty deserted train from Marseilles to Paris, her phone finally rang. Seeing it was Tris, she picked up.

'I'm sorry,' she said before he could speak. 'I should have let you know I was leaving. I just…had to get away.'

'Where are you?' he asked, his voice tight with concern. 'Come back. Whatever happened, sleep on it. Talk to Théo in the morning.'

'I can't.' She sighed tiredly. Staying at the *château* meant once more facing Théo and she no longer had the strength. 'I'm on the train. Look… I'll explain everything when I see you next.' She couldn't relive the horrible humiliation again so soon.

'Connie,' he pleaded. 'Please tell me you're okay. I'm sick with worry. I've never seen Théo so…quiet as when he saw your message. Everyone else is leaving.'

Connie blinked, her eyes dry and gritty from crying. She wished she could reassure her dear friend. But she wasn't okay, not yet.

'I fell in love with him, Tris,' she whispered, clearing her aching throat. 'I know…so stupid. I judged it wrong again. But I just couldn't do it. I couldn't be with him, have his baby and not feel things.'

But Théo had managed to hold back. He'd kept his heart safe the way he'd always done.

'I don't understand,' Tris said in a hushed voice. 'He said he was going to ask you to move in with him.'

'He did.' Connie sighed, the key to his apartment in her bag. 'But living together isn't enough for me. I want all of him, Tris. I love him too deeply to hang around waiting for scraps. And I know him now, know his dreams and fears. Part of him is stuck in the past, still grieving in a way he couldn't as a boy. Still terrified of losing the people he loves. And while he's still holding back, he can't love anyone, including me.'

'Can you blame him for being cautious?' Tris asked quietly, his loyalties clearly torn. 'Every woman he's ever loved has left in one way or another.'

'I know,' she whispered, scrunching her eyes closed, unable to look at her reflection in the glass a moment longer as shame burned her up. She'd promised she wouldn't leave him and then she'd done exactly that. Fled in the night. On Christmas Eve.

'I'm not leaving for ever,' she croaked, the tears back. 'Just until it doesn't hurt quite so much.'

'He's devastated, Con,' Tris whispered.

Crushing pain shot through her. 'So am I,' she said, determined to shield her heart the way Théo had done. 'But he knows I'm committed to him in a way I always will be. We'll still raise the baby together. We'll always put its needs first.'

'Even at the expense of your own needs?' Tris said. 'Your own happiness?'

Connie swallowed a fresh wave of tears. 'Yes. Because that's what parents do.'

A moment's tense silence passed during which Connie sensed Tris's disappointment. She was being cowardly. But she'd been here before and this time needed to be selfish.

'Um… I have to go,' Tris suddenly said. 'I'll um…call you later.' And then he hung up.

Théo closed the front door on the last guest, his shoulders sagging in defeat. Pain seemed to seep through every part of his body. She'd left him. Gone. Fled the *château* without a word of explanation. Without giving him a chance to sift through his thoughts and untangle his feelings and process what she'd said in the library.

Oh, he'd read her message and he understood her reasons for running after he'd been blindsided by her confession that she loved him. But what he couldn't understand was why he was still standing there instead of chasing after her and begging her to give him another chance.

As he re-entered the kitchen, half dazed, Tris hung up the phone.

'Was that Connie?' Théo asked, foolish hope rendering his throat tight. 'Is she…okay?' Maybe she'd changed her mind and was on her way back to him. Maybe they could work through this and start over.

Or maybe he'd simply got what he wanted all along— his precious emotional safety. So why was the full-body agony only getting worse with every breath?

Tris nodded guiltily. 'She's on the train back to Paris.'

Théo scrubbed a hand down his face, a sense of inevitability causing him to slump despondently into a chair at the rustic farmhouse kitchen table where Tris and Victor had opened a bottle of whiskey and had obviously been nursing nightcaps.

Hadn't a part of him always known that this was how it would end? Hadn't he lived his entire adult life waiting to be rejected or abandoned? And he'd somehow doomed himself to relive history repeating itself over and over again.

'I poured you one,' Tris said, sliding him a glass.

Théo gripped it, just to give his hands something to do, but he knew he wouldn't be able to swallow a drop. And he wanted a clear head to make sense of how things had gone so badly wrong.

Perhaps sensing some serious soul-searching was about to go down Victor stood and touched Tris's shoulder. 'I think I'll grab a shower before bed,' he said, casting Tris an encouraging look before leaving the room.

'I can't believe she left,' Théo muttered to himself after another moment of tense silence, debating jumping in the car he kept at the *château* and driving all the way back to Paris.

'Can't you?' Tris challenged loyally, shooting him a dark, accusing look that then turned sympathetic. 'I told you to be careful with her.'

Théo pushed his glass away. 'I thought I was being careful. I never made her any promises beyond being there to help raise the baby.'

'Connie's the toughest woman I know,' Tris said. 'She doesn't really need your help, or your promises. But she loves you anyway. Did she tell you that?'

Théo nodded miserably, closing his eyes on a wave of nausea, picturing Connie's beautiful face as she'd bravely told him how she felt. As she'd given him all of herself, given him everything he wanted but was too scared to reach for in case it seeped through his fingers like water.

'Do you think it's true?' he asked his brother, his voice a pained croak. Could she truly love him, as messed up and emotionally cautious as he was?

Tris frowned. 'Why do you doubt it?'

Théo swallowed, his gut churning. 'Because I've been here before and it all went wrong. Because she promised she wouldn't leave me, only tonight, but she left anyway,' he snapped, frustrated with himself for allowing Connie to walk away thinking he didn't care and feeling as if he might throw up.

'Because she's scared, just like you,' Tris said, glancing

worriedly at Théo. 'Scared to take a chance on love and get it wrong again. To be hurt again. For the past three years she's told herself she's safer alone.'

'I know.' Théo hung his head, his mind spinning in circles. 'And tonight, I proved her right,' he whispered, standing to pace the kitchen. There was too much energy boiling inside him to sit still. How could he have done the one thing he'd wanted to avoid: let her down and hurt her? When Connie had given him everything.

'I can't believe you let her go,' Tris said, shaking his head.

'It's...complicated,' Théo said with a wince at how pathetic that sounded. 'It's not just about us and our feelings. We have to think about the baby...'

Remembering how Connie had accused him of only caring about the baby, he groaned in frustration.

'It's always been complicated,' Tris pointed out. 'That doesn't mean you should give up.'

'We're not giving up,' Théo argued, helplessly. 'We're choosing to put the baby first.'

'You're choosing fear,' Tris said with an unsympathetic scoff. 'Both of you.'

Théo stared at Tris, his heart lurching at how lost he felt and how Tris seemed more emotionally together.

'She said you're stuck,' Tris said, his eyes wary. 'Said you didn't grieve properly when we were kids. Is that true?'

'I... Probably...' Théo swallowed, the heart he'd kept carefully protected all these years cracking open so all the fear and doubt in him spilled free.

Connie was right. Some part of him had never properly processed what he'd lost as a child. He was terrified of losing people he cared about, people he loved. That explained why he'd behaved so abominably tonight. He loved Connie, desperately, so his fear was at its pinnacle.

'Is it because of me?' Tris whispered, his thumb rubbing at a divot in the scarred tabletop. 'Because you had to take care of me because you're older?'

'No.' Théo paced back to the table and rested his palms flat. 'It's because of me. Because Connie is right. I'm terrified to let anyone close in case they leave me. Like Maman and Mémé and Anaïs and now Connie. But it's too late,' he said, certain that alongside the fear his broken heart had exposed were other feelings. Enormous feelings he'd spent weeks denying. 'I love her too,' he finally croaked, closing his eyes against the burn in his chest. 'I have for weeks. I've just been in denial.'

'Of course you do. So tell her that,' Tris said excitedly, as if it were as simple as speaking those three little words.

'I wish I could. I wish she were here.'

After a few tense moments of silence, Tris cleared his throat and stood. 'I love you, Théo, but you know you don't need to take care of me any more. I'm an adult and I'm happy and I want the same for you. I think that's what Connie wants too.'

Théo turned wild eyes on Tris, needing his younger brother's wisdom, a part of him right back there to that scared little boy. 'But what if I tell her, if I try to grab what I want and lose it again anyway? I don't think I'll survive, Tris. Not losing Connie…'

Tris tilted his head in sympathy. 'You just have to take the risk, like the rest of us. Look around,' Tris said sadly, shrugging. 'It's Christmas Eve. A time to hold your nearest and dearest close. Connie is gone and if you don't tell her how you really feel about her, you're unlikely to get her back. What scares you more? That you try and maybe fail, or that you don't try at all and never know if you might have found the perfect love, the perfect family you've always wanted?'

Théo nodded, his lumbering, battered heart restarting as if shocked back to life. 'You're right. How did you get to be so wise?'

'I had an amazing brother and role model,' Tris said softly.

Théo swallowed, the love he'd tried to contain pouring out of him. Love for Tris and their precious little family. Love for his child, but most of all for Connie. Maybe if he caught up with her, told her how he truly felt, he could win her back, persuade her to give him another chance. Persuade her to come back home. Maybe they could work at this terrifying love thing together.

With his mind instantly clear, he marched across the kitchen. Snagging his keys from the hook by the back door, Théo briefly hugged Tris. '*Joyeux Noël.* Enjoy the *château.* The fridge is stocked, there's plenty of wood for the fire and I give you permission to raid the wine cellar.'

'Wait. What are you going to do?' Tris called as Théo flung open the back door and marched out into the freezing cold.

'I'm going to Paris. To find Connie and tell her how I feel.'

'It will take you all night to drive,' Tris called after him, but Théo was already sitting in the car and gunning the engine, which was sluggish from the sub-zero temperatures.

'I'll take the train,' he yelled, slamming the car door. Then praying for a Christmas miracle, he floored the accelerator, sped down the gravel driveway and took the road to Marseilles.

CHAPTER EIGHTEEN

CONNIE ONLY MADE it as far as Avignon on the train before she came to her senses and changed her mind. Tris was right. She'd thought she'd bravely given Théo her whole heart, but she'd still been scared, had still held a sliver back because she didn't want to be hurt all over again and run. But Théo would never deliberately hurt her, and she'd broken her promise and left him the way he almost certainly had expected her to because of his past.

Rushing to the opposite platform in the railway station, she boarded the next Marseilles-bound train. Frustration formed a tight ball in her stomach. The train just wasn't moving fast enough. She needed to go back to the *château* and be fully honest with Théo. She needed to give him the time he'd asked for and seriously think about them living together. She needed to tell him that she would always love him, even if he couldn't love her back.

In despair, she dropped her face into her hands. Tris had been right. Théo had lost every woman he'd ever loved. And in acting out of fear, in clinging to the desire to protect that last piece of her heart, Connie too had run out on him. On Christmas Eve!

With trembling hands, she fired off a text to Théo, hoping he might still be awake even though it was after midnight and now officially Christmas Day.

Never should have left. I'm coming back. Let's talk.
Please.

She'd just about given up on a reply when her phone
pinged with an incoming text.

This is Tris. Théo is on his way to find you but left in a
hurry without his phone. Where are you?

Connie practically howled in agony, her heart thudding painfully.

On the train to Marseilles. Should I change again and
head to Paris after all?

Where was Théo headed? Surely he wouldn't drive all
the way back to Paris alone?

To Connie's relief, Tris's reply came swiftly this time.

No! Get off train at Marseilles and make a wish that you
intercept him there. That's where he's headed.

The thirty-minute journey back to Marseilles felt more
like a thirty-hour-long haul. Plenty of time for Connie to
list, alphabetise *and* rearrange her endless regrets in de-
scending order. How could she have behaved so stupidly,
allowing her fears to stand between her and everything
she wanted? How could she ever have convinced herself
she could be content with so little? Faced with a kind,
honourable and passionate man worthy of her love, her
feelings just wouldn't stay contained. And a man like
Théo was worth fighting for.

As a recording finally announced Marseilles station, Connie grabbed her bag and headed for the nearest exit. The automatic doors seemed to take a year to slowly glide open, then she was out on the platform and hurrying towards the station exit.

That was when she saw Théo, running her way, his face lighting up when he spied her. She froze, her bag sliding from her hand as he ran faster. She couldn't believe they'd found each other.

'Connie,' he said, panting hard as he gripped her shoulders. 'You came back.'

His relief was palpable. Connie nodded, everything she wanted to say to him stuck in her throat, which was clogged by her overwhelming feelings of love.

'I'm sorry,' she choked out. 'I should never have left. I know I broke my promise.'

'No, *I'm* sorry,' he cried. 'I should never have given you a reason to leave.' As if he couldn't be without her in his arms a second longer, he wrapped them around her shoulders and held her close so she felt the rapid thud of his heart against her cheek.

Connie clung to his waist and breathed him in. He smelled like burning candles and pine needles and Théo. 'I was scared,' she admitted, her joy that they were reunited, that they'd found each other, bubbling up.

'Me too,' he said, prising her far enough away so he could peer into her eyes. 'You were right about everything you said. Every word. I'm so glad you came back.'

'I only left because I couldn't face seeing you again,' Connie rushed on, trying to explain why she'd left, 'knowing that I might have judged this so badly, but—'

'No,' he said, cutting her off. 'You didn't judge it wrong. I was just too terrified to say or do the wrong thing because I didn't want to lose you. I couldn't survive losing you, Connie. Not you.'

'But that's just the thing, Théo,' she pleaded. 'I came back to tell you that it's okay. You don't have to be scared. We'll always be a family. You, me, the baby. You could never lose me. I'll never leave you again, I swear.' Even if she had to find contentment as his friend.

'Connie,' he said, swiftly kissing her lips, his stare wild with passion. 'You don't understand. I love you. I want the same things you want. I want for ever with you. I want this Christmas and all our future Christmases. I just panicked earlier because I've messed this up before and it would kill me to lose you. Not just because of the baby, but because I want to spend the rest of my life with you. You're everything I want. I've loved you for weeks, I was just in denial. I'm sorry.'

Before she could speak, he covered her mouth with his. Their lips slid together, breath mingling as they grabbed at each other in obvious mutual desperation. Connie's heart soared out of her chest and she smiled against Théo's mouth.

'You love me?' she asked when she'd pulled back, smiling for joy.

He tunnelled his fingers through her hair and cradled her face, his stare adoring. 'I love you so much I ache whenever we're apart. I watch you sleep. I fantasise about all the places I want to take you on holiday. I've bought you far too many Christmas gifts because I just couldn't help myself, and if you're going back to Paris tonight, that's where I'm headed too, because I won't be able to sleep unless it's wherever you are.'

'Théo…' Connie blinked, happy tears seeping from the corners of her eyes.

'Please forgive me,' he said, pressing his lips to her forehead. 'Please give me another chance to prove to you that I am ready to love you with every inch of my terrified heart. Please let me try to be the man you deserve, because I promise you, unreservedly, that no one will ever love you harder than me.'

'Okay,' she said, laughing through the tears that stung her eyes. 'But there's nothing to forgive.'

'Okay?' He smiled wider. 'I'll take okay,' he said, his mouth returning to hers. And for a long time, despite the cold and Théo's lack of a coat, they kissed on the platform, not needing the excuse of mistletoe, because they had their love for each other instead.

Until Théo had Connie safely back at the *château* and snuggled by the fire with a warm drink, he couldn't fully relax. He'd driven back from Marseilles station with one hand on the wheel, the other hand holding hers, a goofy smile on his face as he'd looked over at her every few seconds. But having almost lost her tonight, he wasn't taking the risk of physically letting her go again.

Now, sitting by the fire in the salon with his arms wrapped tightly around her, he drew her even closer and buried his face against her neck. 'I love you,' he whispered. *'Joyeux Noël.'*

'Joyeux Noël.' She smiled up at him and snuggled closer. 'I'm sorry if I ruined the celebrations.'

'You didn't. You being there made the celebrations everything.' He stroked his fingers through her hair, simply enjoying the beat of her heart against his. 'Everyone rushed off to catch midnight Mass in the village. Besides, *le Réveillon de Noël* is about family and you are my family, Connie.'

Connie pulled back and picked up the gift she'd carried in from the hall table. 'This is for you. I want you to open it.' She held the box out to him, her eyes bright with excitement and love that choked him.

'You first,' Théo said, handing her the gift he'd purchased with Tris.

Smiling his way, Connie untied the ribbon and prised open the box, her face lighting up as she examined the contents and gasped. 'It's beautiful, Théo,' she said, pressing her lips to his then gently fingering the delicate gold chain inside.

'Try it on,' he urged. 'I'll do it up for you.' Taking the necklace from the box as Connie swept her hair aside and turned around, he draped the delicate chain around her neck. 'Tris helped me choose it. So if it doesn't fit, we can blame him,' Théo said, fastening the tiny clasp and then pressing his lips to the back of her neck.

'It's perfect.' Connie turned and smiled. 'I love it. Thank you.'

She kissed him again. They couldn't seem to stop kissing or touching each other.

'Now open yours,' she urged excitedly, pushing the gift his way.

Théo didn't really want to let go of Connie but nor could he deny her a single thing. He opened the box to find a digital photo frame inside. The frame surround was a stylish dark wood and when Connie pressed the *on* button, the display screen came to life with a photo of the two of them together at Tris and Victor's wedding. Instead of smiling at the camera, they were smiling at each other, their expressions so obviously enamoured, Théo couldn't believe it had taken him so long to recognise his feelings for this incredible woman.

'It can hold thirty thousand images,' she said, scrolling to the next photo she'd uploaded. It was Tris and Victor on their wedding day, and then a shot of Tris and Théo as boys, their beautiful *maman* in the centre. 'So there's plenty of space for photos of the baby and any others you want to display.'

With his chest aching that she understood him so well, Théo scrolled back to the first image of him and Connie. 'This one is my favourite for now,' he said, drawing her close for another kiss. 'Thank you. It's a perfect gift. You obviously learned some skills from the gift master.'

She laughed and he swooped in for a kiss he almost couldn't bear to end. 'I can't wait to fill it with happy memories of our family.'

'Neither can I,' she said, reaching for her bag and pulling out his apartment key. 'I want to move in with you, if the offer still stands.'

Théo cupped her face. 'Do you really need to ask? I've never wanted anything more than to wake up with you for the rest of my life.'

With her eyes shining and smiling, she held the key above their heads, the mistletoe keyring dangling above them. 'Shame to pass up on an opportunity,' she said with a seductive smile.

'I will never need an excuse to kiss you,' he said, knowing he would love her for ever. Then, because it was Christmas, and Connie was the best gift he'd ever been given, he pressed his lips to her smiling mouth.

EPILOGUE

Christmas Eve one year later

WITH BABY ELISE asleep after her feed, Connie carefully handed their precious daughter over to Théo.

'I'll just put her down,' he said, looking at their daughter with wonder then gently kissing the baby's forehead before heading for the nursery in their Paris apartment. Connie watched through the baby monitor as he lovingly laid four-month-old Elise in her crib and sighed with contentment.

Théo was the perfect father. Loving, attentive and fun. Somehow, watching him be the wonderful parent she'd instinctively known he would become, Connie fell a little deeper in love with him every day.

'She's so utterly perfect,' he said, sliding next to Connie on the sofa and, with his arm around her shoulders, drawing her close. 'Just like her *maman*.'

Connie smiled, raising her face to his for a kiss. 'And her *papa*.'

'She's so wonderful, I think we should make more babies, don't you?' Théo teased.

Connie beamed indulgently. They had of course already had this important conversation many times in the past year so he knew they each wanted another child to complete their little family.

'One more,' she said, resting her head on his chest. 'And maybe in another year.'

Théo held her close and kissed the top of her head. 'Of course, we can make the next one in the traditional way if you like.' He placed his index finger under chin and pressed his lips lazily to hers, slowly savouring their kiss, the heated look in his eyes making her shudder deliciously.

'Let me just finish my drink and then we can practise,' Connie teased and snuggled closer. 'Because practice makes perfect.'

The rumble of Théo's chuckle vibrated through his chest as Connie relaxed in his arms. The fire crackled in the grate, the warm air carrying the scent of pine. The instrumental Christmas chill music softly played in the background and as Théo's heart gently beat beneath her cheek, Connie had never felt so content.

After a moment, he shifted, producing a small box from underneath the sofa cushion. 'There's one more gift for you,' he said, handing her the velvet box, his dark eyes tender.

'Théo…' she whispered, her heart rate spiking excitedly as she sat up and stared at the box. She prised open the lid and gasped, her stare flying back to Théo's.

'It can mean whatever you want it to mean,' he said about the stunning diamond ring. 'I want to marry you if you want to be married. I want to spend the rest of my life with you and grow old by your side, married or not. I want to raise our family with you and I'll never stop loving you, Connie. Just be mine.'

Connie laughed ecstatically, although her vision swam with happy tears. 'I want all of that too,' she said, pulling the ring from its velvet cushion.

Théo took it from her fingers and slid it onto her ring finger. 'So will you marry me, Dr Dubois?'

Connie threw her arms around his neck and kissed him, her heart soaring with love for this incredible man who'd taught her that love *was* worth the risk. 'I will, Dr Augustin.'

Théo's radiant smile squeezed another drop of love from her heart. '*Joyeux Noël*, my love.'

'I love you,' Connie whispered, embracing their always simmering passion as she brushed her lips over his. 'Happy Christmas.'

* * * * *

If you enjoyed this story,
check out these other great reads
from JC Harroway

One Night to Royal Baby
One Night to Sydney Wedding
Manhattan Marriage Reunion
The Midwife's Secret Fling

All available now!

THEIR CHRISTMA
PREGNANCY SHOCK

ANNIE O'NEIL

MILLS & BOON

To every one of you who can't think of
anything dreamier than curling up with a
Christmas love story. We are kindred spirits.

Also? In case you don't know…
Hygge, the Scandinavian philosophy of comfort,
care and cosiness—especially in wintertime—
is pronounced hue-guh. (Almost like a huge hug,
but not quite, but close enough!)

CHAPTER ONE

IT WAS POSSIBLE Matti's commitment to reinventing herself was verging on...extra.

Surely relocating to Copenhagen and putting her rusty Danish to work at a renowned hospital was enough of a challenge without pushing this particular boundary.

C'mon, Matti. Where's your courage?

It was a word she'd heard a lot lately. *Matti, you're so courageous. A new job in a new country? Especially considering—*

She glanced at her godmother who, as usual, smiled at her without judgement.

'I'm all over this,' Matti assured her, willing the words to spur her to action. 'In it to win it.'

'I know,' Astrid said as if she'd not doubted her for a second. 'Your name means warrior. But,' she continued, 'even the most valiant of warriors feel scared sometimes.'

Matti barked a self-deprecating laugh. Her nervous system was battling something more crippling than fear.

Shame.

A demon she'd been at odds with for years now. And it was time for that demon to take a hike.

She centred herself, willing her wobbly legs to join the party. If she walked away from this self-imposed challenge, she feared she would crumble at all of life's inevitable hurdles. Meaning, her ex-was right. She had changed since the accident. And not for the better.

'Darling,' Astrid finally said, giving Matti's cheek a soft stroke with the back of her hand. 'You know what you're capable of. And so does everyone who meets you. You need to learn to believe in yourself. Remember, you've already taken the doorstep mile.'

'Doorstep mile?'

'It's what we Scandinavians call the first mile away from the familiar. Especially when it isn't working for you any more.'

Matti winced. Talk about hitting the nail on the head.

'Change is frightening,' Astrid said matter-of-factly. 'Setting out into the unknown is the most difficult journey to make. You've done that, figuratively and literally. A new job in a brand-new city.'

'I spent my summers here as a kid,' Matti reminded her, wincing at the testiness of her response. 'I'm still a doctor, so…that's not new.'

Astrid clearly disagreed. 'Visiting your mother's homeland for the summer holidays is different to moving there. You'll be adapting to a different lifestyle. Using a second language. Pushing yourself professionally. All of which takes tenacity. Bravery.' She paused for effect. 'Sometimes a show of strength is knowing when a challenge can wait.'

True. She hadn't been remotely nervous when she'd pumped her first heart back to life. Set complicated compound fractures. Stitched countless wounds. Not to mention the calm steadiness she felt when she'd extracted countless foreign objects no doctor wanted to find inside a human. Achievements she'd once felt proud of until shame had ploughed over everything. Especially her confidence. Which was why she had to do this. Now.

Deep breaths. The only one judging you is you.

She looked down the sparsely populated, curved wooden boardwalk the locals called 'The Snail'. More formally known as the Kastrup Sea Bath, the pier's nickname referred to its unusual spiral shape. A protective wooden wall arced around an enclosed swimming area where someone was climbing out of the water. A couple of dog walkers were enjoying the view. A cyclist was drinking a coffee. Quite good-looking if she wasn't mistaken. From a distance, anyway.

What are you doing, you numpty? You should know better than to judge a book by its cover!

She tipped her head back, eyes closed, took a deep breath, then blinked them open, frowning at a gathering pre-dawn cloudbank. A sign something ominous was about to happen?

Don't be ridiculous. It's weather. Not to mention the fact the water was warmer than the air temperature by several degrees. They'd checked.

More to the point, her natural surroundings were not only stunning, they were at the heart of a gorgeously bustling European capital begging to be explored.

Her mother's native country had always been magical to her. The fjords, the stone buildings, the gorgeous canals, the straight-talking Danes and now the hospital where she hoped to reestablish herself on *her* terms. No more averted gazes or pitying smiles. No more muted conversations falling silent as she passed, head bowed, trying to make herself small as her cheeks burned with frustration. She wanted to leave *that* woman in the UK. The one struggling to cope after her fiancé, only weeks away from vowing to stay by her side no matter what, had decided she was 'too much'. And by 'too much' he meant she repulsed him.

To her surprise, a new reaction to the shame-soaked memories surfaced. She felt disgusted. Not with herself, but with him. How dare he superimpose his selfish, superficial outlook on her? Did he think placing the blame on her would absolve him of guilt for leaving? *Well, screw that. Screw him!*

'I'm ready,' she said.

The revelation must've translated in her tone. Smiling, Astrid held out her tote bag. 'Put your things here.'

Matti gave her godmother's arm a squeeze. 'Thank you for doing this with me.'

'Of course.' Astrid took off her hat and deftly wove her long silver-blonde hair into a thick plait. 'Anything for my favourite goddaughter.'

Matti laughed. 'You mean your only goddaughter.'

Astrid shrugged. 'Semantics.'

Matti rolled her eyes, but the warm exchange served as a reminder of why she'd moved to Copenhagen. Her parents had passed away a while back and, after her personal life had imploded, Astrid was the closest thing she had to family. Not to mention one of the most vibrant, life-loving people she knew. Like her mother, Astrid met challenges head-on.

She plucked off her knitted bobble hat and gave her red-gold hair a fluff so that it covered her neck.

Astrid caught the instinctive gesture but, rather than comment on it, pressed her hands to her heart. 'Such a beauty.'

Matti opened her mouth to refute it but, determined to rewire her brain to embrace the positives, gave a shy smile of thanks. 'You're the best.' She mirrored her godmother's gesture. 'Truly, Astrid. I can't thank you enough. For renting me the barge. Letting me drag you out of bed in the cold—'

Astrid laughed. 'You won't know what cold is until we come here in January. And there isn't anyone else I'd rather have in the barge.' Her tone sobered. 'I should be the one thanking you. With Oskar gone, I… I'm not sure if—' Her light blue eyes clouded with tears. Little wonder. She and Oskar had been married for over forty years. 'I'm so very pleased we can be here for one another. Now—' she put on a bright smile '—I think it's time. Don't you?'

'I do,' Matti agreed, humbled by the reminder that her permanently cheery godmother was in the throes of reinventing herself as well, now that she was a widow. 'Let's do this.'

She toed off her snuggly ankle boots, held onto the railing as she peeled off her socks and reminded herself of the countless therapy sessions she'd spent piecing together the scraps of herself that she'd once taken for granted. Confidence. Pride. Vulnerability. She shivered at the memory.

Astrid, mistaking it as a reaction to the wind, said, 'Just think of the coffee and pastries we'll be having after.'

'Is it *hygge* to skip this part and go straight to pastries?'

Astrid laughed. '*Hygge* isn't a boardgame with rules, my sweet. It's a philosophy. One you must personalise. Whatever makes *you* feel cosy and content is *hygge*. One person's cosy may not be another's.' Proving her point, she dropped her thick coat to the ground despite another fresh gust of wind. 'Bliss.' She closed her eyes, tipped her face up to the sky and spread her arms wide as if offering herself to the universe.

Matti marvelled at how completely at ease Astrid was in her sixty-something body. Not a scrap of Britishness about her. No shame for its imperfections. No sucking in her tummy, or covering herself. No apologies.

Astrid turned to her with a smile. 'I am so grateful to be alive. To have a body capable of experiencing so many different sensations. Hot. Cold. Scratchy. Soft. Smooth.'

Matti joked, 'I might leave cold and scratchy off my list.'

Astrid tsked. 'Shielding yourself from what's unpleasant or frightening means you might not experience the exhilaration of realising how extraordinary you are. How strong. But if it really is too cold for you…'

They shared a look. The weather was not the problem.

Astrid gently cupped Matti's shoulders without acknowledging her reactive flinch at the contact. 'Your mother always said you had the heart of a lioness. Called you her "tenacious adventurer". The fact that you're here is proof.'

Matti gave her a doubtful look. 'You don't think she would've said I'm running away?'

Astrid pulled a face. 'It's what *you* think that matters. You wouldn't have left everything behind if you weren't looking to shake things up, would you?'

'True,' Matti conceded. If she'd succumbed to self-pity and accepted the victim role her friends and colleagues had imposed on her, she would've spent the rest of her life in a numb fog of *Where did it all go wrong?* back in York. Life was for living, even if progress came at a snail's pace. Ha! She was on a snail-shaped pier. It was up to her to set the pace.

Dramatically ripping the snaps of her thick knee-length coat apart, she flung it behind her. 'Time to make like a polar bear!'

'That's the spirit,' Astrid cheered. 'We'll make a proper Dane out of you yet. On you go, then. One, two—'

Matti took a deep breath…*out with the old*…and in she dove.

The shock was instant. Her skin felt as if it had burst into flames. It was the worst thing she could have imagined, compounded by not being able to breathe. Panic threatened to consume her. Helplessness. Everything she'd felt back when—No.

She made herself open her eyes and orientate herself. Though the sun had yet to rise, she could see the increasing glow of daylight above her. Two or three strong strokes and she would resurface. To her surprise, a wash of calm shifted the fear away and by the time she broke through the water a wave of euphoria was surging through her like an orchestral swell of music.

She looked around and saw Astrid treading water not far off, hands raised above the water waving invisible pompoms. 'You did it!'

'I did it,' Matti whispered. She, Matti Meadows, was swimming in the Baltic Sea in Copenhagen on All Hallows

Eve in a barely-there swimsuit. She started laughing. Infectious, joyful laughter born of such a simple act: jumping into really, really cold water.

'Welcome to Denmark, darling,' Astrid said, swimming to her. 'I hope you find what you're looking for here.'

'I suspect I will as long as it's pastry-shaped,' Matti joked, but Astrid's comment struck a chord.

Imagining her future was something she'd been struggling with. Even picturing what sort of impression she'd make at the hospital tomorrow was beyond her. Maybe it was a good thing. Picturing the worst-case scenario came with the danger of manifesting it. Open mind, open heart. That was how she wanted to start each day from now on. She'd done this. And for the first time in ages, she felt proud of herself.

As Astrid set off on some laps, Matti ducked back under the surface of the water, swimming with long, assured strokes that took her further away from the wooden pier. When she surfaced, she saw the pale outline of the moon still hanging in the sky. Instinctively, she tipped up her chin, breathed in a delicious lungful of air and howled.

CHAPTER TWO

WHEN THE TRAFFIC increased on the Øresund Bridge to Sweden, Felix drained his coffee. Time to get to work.

Starting his days out here on 'The Snail' was his way of reminding himself of his place in the world. One soul amongst many.

He was tucking his silver flask into his backpack when a message pinged through from his sister. Another reminder about joining her and her children at Tivoli Gardens for tonight's Halloween extravaganza. The famed amusement park was a huge lure for children and adults. Families. He began typing his standard excuse, 'Sorry, working', when he heard a woman cry out. Or rather…was that *howling*?

He scanned the bay for swimmers, quickly spotting a woman in a pink bathing cap doing a steady crawl close to the dock and then, beyond her, a strawberry-blonde who, sure enough, was howling at the moon like a she-wolf calling in her pack.

As many health benefits as there were from a bracing plunge in the sea, he'd seen enough cases of hypothermia in the emergency department to know not everyone could tell when an endorphin surge turned ominous. He leant his bicycle against the railing, prepared to dive in if necessary, when she turned so that he could see her face.

This was not a woman in trouble. Quite the opposite. She was beaming. Glowing with life. Completely unaware, or perhaps not caring, that she was being observed. She was like a dolphin at play. Plunging her hands into the water to send arcs of droplets up and over her head, only to disappear under the water, surfacing seconds later with a whoop. Utterly carefree. Joyful in a way that nudged at the part of him that had once been the same, before he'd crushed the instinct into submission.

What fuelled her joy? he wondered. Some good news? Born that way?

Didn't matter. He knew why he'd chosen to relinquish that part of himself.

He took hold of his bike when she began swimming back towards the dock. No need for him to intervene. As she climbed out, she called out to the woman in the pink cap that she'd meet her in the sauna. She was around his age, medium height. Pretty. Very pretty, actually. Just his type, if dating was on his agenda. Which it wasn't.

She plucked a thick purpose-made swim coat from the dock. As she turned and swirled it around her shoulders, his breath caught.

Her back, crisscrossed by two thin straps of her bathing costume, was covered in burn scars. Third, possibly fourth degree. There went his theory about her life being carefree. She'd known pain. Fear. Loss. And yet…she was embracing her life as enthusiastically as if she hadn't. Or, the thought occurred, because she had.

He rode to work, mulling over his decision to do the opposite. As he approached the hospital, he felt the thick protective shield he used to deflect emotions thicken around him. There was a comfort in it, yes, but was denying himself access to life's simpler pleasures actually useful?

'Morning, Felix. Ready for the madhouse?'

Felix looked up from where he was securing his bicycle

to greet his colleague who, judging by the fatigue creasing his features, was coming off a busy night shift. 'Is it chaos?'

'Not too busy,' his colleague admitted. 'But it's Halloween today, so prepare yourself for a lot of pumpkin-carving related injuries.'

Felix gave him a wry smile. 'Every holiday has its dangers.' Not all of them physical.

His colleague huffed out a laugh. 'Children's holidays should come with warning labels. Thank goodness we don't have to worry about any of that nonsense, eh?' A committed bachelor, he gave Felix a knowing look as he pulled his bicycle out of the rack. 'Children, I mean.'

The approaching sound of sirens gave Felix the perfect excuse to dodge answering. Discussing the merits of childlessness wasn't a conversation he was interested in having.

As the ambulance pulled into the emergency bay, a couple of attendants in protective smocks and gloves ran out to assist. One of them, a twenty-something junior doctor, was wearing a mask and a cape that were more superhero issue than hospital issue.

'No costume, Dr Beck?' she asked with a hopeful smile.

'I dressed as a doctor,' he said dryly.

Her smile faded, cheeks pinking in embarrassment. She shot her colleague a look like, *Oh, boy, Dr Beck got out on the wrong side of the bed again.*

Her peer shrugged like, *What did you expect? It's Dr Beck.*

This type of exchange wasn't unusual. He chalked them up as confirmation that he'd successfully separated his professional and personal identities so that his private life, which had once been the talk of the hospital, was now off-limits. But something about seeing that woman howl at the moon earlier was still with him. A niggling thought that maybe he didn't want to be *that* guy any more. The curmudgeonly killjoy known for shutting down any attempt at adding levity to a job that could take a toll. Was it truly serving him? Or keeping him outside the orbit of his own life…reinforcing a solitude that, these days, was beginning to feel isolating rather than comforting.

'Here we go,' he said, shoving the thoughts away as the ambulance pulled into the bay.

Still in his street clothes, he pulled open the back doors of the emergency vehicle, stepping to the side so that his colleagues could unload the gurney.

The lead paramedic began rattling off the essential information as the team swept into action. 'Sixty-two-year-old male, presenting with acute chest pain radiating to the left side of his neck and jaw, causing him to fall off his cycle on his way to work, sustaining superficial lacerations to his forehead, left hand and left knee.'

As the paramedic ran through the blood pressure stats, oxygen saturations and other vital statistics, the patient pulled the oxygen mask off his face and gasped, 'My phone. I must call my wife.' He pushed himself up and tugged a mobile phone out of his pocket, collapsing back onto the gurney from the effort and, in so doing, dropped it directly in the path of a steel-toe booted paramedic.

'We'll reach out to them.' Felix scooped up the cracked phone and pocketed it before he could see the damage.

The paramedic eased the patient's mask back in place and, as the team headed into the hospital, cited the fluid drip they'd put in place and, of course, the all-important dose of aspirin to thin the blood.

Felix jogged in after them, calling out to the Chief Resident, Dr Freya Larsen, 'Do we have a free trauma room?'

'Three,' Dr Larsen instructed, then, waving a glittery tasselled child's magic wand at Felix said, 'I was hoping to magic you up early for today's shift.'

Felix raised his eyebrows. He was always in early. Dr

Larsen, a warm-hearted sixty-something surgeon the staff esteemed as a mentor and, at times, an unofficial grandmother, had known this about him since she'd hired him, some ten years back, as a fledgling intern. 'Everything okay?'

'Yes.' She smiled, turning to the large assignment board to erase a couple of names before holding a pen aloft. 'Do we have a name for the new patient?'

Felix glanced at the sheet the paramedics had given him. 'Arthur Neilsen.' He handed her the paperwork then remembered the phone in his pocket and the promise to contact his family. He pressed the phone's damaged screen. A bright, sunlit picture of a large, happy family appeared beneath the fractals of the broken screen. They were all striking silly poses, laughing and looking utterly carefree, apart from Arthur. He was on the edge of the photo, oblivious to the teenage boy wagging a finger at him for being on his phone.

The image hit him like a sucker punch. Felix had been in countless similar photos at his own family get-togethers. Pulling his loved ones close. Chastising anyone on their phone. The past few years? He hadn't even bothered going.

Arthur was a husband, father and grandfather. A man with plenty of reasons to live, let alone reasons to put his phone away. The screen was locked, so Felix pocketed it, making a mental note to check in with him once he'd changed into scrubs.

Dr Larsen tapped him on the shoulder with her wand. 'Do you have a moment to talk about magic?'

'If this is about wearing costumes—'

'No—' Dr Larsen held up her hand, stopping him '—it's about our new hire. The one I told you would be with us through Christmas?'

Felix vaguely remembered something from the previous week's staff meeting. 'Remind me?'

Dr Larsen pointed towards the staff lounge, indicating he

should follow. 'Trauma specialist. Highly skilled. Dr Meadows went straight from medical school to *Médecins Sans Frontières*. Worked in Syria, Ukraine, the Middle East, Southeast Asia and, more recently, in a trauma unit at a public hospital in the UK.'

'Why is she coming here?'

Dr Larsen's eyes twinkled. 'She's developed a keen interest in *hygge*.'

He gave a huff like, *Oh, boy, here we go*. A reflexive response to a cultural philosophy that was, at its heart, about togetherness, family, but had lately morphed into a quest for the perfect soft furnishings or hand-dipped organic beeswax candles. In other words, it had become about things, not people.

Meaning, the next few months would be spent battling a trendy, style-over-substance colleague over buying out-of-budget throw pillows embroidered with words like 'Cozy' or 'Chill Time'.

Alternately, if she was more of a tree-hugging, earth mother type with a large 'non-traditional' family who made her own kombucha, they'd clash over promoting alternative therapies or an insistence on all staff wearing upcycled scrubs covered with butterfly patches or, worse, smiley faces.

In either scenario, he'd be the bad guy, forced to justify his cool, scientific, professional approach to running the department. Emergency centres didn't have space for touchy-feely nonsense. They demanded intense concentration and acute attention to detail.

'Let me guess,' he said to his boss. 'She wants us to practice medicine by candlelight?'

Dr Larsen gave him a look. He was to take this seriously. 'She's keen to see how, if at all, we Danes integrate the concept of *hygge* into our work and patient care here in the emergency centre.'

'We Danes?' he repeated. 'Where's she from?'

'The UK. She's on a two-month contract with an option to extend.'

Rather than breathing a sigh of relief that the tenure would come to an end, Felix busied himself pouring them each a cup of coffee, scrambling to pinpoint areas where the hospital integrated the concept of family and togetherness in a way that didn't interfere with the medical practitioners' day-to-day business.

Dr Larsen beat him to it. 'You'll know that the hospital's recent renovations took patient experience into consideration but, so far, there hasn't been a study on whether we doctors are doing the same.'

Felix took a sip of coffee to stem a comment about his belief that there didn't need to be a study because the doctors were doing precisely what they were meant to: practicing medicine.

In fairness, the renovations had made a positive impact on both the staff and patients. Tactical applications of warm, honey-coloured wood and larger windows in the recovery rooms, for example, had seen more than one patient declare that they felt they were staying in a luxury hotel, not a hospital room. The architects had also added several visitors' rooms with adjoining private gardens, geared towards getting patients who were able out of bed to play board games, chat privately, sit in the sun or, in one case, garden. Surely those changes alone had ticked enough boxes to satisfy Dr Meadows' niche interest in Danish healthcare.

'So,' he tried again, 'how much policy am I meant to overlook to accommodate her suggestions?'

His boss shook her head, displeased. 'It's precisely that attitude that compelled me to pair the two of you together.'

'Sorry? We don't work in teams.'

'Yes, you do,' she said pointedly. 'You are part of a large

team here at the hospital and, from tomorrow, you will also be part of a team of two.' Before he could protest, she continued, 'I think we should call it The Holiday *Hygge* Challenge. Fun, right?'

No. It wasn't. Cutesy names attached to woo-woo projects that kept him away from his actual job was about as close to his idea of hell on earth as it came.

'You'll start tomorrow. All Saints' Day. Fitting, don't you think? A day honouring those who devoted their lives to improving the world around them. Much like a physician. Now—' she pushed her tablet between them and pulled up the staff roster '—I've matched her rota to yours. You'll have November for research and to work out the particulars. You'll launch the project December first, rolling out your innovations through until the New Year.'

None of this was sitting well. 'You do remember I'm the resident Grinch, right?'

His boss shrugged. 'If I remember correctly, the Grinch discovered it was better being part of a community versus looking down on it with disdain.'

Felix asked a question he wasn't sure he wanted answered. 'Are the staff unhappy with the way I run the ward?'

'You run a very efficient ward,' said Dr Larsen.

'Is that your way of saying there's room for improvement?'

She tilted her head and gave his arm a pat. 'Let's not read too much into anything, all right? Keep an open mind. Who knows? Maybe you won't be the Grinch this Christmas.'

Felix shook his head, laughing. 'I wouldn't bet on it. Which does beg the question, wouldn't it be more useful for Dr Meadows to work with someone who is into *hygge*?' His older sister, for example. She loved all of that stuff. Baskets full of blankets. Wood fires. Knitting circles. Baking with her children. Comforts he'd eschewed in his own home, as they reminded him of the life he wasn't living.

By choice, Felix. You're nobody's victim.

His boss gave him a knowing look. 'If anyone needs to examine the benefits of remembering that there are as many good things in life as there are bad, it's you, Felix.'

Felix gave his jaw a scrub. His mentor was doing what she did best. Forcing him to confront something that made him uncomfortable. Not for cruelty's sake, but for growth. Back in the day, it had meant being asked to lead surgeries for anything from a ruptured appendix to a compound fracture. But this so-called *Hygge* Challenge went deeper. Dr Larsen had known him before, during and after his three-year marriage. Knew his ex-wife, her new husband and their toddlers. And, more to the point, that Felix's version of moving on from his failed marriage had been shutting himself off from friends and family, using work as his excuse.

'We're not pulling punches today, are we, boss?'

She gave him a bright smile. 'No. We're not. Copenhagen Central is Denmark's flagship hospital and if we can improve patient experience in the emergency care centre it sets an exemplar for others to follow. I know you'd hate to think there was something lacking in the care you provide. In your bedside manner, for example.'

The comment had the same effect as a matador brandishing a cape at a bull. She had his full attention.

Leading by example was what he thought he'd been doing. But if patients were giving negative feedback about him, Dr Larsen was right to challenge him, even if it made him want to crawl out of his own skin with discomfort.

'You're a wonderful doctor, Felix,' his mentor said, seeing her comments had unnerved him. 'And you can be an even better one. Research has confirmed that actively practising *hygge* reduces depression and anxiety, promotes an increased feeling of community, elevates optimism and gives people a greater appreciation for life's simpler pleasures.'

He forced himself to swallow a counterargument about the application of scientifically based medicine having more merit in a hospital than a knitting circle. This was a time to listen, not argue.

'I know you appreciate low cost, high impact solutions that facilitate shorter recovery times and a reduced likelihood of a return to hospital, Felix.'

He nodded. That was true.

'Dr Meadows wants your project to prove it. And who knows?' His boss gave him an affectionate smile. 'As you explore your options, you might find something that puts some joy back into that big heart of yours.' She gave his hand a pat. 'It's time to let the past go, Felix. Look to the future.' She rose, coffee in hand. 'And to be clear? I expect you to treat this challenge as seriously and respectfully as you would any trauma case.'

'Understood.'

He headed towards the registrar's desk and, after running through a few things, remembered once again the ambulance patient's phone. He handed it to the registrar. 'Would you mind getting this to Arthur Nielsen once he comes out of surgery?'

The registrar typed a few words into the computer then frowned. 'We'll pass it onto his family.'

'No,' Felix corrected. 'Give it to him, please.'

'We can't give it to him,' the registrar explained. 'He didn't make it. Dr Christiansen is ringing the family now.'

Normally, Felix took this type of news in his stride. But hearing it in the wake of the conversation he'd just had—a stern reminder that his crisp, businesslike approach to work was not only affecting his colleagues but his patients—the news came as a blow.

'Right.' An uneasy prickling sensation spread through him. He needed to shake it. 'Anything on the board?'

'Nothing that'll keep you off the floor all day. Sorry.'

Was that what he looked for in a case? A surgery that kept him out of the highly emotive frontline of patients and their loved ones. People who, in many cases, were having the worst day of their life. Or, like Mr Nielsen, the last.

This was exactly what Dr Larsen had been talking about. The weak links in his chain of thoughts. Leading by example meant doing the hard stuff, even if—especially if—it was uncomfortable. Growing pains were aptly named. He was feeling it now.

As much as he wished it, he couldn't bring the patient back to life. But there was something he could do.

He took out his phone and replied to his sister's text. Worst-case scenario? They'd make him ride the roller coaster and talk about feelings. At the same time.

Best case? He'd find a way to channel the version of himself he'd once been. The one who gave his nieces and nephews piggyback rides. The one who didn't avoid family get-togethers, knowing he'd be held to task. The version who would've called Arthur Nielsen's family himself, before it was too late.

CHAPTER THREE

MATTI INHALED A delicious lungful of crisp autumnal air, burnt sugar and apples. She hadn't been to Tivoli Gardens since she was a little girl and had forgotten how magical it was. More so tonight with the vibrant parade of ghosts, princesses, monsters, witches, skeletons, kittens, devils—adult and child-sized—all buzzing with anticipation.

Instead of infusing her with a shared giddiness that spurred her into buying a ticket, she became increasingly aware of how alone she was. She had her godmother, of course. Not tonight, though, and for some reason, it made her feel incredibly exposed. To the point of weakness. Her fingers gripped the edges of her cape so she could pull it round her, when a light caught and flared off one of her gold wrist cuffs.

A timely reminder that she was dressed as a *super*heroine. A warrior who confronted her fears head-on instead of wishing she was invisible.

She released the fabric, set her feet in a solid stance and cupped her hands atop her hips. As if the universe was giving her a nod of approval, a light breeze filled out the folds of her cape so that it billowed around her.

A little girl passing with her mother stopped to stare in wonder.

Matti gave her a wink then headed to the ticket booth. She had a roller coaster ride to take.

As she made her way past a multitude of stalls selling

everything from fresh, hot doughnuts to knitted hats in the shape of a *kraken*, her nerves took a different form. She was not a roller coaster girl. Perform a complicated surgery in a conflict zone? No problem. Get strapped into an open cart that whipped her up and down and all around? It wasn't the sort of thing she had ever wanted to do as a girl. Her parents had been older than most of her friends' parents as a girl. Quiet, academic types, more stimulated by the contents of a book than by a so-called thrill ride. She'd been the same, seeking excitement in cerebral challenges over physical ones. Her accident had forced her to acknowledge that her body played a huge role in her life, a ridiculous-seeming realisation for a grown adult but, for her, a critical one that had led her to this point. Exploring facets of life she'd never really had to before.

Which was why she was dressed as Wonder Woman and joining the queue for a ride that already had goosebumps running up her arms, courtesy of the screams of the passengers racing past.

As the queue lengthened behind her, she suddenly registered the sound of loud voices. A sharp shout. A clatter. A blur of motion. Before she could make sense of what was happening, a large male hand lightly cuffed her forearm. A cool shift of air skimmed across her back as the man shifted her round so quickly that she instinctively grabbed hold of his arms for balance, only to be knocked off-centre yet again as he took the brunt of a collision with a pair of young men dressed as pirates, too caught up in a dramatic plastic sword fight to notice them.

'Are you all right?' he asked in a voice that in any other circumstances would've made her insides go all gooey, but instead, she realised she had plastered herself to his chest like a limpet.

Let go of him, she told herself.

Her body was not listening to her.

Her fingers, insofar as she could tell, were attempting to embed themselves in his lean but well-defined biceps as her nose nestled into his jumper, breathing in an intoxicating mix of freshly hewn wood and burnt sugar. Cardamom and nutmeg. Crisp air and autumn leaves. He was everything and one thing all at once.

'Are you all right?' he asked again.

When she failed to answer, she felt the vibrations in his chest transfer through to her cheek as he called out in a louder voice, presumably to the pirates, to watch where they were going. Not unkindly, but there was definitely a protective note of warning in it.

Questions pinged around her head, but in a blur, as if she were in a magical snow globe, minus the snow but including the magical, comforting feeling she always got when she saw one.

This, she thought. *This* was what she'd wanted to feel when she was with her ex. *Protected*. If the pirates had crashed into her back instead of his, the pain would've been so acute she'd be curled up in a ball on the ground, pleading with someone to ring Astrid to come and get her.

Which is why you need to thank the nice man, Matti.

Filled with gratitude, she willed her fingers to loosen their grip on his jumper and pleaded with her feet to take a step back so that she could look at him like a normal person.

Slowly, she lifted her gaze, letting it travel along the curves of his neck, loitering amidst the soft golden bristles lightly shadowing the curve of his jawline, the full sweep of his mouth, until she reached his bright, sea-blue eyes. He was watching the pirates who, chastened, were now backing away, swords aloft, apologies floating towards them, before resuming their battle.

The moment she took a step back so that she could properly see her protector, she wished she hadn't let go quite so quickly. Rushes of butterflies didn't come to her often, but when they did, she remembered them. And right now, her insides were fluttering with a kaleidoscope of diaphanous wings. He was the kind of handsome that only existed on film posters. Intense eyes, straw-coloured hair, sexy-nerd glasses, a furrowed brow and lips that were begging to be kissed.

Her heart was doing its best to hammer its way out of her chest as questions exploded into her head, one after the other, like popcorn, each begging for priority. What would happen if she clung to him again? Pressed her cheek against his heartbeat? Would it be pounding as rapidly as hers? What would it feel like to run her fingertip along the bristles on his cheek? Trace the light fan of creases fanning out from his eyes. Plunge her hands into his hair and pull those lips to hers in an act of wanton longing—

'Are you all right?' Dream man was frowning, clearly concerned that the only thing she was capable of was staring at him like a love-struck kitten.

She made herself nod yes, deeply regretting not wearing her long winter coat so she could pull it over her head and slink away instead of trying to find a non-awkward, *Yes, that's right, I'm dressed as a superhero* pose.

'Thanks for being a human shield,' she finally managed and put her hand out for a fist bump.

'Pleasure,' he said, but no smile accompanied it. Nor a fist bump.

'Are *you* all right?' she asked. 'You took the brunt of it.'

'I'm—' he began, then stopped to throw a glance at an attractive woman behind them in the queue.

Her heart plunged to subterranean depths. He was married. The woman had to be his wife. And the children around her his children. And here she was, perving over him to the extent that a heated swirl of attraction was spiralling from her tummy down to her cobwebbed—

'I think you should ride with Wonder Woman,' sexy married man's wife said. 'Make sure she's all right.'

Now it was Matti's turn to frown. Why would this scrumptiously delicious man's wife want him to ride a roller coaster with a stranger? Particularly when it was practically obligatory to hold hands.

'I'm sure she doesn't need me to do that,' he said with too quick a glance to notice that she most definitely did. Well, she didn't *need* him. But she wanted him.

Maybe he was right.

'Felix,' the woman said remonstratively. 'Manners.'

Felix!

Great name. It suited him. Were his glasses a costume? Maybe he was supposed to be Clark Kent, which would mean her costume was a perfect match for his. Or maybe they were actually his glasses. She tried to discreetly study him, but Felix—*Felix!*—caught her staring and because she had no poker face whatsoever, saw enough to realise that she most definitely would not mind being thigh to thigh with him.

'Unless,' he began uncertainly, 'you'd like me to barge in.'

'That'd be great!' Matti blurted. 'Barge away. I mean, unless you want to ride with your family. I don't want to ruin any well laid plans. Plans are great, especially when they're well laid.'

Cringe! Verbal diarrhoea was not attractive. *Now he thinks you're an idiot and will never want to have sex with you.*

Sex?

She'd barely learnt his name and already she was imagining having sex with him?

The desire to pull him to her and kiss him resurfaced with a vengeance. She didn't want to give him sweet, soft, tentative pecks. She wanted to kiss him hungrily. Passionately. Now. Now, before he found out anything about her. The accident. The agony of recovery. The humiliation of her broken engagement. And then, because he was someone else's husband and his wife would rightly demand she never set foot near him again, she would preserve the kisses, his scent and the evidence that her body could still feel sexy on the inside in a mental snow globe she would call *The Day I Remembered How to be Brave.*

She searched his eyes to see if, by some wild turn of events, he'd mind being kissed by a complete stranger in front of his wife. The Danes were known for a healthy, open attitude towards sex and bodies—flawed or otherwise. If he wasn't married and kissed as well as she suspected he did, she'd even consider pushing the boat out further. Invite him home for her first ever one-night stand. That way, if he saw her scars and rejected her, her deepest fears would be confirmed. Or, she allowed, seeing as this was entirely hypothetical, if he didn't run for the hills when he saw her scars, she'd take it as a sign that trusting her gut was as important as trusting empirical evidence.

Her eyes dropped to his lips. The reality was, she'd never kiss them. Never know if they'd taste salty or sweet. If he'd tip his head to hers if she closed the small gap between them. Lick his lips in anticipation as she lifted her mouth to his.

They were a shade darker than they'd been at first glance. Fuller. They were also moving.

'It would make sense,' she heard him saying once she'd cleared away the lust static, '...to ride with you. My sister and her family are an even number.'

Matti blinked at him, trying to understand what even numbers had to do with a Scandinavian Clark Kent, when all of the sudden she backtracked. *Sister!* The woman was his sister, not his wife. She was free to throw herself at him. Which, as a real option, was a thousand times more terrifying than the hypothetical one.

One of the children, a blond boy dressed as a Viking, clarified. 'One,' he began, poking his chest, then moved on to his three siblings, Felix's sister and a congenial-looking man eating a candied apple. 'It would be good for Uncle Felix to ride with a superhero,' the boy said to Matti. 'He hates roller coasters.'

She turned to him, delighted. 'You do?'

Felix gave the kid a playful fist-bump. 'Thanks for blowing my cover, pal.' His bright blue eyes returned to her as he sheepishly admitted, 'I do hate roller coasters.'

'Me, too.' She grinned. 'I'm pretty sure I'll scream.'

'I will definitely scream.' Felix returned her smile, but something about the way he looked at her gave her the feeling that she'd just confirmed something he suspected about her. Something he liked.

The attendant beckoned them to a set of cars on the loading platform.

'Go on, Felix.' His sister gave him a nudge. 'You two take the front one. It's the scariest.'

CHAPTER FOUR

FELIX CLIMBED INTO the roller coaster car after Wonder Woman, ignoring his sister's smug smile of satisfaction.

'I'm Matti, by the way,' she said as she tucked her cape around her.

'Felix.'

She put her hand out to shake his, but pulled it back abruptly when the roller coaster attendant instructed them to raise their hands while he lowered the roll bar.

'Safety first,' she quipped. 'Not that riding a roller coaster is a guarantee of safety.'

'Especially when it's over a hundred years old,' Felix said without thinking. 'And made of wood.'

'Maybe I should have gone with the carrousel,' she joked.

'At least this isn't The Demon.' The amusement park's most terrifying ride. 'There was an incident a few years back when the riders were stuck on it for over an hour.'

She pulled a face. 'Riding something called The Demon on Halloween seems like tempting fate, doesn't it?'

He was about to say it was if you believed in fate, something he didn't, but seeing Matti twice in the same day made him wonder if the charged energy buzzing through him signalled something beyond a coincidence. As if the universe was trying, not so subtly, to say, *Pay attention, this woman is going to show you life through a different lens.*

Then again, his logical side countered, there was a slight

accent to her Danish. Chances were, she was a tourist visiting Copenhagen's hot spots, meaning he was reading far too much into what was a coincidence.

'Oh, boy!' Matti grabbed his leg as the clutch of cars in front of them took off with a creak and a lurch. 'We're next.'

He stared at her hand on his leg. Instinct told him to hold it, reassure her, but just as he was about to, she pulled it away, grimacing through an apologetic smile.

'Sorry. You're probably regretting coming to my rescue. I promise it won't happen again. I'll sit on my hands.'

He hoped she didn't. 'Glad to be of service.'

Glad to be of service?

As flirtatious banter went, his was clearly rusty.

'You've been very heroic tonight,' she said.

'Sorry?'

'With the pirates?' she prompted.

'Ah!' That had been pure instinct, not heroism. If they'd crashed into her back, it could have been agony. 'Argh!' he said, waving an invisible sword. 'Avast ye matey!'

She laughed good-naturedly, despite his clear lack of pirate panache.

If anything, he owed the pirates a thank you. He'd instantly recognised her when they'd joined the queue. If the swordfighters hadn't come barrelling towards Matti, he probably wouldn't have said anything to her, just stood there mutely, wondering what it would be like to be with someone who clearly relished life, even the parts that scared them. Then, later, beating himself up for lacking the courage to say hello.

The roller coaster lurched forward.

Matti grabbed his hand, apologised, released it, then grabbed it again as the car began ascending the first arc. 'My hands are refusing to be sat on. Do you mind?'

'Not in the least.' And off they swept.

They both screamed and screeched and, to his surprise,

laughed themselves silly. Felix couldn't remember the last time he'd been so aware of someone. The press of her thigh. The way her fingers naturally wove through his. His body's protective response to hers as the car swerved and accelerated, hurtling down then crawling up, pausing, then, without warning, plunging down again.

At the end of the ride, she thanked him profusely. 'I hope I didn't break your hand.'

He opened and closed it a few times to prove it still worked, wishing more than anything that this was a beginning rather than a goodbye.

His sister bustled up. 'Have you two seen the photos?'

Matti's warm hazel eyes went wide with delight, as if she'd been presented with a birthday cake. 'I bet I look absolutely terrified.'

'Go see for yourself,' his sister said, giving him an indiscreet shove in the same direction Matti had gone when he failed to follow her.

'I'm going to buy a copy,' Matti said, holding the photo up for him to see.

She looked exhilarated. One hundred percent in the moment. And he? He was staring at Matti as if he'd never seen someone more beautiful.

If she was embarrassed for him, she was doing an excellent job of covering it.

'From now on,' she said to him as she handed her card to the merchant, 'whenever I'm scared of doing something, this will remind me that *thinking* about doing something is usually scarier than doing it.'

She began to unzip a hidden pocket on the inside of her superhero belt, then abruptly shot him a look of apology. 'I'm sorry. I wasn't thinking. If you'd like a copy, I'd like to get you one. In thanks.'

'Thanks? For what?'

'Being kind. You've been incredibly kind to me.'

He was about to say it was nothing when he realised that doing so would diminish her gratitude. The way she'd said the word 'kind' made it sound like something precious. Something rare. He couldn't imagine anyone behaving otherwise, but his gut was telling him she'd known enough pain to truly appreciate even a fleeting kindness.

'I'd love a copy of the photo,' he said. 'Thank you.'

'Good answer.' She beamed. After she'd finished the transaction, she handed him the photo and clapped her hands together. 'Well!' She put on a smile that didn't quite make it to her eyes. 'I guess I'd better return you to your family.'

He didn't want to be returned.

He looked around for them, trying to think of a casual way to ask her to join them, when he realised that his sister and her family had vanished. *What the—?*

His phone pinged. A series of saucy emojis appeared, then a message:

We decided you should go on a date. We're going on The Demon then heading home. Stefan says they sell condoms in the gents. Put December 1st in your calendar. Bring the redhead.

He shoved the phone back in his pocket, mortified.

'Everything okay?' Matti gave him a worried look.

'All good.'

Apart from his sister micromanaging his personal life. Then again, if Matti had joined their group, Solveig, who had no filter, would've inevitably recounted every embarrassing story from his past, spilled the beans about his failed marriage, highlighting his refusal to 'rejoin the dating pool'— something she'd been pressing him to do since last Christmas.

'It was Solveig, my sister. She said the kids dragged them

off to ride The Demon.' He made a vague gesture like, *What can you do?*

Matti started giggling.

'What?' He began laughing too, even though he didn't know what was funny. 'Did you want to join them?'

'Not a chance.' She feigned horror, then, eyes locking with his, pinked as she said, 'It kind of seems like they're setting us up.'

He groaned. 'That obvious, huh?'

She pinched her fingers together. 'Little bit. Putting us together on the roller coaster I could buy, but with the photo booth and then a disappearance to a ride they know neither of us would go on?'

'She's not exactly subtle.' Felix gave the back of his neck a scrub. Once a younger brother, always a younger brother.

'Look,' Matti said, taking a step back. 'I don't want to make you uncomfortable—'

'I'm not uncomfortable,' he cut in. 'Well, I am, but only because I don't want to make you uncomfortable.'

'I'm not uncomfortable.'

They gave one another nods like, *Good, good, glad that's clear*, which sent Matti into another round of giggles.

'What are we? Ten?'

'Out of practice,' he admitted.

'Snap.' Matti put out her fist.

He bumped it. She grinned then looked back at the roller coaster, where another set of passengers were screaming as they plunged up and down the track.

'As we're both out of practice, and behaving like ten-year-olds, should we take a page out of their rulebook?'

'If you mean take on The Demon—?'

She waved her hands. 'Definitely not that. I meant, you know how little kids will go up to another kid they like the look of and ask if they want to play or be friends or assign them a role like…' She waved an invisible wand at him. 'You're a knight in shining armour.'

'Yes,' he said, drawing the word out, not entirely sure where this was going.

'They just go with it,' she said with a happy shrug. 'No questions, no third-degree about their past or plans for the future. They just play and then, when their mum tells them it's time to go, they make sad faces and moan, *Aww, do we have to?* They do, and then life goes on. Fancy having a night like that?'

'Only if I get to be a knight in shining armour,' he joked.

She batted her eyelashes at him. 'You've already nailed that.' She held out her hand to him, as if holding hands was also part of the deal. 'You choose what we do next.'

He took her hand in his, the contact feeling both familiar and new, then asked, 'How do you feel about bumper cars?'

CHAPTER FIVE

Two rounds of bumper cars, a carousel ride, a pumpkin-carving contest—which Matti won—and a turn round the Ferris wheel later, Felix automatically took Matti's hand in his as they left the ride and set off down a tree-lined lane aglow with fairy lights.

She grinned up at him. 'Where to next?'

'We're here,' he said.

'We are?' She looked around, confused. They'd just reached a small green, a few metres from a clutch of food stalls and not near any of the rides.

'We are.' Before he could overthink it, he cupped Matti's heart-shaped face in his hands, skimming his thumbs along her jawline. *You are so very beautiful*, he thought, willing his fingertips to remember the softness of her skin, the freckles speckled on her nose, the tug of attraction rising from deep within him.

'Where are we?' she whispered.

'The kissing booth.' He dipped his mouth to hers before his brain had a chance to intervene. The moment their lips met, overthinking wasn't an option. This was no tentative first date peck, a teasing brush of the lips.

This was hunger. Thirst. A longing for more. Kiss after kiss adding fuel to the sparks of attraction he'd felt ever since he'd seen her this morning, proud, fierce, howling at the moon.

When her lips parted beneath his, concern that he'd overstepped or misread things vanished.

What a way to re-enter the world of the living. Kissing like a teenager. In public, no less. Shrugging off his normal reserved behaviour felt surprisingly liberating. Instead of shame at a public display of affection, the rest of the world blurred as a golden, purifying heat flooded his nervous system, reawakening parts of himself he'd convinced himself he had no right to feel any more.

Happiness. Intimacy. Hope.

Approaches to life that, until this moment, felt vulnerable. But, seeing them in Matti, he realised they weren't vulnerabilities. They embodied an openness to life and, as such, were a strength.

He wanted to live in this moment for ever. Touching her. Tasting her. Feeling her body arch into his as if trying to meld their bodies into one.

He cupped his hand over the soft, delicate curves at the nape of her neck, relishing the silky tickle of red-gold hairs that had escaped her plaits.

She shivered.

He pulled his hand back. 'Sorry. Too cold?'

'No,' Matti put her hand over his and placed it back on her neck. 'Not cold. Just…new.' She kissed him again, dissolving his ability to ask, *What? What about this, apart from everything, is new?*

Someone shouted, 'Get a room!'

Matti pulled back and bit her lower lip.

He laughed, strangely delighted. 'That's new, too.'

The tension in Matti's shoulders eased a fraction. 'Kissing, you mean? No,' she corrected. 'You definitely know how to kiss. But not in public?'

'The latter,' he confirmed. Danes were very comfortable

with sex as a topic, but not so much with public displays of affection. 'What do you think?'

'What? About the kissing?'

He threw caution to the wind. 'About his suggestion.'

'Oh!' Matti gave herself a little shake and pulled her cape around her.

His heart sank. Too much, too soon.

She looked up at him. 'What do you think?'

Honestly? He was up for it. Wanted to touch her, caress her, see if he could transfer that extraordinary feeling of light filling his body. Her body language suggested the feeling wasn't mutual.

She ran her finger along her neckline and shivered again. She wasn't cold. She was covering her scars. Should he tell her he already knew about them? That he wasn't worried about them if she wasn't.

He searched her eyes, willing them to tell him what to do. What to say. She was nervous, but not about him. It was more…

You've been incredibly kind…

Her words ran in a loop. He racked his brain, trying to put pieces of the unfamiliar puzzle together, when it came to him. She was nervous about her scars because someone had been unkind to her about them. Which made his blood boil. How someone could be so cruel—

She shivered again.

'Here.' He shrugged off his coat. 'Put this on.'

'I'm fine,' she protested as he swung the coat round her shoulders. 'I don't—' She glanced up at him. 'Thank you. Sorry. Thank you.'

'No thanks necessary,' he insisted, frustrated at how awkwardly he was handling this. He was a doctor, for heaven's sake. He had difficult conversations all day long.

Not with someone you're attracted to.

He took a step back, considered suggesting they call it a

night, then thought, *No. This isn't the memory I want to leave her with.* He pressed his hand to his chest. 'I have a confession to make.'

Her eyes snapped to his. 'A confession? No. That's okay. I don't want to know. Especially if you're already seeing someone and this was a pity date. No! Worse. This was a pity date with kissing. Which means that even though they were the *best* kisses I've ever had, this was a completely awful thing to do. Here, take back your coat. It'll be worse if it smells like another woman when you get home to her.'

'Keep it. Please.'

Instead of putting it back on, she buried her face in the fabric to muffle a cry of despair. Or fury. She peeked up at him. 'It's worse, isn't it? You're married.'

'No.' Definitely not married. He shoved his hands through his hair, gave his head a scrub. 'We need to back up a minute, okay? First. This—you and me? Not a pity date. Unless you ask my sister, in which case she would say it was, but that you were the one taking pity on me.'

'I wasn't taking pity on you!' Matti protested. 'I was eating out of your hand from the moment you saved me from the pirates. I mean, not literally. Oh, God, I'm so terrible at this. Can we cut to the chase? You're seeing someone, aren't you? And your sister doesn't know.'

'No. I'm not seeing anyone.'

'Phew!' She wiped invisible sweat from her brow. 'I'd hate to think I was your bit on the side.'

'You are not a side dish, Matti.' She was everything. Soup to nuts. And yet she couldn't see it. 'Matti, the truth is, I saw you earlier.'

'Where?' She frowned, thinking. 'On the carrousel?'

'No. This morning, at the Snail.'

She looked confused for a moment, then, eyes widening, groaned. 'You saw me howling at the moon?'

He nodded. 'I did.'

'And you didn't ring emergency services?'

'No. Why would I? I don't think you're crazy, if that's what you were suggesting.'

She launched into a long, rambling explanation about how he had ample fodder for believing that she had lost her grip on reality.

As he listened, it occurred to him that her questions and side-tracking banter were Matti's way of wriggling out of his suggestion that they spend the night together. It was, of course, her prerogative to refuse him, but if this was the last time he saw her, he didn't want her walking away feeling less than. He wanted her to be able to walk away head held high, feeling proud of who she was.

'Matti, when I saw you this morning, I thought, what an amazing woman. She swims at dawn, howls at the moon—swims like a dolphin. I wish I could be like her.'

She gave him a doubtful look. 'Don't fib. You don't strike me as the sort of person who howls at the moon.'

Fair. But he wouldn't mind having a go.

'Not before I met you, I wasn't.'

She smiled and looked up at the sky. 'Where's the moon?'

'Matti,' Felix cut in gently, 'it's a compliment, not a challenge. You're an amazing woman. Beautiful, fun-loving, inspiring. I've done more new things with you in the past two hours than I've done in the last decade.' Fun things, anyway. Spontaneous. IVF had been new to him, and divorce, but they had also been soul-destroying.

Matti still wasn't having it. 'It's easy to be yourself with someone you're never going to see again.'

He laughed. 'Not for everyone. Not for me. Being with you makes me feel—' He stopped, wanting to find the perfect word. 'You make me feel alive.'

'Alive,' she repeated, as if the word confused her.

'Yes. Alive.'

It wasn't exactly poetry, but it was the truth. A realisation that the last three years had felt like being half alive. Pretty much how his ex had described him when he'd left.

Only a cold-hearted bastard would let me walk out that door after everything we've been through, she'd said, tears pouring down her face. Though it had taken every fibre of his being to do it, he'd crossed to the door and opened it, leaving everything he liked about himself in his wake. Tonight, he'd had glimmers of thinking maybe, just possibly, he could salvage the version of himself he liked.

'Matti, at the risk of being too plain, you should know that I genuinely enjoyed myself tonight. When we were kissing, I didn't want the night to end. That's why I asked if you wanted to get a room. Very clumsily and awkwardly. It's been a while since I've been intimate with someone.'

'How long's a while?'

'Three years.'

She didn't gasp in horror, just gave a little nod of acknowledgement. No judgement.

'I meant it when I asked if you would like to spend the night with me. The choice is obviously yours, but I am conscious that trusting me might be complicated beyond the usual reasons because of your...um...your situation.'

He groaned inwardly. If he ever spoke this opaquely to a patient, he'd strike himself off the roster.

'Which situation?' she asked, but before he could answer, she understood. The colour drained from her face. 'You didn't just see me howling, did you?'

He shook his head. 'No.'

'You saw my scars.'

'I did.'

She looked around. 'It's getting late, don't you think?

Maybe we should call it a night. Do you know where the exit is?'

'Don't leave yet,' he said, uncharacteristically sticking with what was clearly a difficult topic. 'Not like this. Look, I wanted you to know I saw your scars because if the only thing stopping you from being with me is fear that I'll react badly, I won't.'

She shook her head. 'I don't know.'

He closed his eyes, trying to find a way to convince her to see herself the way he did. She was...*extra*. In the very best of ways. Generous, kind, open, humble, funny, fearless and very, very beautiful.

He scanned the area and saw something that might at least pave the way for a less fraught ending to their night. 'Would you let me buy you a hot chocolate?'

She gave him a sharp look. 'With little marshmallows?'

'As many as you like.'

She gave him a once-over that had just enough playfulness to show she was wavering.

'They might even add those fancy little chocolate curls.'

A few minutes later, they found a bench and sat down with their drinks. Matti's was as large as they came, a hot chocolate with an enormous swirl of whipped cream covered in marshmallows and chocolate curls. She held it up, considering it. 'Drinking this will be about as awkward as continuing our conversation.'

'How do you mean?'

'The only way to do it is to get messy.' She gave a forlorn solitary laugh then took a sip, surfacing, as expected, with a dollop of whipped cream on her nose. She swiped it off then looked at his drink. 'What's yours called again?'

'Dark Night of the Soul. It's dark chocolate and...' he gave the cup a swirl '...not much else. Want to try?'

'No, thanks. I'm all about ghost-shaped marshmallows and whipped cream tonight.'

Whatever brought a smile to her face. His, a suggestion from the barista, was both bitter and sweet. A fitting duo, given the circumstances.

After a few moments of drinking their hot chocolates and watching the world go by, Matti shifted round so that she was facing him. 'Okay. The sugar high has kicked in. Now it's my turn to confess something to you.'

CHAPTER SIX

MATTI KNEW SHE was being slightly melodramatic. Okay, she was being a lot melodramatic, but she was buzzing with nerves. She hated seeing Felix so anxious, especially after having had such a fun night. And that little drink he'd bought himself! Dark Night of the Soul. It sounded and looked like a penance. He'd done nothing wrong. It was she who owed him an apology. She swiped another dollop of whipped cream off her nose, then admitted, 'I'm not scared of roller coasters.'

He blinked, confused. 'Why did you say you were?'

'I wanted to hold hands.' She winced. 'It was stupid. I was hoping you'd offer to hold my hand if you thought I was scared. And I wanted to feel you holding mine if you got scared.'

'I see,' he said neutrally, those blue eyes of his darkening as he took her admission on board. 'And why would you do that for a stranger?'

'Because I like people to feel comfortable in themselves. Life's too short to worry about what other people think.' She gave him an embarrassed look. 'It's a lesson I've been trying to teach myself. I haven't fancied anyone in a long time and the second I saw you I thought *phwoar*…he's gorgeous. And then, better not flirt with him, he won't want to see you naked.'

'That's quite a leap.'

She gave a nonchalant shrug. 'I'm a big leaps kind of girl. Anyway—' she closed her eyes and took a breath before continuing '—I have a past, obviously. A difficult one that made me withdraw from life for a while. When you saw me earlier, at the pier, I was literally and figuratively taking a plunge into a new chapter. One in which I would live my life as if no one was watching. And even if they were, remembering that it doesn't matter what anybody else thinks. It matters what I think about me.'

'Brave. On both counts,' Felix said.

He sounded genuine. Encouraged, Matti continued.

'Tonight, I was challenging myself to go out on my own. And then you rock up looking all Clark Kent sexy. I haven't flirted in a hundred years, so I told myself I should try and flirt.' She raised her index finger. 'But only after I figured out you were with your sister, not your partner. Please refer back to our earlier conversation about being a bit on the side.'

'Noted.' He gave her a serious nod. One with just enough light in it to see he was following her lead on this. Letting her set the tone. Anything else and she'd probably jack the rest of the conversation in and use the hot chocolate sugar boost to high-tail it home.

'It wasn't entirely brave. Flirting with you on the roller coaster seemed safe because we'd never see each other again.'

'And then my sister threw a spanner in the works. Foisted me on you for the night.'

'No!' Matti protested. 'She actually made the challenge better. Scarier, but better.'

He gave her a shy smile. 'Good. I really enjoyed our night.'

'Me too,' she said. 'So much. Especially the kissing. I mean, the other stuff was good, but the kissing was a highlight.'

'And then I went and bungled it up by pressing for more.'

'Not at all,' Matti said. 'I wanted—I want—to say yes, but I got all self-conscious. Not a great way to finish my day of living as if no one is looking, really, is it?'

'Well—' Felix gave his chin a rub '—to be fair to you,

spending the night together would involve a lot of looking. But for the record, when I saw you this morning I saw a woman who seemed completely confident. Free-spirited. And I found it…enchanting.'

'Enchanting?' She gave him a don't-kid-a-kidder look.

'Seriously. How many people splash about in the water like a dolphin? Howl at the moon? You knew there were people around. Knew they'd hear you. Look—' he put his empty cup in a nearby bin then turned back and took her free hand '—I think you're incredibly beautiful.'

Matti's stomach churned. 'But…?'

'There are no buts. I think you're beautiful. When I saw your back, my first thought was, *Wow, there's a woman who's made peace with what must've been one hell of a trauma.*'

'Most people think, *Eww gross, what happened to her?* Or, *Oh, look at the poor lady with the ugly scars.*'

Felix looked horrified. 'Shame on them. I'm sorry you've had that experience. Nothing like that even crossed my mind. Look, I'm not the kind of guy who looks for signs from the universe, but when I saw you this morning, I had this feeling I was meant to see you. I went to work thinking I'd probably be a happier man if I took a page out of your book. Approached life with a bit more verve. As if… What's that saying?'

'Dance as if no one else is looking,' they said together.

She grinned at him. He seemed to know exactly what she'd been through, even though he only knew it was 'something'.

'Why do you find life scary, Felix?'

He winced.

'Sorry. Too personal.'

'No. Well, yes. Let me put it this way, feeling good—the way we have tonight—it's terrifying for me.'

'Really? Why?'

'Because it might end.'

'But you said yes, knowing it would end.'

'True. I thought that would make it easier. Knowing it would end. I guess I pictured the night being like a…' he tapped his lips, thinking '…like a moment in a snow globe.'

Matti almost exploded. 'That's what I was thinking. I love snow globes.'

'And I love knowing an outcome in advance.'

She laughed. 'If I'd known coming here tonight would have led to meeting you, I don't know if I would've come.'

He frowned.

'Not because you're not great,' she quickly covered. 'It's just…the last few years have been a lot. There was this, of course.' She pointed to her back. 'A break-up I didn't see coming. I quit my job thinking that would help, then instantly felt…untethered. My plan was to hide under my duvet for the rest of my life, when my godmother rang me. This was in the spring. Her husband had had a stroke and was in hospital. She said he needed support.'

'She knew what you'd been through?' Felix asked.

'She did. The fact that she asked me to come over, knowing I had all but literally become a bed bug, told me that she was suffering much more than I was. So I came. I wasn't very useful. I can't bake. I'm a terrible cook. I finally realised she didn't want me here to be useful, she wanted me here because she needed someone to be here, you know? Someone she loved, who could help her keep things in perspective. Which gave me perspective. I realised all of my *Woe is me* nonsense was a lot less satisfying than helping someone I loved.'

Felix nodded and sat back on the bench, as if to properly absorb her comments.

When she finished her hot chocolate he asked, 'If you went home alone tonight, would it be better than spending it with me?'

She barked a laugh. 'You're very kind, but I think I've put you through enough tonight.'

He didn't laugh. 'I don't feel like I've been put through anything. And if at any time you want me to go, I'll go.'

'But what about—?' She pointed at her back.

'Oh,' he said, as if she was pointing out some freckles. 'I keep forgetting.'

'Forgetting?'

'Matti—' his voice thickened '—you give a man—*this* man—a lot more to think about than scar tissue.'

'Gosh.' She swallowed. 'Well, in that case… How do you feel about houseboats?'

Matti straddled the front tyre of Felix's bike, holding the handles loosely until she felt him steady the frame behind her.

'Ready?' he asked.

'Ready.' This was another first for her. Riding on someone's bicycle handles like a schoolgirl. A trust exercise in advance of an even bigger one. She gripped the handlebars and dipped her knees, about to jump, when she felt his hands cup her hips. 'What are you—?' she squeaked. He lifted her onto the handlebars as if she were made of spun sugar.

'Comfortable?'

'The chariot of my dreams,' she lied. The short ride to her home wasn't much of a magic carpet ride, but it was fun seeing smiles appear on the faces of the passersby as Felix pedalled them along the quaint streets. He even took the awkwardness out of pulling over to a shop to buy protection by emerging with a rose, handing it to her with a courtly bow.

Soon enough, they arrived at the houseboat, a stone's throw from her godmother's townhouse. When she'd moved in a few days earlier, she hadn't once imagined having anyone other than Astrid cross the threshold and had secretly dubbed it her 'hermit house', so it was a pleasant surprise to feel excited to invite him in.

'This is wonderful,' Felix said, admiring the warm ambience in the small but welcoming canal home.

'It's great, isn't it?' Matti beamed. 'It's my godmother's. She normally rents it out to tourists but is letting me use it while I'm here.' She debated telling him it would be for a couple of months, then remembered the snow globe.

'Is she an interior designer?' he asked.

'She makes pottery,' Matti explained, pointing out a beautiful bowl on the coffee table that matched the various shades of blue the sea had been this morning. 'She says she designs rooms to highlight her creations, but she's over-modest. She's talented at a lot of things. Like picking properties for one. Look—' she pointed to a pair of French windows at the far end of the living area '—it's even got an outdoor porch. Perfect for people watching.'

'There's only one person I'm interested in watching right now,' Felix said, eyes raking over her as if she were a sugar-coated pastry. Astonishingly, she enjoyed it, being admired.

'You're sure you want to do this?' he asked.

'I'm sure,' Matti confirmed.

'As long as you're happy.'

'I am very happy,' she said. And unbelievably lusty. They stood there, looking at one another, when it suddenly struck her that Felix was waiting for her to make the first move, set the pace. A gentleman intent on assuring her she was safe.

'As it happens,' she said in a throaty voice she barely recognised, 'I know a way both of us could be even happier.' She crossed to him, pleased that the height her heeled boots gave her put her in the perfect position to kiss his neck. Something she'd been itching to do all night. She leant in.

His soft groan of approval emboldened her. She began

undoing his coat buttons from the bottom, her fingers grazing his clothing beneath the thick wool, teasing out the task until, shifting the cloth off his shoulders, she lifted her mouth to his. Neither of them noticed his coat falling to the floor.

Before long, the floor was strewn with clothes. Mostly his. Wonder Woman had a far more economical choice of clothes, having lived somewhere warm enough not to bother with the flesh-coloured catsuit she'd worn beneath hers.

'Do you need some help with this?' Felix traced his finger along the neckline of her catsuit, sending a cascade of tingles to her breasts. No wonder she'd had a conical bra, Matti thought, feeling her nipples tighten with anticipation. But first, she had to get out of the catsuit. It had taken her ages and some fairly awkward wrangling to put on. It would be the opposite of sexy to repeat the exercise in reverse and she was feeling sexy. Not in a performative way, but genuinely sexy.

'I'm glad you asked,' she said in that same husky, come-hither voice. She spotted a pair of scissors in a ceramic pot on the kitchen counter. Was this the solution to her problem, cutting the whole thing off to avoid embarrassment?

Dangerous. But maybe in a good way. A sexy way.

Never in her life had she been accused of proposing risqué foreplay. Mixing danger with desire. Tonight, that would change.

She pulled out the scissors, relieved to see they were blunt-tipped, then presented them to Felix. 'Would you do the honours?'

He looked down at the scissors, then back at her, blue eyes glinting with approbation. She'd hoped he'd run with it, and as he took the scissors from her she felt a heat build in her that longed to be sated.

He weighed up the scissors, as if ensuring they were the

right tool for the job. Ran his hand along her thigh. 'If I do this, you won't be able to wear it again.'

'I'll live with the consequences,' she said, all saucy vixen-like.

Who even *was* she? Did it matter? She liked feeling this confident. Provocative. She'd definitely be inviting this version of herself around again. A pang of pre-emptive loss niggled at her. Could she be like this with anyone else? Would she want to? She shoved the questions away.

'I think this particular operation would work best,' Felix said, putting the scissors on the counter then pulling her to him, 'if you were up on the counter. Thoughts?'

'Agreed.' She held her cape aloft. He took hold of her hips and, after she nodded that she was ready, furled the red fabric behind her as he lifted her onto the countertop.

He kissed her once, long and deep, then knelt down, laughing lightly at her growl of frustration that he hadn't stayed for more. Her breath hitched as he unzipped one of her liquid black boots, caressing her calf as he slipped it off with such care it was as if he was unwrapping a precious work of art. Perhaps, she allowed, he saw her in that way. Precious. Singular. After he'd taken off the second boot, she felt a flicker of nerves. She'd already slipped out of the short dress and bodice she'd been wearing when they'd been kissing, so here she was, wearing nothing but a catsuit and a cape.

Still kneeling, Felix looked up at her, his expression earnest, as if he truly understood the amount of trust she was putting in him and that, rather than feeling nervous about it, he felt privileged. It was an unexpected salve to wounds she'd thought would never heal.

She handed him the scissors. She wanted this. She wanted him.

He tucked a finger beneath the fabric at the inside of her ankle, lifting it away from her skin so that there was enough room to slip the cool metal scissors beneath it. His beautiful blue eyes met hers. 'You're sure?'

'More than.'

He made the first cut. As the fabric began to fall from her calf, her thigh, her hip, he traced the scissors' path with his thumb, lighting up her erogenous zones in a way she'd never experienced before. She felt dangerous. Sensual. Erotic. There was no power play in this. It was give and take. And because of that, she knew she could trust him in a way she'd never imagined trusting someone again.

He gave the same care and attention to her other leg, skimming his hands along her bare skin as the cool metal sliced through the fabric. When, at last, he rose, she pulled him to her, showing him with her body how much of an aphrodisiac she found him. His fingers skimmed over her breasts, which were still covered by the catsuit. To her surprise, the fabric made her feel trapped rather than protected. Would wonders never cease?

'Cut it all off,' she instructed.

Felix took a step back, then turned away.

'What are you doing?' she demanded. Then, panicked that this was not the night he'd been imagining, added, 'I hope I'm not making you feel uncomfortable.'

'Not at all. But I want to make sure you're comfortable.' He scanned the room then grabbed a soft cashmere blanket from the back of the sofa, which he spread on the wooden countertop behind her.

'Will you be all right to lie on your back?'

She nodded and lay back, touched by his thoughtfulness. Barely a second passed before her thoughts dissolved into sensation. He slid his fingers beneath the slim rectangle of fabric between her legs, holding it away from her delicate skin before, in one sure move, he cut the fabric in two. She gasped with pleasure when he cupped her, then gently shifted his thumb against the tingling, sensitive bean above her sex. It felt luxurious, being touched this way. But he'd only just begun. One sensation melted into another, pleasure piled upon pleasure as he slid two fingers inside her, releasing a throaty sigh when he felt how wet she was.

If this night never ended it would be too soon. And no way would it all fit in a snow globe.

Felix held the scissors aloft. 'There's still a bit more to go.'

'If you don't cut it all off right now, I might spontaneously combust.'

He slid his fingers from her, slicking the dew in circles over her clitoris, pressing his hips against her inner thighs. Still lying back, she wrapped her legs around his hips, holding him close. In a move she thought only a surgeon could pull off, he cuffed the loose fabric around her waist, pulled it taut, and in one fluid move scissored the remaining fabric away from her belly, her chest, her decolletage, finally snipping the fabric in two at her shoulder.

She pushed herself up, wanting to feel her breasts against his chest, but he held up his hand. 'Not yet.'

'Tease.'

'Perfectionist,' he gently corrected, easing what remained of the catsuit from her shoulders until she was completely bare, apart from the cape.

'You're so beautiful,' he whispered.

'I don't know what you've done to me,' she whispered against his lips, 'but I believe you.'

'Good.'

He pressed his mouth to hers and kissed her with such tenderness she all but mewed with pleasure, succumbing to the instinct when her breasts finally pressed against his chest. Skin against skin. There was nothing like it.

The world around her vanished. If she'd thought their first

kisses felt like an internal fireworks display, the electric currents running through her now would light a nation.

She raked her nails down his back, relishing the sounds she drew from him. Touching him was like discovering two people. Herself and him. The solid expanse of his chest. The taut tenderness of her nipples. The tickle of hair at the waistband of his boxers. The ache of desire between her legs. The tip of his erection, wet with desire for her.

'I want you,' she said. 'Now.'

'Your wish, my command.'

CHAPTER SEVEN

THE HANDFUL OF seconds it took to get protection felt like an eternity, but returning to her was all the reward Felix needed. Matti's hazel eyes were glistening, the flecks of gold molten with the same desire he felt for her. She pinched the condom with her fingertips. 'May I?'

'Please.' He slid his boxers off, kicked them away and stood before her, amazed at how natural it felt to be with her. This was a landmark moment for both of them. The first time he'd been with someone since his marriage. The first time, he presumed, she'd been with someone since her accident. He'd thought sex would never be the same for him after what he'd been through. Something that would never make him feel whole in the way it once had. But he'd been wrong. This felt richer, deeper. Bereft of any expectation beyond ensuring Matti knew how extraordinary she was.

She was still wearing her cape. He sensed the decision wasn't out of shame, or a desire to role-play. More...a lingering need for a safety blanket, however slight. A film of protection he hoped she'd ultimately realise she didn't need. Certainly not with him. But he got it. He didn't need a condom to prevent her from getting pregnant, but had bought them anyway.

He sucked in a breath when she took his erection in her hand, gently sliding the protection into place. She took her time, teasing the roll down slowly, clearly enjoying the twitches and pulses of reaction from his penis. When she finished, she gave him a shy smile. 'I hope that was okay. It's been a while.'

'More than okay,' he said. 'If you're uncomfortable, we can stop at any time. I don't want you to have any regrets. Not now, not in the morning.'

'Thank you, Felix.' She gave his cheek a gentle stroke, his lips a soft kiss. 'I feel safe,' she assured him. 'And the same goes for you. If you think you're going to regret—'

'I won't regret it.' He cupped her bottom and pulled her closer to the counter's edge, his penis upright between them as he brushed his fingertips along the curves of her breasts. She arched into him, the tips of her nipples taut against his chest. He pulled back, enjoying the moment when her groan of frustration became a moan of approbation as he ran his tongue around her areola, then took the crimson nub of her nipple in his mouth. She wove her fingers into his hair with a sigh of satisfaction.

'Don't stop,' she whispered.

He wouldn't. Her body was ambrosia to him. He couldn't get enough. Sucking, licking, stroking her breasts, grazing his teeth along her nipples. It took a Herculean effort to fight the tugging ache in his scrotum as she arched into him, asking for more until, finally, she whispered to him to please, *please*, put himself inside her.

'I will,' he assured her. 'But there's something I want to do first.'

He took hold of the strips of fabric holding her cape in place. 'May I untie these?'

She nodded, but the sheen of emotion turning her hazel eyes to liquid gold was impossible to miss. This was a moment he had to get right, for her.

He'd spotted some lotion he knew would be suitable for her back on the counter and reached for it. 'This okay?'

Tears clung to her eyelashes, spilling when she nodded. 'Perfect.'

Rather than move behind her, he stayed where he was, his erection like a flagpole between them. He wanted her to have visual proof that touching her back would not change his body's response to her. He hadn't come here tonight because of her physical beauty—which was saying something because she was stunning. He'd wanted to be here, with her, because she made him feel seen in a way he hadn't experienced in years.

He warmed some lotion between his hands then spread his fingers wide to slide them along the arch of her buttocks, up to the dimples below her waist. She buried her head in his neck.

'Okay?' he checked.

'More than,' she whispered, clasping her hands behind his neck.

When the petal softness of her skin gave way to the raised, damaged skin, a rush of gratitude bowled through him. Being trusted in this way was far and beyond the trust his patients put in him. It was humbling. Made him want to be the type of man she deserved.

He swept his hands along either side of her spine, stopping when she inhaled sharply as he reached the curve below her shoulder blades.

'Too much pressure?'

'No. It's perfect.' She pressed her hands against his beating heart and locked eyes with him. 'I can't tell you how amazing this feels, but if you feel uncomfortable in any way—'

'I don't.'

A few more tears fell. 'You don't need to keep checking in. I know you won't hurt me.'

The simple statement was anything but. Hurt her physically? Not a chance in hell. Emotionally? He'd savage himself first.

'You're in charge here,' he reminded her.

'No.' She shook her head. 'I don't want that. I'll stop you if I need to, but I don't want to be treated like I'm different. Please don't wrap me in cotton wool.'

The plea was raw. A frustrated mix of anger and desire.

'Believe me,' he said, 'there are many things I want to do to you right now. Wrapping you in cotton wool is not one of them.' He'd do it, of course, if that was what she needed. Judging by the look on her face, it most certainly was not.

'If it's a long list,' she said, allowing a playful note to surface, 'you better get busy.'

'Try and stop me.' Felix thumbed away another tear skidding down her cheek, then, with intent, pressed his hands against the base of her spine and swept them up the length of her back until he reached her neck, circling it lightly while he pressed his mouth to hers for hungry, searching kisses that made him realise the boundary they'd set—being together for one night only—would not be enough. He wouldn't break the promise, but he'd use every moment he had left, devoting himself to giving her pleasure.

The way she responded to his touch—soft whimpers, throaty moans, nails digging into his skin—told him she'd abandoned any attempt at restraint. He gave himself permission to do the same. Responded to her body out of instinct. Stroking, skimming, brushing, caressing the lotion over her back, her thighs, her calves, her feet until she pulled him to her, their bodies so close he could feel her longing pulse against the base of his cock until, finally, he couldn't bear even that slight distance between them. He took his penis and held it between her legs, pressing it gently between the folds of her sex, in and out, in and out, just the tip. He was driving himself insane, but knew holding back would be worth it. He wasn't wrong.

She gripped a fistful of his hair and pulled his mouth to

hers. He spread his hands across her buttocks, tipping her hips so that he could push deeper into her until, at last, he was completely surrounded by her. Paradise. They lost themselves in motion.

Being with her released something new in him. A sense of safety in admitting he was completely available to her, powerless to fight his desire, as if she was a potent aphrodisiac. He was bewitched. By her scent. Her hair. Her skin. The throaty murmurs of pleasure that were almost like purring. She trusted him with her vulnerabilities far more than he would've trusted himself and for that alone he would be forever grateful.

They moved in synchronicity, slowly at first, building to that perilous plateau—the point when he knew he would lose all control. She crossed her ankles at the base of his back and, clearly sensing he was reaching the point of no return, began squeezing his cock with her sex, digging her nails into his shoulders until, at last, luxuriously powerful waves of release were unlocked. Their breath came in short, gut-deep bursts until, finally, the shared unity of reaching the sexual apex rippled through their bodies.

They stayed that way, as one, staring at one another half-dazed. It was impossible to pinpoint exactly what it was he was feeling. She held his face in her hands and gave him a soft kiss. 'Thank you.'

'Thank you.' He returned the kiss. 'That was very, very memorable.'

She gave her arm a light pinch. 'Are you sure I'm not dreaming?' She repeated the gesture on his bicep. 'Are you real?'

'As real as the kitchen counter you're sitting on,' he confirmed.

A naughty smile caught the corners of her lips. 'Countertop sex is *so* much better than I thought it would be.' She gave his chest a pat as if congratulating him. 'You were definitely the right man for the job.'

'Glad to be of service.' He gave her a salute.

'Oh, no, no.' She clapped her hands to her cheeks in embarrassment, her eyes wide with horror. 'That sounded awful. Like I'd put "Have sex with a hot stranger" on a to-do list.'

'It would definitely make me curious about the rest of the list,' he said, switching to a businesslike tone, 'Milk, bread, have sex with a stranger after a roller coaster—'

'Stop!' Matti laughed then suddenly tipped her head back to let out a growl he couldn't quite define. When she looked at him again, he felt as if she'd just peeled away yet another protective layer. 'This is so out of character for me. I don't know how on earth you've gone through three years without women launching themselves at you, begging for sex.'

Now his laugh turned into a groan. 'I can assure you, no one has thrown themselves at me.'

She pulled a face. 'Why not? You're perfect.'

'If only.' Matti had met a version of himself he hadn't been sure existed. His colleagues, pretty much the only people he saw, knew a far less friendly version. 'Tell me,' he said, 'what do you see? I'd like to see myself through your eyes.'

'Well,' Her eyes skated over his face as if hunting for the right words. 'I see a kindred spirit. We're both a bit lost, maybe? But are so used to putting on a brave face we don't know how to admit to ourselves, let alone others, that we need their support.'

She was good. He nodded for her to go on, but she thought for a moment before continuing. 'Well, after you saved me from the pirates, you said you hated the roller coaster. That comforted me.'

'Why?'

'Because it told me you were honest. Brave about some things but not everything, and honest enough to admit it. I couldn't have kissed you, let alone imagine sitting here like this, naked, unless I trusted you here.' She put her hand over her heart, then moved it to her gut. 'I was terrified of being intimate with someone again. It hadn't occurred to me to "break the seal" with a stranger, because I knew it would be emotional. You made me feel safe enough to know I could have all the feelings. What surprised me was how good the feelings were. I thought having sex again would only remind me about what I lost.'

He nodded. He got that. He'd wanted to remember who he'd been before life had thrown him a curveball that had changed everything and had, instead, unearthed a new version. One that needed work, but one that was worth working towards.

She put her hand on his heart. 'There is no way I can properly thank you for tonight. It was so much more than sex for me. But if there is anything I can do, I insist, I *implore* you, please ask for it.'

What could he say that wouldn't sound trite? He tried to summon a worthy response. It was he, not her, who owed the debt of gratitude, but everything that came to mind sounded as if he was regurgitating a greeting card. What he was feeling right now was too unwieldy, too monumental, to condense into a phrase or sentence, so he opted for dropping a kiss onto her forehead, then held her to him, breathed her in, willing the sense of peace that she'd unearthed in him to stay within reach as a reminder that there was at least one person who thought he was good, kind. No words of thanks could match that knowledge.

A nearby church bell tolled, signalling the arrival of a new day.

'I'd better get back,' he said reluctantly, wishing more than anything he could hold her in his arms, fall asleep with her, make her coffee in the morning. 'I don't want to turn into a pumpkin.'

'Handsome princes don't turn into pumpkins,' she lightly teased, but he heard the same thing in her voice he'd heard in his own. Regret that this was goodbye.

She slid off the counter and said she was going to get a bathrobe. He gathered up his hastily discarded clothes, smiling at the ferocity of their passion when they'd first come in. He dressed and as he shrugged on his coat, Matti came out of the bedroom in a cosy sky-blue dressing gown.

'You're sure you're all right going back on your bike?' she asked.

It wasn't an invitation to stay.

He nodded. 'One of the safest cities in the world.' He was at the door now, wondering whether or not to kiss her goodbye, but when she stayed put and gave him a little wave from where she was, he realised she'd already begun to seal the night in that imaginary snow globe of hers. Capture the fairy tale.

He'd have to do the same.

As he rode along the deserted streets, a bone-deep ache to be the man he'd been tonight held him in its grip until, turning the lock on his flat, he made himself wait, only opening the door after a reminder that fairy tales were nothing but fantasy and that he knew, more than most, that dreams had a way of not coming true.

CHAPTER EIGHT

Matti arrived at Copenhagen Central Hospital feeling bright-eyed and bushy-tailed. She'd started the day with another swim out at The Snail. A part of her had been hoping to see Felix, but when she hadn't, she'd told herself it was for the best. Especially as she had her shiny new job to distract her from remembering pretty much the most erotic and generous lovemaking she'd ever experienced.

She entered the main doors to the emergency care centre which, given the early hour, wasn't too busy. A friendly-looking woman in her early twenties was logging a patient in at the main reception desk and, a couple of metres behind her, a male doctor wearing a traditional white coat over a pair of dark blue scrubs was examining the intake board. For a split second her heart soared, thinking it was Felix, but as he disappeared into the patient area it sank again. Something about the way he held himself didn't match up. This guy was tense. A bit edgy. She'd bet Felix would rock a pair of scrubs.

Matti, she warned herself. *What happened in the snow globe stays in the snow globe.*

She gave herself a shake and went up to the reception desk. 'Hi, I'm Dr Mattie Meadows. I was told to ask for Dr Beck.'

'Oh,' said the receptionist, almost apologetically. 'Really?'

'Yes.' Matti checked the email she'd had from Dr Larsen again. 'Apparently, he's going to show me the ropes.'

The woman leant closer towards her and in a low voice

said, 'Don't pay attention to his grumpiness. He's a good doctor, but a little short on charm.'

Matti tapped the side of her nose and smiled. 'Thanks for the heads-up. I'll make it a personal mission to see if I can squeeze a smile out of him.'

The woman laughed. 'Good luck with that!' She waved her hand between them as if clearing the moment away. 'I'm Sofie, by the way. And Dr Beck's not that bad once you get used to him.'

'Noted.'

She looked up when someone pushed through the doors of the patient area and froze. If hearts could literally jam in a person's throat, hers was doing it now.

The doctor in the white lab coat? It had been Felix. More accurately, it *was* Felix. And he did not look as if his tummy was full of butterflies. Which did beg the question, why was hers?

Through a buzz of brain static, she heard the receptionist say, 'Dr Beck? This is Dr Meadows. She said you were expecting her.'

He looked at Sofie, then at Matti, his expression darkening as if he was living his worst nightmare.

Oh, no. No, no, no, no, no. This wasn't how she'd imagined he'd react if their paths crossed again.

She forced a smile. 'Hello, there.'

No response other than a muscle twitch at the base of his gritted jawline.

Matti's butterflies fled the scene and were swifty replaced by a healthy dose of indignation. She wasn't exactly running around the room screaming, *Oh, my God, this man's seen me naked!* The least he could do was say hello.

'Sorry, Dr Meadows.' Sofie gave her an apologetic smile. 'He does normally speak. Dr Beck?' she prompted. 'Not had your morning coffee yet?'

He gave her a distracted headshake, eyes still glued on Matti, but still no greeting which, frankly, was silly.

Right. Time to put on her big girl pants.

She crossed to him and extended her hand. 'Dr Beck. It's so nice to meet you. I'm guessing from your expression that you weren't expecting me, or, if you were, weren't looking forward to it.'

His eyes widened at her forthrightness. The huffed laugh and instinctive lift of his chin indicated she'd hit the nail on the head.

'Oh, well,' she said with a shrug, widening her fingers and giving them a little wiggle to remind him he had yet to shake her hand, 'we're both professionals. I'm sure, with an open mind, you'll soon see I will be an asset to your team. Things can't be too different here in Denmark to England.' At which point, she realised she'd been speaking in English. Oops. Nerves. 'I've no doubt you'll set me straight if you find otherwise,' she added in Danish, just to prove she could.

'Nice to meet you,' he said woodenly, finally reaching out to shake her hand.

She would've liked to have shot a jaunty, *He speaks!* to Sofie, but as his fingers slid across her palm, her nervous system sent a rush of warm, glittery tingles to an area of her body that was definitely not work appropriate.

She dropped her gaze to their hands, half expecting to see a cloud of fairy dust. There wasn't. *Because this is real life. Matti. In a real hospital. With real patients. And you're a real doctor who wants to be taken seriously.*

When she looked up again, she caught a glimpse of the man she'd met last night, so fleeting she wondered if she'd imagined it. *Why are you hiding him?*

'So,' he said, ending the handshake. '*Hygge.*'

He said the word, which always sounded like a hug and a sigh to her, as if it were a bad stench.

Oh, boy. She had definitely imagined it.

'Yes, indeed.' She arched an eyebrow at him. '*Hygge*.'

'In an emergency department?'

His voice wasn't exactly dripping with sarcasm, but the verbal sparring struck an exacting blow to her too-tender heart.

Determined not to crumble at the first belligerent, blonde and blue-eyed hurdle, she deflected her pain with humour. Half cupping her mouth, she stage-whispered to Sofie, 'Out of curiosity, does his word count increase after he's had a coffee?'

The weight of his hard stare landed on her like a pile of bricks.

She narrowed her gaze and returned the hard stare. 'If you think I'm here on a whimsical jolly, you're wrong. I'm here to practice medicine. Just like you. And to help people,' she added pointedly. 'People who are at their most vulnerable.'

He winced. As well he should.

'As you may or may not know,' she continued, 'before I worked in a traditional hospital, I spent a lot of time in conflict zones.'

He shifted his weight back on his heels, crossed his arms, nodded. He was listening.

'We were always short on resources and, of course, the environment around our makeshift set-ups were impossible to control. We did the best we could with what we had but, as you know, it's not just the physical wounds that cause damage. Living in a state of fight or flight can double it.'

It occurred to her that Felix's silence was his version of flight. If he didn't engage, he was out of the fray. Too bad. She was here to fight for what she believed in.

'When I returned to the UK to work in a traditional hospital, I was expecting it to feel… I don't know…*infallible*.'

He nodded distractedly, pulled a phone from his pocket and thumbed it open.

Matti was wide-eyed. He knew she'd been in hospital for

her burns. As a doctor, he would also know she'd been there for months, so her insight was from both a patient and a doctor's perspective. And he was reading his phone?

'Copenhagen Central has an incredible set-up. Advanced imaging systems, ergonomic chairs...*snow globes* absolutely everywhere.'

He looked up at her, startled. 'Sorry?'

Yes, you should be.

'I was saying how much I like the renovations here at Copenhagen Central.'

'You've done your research.' He sounded impressed, which irritated her.

'I didn't just pick up a dart and throw it in a map.'

He heard the testiness in her voice and pocketed the phone.

'I was here a few months ago, when they were adding the finishing touches.' *Remember? I told you last night about being here with my godmother.*

He nodded, as if the memory was coming back to him. 'In the Intensive Care Unit.'

'Palliative,' she corrected, slightly mollified that he'd remembered her telling him that she'd been here. 'I was impressed by the high standard of medical care my godfather received and, more to the point, was particularly struck by the environment the staff created.'

'How does it differ from the care offered at your hospital?'

'My *former* hospital,' she corrected. Had he erased nearly everything she'd said last night from his brain's hard drive?

Maybe he was too busy picturing her naked.

And maybe Santa Claus would walk in and tell her all of her dreams were about to come true.

He picked up a tablet from the counter and tapped something into it.

What the actual—?

This was important to her. If the project worked the way she hoped, it would have a positive impact on the patients. She'd quit her job for this. Sold her flat, left nothing in storage. She hadn't wanted a safety net. And right now, she was freefalling.

'The patients—the ones in Palliative Care—seemed to have this extraordinary sense of peace. Security. I know this sounds counterintuitive, but they had a sense of well-being that made the journey they were on less stressful. And everyone I spoke to put it down to *hygge*.'

He tapped on his screen, glanced at her. 'And you think this is transferable to the emergency care centre?'

'That's why I'm here. I want to find a way to transfer that bone-deep understanding that we, the physicians, are looking after our patients—medically and on a personal level—versus treating them as a series of boxes to be ticked on an electronic device.'

Felix looked up from his tablet and met her gaze. *Touché.* He pocketed the tablet.

'And you think knitting or decorating biscuits would accelerate the healing process?'

Instead of taking his question as a barb, she registered it as cautiously curious. There was no way the man she'd met last night wouldn't be a champion for patient care. He had to be buried in there somewhere.

Matti held her hands open, book style. 'Look. Science-based, high quality medical treatment obviously needs to be at the heart of any emergency care centre.'

'What a relief,' he said dryly. 'And here I was thinking you wanted to replace the pharmacy with a pastry stall.'

She heard Sofie suck in a sharp breath behind her.

'Perhaps you're the one who needs a pastry, Dr Beck,' Matti said in a saccharine voice. 'I think you need some sweetener.'

As gratifying as Felix's wide-eyed response was, a muted, 'Oh, snap,' from Sofie reminded Matti that she wasn't just making a first impression with Felix, she was making it with all of the staff.

She readopted her professional tone and continued. 'As I'm sure you know, Dr Beck, the definition of medicine is the diagnosis, treatment and prevention of disease or injury. The root word of *hygge* means "to think". Thinking about a patient as a person is every bit as important as thinking about them as something that's broken.'

'Speaking of which,' Felix said, 'I've got a patient with a broken arm to see. I'll be sure to take your comments on board.' Then he turned and walked away.

Matti turned to Sofie in disbelief.

Sofie gave her an apologetic smile. 'I warned you.'

Matti pretended not to understand. 'About Dr Beck? A teddy bear. I think he likes me'

Sofie gave her a sympathetic smile. 'Felix is…' She shot a quick glance over her shoulder then leant in to whisper. 'He used to be normal. Fun. He got married a few years ago—'

Matti normally nipped hospital gossip in the bud, but she was skating on thin ice here. Perhaps, rather than gossip, it would be insight. A means of understanding why having his personal life collide with his professional one had gone down so badly.

'A couple of years into his marriage,' Sofie was saying, 'he started to change. Wasn't as happy. He worked all the hours he could. Cancelled dates with his wife, saying he had to cover shifts when, really, he didn't. He wasn't doing anything awful,' she quickly clarified. 'He'd be in a lab researching. Observing surgeries. All sorts. None of us could understand why he was avoiding his wife because he'd seemed so in love. It wasn't a surprise when we heard they had divorced. That was three years ago, now.'

Matti bit her lip. Her own breakup had been awful, and she hadn't even made it to the altar. She couldn't imagine what ending a marriage would feel like. It was clear Sofie thought Felix was to blame for the end of his relationship, but she withheld judgement. Her ex, a PR manager, had done a brilliant job of convincing their mutual friends she'd been the one who'd called off the wedding.

'You'd think he'd have moved on by now. Found someone new,' Sofie said with a shrug, then brightened. 'Wouldn't it be great if you could *hygge* him back into the man he used to be?'

'It would,' Matti said cautiously, thinking…that version of Felix was alive and kicking but, for some reason, he kept him hidden.

Sofie waved down a woman entering the main doors wearing hot pink scrubs tucked into cosy fleece-lined boots. 'Hannah? Would you mind showing Dr Meadows to the changing rooms?'

'Sure.' Hannah gave her a warm, open smile. 'First day?'

'Yes, indeed,' Matti confirmed.

'She's going to be working on a project with Dr Beck.' Sofie gave Hannah a meaningful look. 'They've just met.'

Hannah rolled her eyes. 'Our resident care bear!'

Matti laughed, but it was tinged with nerves. She'd never been in this situation before and if Felix had the power to end her project before it had begun…

Her nerves must've shown because Hannah quickly assured her, 'You'll be fine. Felix is a great doctor. He just takes a little getting used to. C'mon. I'll give you a tour.'

Hannah, a trauma nurse, showed her around the department asking the usual stream of questions—where are you from, why are you here and what have you done in Copenhagen so far? When they arrived at the changing rooms, a handful of doctors and nurses were either getting ready for their shifts or coming off one. Hannah pointed out a free locker for Matti to store her things in then called out to the group, 'Hey, everyone, we've got a team member. This is Dr Meadows—'

'Matti,' she gently corrected.

Hannah grinned. 'Matti. She's a trauma specialist from the UK,' she continued. 'Not only has she had a swim out at The Snail, she's going to be working on a special project with Dr Beck.'

A chorus of admiration for her swim mixed with playful groans and apologies for the 'resident grump' gave way to a steady flow of friendly questions.

To her relief, the group seemed really excited about her project, offering her suggestions off the top of their heads, along with invitations to join their families, especially in the build-up to Christmas, so that she could see the philosophy in practice.

While they chatted, Matti selected a pair of green scrubs from the rack, then headed towards the bench opposite her locker.

For the past two years she'd been changing into work clothes in private. She'd promised herself that would change. If she hadn't seen Felix this morning and, worse, had a terse run-in with him, she wouldn't have hesitated, but the encounter had taken the glow off the confidence she'd felt last night.

She took off her fleece and, after reminding herself that this was the last place on earth she needed to be nervous, pulled off her sweatshirt. She took one of several long-sleeved polo necks she had in her tote to put on under her scrubs, but the shifting of fabric reminded her she needed to apply some moisturiser to her back. An awkward but non-negotiable task. She opened her pot of skin cream—a delicious mix of olive oil, beeswax, honey and bee pollen—scooped some up and twisted her arm round towards her back.

'Hey—' Hannah touched her shoulder '—want some help?'

Matti froze, bracing herself for a pitying expression, but

when her eyes met Hannah's, her face showed little more than a friendly smile. She held out her hand for the moisturiser. 'I love that brand,' she said. 'I always slather myself in it after a swim. Especially this time of year.'

Matti wanted the help. Needed it. She'd felt comfortable asking her godmother to apply some when they were in the sauna, as switches from one extreme temperature to another had a way of wreaking havoc on the temperamental scar tissue, and last night when Felix had massaged some into her back she'd…she'd been in raptures. Especially as her fiancé had always refused to help her 'because you always flinch and it's really hard for me to look at'. As if he was the one getting the raw end of the deal.

He's out of the picture now, Matti.

'Sure,' she squeaked, handing over the pot.

She's a nurse, Matti. She's used to tending to wounds that make other people recoil.

Hannah gently applied the cream, chattering away about the pastry shops near the hospital she thought Matti should try. 'My favourite has biscuit-decorating nights in December. You'll love it. I bring my children.' She laughed. 'By the end, everyone's covered in frosting and has eaten more than they've decorated. It's super messy, but fun.'

Just like life, Matti thought. *Messy, but fun if you focus on the positives.*

'There you go,' Hannah said, handing her the pot. 'Just say if you need more later. See you out there.' And off she went.

This, Matti thought as she pulled on her top. *This* was the feeling she wanted patients to have. Being treated as if she was perfectly normal, despite needing support.

She'd been right to come to Copenhagen. Right to believe that an injury or illness didn't have to make you feel like a victim. All of which gave her the boost she needed to convince Felix that his time working with her would be time well spent.

CHAPTER NINE

'LET'S GIVE MR JOHANNSEN some privacy, shall we?' Felix said to the intern who'd been assisting him. 'To speak with his loved ones.'

'Surgery two is expecting us.' The doctor, who'd been unlocking the patient's bed wheels in preparation to move him, looked bewildered. Felix was never one to waste time getting to surgery.

Matti's words were still echoing in his head. *Thinking about a patient as a person is every bit as important as thinking about them as something that's broken.*

It didn't sit well with him that she might have felt like that when she'd been in hospital. A body being dealt with in a clinical way without factoring in how she was feeling. Not that he'd considered her feelings when he'd short-circuited at the sight of her. His entire body had shot to high alert and, instead of offering her courtesy, he'd fled the scene. Just as he'd done last night when he'd caught himself imagining a future with her. He glanced out of the window, half expecting a spectral figure to be laughing away. *You can run*, it would be saying, *but you can't hide.*

'Dr Beck?' His intern was looking at him as if he was the spectral figure.

'Right, yes. Mr Johanssen?' He crossed to the patient's bed. 'I understand you left your mobile phone at home and wanted to ring your family?'

'Yes. Yes, I would.'

Mr Johannsen, a middle-aged man, had arrived complaining about pains in his chest and left arm, meaning his body was presenting with symptoms of a cardiac arrest. He'd been given aspirin, oxygen and run through a series of tests that had determined he'd need surgery. A surgery he stood a better chance of surviving if he went into it without any additional emotional stress.

Felix unlocked his phone and handed it to him. 'Let your family know we're going to look after you. If you keep them on the line when you're done, we'll make sure they know where to find you when we've got you in Recovery.' He motioned the intern to join him outside the room.

The doctor, a dark-haired woman in her late twenties, locked the bed wheels down and, along with the nurse who'd been assisting them, exited the glass-walled room. Felix slid the door shut.

'Sorry, Dr Beck,' the intern said, openly confused. 'Am I missing something?'

'We both were,' Felix said, eyes on the patient. He'd bet Matti would've had him on the phone long before now. He was kicking himself for such a simple oversight. Especially after yesterday, when he'd completely forgotten to hand over a patient's phone, only remembering when it was too late.

Not every case had the space to allow for phone calls to loved ones, but this one did. It was an element of patient care he and his team needed to be factoring in with each and every case. An element of care, he found tough to admit, he'd been neglecting.

'Watch,' he said. 'Note his BP stats now, during his call and after.'

Silently, they did as he instructed. As anticipated, the patient's face relaxed when, after dialling the number, someone answered. As they spoke, the numbers on the blood pressure monitor slowly crept down. This wouldn't be true of all patients, but there was usually someone or something that could reduce a patient's stress levels.

Point one to Matti.

He shook the thought away. That wasn't right. Or fair. She wasn't here to notch up points. She was here because she knew exactly what it was like to be a patient and had, in her time with her godfather, seen the positive effects of being treated like a person. Something he had failed to do when yet another shift in his universe had brought her here to Copenhagen Central.

He'd drawn such a wide line between the man he'd been last night and the man he showed the rest of the world it felt like being two different people. The intern shooting him nervous glances was familiar, but his reaction to it was new. He didn't want her to be frightened of him. Nervous. They didn't need to be friends, but they did need to respect one another.

Respect had to be earned,

'So, what's stopping you?' a voice in his head asked. A voice that sounded a lot like Matti's. *Earn her respect.*

'Right.' He handed his tablet to the intern. 'Talk me through the case.'

'Mr Johannsen has been experiencing discomfort since last night,' she began. 'He put it down to a heavy meal and decided a night's sleep would sort it, but he began experiencing chest pain at work during a meeting, then again when he realised he'd forgotten his phone at home…' She continued, running through the protocols they'd already seen to. Thrombolytics to break down any blood clots, namely fibrin, a protein that blocked blood flow through the coronary artery. Nitroglycerin. Beta-blockers to improve blood flow.

'And, of course,' she continued, 'he's had a coronary angiography.' She looked at her watch. 'We should probably get him up to Theatre.'

Felix looked at the patient who, despite being hooked up to various monitors and an IV, moments away from being wheeled into surgery, was now smiling, laughing. He cleared an unexpected hit of emotion from his throat. This was a moment the patient they'd lost yesterday should've had. Yes, they still might have lost him, but the call would've been a solace to his loved ones.

'When he's finished on the phone, take him up. Are you comfortable leading?'

The intern looked at him in amazement. 'Seriously?'

Felix nodded. Part of managing a team meant trusting them. A courtesy he knew he didn't regularly extend to his staff, thinking that if it went wrong he'd rather bear the burden of guilt.

He shook his head. No. This wasn't right. He hadn't told her about the sacrifices he'd made. The part of his heart he'd ripped out of his chest to give his wife what she'd always wanted.

'Dr Beck?' the intern asked. 'Was that a yes, you can do the surgery, or a no? You shook your head both ways.'

Felix almost laughed. Yup. Today was certainly going to be interesting. 'You're ready to lead,' he assured her. 'Page me if you have any concerns.' He headed back to the patient board, mulling over his conversation with Matti. He'd turned what could have been a briefly awkward situation into a confrontation. In rejecting her suggestions, he'd basically rejected her. If she was still here, he'd need to eat humble pie to start earning even a crumb of respect.

Why had he been such an ass? He knew *hygge* wasn't solely about knitting mittens or sitting by the fire with a good book. It was about family. Togetherness. Supporting and feeling supported by colleagues, loved ones.

He thought of the lengths he'd gone to, trying to give his

wife what she wanted most—children—and his failure to do so.

She'd said she'd find a way to move on, that they'd make do as they were, but he loved her enough to know she would never be able to move past this particular hurdle. They weren't, despite their many attempts to convince themselves they could fill the childless void, one of *those* couples. The kind who were completely content with one another. He'd tried to talk to her about it, but she'd insisted she was fine even though it was clear she wasn't. So he'd found a way to prove it to her. When she'd asked for a divorce, it should have been a relief. It had, after all, been the goal. But, like their efforts to have a child, it had felt like another failure.

'Hi, there.' He turned at a soft tap on his shoulder.

Matti.

She gave him a polite smile. 'Want to put me to work? Oh!' She handed him a form. 'My Patient Safety approval form. Dr Larsen has a copy but I thought, given your response to the *hygge* project, you'd want to be assured I'm properly qualified to practice medicine in Denmark.'

He gave the document a scan and returned it. Now to the more onerous task. Earning her respect. And, just as important, her trust.

'So,' he began in an awkward, jovial tone. 'The Holiday *Hygge* Challenge. Where do we begin?'

She gave him a look. 'So… I take it we're not going to address the elephant in the room?'

'I think you just have.' He swiped his hand over his face. 'I owe you an apology.'

'You think?'

'I know. I'm sorry. I didn't expect to see you.'

'I guess that snow globe had a different concept of preserving a moment.' A smile teased at the corners of her lips. 'Look. This is awkward for both of us, so how about we wipe the slate clean? What would you think about me shadowing you so I can see how you run the department?'

It was an olive branch he didn't deserve, but he took it.

'Sounds good. Unless you'd like to lead and I can jump in if necessary.'

She shook her head. 'This isn't my turf. If the situation warrants it, I'm more than happy to get stuck in, but—' she gave him a too innocent smile '—I'd like to see how you approach patient treatment.'

A flash of memory came to him. A pair of scissors in his hands. Matti offering herself to him. Her trust. Her vulnerability.

He shook his head, willing the image to park itself closer to the North Pole. The clean slate plan was going to be difficult to achieve.

'Well,' he said after giving the patient board another scan. 'How about we do a two-for-one?'

She gave him a confused look.

'I've got a seven-year-old who needs some stitches…'

Her eyes lit up, making the connection. 'Sewing a patient. *Hygge.* Cute,' she said dryly. Then, as he turned his back to her to lead the way, he heard her whisper, 'Very cute.'

CHAPTER TEN

'DID YOU SWIM again today?' Hannah, the nurse Matti had met yesterday, gave her a friendly smile as she opened a nearby locker.

Matti had already changed into the lightweight polo-necked shirt she wore under her scrubs, and wondered if the question was her colleague's polite way of asking if she needed her back moisturised. The thought, annoyingly, instantly conjured a memory of a naked Felix, massaging slicks of lotion along her back.

When he'd stood in her doorway, about to leave, she'd seen the same questions in his eyes she'd been asking herself. Was one night enough? Were they closing down a beginning because they feared an end?

For every part of her that longed for another magical night, there was a part of her that wished it had never happened. They'd stumbled through the work day together yesterday but, despite the odd moment of being so engrossed in a patient's case they forgot to be awkward, it had been awkward. Nor had they sat down to seriously discuss the *Hygge* Challenge. Something she was hoping to rectify today, even if he thought her project was a waste of time.

'Matti?' Hannah waved a hand in front of her face. 'Earth to Matti.'

Matti started, embarrassed. 'Sorry. Away with the faeries.'

'Lotion?' Hannah prompted.

'I'm okay, thanks,' Matti said, flicking her ponytail out from her neckline, only to realise it was her damp hair that had cued the offer, not a covert attempt to play the Good Samaritan. She made a mental note to stop weaving her fears into the subtext of every exchange she had. 'My godmother helped me out after the swim.'

'Cool,' Hannah said, then, after a quick look round, lowered her voice. 'I'm glad Felix the Grouch didn't scare you away yesterday. Saying that, he was different from how he normally is when he was around you.'

'Was he?' He'd barely met her eye the entire day.

'Yeah. We think he was trying to be nice. It obviously doesn't come naturally, but, for what it's worth, we're all rooting for you. It's about time he got shook.'

'Shook?'

'You know, rattled. He's a great doctor. The best head of department we've had for a long time.'

She paused, as if considering whether or not to say something. Matti could guess what it was.

'I heard he had a rough time a few years back.'

Hannah nodded. 'Yes. It changed him. But because he'd set such a great precedent, the way he runs things now doesn't really get challenged. Being part of your Happiness Challenge—'

'*Hygge*,' Matti corrected.

'Happy. *Hygge*.' Hannah grinned. 'They're the same thing, really. Anyway, you got to him yesterday. I've never seen him show off before.'

'Show off?'

Hannah gave her a *what an innocent* look. 'He wanted to impress you. He was insisting patients call their loved ones before surgery. Found spare chairs for the waiting room. All sorts.'

Matti shook her head. 'I thought he was doing it to prove

my project was redundant. That you and the rest of the team already factored *hygge* into your work ethos.'

'No,' Hannah said firmly. 'He's normally all "efficient, efficient, efficient". He'd get annoyed when he saw us taking a bit of extra time to do something outside of the job remit. Either way, we're glad you're here. We can't wait to see what he's like when you finish your project.'

Huh. Wasn't that interesting? Matti held up her hands like, *Who knows what's going to happen?* 'I guess it'll be fun finding out.'

Hannah laughed. 'Fun? Are you sure we're talking about the same Dr Beck?'

The tall, blue-eyed sex god who she had to remind herself not to launch herself at whenever they were alone.

'One and the same.'

'Well, good luck to you,' Hannah said, closing the door to her locker and twirling the lock to set it. 'If you're ever in need of some moral support, we're here for you.'

They headed out to the patient board which, to their surprise, was clear.

A clean slate. Hopefully, a good sign for the day.

'Hey look.' Hannah pointed towards the reception area.

Matti did a double-take. A pair of orderlies were deep in discussion about how they should hang some rather worn-looking tinsel along a wall. 'Christmas decorations already?'

'You bet.' Hannah grinned and called out to the receptionist, 'Sofie, we Scandinavians are obsessed with Christmas, aren't we?'

'Yes, we are,' Sofie sing-songed. She held up her fingernails as evidence. Yesterday they'd been orange and black. Today? Glittery bright red. 'We're ob*sessed*.'

'Obsessed with what?' asked a very familiar caramel voice. One that wasn't quite as melty as it had been the first time she'd heard it, but a degree or two warmer than yesterday.

Sofie, flustered, said, 'We were just explaining to Dr Meadows that the holiday decorations are going up today because we Danes adore Christmas.'

Matti willed her expression to appear neutral, but when she turned to face Felix her face instantly did its own thing and smiled.

Felix gave her a nod of acknowledgement, nothing more.

Her smile fell away. Good grief. She didn't like this clean slate. Time to throw some glitter on it. 'I think it's a delightful obsession. And very *hygge*, don't you think?'

Felix folded his arms and adopted a 'thinking pose', an elbow perched on one of his hands, while the other held his chin, his index finger tap, tap, tapping those beautiful lips of his. 'I would say strongly embrace rather than obsessed,' he said. 'Obsession isn't healthy. But yes.' He shifted his gaze to Matti. There was a twinkle in his eye she hadn't expected. 'We're big fans.'

'What do you like to embrace?' Matti asked him.

He arched an eyebrow at her.

Too late, Matti realised how easily her comment could be misconstrued. 'At Christmastime,' she fumbled. 'You know, things, activities.'

Felix's lips twitched with amusement. He was enjoying this. Watching her scramble for her dignity.

She turned to Sofie and squeaked, 'Anything in particular you look forward to?'

'Family time,' Sofie said without missing a beat.

Hannah agreed. 'And friends, of course. Sometimes more than family,' she added with a laugh. 'What about you, Dr Beck?'

Eyes still on Matti, he said, 'Unwrapping presents is always fun.'

Her cheeks went crimson. If this was his way of suggesting he'd like to 'unwrap' her again— Before she could finish the thought, a set of butterflies took flight round her heart without her permission.

'Dr Beck,' Hannah chided. 'Surely you know it's better to give than receive.'

'I do,' he said, those beautiful baby blues of his still on Matti.

'Ooh!' Sofie pitty-patted her hands together with a squeal of delight that, mercifully, gave Matti an excuse to end her staring contest with Felix. 'What about putting up the tree? I *love* getting the tree!' She also loved lighting the candles on the tree. The first of December, when the whole family gathered together for a huge feast. Present-wrapping. Snuggling under blankets. Giggling with her nieces and nephews as they stumbled about ice-skating on the lake near her family's cabin. Roaring woodfires. And the list went on.

'What about you, Matti?' Hannah asked when Sofie paused to draw breath.

Matti took a moment, then decided to give Felix a dose of his own medicine. 'Buns.'

Felix choked, disguising it as a cough.

'Baked goods,' she clarified. 'Pastries.'

'Good choice.' Hannah reminded her about the bakery she'd recommended the day before. Felix still had his hand over his mouth, possibly covering a smile if the crinkles by his eyes were anything to go by.

About time, Matti thought, allowing a smile of her own as she remembered the moment when she'd first touched his derriere.

'I'll tell you what I don't love,' Sofie said. 'These tired old Christmas decorations.'

The orderlies were wrestling a tangle of tinsel into submission. Although, judging by their expressions, it could've been the other way around. Next to them, a heap of white and green branches were presumably waiting to be made into a tree. A tatty snowman made of felt stared back at them with his solitary coal-coloured eye.

Matti was just about to ask how they would decorate the reception area if money was no object when a friendly-looking middle-aged woman wearing a beautiful green shawl came through the main doors carrying a large knitting bag. She scanned the room as she made her way to the reception desk. 'If you don't mind my saying, your decorations seem a bit past-it.'

Sofie agreed. 'We were just discussing that.'

'You know,' the woman said, putting her bag on the counter, 'if you let my knitting group loose in this place, we'd turn it into a winter wonderland in no time.'

'That would be amazing.' Matti's imagination instantly ran riot, filling the clinical surroundings with soft seasonal decorations that would definitely provide more comfort than a one-eyed snowman. This woman seemed heaven-sent.

'Hygienic?' she heard Felix say behind her.

He had a point, but she wasn't going to let him steal her thunder. Not yet anyway.

'I'm sure you'll all be busy making presents for loved ones.'

The woman laughed, winced, then explained how their families had begged them not to gift them any knitwear for Christmas. As such, the group had decided they'd spread their wings and try to find something creative to do as a group. 'We were thinking of knitting a miniature version of Stockholm, but…'

Matti couldn't help herself. She pounced. 'Decorating here would bring so much joy.' Felix cleared his throat behind her. She pressed on. 'Would anyone mind if any of the decorations didn't survive the holidays?' She decided against going into detail. No one wanted to think about vomit on a knitted Santa. For example.

'Of course not,' the woman said enthusiastically. 'Every time I make a toy for Dogmar, it gets destroyed in minutes.'

'Dogmar?'

'My dog,' she said, pressing her hand to her chest as her breath hitched.

Matti laughed. 'I bet he appreciates your efforts.'

'I appreciate him,' she said. 'That's why I do it.'

'Tell me,' Matti asked, 'does knitting relax you?'

'Always,' she said, then conceded, 'maybe not today.'

'Oh?' All of a sudden, Matti's brain began putting fragments of information together. The woman's careful, almost cautious, gait as she'd made her way to the admissions desk. Her laugh, curtailed by a wince. The light sips of breath, rather than a more natural rise and fall. Matti came out from behind the reception desk to help guide her to a seat, only to see Felix heading towards them with a wheelchair.

'I'm so sorry,' Matti said. 'I was so enthused by your offer, I neglected to ask you why you'd come.'

'I had a little accident,' she said. Then, as if acknowledging the reason opened the floodgates to the pain she was experiencing, she wavered. Matti put an arm around her waist to steady her while Felix locked the chair in place.

'What's your name, love?'

'Frida.'

'Frida—?' Hannah asked, holding the chair steady as Felix and Matti helped lower her into it.

'Frida Clausen,' she said, again pressing her hand to her chest.

Felix knelt down in front of her so she wouldn't have to strain, looking up at him. 'Are you feeling heart pain?'

'No. Maybe. It's—' Her chin quivered as she haltingly continued. 'I was walking to my knitting group. Oh, this is too embarrassing. It's probably nothing.'

'No, no,' Felix said gently. 'Go ahead.'

Frida shot Matti a look like, *Do I have to?*

'We're here to help,' Matti assured her, giving one of her

hands a squeeze, then discreetly pressed her fingers to the pulse point on her wrist. It wasn't racing, but something felt off.

Frida's breath hitched again. 'I was so excited to show them a new pattern, I ran up the stairs far too quickly and I tripped.'

Matti glanced at Felix. He looked as perplexed as she was. No broken bones as far as she could see. Her hands weren't scraped. No cuts. No bruises on her forehead to indicate a concussion.

'I was holding my knitting bag when I fell and—' she took another sip of breath then pointed at her chest '—I think something happened in the fall.' She glanced nervously between them, then abruptly her face drained of colour.

Felix knew better than to wait for the rest of the story and began wheeling her towards the exam rooms. 'Dr Meadows?'

While Matti grabbed Frida's knitting bag, Hannah said she'd try and find out which knitting group Frida belonged to. Matti jogged after Felix, grabbing a pair of protective gloves along the way. She arrived in the room as Felix was asking Frida if she had any allergies they should know about and if there was anyone she'd like them to call.

'No, I—' She waved her hands. 'I don't want a fuss. I feel so silly.'

'No, no,' Felix assured her. 'Accidents happen.'

Matti lowered the bed to an appropriate height then helped Frida out of the chair and onto the bed.

'My shawl!' Frida cried as Felix wheeled the chair out of the room.

He stopped short. 'I'll put it here for you, with your bag, all right?' He folded it carefully then draped it on the back of the visitor's chair in the corner, giving it a final smoothing stroke before he left.

The pair of them watched him leave. As gratifying as it would be to think he'd been so careful with the shawl to prove he knew a thing or two about patient care, something told Matti it hadn't been a performance. This was how he showed he cared. Not in flowery speeches or sentimental declarations, but with an extraordinary attention to detail. Like saving her from the pirates. He hadn't said a word about her back. He'd seen a problem, stepped in and solved it without any expectations in return.

Her heart felt like a balloon filling with helium. She knew she'd been right to trust him. And if she wanted him to do the same, she'd have to show him, in a way he understood, that they wanted the same thing here at Copenhagen Central. Unparalleled patient care.

'He's a bit of a dish, isn't he?' Frida said.

Matti made a vague noise by way of answer. 'Now then, Frida. When you fell, do you think you fell on a knitting needle?'

'I think so...' Tears bloomed in Frida's warm brown eyes. 'I was too afraid to look. But it hurt so much, my friend insisted on bringing me here. She's parking the car.'

Matti nodded, relieved to hear she had a friend to support her. 'Where does it hurt?'

Frida made a vague gesture over her loose-fitting jumper which, as far as Matti could see, bore no sign of bloodstains.

'I think we might need to take a look under your lovely jumper,' Matti said just as Felix returned. He pulled open a drawer and held up a pair of scissors. 'Will you need these?'

'No!' Frida cried. 'Not this one.'

'It's loose enough that we may not need them,' Matti said. 'Let's give it a go. If you could just lie back for me...'

Frida closed her eyes, then let her head sink into the pillow behind her.

Matti eased the sweater up while Felix put on some gloves on the opposite side of the bed. There was no visible injury at Frida's waist or stomach but, soon enough, they found the source of her pain.

The jagged edges of a wooden knitting needle were protruding from her chest at the centre of her bra line. In other words, it had pierced through her sternum. Only a centimetre or so was visible but, judging by her shortness of breath, there had to be at least a few centimetres beneath the skin. She could be suffering from a pneumothorax if it had punctured her lung, or something much worse if it had hit her heart. Matti looked at Felix and mouthed, 'CT?'

He nodded and left the room.

'Frida?' Matti explained that her suspicion about the knitting needle was correct and that they wanted to take some images before making a plan.

Frida tried to push herself up. 'I shouldn't have come in. I'm being silly. I have a pair of tweezers in my bag.'

'You let us look after that side of things,' Matti said, gently holding her in place. The needle was much bigger than a splinter. Removing it would likely require surgery, not tweezers.

Frida grabbed Matti's wrist. 'I need to check my bag. Make sure it wasn't one of the rosewoods. They were my grandmother's.'

'I'll get it for you,' Matti said. 'While we check your stats, why don't you tell me about your grandmother?' She wrapped the cuff around Frida's arm and listened attentively, relieved to see her patient relax as she recounted how her grandmother had been the one to teach her how to knit.

'It must've taken me a year to finish that first scarf,' she said, closing her eyes and smiling as if she was picturing it now.

Matti clipped the heart monitor onto her index finger and asked follow-up questions, all the while marvelling at how the human spirit was often so much stronger than the body. Time and again, she'd seen patients who completely forgot about their plight when something else worried them more. Their home. Another patient. A loved one.

Or a carpet like the one her fiancé had refused to let her roll on when her back had been on fire.

'I really hope it wasn't one of the rosewoods,' Frida said, then, as if her situation had finally caught up with her, she gave a heart-rending sob. 'I can't believe I was so careless.'

'Hey,' Matti soothed. 'It was an accident.'

'A foolish one,' Frida said, as if remonstrating with herself.

'Not foolish at all,' Matti corrected. 'Accidents are just that.' It was a mantra she'd repeated to herself on a loop when she'd been the one in Frida's place, frightened, panicked, trying to piece together how she'd managed to turn a relaxed Saturday morning into a nightmare.

A light knock sounded on the door.

It was Felix. Matti handed Frida a clutch of tissues. 'We're going to take care of you, all right?'

Frida sniffled into her tissues then gave Matti a watery smile while Felix slid the exam room door open for a radiologist who wheeled in a high-tech mobile X-ray machine.

Matti was confused. She'd said CT scan. She pointed at the machine questioningly.

'The tech was free, so I thought we should get some images straight away,' Felix said.

'Honestly,' Frida said. 'This is too much fuss. I bet I could pull it out with my—'

Matti caught her hand in the nick of time. 'We need to leave it where it is for now, all right? It's important to know exactly how deep it is before removing it.' She held Frida's hand between hers. 'I know this is frightening, but it's important to take things step by step. After we get your stats and take some X-rays, we'll probably need a different type of imaging and then we will know the safest way to take it out, all right?'

She didn't have to turn around to know Felix was shooting daggers at her. But she was pretty sure he didn't want her pointing out that an X-ray wouldn't show a wooden knitting needle. It could be that taking X-rays first was protocol. Every hospital had slightly different rules of procedure, something she'd wrestled with when she'd come back from fieldwork where thinking outside the box was not only the norm, it often saved lives.

'I feel fine,' Frida said unconvincingly. 'I think it was just panic that made me feel faint. I'm not a big fan of hospitals.' She gave them an apologetic smile.

'Don't worry,' Matti said. 'Your secret's safe with us. And, for the record, your body's been your ally.'

'How so?'

'It gave you little signs that you should have it checked out.'

Matti was sugar-coating reality. If Frida had seen the shard earlier and pulled it out she might not have made it to the hospital alive.

'Dr Meadows?' Felix touched her elbow. 'We need to step out of the room while the imaging is done.'

'Do you have to go?' Frida asked, her anxiety visibly increasing.

'Only for a moment,' Matti assured her. 'We'll be right outside the door.'

'Would you be able to see if my friend's made it in?'

'Of course.'

Matti made a note of her name, then left the room with Felix.

'How're her stats?' Felix asked.

Matti ran him through the ones she'd taken. Nothing too out of the ordinary, but once that needle was extracted it might be a very different scenario.

'Next steps?' he asked in the same, almost brusque tone he'd used yesterday.

Matti held up her finger as if to pause the conversation.

'I'm just going to nip out to Reception to see if her friend's here.'

He frowned, displeased.

'What?'

'Shouldn't you be focusing on the patient?'

She looked Felix square in the eye. 'I am. She's in a stable condition and would benefit from knowing her friend's here to support her. Especially considering she's going to be incredibly frightened once we get the CT scan results and tell her she'll need surgery.'

'What CT scan results?' Felix asked, openly annoyed now.

'The ones we'll need because a wooden knitting needle won't show up on the X-rays,' she blurted.

Felix glared at her and then, as the penny dropped, gave his jaw a scrub in frustration. He clearly didn't like making mistakes. Instead of an apology, he pointed at her tablet. 'What's her friend's name?'

'Why?'

'I'll find her. You call CT and Surgery. Book both. You'll lead.'

She told him the name and he left without another word.

The exchange should've felt barbed, loaded with a sting. It definitely would've sounded curt to an observer. But Matti knew neither of those things was true. If there was one thing she knew about trauma surgeons, it was that they loved unusual cases. And he had given it to her. His version of making amends. And in that moment, she did the one thing she'd promised herself she wouldn't.

She fell a little bit in love with him.

CHAPTER ELEVEN

After Felix met with Frida's friend, he signed out an overnight patient who'd been cleared for release, updated the board, then, after ensuring the rest of the team was up to speed and supported, headed to the surgery unit. He took the stairs to the observation room above the operating theatre in twos. Every seat in the small room was taken. A dozen doctors and nurses cracking knitting jokes—all of which died out when they realised who had just walked into the room. A junior doctor offered him her seat.

'I'm fine standing,' he said, then, as if Matti had whispered in his ear that he'd sounded curt, added, 'Thanks for the offer.'

A few looks of surprise were exchanged. A day ago he would've dismissed the moment, but today it bothered him. He prided himself on running an effective and efficient team. But if Dr Larsen was right—that he was achieving his goals by inducing discomfort amongst the staff, it was an issue she'd rightly called out.

Sure, he'd needed some time to lick his wounds after the divorce, but he should never have let his personal demons affect how he treated people. Not his colleagues or, he admitted, his family. A loving gaggle of souls he'd kept at arm's length for too long.

'Can someone catch me up?' he asked the room.

The same junior doctor timorously raised her hand.

He gave her a nod to go ahead.

'Pre-op, Dr Meadows did a focused abdominal sonography examination after the non-contrast CT scan showed that the needle had penetrated Frida's sternum.'

He let out a low whistle. The sternum usually served as a protective shield over the heart, lungs and major blood vessels. He trained his eyes on the monitors showing the detailed work Matti was in the throes of as the junior doctor explained that the needle point had nicked the heart's right ventricle, which had caused internal bleeding. Frida hadn't been in acute respiratory distress, but they'd put her on an oxygen mask just in case. Her blood pressure was normal and there hadn't been any muffled heart sounds, so she'd brought her to surgery for a median sternotomy to remove the foreign body. The doctor concluded, adding, 'Dr Meadows is an amazing diagnostician.'

'And surgeon,' said another.

'What makes you say that?' He hoped his question didn't sound as if he doubted Matti's ability. He'd read her CV, her references. All glowing. Each referee had added a personal note commenting on her skills being matched by the level of personal care she gave her patients. He was pretty certain if he asked for references, they wouldn't contain the same level of affection that shone through in hers.

'She's incredibly fast,' one observed, clarifying, 'efficient, I mean. Not chaotic. It's like she's doing it by muscle memory.'

There were murmurs of assent.

'She knows how to lead a team,' someone else volunteered.

'She quoted Hippocrates,' said another.

Felix smiled. 'Any wound to the heart is fatal?'

'That's the one,' said the doctor, surprised Felix had guessed it.

'What was the context?' Felix asked.

'Before they began, she asked the team if they felt up to proving Hippocrates wrong.'

'They're doing it,' said another, pointing to the monitor, which showed Matti completing and tying off a final stitch to the right ventricle. She handed over the closing elements of the surgery to the team, assuring them that she had full confidence in them while tactfully making it clear she'd be close by if they needed her.

The observation room gave her a standing ovation when she looked up on her way out of Theatre. To their delight, she curtseyed her thanks.

When her eyes lit on him, he froze. What was he meant to do? Smile? Give her a thumbs-up? Make fake crowd noises? He gave her a nod.

He caught a nurse giving one of her peers an eye-roll like, *Dr Meadows aced a once-in-a-lifetime surgery and he gives her a nod?*

It was true, but this wasn't a well done nod. And something about the way Matti's eyes had sparked a little bit brighter afterwards told him she knew what the nod meant.

They were on an even playing field—and they were on the same team.

His pager sounded, calling him back to the ER. When he arrived at the desk, he checked the board. There weren't any new patients that he could see, but a quick glance at the waiting room indicated otherwise.

'What's up?' he asked Sofie.

She grinned. 'Frida's friends are here.'

He took a proper look at the waiting room. It wasn't just full. It was full of knitters. Men and women with various projects on the go, some helping untangle balls of yarn, others examining patterns, all of them chatting away, smiling.

'You paged?' Felix asked Sofie.

'Well…' She looked at him as if it was obvious. 'I thought you'd want to handle…' She trailed off.

'Handle what?' he asked, realising as he spoke that she'd assumed he wouldn't want them there.

The waiting room was for patients. It was also for loved ones anxiously awaiting news. He found himself asking, *What would Matti do?* She'd speak to them.

'Thanks, Sofie.'

He found the friend who had brought Frida here, a gentle, grandmotherly type, and explained she would be coming out of surgery shortly but that she wouldn't be able to see visitors for at least a couple of hours, if not more.

'We're happy to stay,' the older woman said. 'She doesn't have much in the way of family, so we wanted to make sure she knew her knitting family was here, supporting her.'

Felix was about to suggest they find a nearby café when he recalled the initial exchange with Frida. 'You know what I think would make her day?'

A few hours later, Felix caught up with Matti at the coffee station.

'Hey—' she smiled at him '—want a cup?'

'I'm all right, thanks. How's Frida?'

'Doing well,' Matti said. 'She's out of Recovery and on the ward now. Her friend was waiting right by her bed when she came out. I suspect I have you to thank for organising that.'

He shrugged it off, but had to admit it felt nice to have someone leap to a nice conclusion about him. 'Interesting surgery?'

Matti lit up. 'So interesting. You've got a great team here. We're waiting for the results of a couple of tests I requested, but hopefully, beyond a small scar, recovery won't be too much of an ordeal for her.'

'Have you been into the reception area?'

She shook her head. 'Back-to-back patients. Why?'

'I think you should have a look.'

She stared at her coffee cup. 'Am I going to need a few more of these?'

'No, no. It's something…something you'll like.'

'Oh?' Her smile brightened. 'Sounds intriguing. Can I have a hint?'

He shook his head. 'Better as a surprise.'

They headed towards the reception area. Matti stopped short of it and grinned mischievously at him. 'Should I close my eyes before going in?'

As tempting as it was to step behind her and cup her eyes for a big reveal, he didn't want any reminders of how good it felt to touch her. 'No.'

Her smile faltered briefly. Wrong decision again. One he hoped she'd forget as soon as she went into Reception.

'Please. After you,' he said, holding out his hand for her to lead the way.

The moment she saw the waiting room she squealed with delight and raced into the centre, turning like a child whose dreams had all come true. 'Are you magicians?' she asked the handful of knitters who remained. They beamed with delight. 'I'm in awe,' she said. 'What talent you all have. What big hearts.'

Felix leant against the reception desk, watching her explore. What had once been a sterile, not entirely welcoming reception area, was now a woollen Winter Wonderland. Strings of colourful mini-mittens and knitted 'paper' chains replaced the lacklustre tinsel. Frosty was still there, but he had two eyes, a bright orange knitted carrot nose and an impressively tall chimney pipe hat complete with a holly berry swag at the centre. He also, unsurprisingly, had a new scarf. The fake tree was barely visible beneath all of its new ornaments.

Matti inspected everything, clapping occasionally, giggling, until she reached the reception desk, where she swooned with delight when she saw the row of knitted characters perched on the counter. They had big pink noses peeking over thick white beards, arms held wide so that they looked like a tiny welcoming committee.

She grinned at him. 'Are these little Santas?'

'They're gonks. Scandinavian hobgoblins.'

She looked at him, confused.

'Mythological creatures,' he explained, much to Sofie's amusement. 'A mix between a gnome and Santa Claus. It's believed that they sneak into homes and barns for warmth during the winter months. If they're treated well, they bring good luck. If not, they play mischievous tricks.'

'Oh, well, in that case,' Matti said seriously, 'I will do everything in my power to treat them well.' She curtsied to the gonks. 'Good day, gentlemen. Welcome to Copenhagen Central.'

As she introduced herself to them, shaking their little hands without any sign of self-consciousness, a part of Felix's heart melted. Watching her made him realise that he'd shut himself down to the point he'd completely stopped taking joy from life's simpler pleasures. As if they were something he didn't deserve.

Matti caught him staring at her and coloured. 'Sorry. Kid in a candy store. Frida has an incredibly supportive group of friends.'

'She does,' he confirmed. 'There were about twenty of them here earlier. It was—' How to describe the scene? 'It was pretty remarkable how they managed to achieve so much without interrupting any hospital work. One gentleman even gave a couple of children who were waiting a lesson. They made snowflakes for the tree.' He showed her then asked, 'What do you think about asking them back? Seeing if anyone fancies giving more lessons?'

'I think that would be amazing.' She pressed her hands together in prayer position, her warm eyes glassing over as she imagined it. 'I wish I'd been here. It must've been like Santa's workshop. I can't wait until Frida sees it. What a special group of friends.'

'That they are,' Felix said, suddenly thinking of his own friends, once a large circle of interesting characters that, thanks to him, had shrunk to, at best, two or three. They'd tried reaching out, getting him to rejoin the human race. But he'd pushed them away too hard and for too long. A mistake, he realised. One he'd have to rectify.

'Felix, this is so inspiring. I bet there are other groups we could approach to teach small classes. Like…a wreath-decorating day? Didn't someone mention a bakery that does biscuit-decorating?'

He was about to say not to get carried away, that this was a hospital not a crafting workshop, but caught himself. Shutting things down before he'd given them proper consideration was exactly why his boss had paired him with Matti. He pulled his phone out.

'Let's start a list. Maybe visit some Christmas market vendors. I could reach out to the charities who already work with the hospital and see if they have any suggestions. Perhaps…' He shook his head, waved the half-formed idea away.

'Go on,' she encouraged.

'I was just thinking about the volunteers who come by with care animals. They visit with the patients, but never come down here. Maybe worth asking if they could do a round or two?'

'Great idea. I know I'd benefit from a cuddle with a fluffy hound.' She beamed at him. 'I'm so in love with this project.'

Her enthusiasm was infectious. To the point Felix barely realised he was stepping towards her, arms outstretched to pull her into a hug. But he did realise. Instead of manning up and following through on the uncharacteristic gesture, he lurched to a halt and whipped his hands up as if Matti was holding him at gunpoint. 'Double high-five?'

'Okay.' She gave him a curious smile. 'Why not?' She patted his hands, bemused, then realised Sofie was watching the pair of them as if they were a brand-new television series.

She gestured for him to follow her back to the patient board.

'Hey,' she said quietly. 'If this is too uncomfortable, working with me after…you know…snow globe night, I can speak with Dr Larsen. Explain that the project doesn't really need to be a two-hander.'

Snow globe night? That was how she thought of it? It made sense. One perfect night sealed in glass. Something to look at, but not to touch.

'No. Don't,' he said, frustrated with how awkwardly he was handling this. 'It's interesting seeing the world through your eyes.'

She frowned. 'This isn't about what I see, Dr Beck. It's about what the patients see and, more importantly, what they experience when they're here.'

'Felix,' he corrected. 'Look, if you'd rather work on your own, I respect that. But if you think I could be of use—as the ward's resident fun sponge—I'm happy to help. Who knows? You might even turn me into a cock-eyed optimist, like you.'

A flash of irritation crossed her face. The tacked-on comment was a mistake.

'This isn't a joke to me, Felix,' she said. 'If you want to disguise your hurt and pain as pragmatism or—what did you call it—?'

'Being a fun sponge,' he said, regretting that turn of phrase as well.

She made a guttural noise. 'Sucking the fun out of something doesn't make it any easier to handle. It makes it worse, in my opinion. An optimistic outlook means you stand a much better chance of finding joy or beauty when you really, really need a reminder about life's perks. Unexpected birdsong. A rainbow. A snowflake landing on your nose. Those tiny moments are precious counterbalances to fear, vulnerability, pain, because the reality is, bad things are always going to happen, no matter how optimistic you are.'

Too late to stop himself, he quipped, 'That's a pessimistic conclusion.'

She shook her head and looked away with an annoyed huff.

He'd just proved her point. Given her a classic example of someone hiding behind cynicism as a shield. He could really be an ass sometimes. No wonder his friends had given up on him. His interpersonal skills were broken. Matti was handing him an opportunity to change for the better on a silver platter and his instinct was to shut it down rather than admit he found contemplating his own future terrifying. Just as he had when he'd been told he and his wife had 'unexplained infertility' issues.

'Listen—' Matti broke the silence '—I'm sorry if that sounded preachy, Dr Beck.'

It hadn't, but her use of his formal title stung. She wasn't angry. She was disappointed in him. And it hurt.

'I didn't think I'd have to explain to you, of all people, how important this project is to me on both a personal and professional level.'

She didn't. And if he could reach into his chest and pull his heart out in apology, he would. A thousand times over.

'If you find the time, I'd be grateful if you could email me a list of the charities you mentioned. I'll speak with them.'

Meaning, she didn't trust him to do it.

He nodded. 'You'll have a list asap.'

'Thanks. And look. I know you were shoe-horned into working with me. Let's see how we go for the rest of the week. If we make progress, great. If not, I'll let Dr Larsen know you're a free agent.'

He didn't want to be a free agent. He wanted to work with her. Prove he wasn't all bad.

Be honest, asshole, said a voice in his head.

Fine, he told the voice. *I like her. A lot. Professionally and personally. And it's terrifying me.*

That's better, said the voice. *So what are you going to do about it?*

'Fair enough,' he said to Matti. 'I've got more than enough to do as it is.' As the words came out of his mouth, he felt his cell structure shape shift back into the cool, distant version of himself. Only this time, instead of feeling protective, his defence system felt like a prison.

CHAPTER TWELVE

MATTI SHRUGGED OFF her coat and dived straight into the water. She needed to reharness the energy she'd had at the beginning of the week. And the confidence.

Her body flooded with adrenaline as the shock of cold water took effect. The hit of elation followed but when, after a few strokes, she resurfaced, she caught herself turning back to look at the pier, hoping to find Felix was there.

Surprise, surprise. He wasn't.

A jagged spear of disappointment lanced her physical high, piercing the fragile confidence she'd been clinging to all week.

A salty sting of tears rose in her throat. She dived under the water again, screaming with frustration. Which was stupid. She surfaced, choking and spluttering. It served her right. This was what happened when she handed someone the power to control her mood. She'd done it with her fiancé and the results had been devastating. Falling back into that mindset after vowing never to do it again scared her.

She started swimming, using each stroke to recount how she'd reached this point.

After she'd gone all bristly and defensive about the *Hygge* Challenge a few days back, they'd finished what was left of the workday walking on eggshells. It had been awful.

That night, she'd turned their talk over and over in her head, ultimately concluding that she owed Felix an apology. Her project was personal. Too personal. To the point she'd basically told him to shove off. And for what? A mistimed joke? Because he'd challenged her? Approached life differently? He had every right to ask questions and to receive a considered answer, not an ultimatum. This was, after all, his department, his home, and she was a visitor. She'd seen the hurt in those sea-blue eyes of his before he'd shut her out. It stung to know she was as capable of lashing out as anyone. And in the workplace? Doubly bad.

The next day, armed with pastries and an apology, she'd arrived at the hospital only to discover Dr Larsen was running the department as Felix had taken a few days' personal leave. She'd tried and failed to hide her disappointment. Dr Larson had taken her aside and asked if something had happened. She'd said no, going to great lengths to compliment Felix, his work ethic, his enthusiasm, his commitment to the *Hygge* Challenge, to the point Dr Larsen had started laughing. 'That doesn't sound the Felix Beck I know.'

She wanted to say he was actually really lovely. Under certain conditions, anyway. Snow globe night had been magical. An otherworldly reminder of the woman she'd once been. Confident. Strong. Able to take a joke, even a bad one. But, like Felix, she'd been different at work. To the point she'd driven him away.

After her swim, she headed to the hospital. Again, no Felix. But when she checked her work email, a rush of nerves accelerated her heartbeat.

There was a message from him.

Convinced it would say she'd made things so impossible for him he'd left the hospital altogether, she held her breath as she clicked it open. It wasn't what she had expected. The email was professional, polite, and contained the list of charities they'd spoken about, along with some suggestions of other groups he thought might interest her. He'd even reached out to Frida's friends, who had not only set up a visitation rota to support her while she recovered from her surgery, but had created another for the emergency centre reception area so they could share their passion for knitting with anyone who was interested.

Matti read it again in disbelief. Who was this man? Yes, he blew hot and cold, but this? This was from a heart of gold. Unless, she thought, this was his way of covering his tracks professionally but backing out of working with her because she was 'too much'. She kneaded her fingers into her scalp, trying to massage her thoughts into an order that made sense.

When the mechanical click and hum of the main doors sounded, she looked up, half expecting to see him. It wasn't. She stood as the small group—a pair of women and an older gentleman—approached, then smiled as she realised they were carrying baskets of yarn and knitting needles. When they reached the reception desk, they asked for her.

'That's me.' Matti grinned, barely registering that Sofie wasn't remotely surprised that a mobile knitting shop had appeared out of nowhere. 'I'm guessing you're from Frida's knitting group.'

'We are,' the trio said in unison, laughing at the unplanned harmony. The younger of the three, a cheery blonde, asked, 'Where would you like us to set up the Knitting Nook?'

Sofie cut in. 'Sorry. If you wouldn't mind waiting just a moment,' She turned to Matti. 'Dr Beck had a health and safety concern he wanted to address before they settled in.'

Matti went from thrilled to furious in no time flat. Felix had been the one to set this up and now he was putting a halt to it? If this was his way of proving his point from the other day, he could take a flying—

'Ah!' Sofie pointed to the service entrance. 'Here we go.'

Two delivery men were pushing large carts carrying not one, but seven beautiful wooden rocking chairs, two of which were child-sized, along with a large pile of colourful wool blankets and a fluffy stack of fleeces.

'I think some lumbar cushions are coming as well,' Sofie said, pulling out a clipboard and running a pen along it, ticking things off as the delivery men began unloading the chairs into a corner that had been cleared of the hospital's standard bench seats.

Felix wasn't proving his point. He was proving hers. That sometimes good things could happen.

'I—' Her vocabulary failed her. 'What—?'

Sofie gave a happy shrug. 'Dr Beck said the Knitting Nook should have ergonomic seating.'

'How thoughtful,' Matti said, suddenly torn. On the one hand, it was an incredibly thoughtful gesture. On the other, it would've been a thousand times better if he was here, too.

So what? You could kiss him?

No. Well. Yes.

She didn't know! His disappearing act had hurt her. Reopened the emotional wounds her fiancé had made when he'd left her at a time she'd needed his support. Was this a genuine olive branch or a gesture meant to serve as a farewell?

Sofie put the clipboard away and began rearranging the gonks on the countertop. 'He said he'd treated enough knitters with sore necks and backs to know proper seating was important.'

'How thoughtful,' Matti managed.

Sofie misread her bewilderment for sarcasm and gave her a *Honey, he's a tricky one* look. 'We're used to Dr Beck going cucumber, but sometimes he pulls a rabbit out of his hat and the next thing you know, there's a Knitting Nook.'

'Going cucumber?' Matti hadn't heard that expression before.

'He's, you know…' Sofie made a grumpy face. 'Like a storm cloud most days.'

'And sometimes the sun comes out,' Matti finished for her.

She watched as the Knitting Nook swiftly took shape. Soon enough, all seven chairs had takers, and the soft click-clack of needles was mixing with the steady hum of hospital activity.

The only thing missing was Felix.

* * *

Towards the end of her shift, Matti was asked to see an elderly patient who'd been brought in by paramedics after he'd been found slumped on the kitchen floor, delirious with pain.

Matti's first suspicion was that he might be suffering from a UTI. Urinary tract infections were common in elderly patients, particularly if they didn't drink enough water or had an enlarged prostate. If treated quickly, they were easy enough to resolve. But left untended, the complications were far more serious.

Hannah, the nurse who had overseen admitting him, was in the room when Matti entered. 'Hey, Dr Meadows. This is Mr Hendersen.' She lowered her voice. 'At least, we think that's his name.'

'Oh?' The patient was a dead ringer for Santa, but not a jolly one. He was clearly in discomfort and his pale blue eyes seemed to be looking through rather than at her. 'Hello, there. I'm Dr Meadows. Mr Hendersen, is it?'

He shook his head.

'Oh, dear. Apologies. What's your name?' He shook his head again, which made Matti wonder if, perhaps, he spoke another language. She asked Hannah if she'd tried any other languages.

'Swedish and German,' Hannah said, adding, 'and English.'

Matti frowned, then tried speaking to him in French. Again, the man shook his head. 'Who rang the paramedics?'

'From what I gathered,' Hannah said, 'the next-door neighbour heard noises coming from the flat when they were on their way out. Thankfully, they had a spare key for emergencies and were able to get to him.'

'I'm presuming then, he isn't the owner.'

'The neighbours think he might be the owner's father, but sometimes they let the flat out to holidaymakers. He didn't have any identification that they could find and the owner wasn't home.'

He groaned and grabbed Matti's wrist, squeezing it tightly as his watery, red-rimmed eyes appealed to her for help.

She felt for him. Alone. Frightened. Being addressed by the wrong name, but in no fit state to explain his situation.

'We're going to help try and ease whatever's troubling you, all right,' Matti assured him, hoping a soothing tone and a comforting smile gave him some assurance. She quickly ran through the stats Hannah had entered into the tablet. High temperature. Weakness. Distress. Lack of mental acuity.

'Do we know if the neighbour has contacted the owner of the flat? It'd be useful to know if he has any allergies.'

'I would imagine so, if they had a key,' Hannah said. 'But no one's been in touch. We can run a spot test for penicillin.'

'Great. A urine sample would be useful as well. Shall we get him into an exam robe?'

Hannah nodded. 'We're just going to take your shoes off, sir. All right?'

They went to opposite sides of the bed and undid the laces of his shoes, sturdy, well-polished, old-fashioned leather brogues. Matti frowned when she saw his socks. They were wool, and woven in a traditional Scandinavian pattern, but in dire need of darning. Each of his big toes was poking out. The nails weren't in great shape. Patients with diabetes often presented with nails in this state. Perhaps, if he had diabetes, he was hypoglycaemic. She tried to take one of the socks off, but the moment she made contact, he kicked out his foot, almost catching her in the stomach. She knew he wasn't trying to hurt her but that pain had overridden his impulse control. Not dissimilar to the way her personal flashpoints had overridden her impulse control with Felix.

'Do you think he might have dementia?' Hannah asked in a low voice.

She hoped not for his sake. There'd been such a spike in dementia cases in recent years. It broke her heart to see patients wrestle with the changes that, in too many cases, they were powerless to control. Not to mention their loved ones' heartache.

'Once we get him into a gown, let's test him for diabetes and get a urine sample.' Matti had treated more than a few older men for UTIs who'd presented with dementia symptoms. A strong infection often made them delirious with pain.

Despite some resistance, they managed to get his trousers off. He was wearing incontinence briefs and, based on what she saw, Matti was persuaded a urinary tract infection was to blame, but she'd still do a few other tests to make sure they didn't miss anything.

'We're going to make sure you don't have a penicillin allergy,' she explained to him. 'If it's a UTI we'll pop you on an antibiotic drip. It will help you feel better.'

He caught her wrist and started speaking in a deep, urgent stream of words she couldn't make out. She looked at Hannah, who shrugged, equally confused.

'I'm sorry,' Matti said, wishing she could ease his anxiety. 'Could you repeat that?'

He did. She still didn't understand.

'He might be from Zealand,' Hannah said uncertainly. 'I recognised a couple of words. It's an island to the east. A lot of the older residents still speak the local dialect. Dr Beck speaks it, I think.'

Matti shot her a look. 'I'm sure we can muddle through.'

'Hey—' Hannah made a show of trying to catch Matti's eye '—you don't have to say anything if you don't want to, but if he's making your life difficult, you're within your rights to call him on it.'

If only it were that simple.

Their patient moaned something and again, neither woman could understand him.

'Hannah, is there any way to find out if anyone else on staff speaks his dialect?'

'Yes, but…' She twisted her mouth as if debating whether to say something.

'What?'

'Dr Beck is closest.'

Matti's heart stopped. 'He's here?'

Hannah grimaced apologetically. 'I just saw him in Reception.'

He'd come back. Meaning, she'd have to talk to him. Which was a good thing. And a scary thing. And, more pressingly, a useful thing.

Hannah tentatively stepped towards the door. 'Shall I fetch him?'

'No. I mean yes. Obviously. That would great. For the patient, obviously.'

'Yeah,' Hannah said, giving her a side-eye. 'For the patient.'

'Thank you, Hannah,' Matti called after her. Cheeks burning, she took her patient's hand and gave it a squeeze, almost seeking rather than giving comfort. 'We're getting someone who can explain everything to you. He's very…' Maddening? Wonderful? Impossible? Infuriating? 'Capable.'

Before she had time to gather her emotions, she heard Felix's voice outside the room. She willed her face into a neutral, professional smile which instantly turned into a lovesick kitten face when he appeared in the doorway. Not the best of ways to reestablish her professional authority.

'Dr Meadows.' Felix gave her a tight nod, his expression unreadable. When their eyes met, it was a different story. He was a storm of emotions. Just like her. He broke eye contact and began speaking with the patient.

As the two men spoke, the patient relaxed his grip on Matti's hand. Whatever Felix had said to him had given him comfort. She, on the other hand, was a basket case.

'This is Ivar Ellegaard,' Felix explained, switching back to Danish. 'He's quite confused, but if I understood properly, he's visiting Copenhagen from one of the islands. He did a house swap.'

'Thank you, Dr Beck, for the translation,' Matti said, then, bizarrely, curtsied. What was with all of the curtseying?

Mortified, she turned her attention to Ivar. Even though she knew he couldn't understand her, she said, 'I'm sorry we got your name wrong, Mr Ellegaard. We'll do everything we can to look after you, all right?'

She wanted to apologise to Felix too, because it was the right thing to do, especially given the success of the Knitting Nook, but she could feel him giving her one of those deep, penetrating, unreadable looks of his and since her entire emotional repertoire was desperate for any excuse to surface, she put on her most professional voice and turned to him, actively avoiding eye contact. One look into those sea storm eyes of his and she'd be a puddle.

'I believe Mr Ellegaard is suffering from a UTI.' She ran him through what they knew so far. 'Would you be kind enough to ask him if he has any allergies? I'd like to get him on an antibiotic and hydration drip if appropriate.'

Felix had another exchange with Mr Ellegaard. 'He's had blood in his urine for a couple of days now but wanted to wait to see his own doctor back home. He doesn't have any allergies.'

She'd been right. UTI. They discussed which antibiotic would be best and the additional tests required to check on his kidney function.

'I'll go,' they said at the same time, repeated it, then turned it into a staring match.

Felix broke first. 'He said you remind him of his granddaughter. You should stay with him.'

'But I don't speak—' Matti called out pointlessly, as Felix

had already left the room. 'I guess we'll have to see if I can transcend the language barrier,' she said to Mr Ellegaard.

She gave him a smile and, seeing his pillow had slipped, adjusted it, asking, 'Do you have grandchildren?' To her surprise, he replied. Heaven knew what he'd thought she'd asked him. It occurred to her that he might understand Danish but felt uncomfortable using it, so she carried on the conversation. 'I bet they wish they could be with you.' She began prepping a tray with alcohol pads, a tourniquet, saline flushes and gauze dressing, all the while chatting away to Mr Ellegaard even though, or perhaps because she knew he couldn't understand her.

'If you were my grandfather I'd be asking for advice right now. Once you were comfortable,' she amended. She told him the nutshell version of the last few days. He nodded and made listening noises as if he was taking in all the drama and giving it careful consideration. As she prepped his forearm for the cannula, she said, 'I really like him. Professionally, obviously. But… I also *like* him, like him. Which makes things complicated.' She gave his arm a wipe with an alcohol swab. 'You know how I told you were we…together. It was meant to be a one-night thing, where we never saw one another again, but then it turned out we were working together.'

Mr Ellegaard made a noise like, *Who'd have believed it?*

'I know, right? I told myself to be professional, we had a deal—one night only—but my feelings aren't obeying my brain and because this project means so much to me, I'm way too sensitive about it and kind of accidentally went a bit OTT on him the other day.' She opened a fresh alcohol swab and wiped his arm again, then, realising she'd already done it, looked at him incredulously. 'See? My brain's all over the place. And no wonder. This is the first time we've seen each other since I snapped at him. Lectured him really. About optimism, of all things. I mean, how ridiculous is that? Getting up in Felix's super sexy, kiss me face about optimism.

He hightailed it which, of course, made me feel abandoned and sorry for myself, but I still owe him an apology, right?'

Mr Ellegaard said something which, of course, she didn't understand but, whatever it was, it sounded insightful.

'I know. I'll apologise. Pretending nothing happened would be the British way to deal with it, and the Felix way, but if I don't then I'm not exactly leading by example.'

He gave a small shrug like, *I trust that you'll make the best decision.*

'At the very least I should tell him that his objectivity is actually pretty useful. Not to mention his contacts. Did you see the Knitting Nook when you came in?' She doofed her forehead. ''Course not. You came in with the paramedics. It's amazing. I might ask them to knit you a fresh pair of socks. You're going to feel a little pinch when I put the needle in. There we go. A bit of tape to keep it in place.'

She gave him a smile. 'You're right. I'll apologise and assure him the project will be better if we both work on it. I won't do it in a way that makes him think I want to date him or anything, because a: he clearly has zero interest in me that way and b: if there's one thing I know about relationships it's that just because someone gives you butterflies, it is no guarantee they'll stand by you when the chips are down. And if by some miracle Felix *does* want more sexy times, I will lock myself in a suit of armour if I have to, but I will resist. Because I am woman. Not only can I roar, I can howl.'

She proved it, but quietly, then tidied up her tray feeling strangely chipper after her 'chat' with Mr Ellegaard. 'Okay, all we need to do now is wait for Clark Kent to show up, get you on some meds, and apologise in a way that makes it clear no sexiness will be happening. Even if he walks in carrying an armful of mistletoe, I will resist.'

A light knock sounded on the door. To her horror, it was Felix.

CHAPTER THIRTEEN

MATTI NEARLY JUMPED out of her skin when she saw him. 'Dr Beck! My goodness, fancy meeting you here!'

He held out an IV bag to her. 'Hannah asked me to bring this in.' She'd said a few other things, too. *Don't be an asshole to Matti* was the nub of it. He knew. He was trying. In his own clumsy way. But having overheard Matti speaking to Mr Ellegaard, he knew he wasn't the only one battling an emotional firestorm.

Matti took the bag with a brisk, 'Thank you. Don't let me keep you. I'm sure you're busy.'

'You don't want me to stay?'

'Me? No.' She hung up the IV bag and, realising it meant she wouldn't have a translator, floundered. 'I do want you to stay. For Mr Ellegaard, obviously. Not me.'

He hadn't heard everything Matti had said, but he'd heard enough to know that leaving the way he had, without an explanation, had hurt her. And that she wasn't the only one wrestling with her emotions.

He'd had a remarkably similar conversation with his sister only yesterday. Unlike this gentleman, his sister had given him an abundance of feedback.

'I've updated his chart on the system,' he said. 'To include the antibiotics and hydration fluids.'

'Good,' Matti squeaked as she attached the drip to the cannula. 'There you are, Mr Ellegaard.' She gave him a smile, then, in a rush, said to Felix, 'I'm sorry. I was oversensitive the other day. When you didn't come in to work I was concerned it was because of me. Which is probably making myself far more important than I am to you, as you are clearly very professional and honour work agreements as well as other out of work agreements, all of which is to say, The Knitting Nook is really wonderful. Thank you for organising it.'

'I'm glad you like it,' he said woodenly instead of pulling her in for a relieved hug and telling her he was the one who should be apologising. God, he wanted to hug her.

'I do like it,' she said. 'More importantly, so do the visitors and patients.' She shot him a tentative smile. 'Can we clean the slate again?'

'We can.' *Don't stop there, Felix.* 'I owe you an apology as well. And an explanation.'

Matti swallowed nervously. 'No. You don't owe me anything.'

Hannah came into the room, took one look at the pair of them and turned back around. 'I'll come back.'

'No,' they both said, then laughed.

'We need your help,' Matti said. 'With the patient.'

Hannah gave her a look like, *You're not fooling anyone.*

Felix explained to Mr Ellegaard that he would be nearby if he needed anything, and that they would find someone to sit with him who spoke his dialect. If he could rest, he should try. As if that was the cue he'd been waiting for, the elderly man nodded and closed his eyes.

'Hannah, could you please check with the translation team? He'll likely be in overnight, so if they could contact his family as well, that'd be great. I need a word with Dr Meadows.'

'Yes,' Matti said. 'We're having a word. About professional matters.'

'Sure,' Hannah said, giving Felix a *Don't you dare hurt her* glare as she left.

Felix pulled the curtain around Mr Ellegaard for privacy then followed Matti out of the room. 'Shall we have a quick chat in the staff lounge?'

'I don't want to keep you if you're on shift.' She looked about as excited to speak with him privately as a ten-year-old being asked to clean the bathroom.

'I'm not rostered until next Monday.'

It was Friday.

She frowned. 'Then why are you here?'

'To find you.'

'Ah.'

He gestured to an empty patient room. Matti went in, her expression more suited to being led to the gallows.

Once inside, he gestured to a chair. 'I think we need to clear the air. I need to clear the air. Explain my disappearance.'

A nurse opened the door, about to usher a patient in, when she saw them. 'Apologies. I thought the room was free.'

'It is,' Matti said, scooching past Felix as if she was afraid of any physical contact.

'You're off shift soon, aren't you?' Felix asked, meeting her brisk pace. She wasn't going to get rid of him that easily.

She nodded warily.

'How would you feel about going to a Christmas market? For research.'

'Research?' She stopped and pulled a face. 'With you?'

'To talk,' he acquiesced, adding, 'it'll be research, too. We can have a drink in one of Copenhagen's most seasonally *hygge* settings.' He braced himself for a no, but her hazel eyes softened.

'Do I need to wear a costume?' she joked, then turned red and waved it away. 'Sorry. Too soon. Definitely too soon.'

They arrived at a side street near the Christmas market on their bicycles. The night was clear and the air held the distinctive scent of frost. It was a very romantic setting. Maybe the staffroom had been the better option.

'Oh, my goodness.' Matti blew on her hands. 'It's chilly out. I should've commissioned a pair of mittens back at the hospital.' She glanced up from her bicycle lock. 'Speaking of which, Frida came down and joined the Knitting Nook for a little bit this afternoon. I'm so glad her accident didn't put her off knitting. Well done again, for organising it.'

'As much as I'd like to take the credit,' Felix said, 'Frida's friends set most of it up themselves.'

'But you gave the okay, didn't you? And organised those lovely chairs.'

'Yes, but getting them was my sister's idea,' Felix admitted.

She brightened. 'Oh! How is she?'

'No, this was my other sister. Dana. But they both love a project. Especially if it has to do with Christmas.'

They also loved anything to do with Felix's personal life. Neither one of them had been shy about letting Felix know what they thought of him when he'd let his marriage go down the drain. They also had opinions about Matti. Lots of them.

'Are they younger than you?' Matti asked.

'Older.'

'Huh.' She scrutinised him as if trying to imagine it. 'I had you pegged as a protective older brother.'

'Protective, maybe. But believe me, if I think I know better than them, I am quickly disabused of the notion.'

She snorted. 'That'd be fun to see. I mean, not in a mean way. I just like watching siblings.'

There was a wistful note to her voice, as if being an only child had been a bit lonely.

As they walked towards the market, Matti dug for more information on his sisters. 'Do they live here, in Copenhagen?'

'About an hour away. By the sea. We grew up there.' He sounded like a robot.

'Sounds lovely.'

'It was. *Is*. It is lovely.'

What a wordsmith. Talking about his childhood home was tricky. Going back even more so. He'd always thought he'd raise his own family there, but when that proverbial ship had set sail, he'd found going home too difficult.

'Would you go back?' Matti asked. 'To live there?'

'No.'

Matti went wide-eyed at his blunt response. 'Okay.'

'Not because it isn't great. But I'm at home here in Copenhagen.' He could be anonymous here, unlike the village he'd grown up in, where everyone knew everything about everyone. But anonymity, a bit like being an only child, could also be lonely.

They rounded the corner and, as anticipated, Matti cooed with delight. The Nyhavn Christmas market was one of his favourites. Set along a cobbled harbour and ringed by colourful seventeenth-century townhouses, every stall, restaurant and boat was bedecked with festive lights. As it was early November, the crowds weren't huge, but there was still a nice buzz about the place.

'What do you think?' he asked. 'Does it give you that *hygge* feeling?'

'A hundred percent,' she breathed. 'It's amazing. I could totally imagine falling in—' She stopped herself.

Falling in love here, he silently finished. Yeah. He could see that. And if he was about to tell Matti anything other than what he had promised himself he would, he could imagine starting that journey now.

When she blew on her hands again, he pointed her towards the heart of the market. 'Let's find you some mittens.'

They set off for a clutch of stalls where he was sure they'd find some knitwear. Sure enough, they found a stall and Matti, who didn't seem to do anything half-heartedly, instantly went into raptures, examining and modelling several pairs before picking up a huge bright red set with cream-coloured holly leaves knitted into the pattern. She started to put one on, then stopped, took it off and examined it. The mitten had two sleeve cuffs, but only one section for the hand. She whispered, 'Do you think we should tell them this pair's not right?'

The vendor saw her confusion and joined them. 'Ah—' she beamed '—you found our love gloves.'

Matti examined it, then grinned as she figured it out. 'It's a mitten for two! So you can hold hands.'

'Yes, exactly.' The woman smiled. 'You and your partner can hold hands without getting cold. And here—' she pointed out the two single mittens alongside it '—these are for your other hand. Please, try. Both of you.'

'Actually—' Matti picked up a pair of evergreen-coloured mittens with a similar holly leaf pattern in cream '—I'll take these, thanks.'

After paying for them, she gave him an apologetic look. 'Sorry about the love glove thing. I wouldn't have made such a show of it if I'd known.'

'It's fine.'

She huffed out a sigh, clearly frustrated. 'Can I be honest?'

'Please.' He braced himself.

'I don't really know how to behave around you.'

Precisely the reason they needed to talk.

'Let's get some *gløgg* and a snack.'

'Mulled wine?' She gave a dry laugh. 'Do you need the Dutch courage or do I need to be drunk to hear whatever it is you're going to say?'

'It's to warm us up,' he lied. He needed the Dutch courage. 'C'mon.' He pointed her down the cobbled street to an outside bar. He ordered while Matti found a vacant table under a heat lamp, made cosier still by the chair coverings, thick, snow-coloured fleeces.

'So cosy,' she said, nestling into the chair. She took a big swig of her wine then looked at him. 'Right. Lay it on me.'

He took a drink, then, after a beat, began. 'I was really thrown when you showed up at the hospital. Doubly so to find out we'd be working together.'

She snorted and held up her mug. 'You and me both.'

They clinked.

Felix took another drink then made himself continue. 'As you know, you were the first woman I've been with in a while and I don't think I would've done it—not that it wasn't great—but I don't think I would've done it if I'd known we were going to be working together.'

'Again,' Matti said, 'snap.'

'This isn't a comment on your skills. You're obviously a great doctor. It's more that you're you, you know?'

'I'm not sure,' she said warily.'

'You're this big beaming ray of positivity. Forward-thinking. Dreamscaping. Blue sky thinking—all of those positive things.'

'Like optimism?'

'Like optimism,' he said. 'I guess, knowing that you'd been through something truly awful but had still managed to find a way through it, to stay optimistic…it made me realise that my coping mechanism—shutting people out—wasn't doing what I wanted it to do.'

'Which was…?'

'Making sure I never hurt as badly as I did when I got divorced.' Felix sat back, a bit shell-shocked that he'd said it. 'I presume someone, if not everyone, at the hospital told you I used to be married.'

'They did.' She winced. 'I'm sorry you went through that and I'm sorry I listened to what they said. I don't normally listen to work gossip, but—'

He held up his hands. 'Don't worry. I'm used to it.' He put on a funny voice. 'Don't take his bad mood personally. He's a block of ice that will never melt. It's him, not you. That kind of thing?'

'More or less.'

He shook his head. There was a time when he'd actually liked being described as an impenetrable fortress. Proof, he thought, that he'd wrestled his emotions into submission. But ever since Matti had bounded into his life and showed him how his behaviour affected not only her but his colleagues, he'd realised how unpleasant he must be to work with. And that had to change.

'I wasn't always such a grouch.'

'Break-ups are hard,' she said with an air of understanding.

'They are,' he agreed. 'Especially when you still love the person, but know they'd be better off with someone else.'

She tilted her head to the side, confused.

He told her the basics. He'd married his sweetheart from university. She wanted a family. A big one. Children had always been her number one dream.

'You didn't want them?'

'I did,' he said. 'But, despite trying absolutely everything, we couldn't have them.'

'Do you know why?'

He held up air quotes. 'Unexplained infertility.'

She grimaced. As a doctor, she knew how frustrating that kind of diagnosis could be. They were scientists who liked to believe that if they looked hard enough, they'd find an answer.

'I'm sorry. That must've been awful.'

'It was,' he said. Every time his wife got her period, it was like watching someone's heart break all over again. 'When it became clear that it wasn't going to happen—us having children—she said it didn't matter, but I knew it did. I saw how difficult it was for her to be around my sisters and their children. Her friends who wanted to be "bump buddies".'

Matti shuddered. 'I can't imagine. Did you—' She stopped herself and apologised. 'Sorry, this is your story to tell.'

'Did we consider adoption?'

Matti nodded.

'I would have. She wasn't against it, but what she really wanted was children of her own. As much as she tried to warm to the idea of adopting, it never lit her up, so we didn't pursue it.'

'Did she end the marriage?'

'No.' The word came out harshly, weighted with remorse. 'She did, technically, but the reason she did was because I created an environment that didn't give her much choice.' He stopped, regrouped. 'She is faultless in this. Told me she wouldn't leave me. That we'd muddle through somehow, but I didn't want her to muddle through. It wasn't fair. I'm not proud of the decision I made, and less proud of how I ex-ecuted it, but I knew the only way she would leave me and find someone who she could have children with was if I be-came someone she couldn't love any more.' He explained how he'd turned in on himself, became a workaholic. Partly out of shame that he couldn't give her a child, partly out of a belief that she'd eventually realise 'muddling through' was a far cry from being happy.

He gave his lukewarm wine a swirl, drank some, then looked at Matti to gauge her reaction. To his surprise, her expression wasn't scornful or pitying. It was compassionate.

'I'm so sorry you felt it was your responsibility to give her what she wanted. It must've felt awful becoming someone you don't seem to like very much.'

His throat thickened. She'd nailed it. He wasn't angry at life, or with his wife for leaving. He was angry with himself for not finding a better way out of an extremely complicated situation. Who knew? If he'd handled things differently... He hadn't. Meaning, he'd made his bed so now he had to lie in it.

Matti sat in silence for a few moments, then asked, 'Are you still in love with her?'

'No,' he said. 'I have love for her in my heart, of course. She did nothing wrong.'

'Nor did you,' Matti parried.

'I was cruel.'

'That's hard to imagine,' she said. 'The man I met at Tivoli, the one in the snow globe, I think he's the real you. And even though you're all dark and stormy at work, that other version is still in there. I mean, those rocking chairs, for example. Heartless people do not engage in acts of kindness.'

He gave a humourless laugh. 'That's very generous of you, but I hurt her. And I'll never forgive myself for being cruel.'

'A truly cruel person wouldn't be torturing themselves after giving the woman they loved a choice.'

He shook his head. 'I didn't give her a choice.'

'You did. She was an adult woman. She had a choice. She could have called you on your behaviour. Really worked on the relationship, but instead, she took the key you'd dangled in front of her and left.'

He hadn't thought about it like that before. His sisters had, but no matter which way he turned it over in his head, he knew, deep down, that he bore the blame.

'She did the best she could in a bad situation.'

'Is she happy now?' Matti asked.

'Yes.' She'd met someone shortly after they'd split, had a child nine months later and then, after a year, another.

'And how about you? Are you happy?'

He laughed. 'I can't say I love being the office fun sponge.' Even less so since Matti had come into his life.

She gave him a side eye. 'Felix, can I tell you something?'

He opened his hands. 'Please.'

'You are not a fun sponge.'

He rolled his eyes.

'Don't do that,' she said. 'Diminish yourself. You did what you thought was the right thing. Was it perfect? Maybe not. But what is? It's not like we're born knowing how to handle crises. You were sad after your marriage ended. That's normal. But you don't have to keep punishing yourself for what you think your ex might be thinking about you. Who knows? Maybe she tells everyone you're great.'

He raised his eyebrows at her like, *I doubt that.*

She shrugged. 'For what it's worth, I think you're at a crossroads. The kind where you have to decide if you want to embrace the fun sponge or embrace the fun. And, for the record, I don't think someone who's as awful as you portray yourself would be capable of giving a woman pretty much the best orgasm ever.'

He spluttered his wine.

'Say, "Thank you, Matti", she instructed.

'Thank you, Matti.' He gave her a bashful smile. 'Believe me, the pleasure was all mine.'

'Not all yours,' she riposted. 'That's the point I'm trying to make.' She looked away then back. 'When you left work after our fight, you didn't run off to a cave for some ritualistic self-flagellation or anything. You went to your sisters'. People who I'm guessing know the real you. People who will comfort you, but who have no qualms about giving you guff if they think you've messed up?'

'True,' he said. 'And again. I'm sorry I didn't let you know I was leaving. I should've told you, but I'm used to—'

'Not considering what anyone else thinks?' Matti finished for him. She scrunched her nose. 'Sorry. That was mean.'

'No,' he acquiesced. 'It's fair.'

He'd hurt her. He deserved it. Which was why he'd thought that keeping himself out of her hair for a few days would be a good thing, when actually, what he'd really done was kick the can a bit further down the street.

'It was actually my nephew's birthday. My sister, the one you met, invited me down for a few days to spend time with her and the children. Her way of cornering me into telling her how our night went at Tivoli.'

'That was brave of you to go, then,' she said.

'Well—' he gave a one-shouldered shrug '—it was either an interrogation by my sister or flagellating myself in a cave.'

Matti laughed. 'I hope you didn't feel that bad about our fight.'

'Don't you mean *two professionals offering one another opposing opinions*?'

'Ha!' She swatted the air between them. 'I was having a tantrum. You were right to challenge me.'

'It wasn't a challenge. It was a defence mechanism. If you tell yourself that life is awful long enough, it's no surprise when bad things happen. And when a good thing happens—like meeting an extremely sexy superheroine in a queue for the roller coaster…'

Matti fluttered her lashes at him. 'Please, do go on.'

'Flattery will get me everywhere?'

'Maybe not *everywhere*,' she acquiesced, lips still parted as if she was about to admit to something. He saw her decide against it. 'We were talking about our fight.'

'Disagreement.' He smiled. 'When I got home after work and sat down in front of my defrosted meal for one, I went over it again. Tried to justify my stance as a cynic, then thought: Is this the man you want to be? The example you want to set for your nieces and nephews. Teach them that when life gets tough, the best thing to do is prepare for the worst-case scenario, build a fortress around yourself, then push everyone away instead of admitting that you'd made a mistake.'

'It's tricky terrain,' Matti said. 'Admitting you could be better to the people you love most, knowing they'll hold you to it—scary stuff.'

He tapped his finger on his nose. 'Exactly. My sister told me I was an idiot. Acting like I was special because things hadn't gone my way.'

'Youch,' Matti winced. 'I bet she told you nice things, too.'

She had. But mostly she'd focused on what an idiot he was for not asking Matti out again. The truth was, he didn't know if he trusted himself, which explained why he'd fallen straight into his old pattern of sabotaging something good.

'Anyway, that's my very long-winded way of saying I'm sorry I was a jerk. I'll work on being better.'

'That's very kind,' Matti said. 'And I'll try not to be hyper-sensitive about the *Hygge* Challenge.' She gave him a curious look. 'How was it at your sister's, being with the children?'

'Awkward at first,' he admitted, giving her a rueful smile. 'I think, instead of looking at children as something I'll never have, I need to enjoy the kids who are in my life and the benefit of being able to give them back. Especially when their sugar high is wearing off.'

Matti laughed. 'There's definitely a plus side to being the one who gets to walk away.'

'That sounds like the voice of someone who doesn't want children.'

Her smile faded and, judging by the sadness shadowing the warmth in her eyes, he realised he'd got that very, very wrong.

CHAPTER FOURTEEN

MATTI CONSIDERED LYING. Offering a flippant, *Who knows?* then escaping to the bar for another round. But Felix had been honest with her. She needed to do the same.

'Actually, I always imagined having a big family.' She quickly qualified, 'I probably won't have one, things being what they are, but as an only child, I always loved visiting friends who had lots of siblings. My parents were older when they had me. Quiet. Academics. Happiest reading in front of the fire.' She missed them terribly and was so grateful to have her godmother to give her advice.

She pointed out a family at a nearby table, laughing and teasing one another as they settled in. 'That's what I wanted. Loud. Boisterous. The kind of family that like board games and water balloon fights. Aren't fussed if things get messy.' She became absorbed in watching the family. Smiling as the parents dealt with a squabble over two steaming plates of frites. The father pretended to gobble down the lot. His children begged him to stop, promising to be good, pleaded with their mother to intervene. The mum gave him a playful bat on the shoulder, after which he made a show of dividing them up. The mum dunked one in mayonnaise and offered it to her husband, eliciting another round of laughter when a dollop dropped on his chin.

She started when Felix asked, 'Not met the right guy yet?'

It would be truthful to say no, but again, he deserved an honest answer.

'I thought I had. He was charming, had a good job. A big family who treated me like one of their own. We got engaged. And then, a few months before the wedding, this happened.' She patted her back.

'Were you still working with *Médecins Sans Frontières*?'

'No—' she blew out a puff of air, watched it cloud then dissipate as if to remind herself that nothing was permanent '—I was back in England.' She steadied her breath before continuing. 'I was at my fiancé's flat. We were making brunch for some of his friends, disagreeing over serving platters. I had my back to the gas hob, which was on, and all of a sudden… whooosh! My lovely, floaty, highly inflammatory dress was on fire.'

Felix swore under his breath. 'Terrifying.'

'It was,' she confirmed. 'Chaos. Instead of dropping to the floor—it was wood so, for some reason, I didn't do it.'

'I don't know if I'd be thinking straight either, if I was in your shoes.'

'Well, either way, I ran to the dining room to roll on the carpet.'

'Stop, drop and roll. Smart.'

'Yes, but—' she shook her head '—I hadn't considered the possibility that my fiancé wouldn't want it damaged.'

'What?' Felix stared at her in disbelief. 'I'd have wrapped you in it straight away. Carpets can be replaced.' Felix swore again. 'Forgive me, but that's pathetic. Tell me you ditched him.'

'Nope. It all happened so fast, I guess I hadn't really digested it. I had a lot of time to think about it in hospital, but because saving a carpet would be the last thing on my mind, I spent ages trying to see it from his perspective, to understand how that was more important than the person he wanted to marry.'

'There aren't any reasons,' Felix growled.

'Everyone has a different response to fear. Some freeze. Some run. Others, people who are trained to work in stressful situations, like doctors, dive in to help. He was none of the above.'

Felix shook his head in disbelief. 'Tell me he called the paramedics.'

'He did.' She'd heard him telling the dispatcher that they had to hurry because he didn't 'know what to do about it'. *It.* As if she were a burst pipe or a plugged toilet, destroying the well-laid brunch plans.

'Mercifully, there was a jug of water on the table, so I poured it down my back, doused the flames, got in the shower till they came.' She'd been shaking so hard it had taken three of them to get her out.

Felix looked horrified. 'Did he even try to redeem himself?'

'He came to the hospital a few times, drove me home when I got out. But he broke up with me then. Said I was "too much".'

Felix shook his head in wonder. 'I don't even know what to say. As a man who has made some big mistakes in his time, I can't imagine stooping that low. For what it's worth, sounds like you dodged a bullet. You deserve better.'

Someone like you?

She shook the thought away. They were both healing from big emotional wounds. Not the best of foundations upon which to start a romance. Or was it a more honest way?

'On the plus side,' she said with a cheeky grin, 'all of those weeks in hospital meant I got firsthand experience as a patient. Counting down the seconds until the next busy nurse or doctor came in, checked my chart, asked me how I was from a clinical standpoint versus a proper "How *are* you?" and a chat. I'm not trying to disparage the staff, but it was all really clinical. Maybe because they knew I was a doctor, they thought I didn't need mollycoddling. Or I didn't ask for it because I knew they were busy.'

Felix rubbed his eyes. 'You're still a person, Matti. You should've felt it was okay to let them know how you were feeling. What about your friends?'

'After I got dumped, all I could see was pity in their eyes when they visited. That depressed me even more. I didn't want to be pitied. I wanted to be... I don't know...silly. Watch dumb movies and talk about make-up. Normal. I basically shut them down. Told them I needed me time. So, in some ways, we're birds of a feather. Pushing people away when we needed them the most.'

'All of which led you to *hygge*,' he said.

'Yup. All of which led me to *hygge*.' *And to you, the one person I shouldn't fall in love with.*

Felix tipped his head to the side, cupped his chin, tap, tap, tapped his lips with his index finger. 'If we don't succeed, or the project doesn't turn out how you imagined, how will you handle it?'

'Poorly,' she said through a laugh. 'No. Not true. I'd be disappointed, obviously. But we're only, what? A few days in and we've already got a Knitting Nook.'

Felix smiled. 'True, although if Frida hadn't had that particular accident—'

She cut him off. 'Someone else would've come in and inspired us in a different way. If I understand it properly, *hygge*'s more of a mindset than things. Making sure we're treating the person with what comforts them as well as their symptoms.'

'Cheers to that,' he said, lifting his clay mug to clink it with hers. 'And long may it continue.'

They clinked and smiled at one another, laughed when they realised both of their cups were empty.

'Another round?' he asked.

'I'm okay, thanks,' she said, giving a happy sigh as she looked around at all of the happy faces. 'Now *this* is a moment that belongs in a snow globe.'

Again, that soft smile appeared on his lips. The one that unleashed a spray of sparks. A glittering feeling of...possibility.

They rose but, not trusting herself to resist a goodnight kiss, she said, 'You know, I think I'm going to do a little Christmas shopping for Astrid. You go on. I'll see you at work on Monday.'

He studied her, as if making sure there wasn't something else at play. 'You sure?'

No. She wanted him to stay and to hold hands in the same mitten and kiss by the canals and a thousand other things, but giving in to those feelings could easily derail the *Hygge* Challenge. She couldn't lose both Felix and the project, even though it meant keeping her feelings to herself.

'I'm sure,' she said.

'All right, well, I guess this is goodbye.'

They stared at one another awkwardly. What was she meant to do? Give him a handshake? That felt wrong. He wasn't a hugger. But then, as if to prove her wrong, Felix took a step towards her just as she went in for a fist bump. She grabbed hold of his arms to steady herself, then looked up at him.

A mistake. He was such a beautiful man. More so now that she knew him better. And those lips of his. Just a lift of her heels and she'd be close enough to—

Felix gave her arms a steadying pat then stepped back. 'You have a good night, Matti.' He held out his fist.

Right. They were playing it cool. She bumped it.

The next morning, Matti finished brushing out her hair, twirled it into a messy top bun, inspected her reflection, then did a double take. There was something different about her.

She was smiling.

For far too long the last look she gave the mirror before leaving for work had been a frown or a lacklustre *That'll have to do* shrug.

Today? There was a contentment about her. A confidence that took her by surprise. After Felix had left, she'd poured her pent-up emotion into exploring the Christmas market. Kissing after they'd bared their souls to one another would've been weird. A mantra she'd repeated over and over as she'd weaved her way through all of the loved-up couples enjoying the market, a few of whom were showing off brand-new love mittens.

The friend zone was fine. Better than fine. Admitting to their personal struggles had not only given them a greater understanding of the other, it gave them more room to be human. Flawed, wonderful, stressed, joyful, defensive, vulnerable. The lot.

If she'd kissed him, there was every chance the friendship would implode. Plus, if she had kissed him, one thing would have possibly led to another and then she wouldn't have met all of the delightful craftspeople she'd spoken to. Wooden toy makers, glass blowers, specialist bakers. She'd even met a Father Christmas who had volunteered to visit the emergency centre to hear people's holiday wishes. She'd also found a present for Felix. One she wasn't entirely sure she should give him.

As she rode her bicycle in to work, a flickering of a dream she'd had came back to her. It had been an all too familiar one at first. Her recurring nightmare. The one where she woke up in a dark hospital room, strapped to her bed, alone, no call button, no sounds coming from the dark corridor, apart from the telltale crackle of an encroaching fire. Panicked, she would scream for help, but no sound came out. She kept trying, but no matter how hard she tried, her pleas were voiceless. This time, instead of waking to the dark, clinical room, her eyes had blinked open to find a Christmas tree twinkling away in the corner, bedecked with miniature snow globes. There was a rocking chair beside it. In it, nestled under a blanket, was Felix, dressed as a gonk.

CHAPTER FIFTEEN

DR LARSEN WELCOMED Felix and Matti into her office, offered them the requisite cups of coffee, which they refused,
then settled behind her desk with an expectant smile. 'I hope
the last month has been interesting for you both.'

'Without a doubt,' Felix said, looking to Matti, who gave
an enthusiastic nod of agreement.

Dr Larsen looked pleased. 'It's *Hygge* Hospital launch day
tomorrow. Let's see what you've got lined up.'

Half an hour later their boss sat back in her chair, clearly
delighted with what she'd heard. 'I don't know who's more
excited,' she said, 'the staff or the patients.'

'Hopefully, all of the above,' Felix said, sharing a com-
plicit smile with Matti.

Dr Larsen caught the shared smile and, judging by her expression, was filing it away under Human Resources. 'Are
you both sure you can handle managing it on top of your
regular workload?'

Was that her real question? Or was she asking them if they
were pushing the boundaries of their working relationship
into something far more personal?

'Actually, the way we've set it up means there's not much
for us to do at all. See?' Matti put a folder next to the calendar chart which detailed all of the proposed activities. 'Each
event has a volunteer host. We've put them in touch with the
hospital administration to make sure all of the appropriate

health and safety protocol are in place and that nothing will interfere with regular hospital duties.'

'It looks wonderful,' Dr Larsen said, flicking through the notebook. 'Building a gingerbread village. Wrapping presents. Decorating biscuits. I'm tempted to join in some of them.'

'Please do,' Matti said. 'The more the merrier.'

Dr Larsen smiled and sat back in her chair. 'Tell me, how did you two find working together? Any unexpected hiccups? Problems we should address before things get underway?'

Felix sucked in a breath, not entirely sure how to respond. There had been hiccups along the way. No doubt about it. The odd butting of heads. But once they'd found their stride, coming in to work each morning had begun to feel like waking up on Christmas Day. As if each day held the promise of something to look forward to.

To his surprise, Matti cleared her throat and with a serious expression said, 'There is one problem I'd like to flag.' She threw Felix a look. 'I'm afraid Dr Beck has been incredibly resistant to the suggestion that he wear an elf's costume for the duration of the month.'

Felix disguised a snort of laughter as a cough. This again?

'An elf's costume?' Dr Larsen looked between the pair of them, unsure if it was a joke or an issue Matti was genuinely trying to press.

'She found some holiday-themed scrubs,' he explained, mirroring Matti's serious expression. 'But I felt, as senior resident, dressing as Santa would be more appropriate.'

'Do you see what I've had to put up with?' Matti threw up her hands. '*Hygge* is about community. Not ho-ho hierarchy.'

'I see,' Dr Larsen said carefully, at which point Matti broke character.

'I'm sorry—' she laughed '—I'm being silly.' Matti gave him a quick glance then said, 'Seriously, Felix... Dr Beck has been absolutely brilliant. I'm sure he'll try to deny it, but he's been the real backbone of this project. I can't imagine having done it with anyone else. So thank you for pairing the two of us. I'm sure I don't need to tell you what an asset he is to Copenhagen Central.'

'Quite the high praise, Dr Beck,' said Dr Larsen.

'Matti's being modest.' Felix held up his hand to stem her protests. 'This was her brainchild. All I did was make a spreadsheet.'

'Rubbish!' Matti protested.

'No, seriously. Not just anyone could have spearheaded this project.' He realised, as he spoke, how true the statement was. The enthusiasm she brought to each day was as nourishing as sunlight. 'Dr Meadows has a way of teasing a smile out of the surliest of souls, and I'm including myself in that category. I don't think there's a single person who's come into the emergency centre over the past month who hasn't offered to come back as a volunteer.'

'That's only because you were so good about structuring everything,' Matti countered. 'Felix has turned my envisioned concept into a reality. And, of course, I want to thank you, Dr Larsen, for letting me do this in the first place. It was a risk for you, and I'm forever grateful.'

Dr Larsen took the compliment like a Dane. Awkwardly. 'We'll see what you have to say at the end of December. What about you, Felix? Any surprises along the way?'

Yes. Too many to count. The past month had changed him. The walls he'd built around himself had begun to dissolve. Working with Matti didn't feel like work. Nor did the time they spent out of hours, scouring the city for ideas. Even when they weren't together, he was making notes of things he wanted to tell or show her. They had, he realised, formed a friendship. A relationship step he'd missed with his wife. They'd been friendly, of course, and loved one another. But when things had gone wrong they'd sought comfort elsewhere, as if they no longer trusted one another with their vulnerabilities. He felt as if he could tell Matti just about anything. She always had an interesting, non-judgemental approach, but didn't pull punches either. The difficulty was keeping his attraction to her in check. After the near kiss at the Christmas market, he'd struggled to lay the instincts to rest.

'It's been a real eye-opener,' he said neutrally. 'Seeing *hygge* as an active practice.'

Dr Larsen narrowed her eyes at him, unsatisfied with his vague answer. 'So you think it's been a good use of your time? Hospital resources?'

Felix nodded. 'As you know, I like to question things. What surprised me was how much I questioned myself.'

'How so?'

He glanced at Matti, who looked just as curious as his boss. 'I know children enjoy crafting and decorating biscuits and all that, but I didn't recognise how important it was for adults to take time out to do the same.'

'Don't tell me you've taken up crafting?' His boss looked amused, picturing him, no doubt, wrestling with piles of glitter and a stack of pipe cleaners.

'No,' he admitted. 'But I can confidently say my paper snowflakes have seen improvement.'

She studied him for a moment. 'Did you enjoy it? Making the snowflakes.'

'I—' He had, but mostly because he'd been doing it with Matti. 'Sure.' It wasn't a convincing answer.

Dr Larsen looked at the pair of them, then spread her hands on her desk like a Prime Minister about to lay down the law. 'As you two have clearly devoted a lot of energy into setting this up, I don't want either of you spending any more personal time here at the hospital. Even if it's to decorate biscuits.'

'Oh, I don't think that's possible,' Felix protested at the same time Matti that insisted they needed to be here to oversee the activities.

'It's more than possible. It's mandatory,' Dr Larsen said calmly. 'You've set up a robust infrastructure. I'm sure I don't need to remind you that *hygge* is about taking care of yourselves. There are time limits to the working week for a reason.'

'But—' Matti protested.

Dr Larsen tutted. 'Enough. You've organised everything down to the last letter. If you want to knit or make snowflakes or decorate biscuits on your own, have at it, but only if you're doing it because it's fun.'

'We can do that here—' Felix began.

Dr Larsen held up her hand. 'No. As much as I value you both, I will fire you on the spot if I hear you've come anywhere near the hospital.'

'What if there's an emergency?'

'Felix—' Dr Larsen tsked '—this is an emergency centre. Everything is an emergency. Which is why it's staffed with professionals trained to deal with such matters.'

Matti sent Felix a panicked look. 'What if it's fun to come in?'

'Fired,' said Dr Larsen.

Felix and Matti stared at one another in disbelief. Which was when Felix realised what Dr Larsen already knew. He and Matti were devoting every waking hour to the project not only because they believed in it, but because it meant they got to be together.

Dr Larsen's expression softened. 'I know how much work went into this,' she said. 'That's why I think you'll both benefit from actively practising what you preach.'

Matti opened her mouth to say something but clamped it shut when Dr Larsen's phone rang. She looked at the caller

ID. 'I've got to take this.' She made a shooing gesture. 'Off you go,' she said with a cheery smile, then took her call off hold, making it clear that the discussion was over.

They left the office in silence, each lost in their own thoughts.

When they reached the staff locker rooms Matti turned to him. 'Why does being told to get a life feel like a punishment?'

Because it was. Apart from a freezer burnt dinner waiting to be defrosted, his calendar was wide open. An entire night to decompress from a day's work used to sound like heaven. But he'd grown used to spending his evenings with Matti, assuring one another that, despite the fun they were having, it was work.

'Do you think we're workaholics?' she asked.

'No,' he said, meaning it, then flip-flopping, admitted, 'Maybe? I'd rather be doing something than nothing. Helping people is the only thing that makes me feel good about myself.'

That wasn't true either. Not entirely, anyway. Winning one of Matti's smiles made him feel good. A laugh. Catching himself about to say no to something then changing it to a yes.

'I'm the same,' Matti said forlornly. 'I guess she's saying we need to figure out other ways to feel good about ourselves because that's the ethos we're trying to foster in our patients.'

'It sounds…decadent.'

'It does.' She burst into giggles. 'We're so ridiculous. We just spent an entire month justifying having fun in the name of work but ask us to just have fun? Disaster. Why are we like this?' She searched his eyes for an answer.

Because they wanted to spend time together without admitting that their feelings for one another weren't entirely platonic.

'Well…' he began cautiously. 'Remember when you asked me about addressing the elephant in the room?'

'Yes.' Matti's cheeks pinked. 'But we said we weren't going to do that again. And we're good like this, right? As friends.'

'Yes,' he said slowly. 'But…given that it did happen, and that work kind of requires certain boundaries…'

'Felix,' Matti deadpanned. 'Are you suggesting we couldn't spend one night together as just friends?'

She was pushing the friend zone. He had to respect that. 'We could certainly find out. How about getting some dinner to take away and we could play a board game? Watch a film? How about we invite Astrid?'

She smirked. 'What? To supervise us?'

'Not at all,' he lied. 'We're friends, right? We don't need supervision.'

They did. They most definitely did. The air between them crackled with electricity. He wanted to kiss her. He should kiss her. He reached out and brushed his fingers against hers. Her breath hitched. Yes. Decision made. He was going to kiss her.

His phone pinged with a text, breaking the spell.

Matti took a step back. 'You get that. And look, I should probably check in on Astrid. We have spent a lot of time working on the project, so…'

He took out his phone and scanned the text. 'It's my sister. A threatening reminder about *Julemiddag*.'

'Sounds scary,' Matti said.

'Sometimes,' he admitted. 'It's the family dinner I told you about. The one we have on December first to mark Advent. They're putting up the tree.'

'Ooh. That actually sounds fun.' She glanced at the locker room door as if she was suddenly itching to get away. 'Look. You've clearly got stuff on, so let's forget about tonight. Rain check?'

'Why don't you come tomorrow?' he asked on impulse. 'To my sister's? She's a great cook.'

'Oh, no.' She shook her head. 'It sounds like a family only thing. I'm sure I'll be doing something with Astrid. It's her first without Oskar.'

'Bring her with you,' he said, unexpectedly excited by the idea of bringing her home to meet his bonkers family. 'Astrid's more than welcome.'

She hesitated, tempted. 'I wouldn't want to impose.'

He laughed. 'I promise you, my sister would love it.' *So would I.*

'Let me ask Astrid.' She tapped out a text, stopping to ask, 'Would we need to bring anything?'

'Solveig always makes more than enough but…' Felix scanned the text again. 'How about a sweet of some sort? Holiday biscuits?'

'I'll just ask…' Matti typed some more then gave a satisfied nod after the telltale whoosh sound. 'Meet in Reception for an update?'

'You got it.' As he got his things together in the locker room, he caught his colleagues giving him some strange looks. He was about to ask why when he realised he'd been whistling a Christmas carol. He hadn't whistled in years.

Ten minutes later, Felix entered the reception area and found Matti admiring a multicoloured scarf that a young boy was knitting with a volunteer. She looked up and smiled. 'Look at this.'

He was happy enough looking at her, but, as ever, Matti's infectious enthusiasm drew him in. He oohed and aahed at the boy's efforts. It was more of a series of knots and holes than a scarf, but he looked so proud Felix gave him a round of applause.

'He's going to knit a dinosaur into the pattern if he's here long enough,' Matti explained, giving a wink to the woman who'd been helping him.

'And a heart,' the little boy added.

Felix admired the lad's optimism. It struck him that his invitation to Matti was similar. Meeting his family could easily send her running for the hills, but there was a chance, however slight, that she'd see yet another side of him. One that might clarify the friend zone conundrum.

'It's looking good,' Felix said to the boy. 'Are you going to wear it to school?'

'No, it's for my mum. She can wrap it around her ankle to make it heal faster.'

Matti explained that the boy's mother had been wheeling the family's Christmas tree home on her bicycle, hadn't seen a kerb and had taken a bad fall. A passing driver had seen the incident and had brought them here.

'Quick, hide it,' Matti whispered to the boy. 'Your mum's coming.'

'*Mor!*' He raced over to a woman being pushed in a wheelchair by a porter. She had a blonde pixie cut, a bright red coat and a matching red walking boot that went up to her knee. Her son excitedly showed her his handiwork.

Felix's chest tightened, part pain, part joy. The mum admired the truly awful scarf, wrapped it around her neck even though one end was still attached to a needle, then realised her mistake and put it round her ankle.

The porter wheeled her over to the Knitting Nook, where she thanked the woman who'd been helping him.

'*Mor?*' The little boy tapped his mum's arm as the volunteer discreetly whipped the scarf into a more serviceable condition. 'When are we coming back? I need to finish my project.'

She threw the group a disbelieving look like, *What have you done to him?* She said she had to come back in a couple of days to ensure the fracture in her foot was being properly supported by the boot. He clapped his hands and asked the volunteer if she'd be there.

'I won't, but one of my friends will be here. If you bring your project back, we'll help you get it just right for Christmas.'

After another round of thanks they left, and Matti warmly thanked the volunteers, impressed not only by their teaching skills but by their generosity in looking after the woman's son while she was seen by the doctor.

'I've never done a dinosaur scarf before,' the volunteer said, clearly excited at the prospect.

After wishing them a good night, Matti virtually skipped out to the bike rack. 'How wonderful was that?'

'Pretty wonderful,' Felix said, willing the knot in his chest to loosen. Maybe inviting Matti and Astrid to his sister's hadn't been such a good idea after all. There was a reason she'd resisted discussing being anything but friends. It hit him like a ton of bricks. He'd never be able to give her the family she'd said she wanted.

Matti's phone pinged. 'Ah!' she said after reading the message. 'Astrid says she'd love to come, but on one condition.'

'What's that?' Maybe it would save both of them the embarrassment of cancelling.

Matti gave him a hybrid grin, part apologetic, part hopeful. 'She wants us to come to her house tonight to help her and her bestie decorate biscuits.' Her forehead crinkled into an adorable pleat of hope as she batted her eyelashes at him. 'Please come.'

A sweetener to soften the blow?

'Pretty please?'

As if had the power to say no.

CHAPTER SIXTEEN

MATTI PUT DOWN the empty piping bag and shook her wrists out. 'Oof! And here I was thinking a three-hour surgery was tough!'

Felix gave her a look that said he was feeling it too. 'Better not tell Dr Larsen.'

They giggled like naughty schoolchildren.

Astrid's girlhood friend Yrsa, a feisty, sparkly-eyed cellist with a thick plait curled round her head, frowned when she realised they'd put down their piping bags. She'd been there since morning, had been baking with Astrid all day, and hadn't stopped moving since they'd arrived.

At a rough guess, they'd decorated about ten dozen biscuits and, after some training, had also helped put together some *julehjerte småkager*, heart-shaped biscuits that had the same tell-tale 'weave' as the paper Christmas tree decorations that had inspired them. The bonus, of course, being that these were edible.

Matti spied one that had lost a corner. 'I'm going to save the aesthetics of the table by taking this one out of action,' she announced, wondering, as she took a bite of the soft, sugary treat, how she could still be hungry after eating several of the open-faced mini sandwiches Astrid had made for them.

She munched away, admiring their handiwork. The gingerbread biscuits were gorgeous. Snowflakes, mittens, Santa and elf hats, holiday jumpers and, of course, miniature Christmas trees.

'Astrid—' Felix held up a Christmas tree biscuit he'd just finished decorating '—I'm embarrassed to include this one.'

'If you're asking permission to eat it,' she said, 'permission granted.'

Felix didn't need telling twice.

It was obvious that Astrid was the artist amongst them. Her biscuits were decorated with precision and delicacy, to the point that the miniature sweaters and mittens looked real.

Felix's, on the other hand, did not. Nor did Matti's, to be fair.

'I'll never be as good as you are, Astrid.'

Her godmother clucked. 'It's just practice is all.'

'No,' Matti corrected. 'You and Yrsa have a gift. I can't believe you made all of these in one day.'

'Pfft,' Yrsa dismissed the compliment. 'This is nothing. You should've seen what we used to do a few years back. We would've done five, ten times this amount.'

Matti made bowing gestures to show how impressed she was. A brightly coloured tin of Astrid's biscuits had been a mainstay of her childhood, but she'd never been here to help make them. So much work! A rush of emotions hit her as she remembered how excited she'd been as a little girl when she'd come home from school and spied the brown wrapped box with string around it, addressed to her in Astrid's equally beautiful calligraphy.

Felix debated doing another, then decided against it and stretched out his palms. 'We should've started training back in November.'

Matti guffawed. 'I don't think any amount of training would have us on the same level.'

Astrid rose to put on the kettle and clucked. 'You two have other talents. I faint at the first sign of blood.'

Matti climbed out from the cushioned bench she'd been sitting on and gave her godmother a hug from behind. 'Don't you worry, oh, godmother of mine. I'll be your nurse whenever you need me. I can't guarantee the catering will be as good…'

Her godmother patted her arm and tipped her head to Matti's. 'That's a lovely offer, but remember, you've got that job in Cambridge to think about.'

Felix frowned. 'What job is that?'

'Oh—' Matti batted it away, realising her time here had diminished her desire to get it, to the point that if Astrid hadn't brought it up, she wouldn't have remembered at all '—a pie-in-the-sky job. I'll never get it.'

'What is it?' he pressed.

Not close enough to you. She told him about the job, adding, 'Total long shot.'

Lead research clinician for emergency medicine at a university hospital. It was the type of dream job that, for someone like her, would lift her career to another level.

'They'd be foolish not to consider you,' he said.

Did he want her to go?

She gave a nervous laugh. 'I'll probably be begging Dr Larsen for an extension to my contract here.'

Felix echoed her laugh and Astrid tutted. 'Don't sell yourself short, darling. You've worked hard and deserve whatever job you wish.'

Matti could tell what Astrid was really saying. She didn't have to feel obliged to care for her in the coming years. It didn't sit well. Even though she knew her godmother had a large group of friends, Astrid was family to Matti. The instinct to say she'd be here for her was heartfelt. But was it realistic?

'Well, I haven't heard anything yet, so, like I said, it was a long shot.' She gave her godmother a tight hug.

Astrid gave Matti's hand a pat then adopted her loving but decisive Danish tone. 'Let go of me, Matti. I don't need pushing round in a wheelchair just yet. Let me get this tea ready, will you?'

Matti planted a sloppy kiss on her cheek, then, after stifling an unexpected yawn, followed Astrid's instructions about which cups to bring to the table.

When she sat back down, Felix threw her a questioning smile. He'd been thrown by the information and, if she was reading him right, was unsettled by it.

'Honestly,' she said as if the whole thing was a misunderstanding, 'I'll never get it.'

'Here we are.' Astrid carried over the pot and poured fresh mint tea into grey-blue mugs that matched the sturdy ceramic pot. 'Felix.' She handed him a cup, pausing a moment to look at him after he'd accepted it. 'The ceramic glaze matches your eyes.'

'Glazed?' he joked, then apologised. 'Thank you. If it was a compliment.'

Matti laughed. 'You Danes are so terrible at accepting compliments.'

'Is that so?' Astrid replied, handing her a steaming mug. 'If I remember correctly, the English aren't exactly known for it either.'

'Well…' Matti floundered '… England isn't *that* far from Denmark.' She put the mug down and covered her mouth to stifle another yawn. 'Gosh, sorry—' she shook her head '—I don't know why I'm so tired all of a sudden.'

'You've had a long day,' Astrid said, then tipped her head at Felix. 'The both of you.'

They looked at one another for evidence. In this light, his eyes did match the blue-grey pottery. Thoughtful. Considered. And decisive. As if he was ready to call it a night. She stifled another yawn.

'Right, ladies.' Felix rose. 'I'm going to take that as my cue to leave Goldilocks to get to her bed. Unless—' he looked round the kitchen '—is there anything I can do to help clean up?'

'Yes,' Matti said through yet another yawn, 'please, put us to work.'

'No, no.' Astrid smiled at Yrsa. 'We've got our system. You two will only get in the way.'

Felix laughed. 'You sound like my mother.'

'A woman who knows her kitchen?'

'Yes. Tomorrow will be tricky for her as she'll be in my sister's kitchen. I hope you don't mind fireworks.'

Astrid smiled at him. 'I'm sure it will be a lovely evening, fireworks included. Thank you for including us in it. It'll be nice to share *julemiddag* with a family.'

'You might not be saying that after you meet them,' Felix joked. 'Yrsa, you're welcome to join us, too.'

Matti's heart swelled at the invitation. He had such a big heart. Not seeing him every day would take some getting used to.

Yrsa was clearly not under the same spell. She refused him with a curt, 'I don't like children. Grown ones, like you, I can take. But anything under the age of sixteen…?' She gave a dramatic shudder then swiftly put a tin of biscuits together and handed it to Felix. 'For the journey home.'

Astrid gave Matti one as well, kissed her on the cheek, then said to Felix, 'I hope you'll do the gentlemanly thing and see my goddaughter reaches her front door safely.'

He held up his fingers as if he was taking an oath. 'I promise to deliver her home safely.'

When their eyes met, she still saw that hint of sadness in them. They put on their coats and Matti had to laugh when Astrid and Yrsa began fussing over Felix's lack of a scarf. He insisted he was fine, but they overruled him.

This, Matti, thought as Astrid wrapped one of Oskar's

scarves around Felix's neck, tweaking it this way and that before giving his lapels a satisfied pat. *This is hygge.*

She knew that for a fact. What she didn't know was how to define what she felt for Felix. Something told her she'd figure it out soon enough. Maybe, she thought, after another awkward fist bump at her door, she'd find out sooner if she found some mistletoe.

CHAPTER SEVENTEEN

FELIX BEGAN TO feel stupidly nervous when, after a lovely drive, his sister's house came into view. 'Here we are.'

'Oh, wow.' Matti sat up straighter. 'It's beautiful.'

'Yes,' he said, but he wasn't talking about the house. Matti was glowing today. She'd put it down to a good night's sleep, but there was something else he couldn't put his finger on. He'd miss her when she left. Much more than he cared to admit.

He'd wondered if her sudden spate of yawning was a cover. A way to dodge answering more questions about this mystery job in Cambridge, but when he'd walked her home she'd seemed genuinely tired. He'd read too much into it. It had been an uncomplicated evening with good food, lively conversation and plenty of laughter. It shouldn't have been a surprise to hear she'd applied for another job. Her contract would be finished in thirty days. Too soon, he'd thought as he'd ridden his bicycle home past the places he wanted to show her.

Agnete and the Merman beneath the Højbro Bridge. The library at Copenhagen University. An astronomical clock set to run for another two thousand years. A museum exhibit about nose shapes. His favourite *smørrebrød* stall, which only opened in the summer months and, of course, Sankt Peders Bageri, the country's oldest bakery, which still sold 'Wednesday snails'—the world's best cinnamon rolls.

When he'd arrived at his flat, a place he'd long considered

his refuge from the world, he saw it for what it was. A soulless set of rooms. Three years he'd lived there, and there wasn't one thing that made the place distinctive to him. He'd slept poorly and, having risen early, went to his favourite bakery to get pastries and speciality coffees for the ride.

They had chatted away throughout the journey, skipping about from one topic to the other. The car was filled with the rich piney scent of the Advent wreath Astrid had made for his sister, correctly assuming he wouldn't have made one of his own. And, of course, there was a stack of tins filled with delicious biscuits.

Inviting Matti to his sister's had seemed a great idea at the time, but today, knowing in his heart that Matti would never consider him partner material, he was regretting it. His sisters and mother did not understand the concept of an inside voice.

And as if they'd been lying in wait, the three women burst through the front door and launched themselves at the car.

His sisters bypassed him entirely, pulling open the car doors, peppering Matti and Astrid with so many questions they barely had time to answer one before another landed.

'Felix!' His mother spread her arms wide for a hug then, seeing the women had gathered at the back of the car to unload the gifts Astrid and Matti had brought, released him, gave his arm a swat and said, 'Why aren't you helping your guests? I raised you better than that.' He turned to help, only for her to grab his arm and yank him back to her side. She nodded at Matti. 'I understand your sister did some match-making.'

The night at Tivoli.

'She did.' He'd leave it at that.

'Looks as though she did a good job.'

'Matti's… Yes…' He stopped, not wanting to go there. 'Solveig did a good job.'

'And the intimacy. How is she in bed?'

He cringed. 'She's called Matti, Mum.'

'Matti,' she repeated slowly, as if she was tasting something new she wasn't sure about, then deciding it met with her approval, smiled. 'She looks vital. I hope the two of you are having lots of sex.'

He scrubbed the back of his neck. *And so it begins.*

His mother, a sex therapist, had never shied away from quizzing her children about their sex lives. She'd been very supportive when he and his ex had been trying to conceive and upset, of course, when his marriage had ended, but had been uncharacteristically silent in the aftermath. He'd anticipated the opposite—being drilled with questions, asked for proof that he'd done everything possible to save his marriage. But she had never pressed. Or maybe, the thought occurred, he'd been deft enough to dodge an interrogation.

'Well?' She gave him a nudge with her elbow. 'She's very pretty. Is she good in bed? Anything you want to talk through?'

He gave her a quick hug. 'No, Mum. Thanks for the offer.' He considered asking her to keep her questions family-friendly for the rest of the day, especially as Matti's godmother was here, but this was the woman who'd subjected him to the most embarrassing puberty ever. Handing him condoms in front of girlfriends, telling them to be safe, suggesting which sex toys to try if they were finding orgasm difficult. She was also the woman who'd taught him never to judge a person by their appearance. Bodies, she said, came in all shapes and sizes. But they all had one thing in common, a need to be touched. She wasn't wrong. The night he'd spent with Matti had been as curative for him as she'd said it had been for her. Though they'd decided to keep their relationship platonic, he had struggled with it. Touching her, holding her, kissing her, it had felt so right. So natural.

'She looks like a Viking princess. No, Freyja.' His mother

gave him a playful nudge. 'Especially with that marvellous hair of hers.'

Freyja, definitely. The goddess associated with a ream of attributes: love, beauty, fertility, sex, gold, magic.

'You must come to me if you need any help with your sex life.' His mother arched a knowing eyebrow. 'I'm assuming you're a bit rusty in that department.'

No answer was answer enough. Before she could quiz him further, his sister Solveig released a piercing whistle that would have dogs howling in the North Pole. A stream of nephews and nieces poured out of the house and crowded around the car, where they were each assigned a package to bring into the house.

His mother, unfortunately, wasn't distracted enough to drop the subject. 'There's nothing to be ashamed of if you're struggling, Felix. She's a doctor, right. She'll know that penises don't always perform on command.'

'My penis is doing just fine, thanks, Mum.'

A glint of satisfaction lit her eyes. He would never play poker with his mother.

'Will you be bringing her for Christmas Eve?'

'Mum, it's not like that. We work together. Her contract ends at the end of the month.'

His mother shrugged as if that was by the by. 'Contracts can be extended, sweetheart. Especially if there's a good reason to stay.'

'It's a work relationship,' he reiterated, not sure if he was saying it for her benefit or his.

'I met your father at work. And if she's not a prospect, a short contract might be a blessing in disguise. You don't have the pressure of pretending it's not a rebound.'

'Mum!' he growled. 'If I want dating advice, I'll ask for it.'

'Oh, darling,' she said. 'No, you won't. You're too private. Luckily, you have a very nosy mother to help. Since your time together is limited, you should be having sex around the clock. I'm sure your sister wouldn't mind if you used one of the rooms—'

'Hi.' Matti appeared in front of them as his sisters swept Astrid up the path to the white clapboard house.

She gave them a cautious smile. 'Sorry, am I interrupting a private conversation?'

'Not at all,' they both said, but for different reasons.

'Matti, this is my mother, Karolin.'

'Pleased to meet you, Mrs Beck. Mathilde Meadows.'

His mother repeated her name as she had earlier, but this time as if savouring a chocolate. 'Please, call me Karolin.'

'Thank you, Karolin. It's nice to meet you. Astrid, my godmother—we're so touched to be included in your family gathering.'

'Of course. Any friend of our Felix is welcome.'

Felix was about to usher them in, hoping a group setting would curtail his mother's urges to quiz Matti about their sex life, when Matti said, 'Karolin, I thought you should know, your son's penis is in excellent working order. I hope that alleviates any concerns you might have.'

Felix was speechless. What had possessed her to say such a thing? He looked at the house and saw his sisters giggling in the doorway. Question answered.

'I'm delighted to hear it. Thank you, dear, for being so frank.' She shot Felix a look like, *See? It's that easy.*

'Pleasure.' Matti gave them both a bright smile. 'Also, as I was raised in the UK and I am half English, from this point on I'm going to pretend this conversation never happened.' She was still smiling, but the message was clear. The topic was closed for discussion.

Bravo, Matti. He'd never seen anyone shut his mother down with such charm. If they were a couple—

They weren't, he reminded himself sternly. *So stop living in the land of 'what if'.*

'Right you are, love.' Felix's mum hooked her arm through Matti's. 'Let's get you in out of the cold and you can tell me all about this *hygge* project of yours.'

Matti threw Felix a look as they set off and mouthed, *'Sorry. Your sisters made me!'* But the sparks of gold lighting up her eyes weren't from the setting sun. She was enjoying herself. So different from his ex, who had always felt visiting his family was akin to enduring an inquisition.

A penny dropped.

His mother hadn't pressed him about his failed marriage because she'd seen the writing on the wall long before he had. Infertility or no, the marriage had never been destined for success.

CHAPTER EIGHTEEN

MAYHEM. IT WAS the only word Matti could think of to describe the atmosphere. Not to the point it was chaotic. More a giddy buzz of excitement and activity.

The sun was setting beyond the large picture windows looking out over a lawn that sloped down towards the beach, giving everything a gold-tinted lustre.

Each of the rooms she'd caught glimpses of as they'd ushered her into Solveig's large, sprawling home looked inviting—big cushiony sofas, perfectly worn leather armchairs, swags of evergreen draped along the wooden stairwell and a picture-perfect tree which Felix's seven nieces and nephews were decorating with strings of Danish flags and other homemade decorations.

It was picture perfect but, more importantly, it felt like a home. Welcoming in a way that had instantly made her feel at ease. They weren't at all like her ex's family, also picture perfect but very aware of maintaining a particular type of decorum, to the point she'd always felt that being on her best behaviour outweighed having fun.

The family were genuine straight-talkers, offering an honesty they expected in return. Which was why, when his sisters had pounced on her and Astrid upon their arrival, they'd said she should be herself, no pretence allowed, particularly with their mother.

'Sorry about all of this,' Felix said, having gently extracted himself from a tangle of nieces and nephews begging him to help with the tree.

'No apologies necessary,' she assured him. 'I feel like I've just entered Christmas land.'

He laughed. 'They take the country's passion for the holidays to another level.'

'I like it. It's a good level.'

'Drinks are help yourself,' Solveig called from the open-plan kitchen. 'Dinner won't be long.'

'How about a drink?' Felix asked. '*Gløgg?*'

She shook her head, stomach churning at the thought of alcohol. 'Just a soft drink, if that's all right.'

'No problem.' He leant in and conspiratorially said, 'I wouldn't blame you if you wanted something stronger.'

'I feel tipsy without the benefit of alcohol,' she said truthfully as two of Felix's nephews raced between them.

'You and me both.' He laughed, then paused, his expression sobering as if he'd seen something that concerned him. 'Are you feeling all right?'

'Absolutely.' She lowered her voice. 'I hope that was okay, me saying what I did to your mum.'

He laughed, embarrassed. 'It was perfect. Just enough information to stop my mother from asking for a blow-by-blow account over supper.'

Matti did a 'phew' swipe across her forehead, relieved, but after he'd excused himself to get their drinks, she wondered if he'd invited her here to act as a kind of beard. A 'show and tell' exhibit for his family to prove he had a love life.

He didn't strike her as someone who played those kinds of games, especially without warning. Paranoia, she decided, dismissing the notion. She crossed to the wood stove, a chic inset where flames danced away behind a clear glass window.

Despite the nature of her accident, she had always loved fires and this one, complete with an aesthetically pleasing pile of logs on the hearth, had the added warmth of being surrounded by scores of black and white family photos, all taken by the same person, judging by the style. Whether it was a group photo or a solo shot, the photographer had a way of capturing the subject's mood to great effect. Anticipation, joy, hilarity. It was a wall of happiness.

'Welcome to the madhouse,' a rich male voice sounded beside her. One that had to be related to Felix.

Matti turned and smiled. The voice belonged to a tall, lean silver fox with a hint of sea captain's aesthetic about him. He had a white, tidily trimmed beard speckled with hints of gold and a thick thatch of hair on top. He was looking at the photographs with an affectionate smile. When he turned to her, she started. 'Gosh. Now I know where Felix got his eye colour.'

He smiled and held out his hand. 'Jakob. Felix's father.'

She shook his hand and introduced herself.

Karolin appeared with a tray covered in delicious-looking canapés. 'Take several,' she encouraged. 'Solveig will only believe it's delicious if this platter comes back empty.'

Matti laughed, took a serviette and selected a trio of canapés.

'Is that it?' Jakob said, narrowing his eyes to inspect her. 'You're not one of these dieters, are you?'

'Oh, no,' Matti assured him, then, to prove it, took a miniature choux bun filled with sour cream and topped with a mini mountain of caviar and popped it into her mouth before adding another one to her serviette.

'That's better.' He smiled, barely managing to take some for himself before his wife swept off to the next group. Matti looked round, hoping Felix hadn't forgotten to bring her something to drink. The canapé, which looked delicious, had a strange metallic aftertaste. She'd had similar canapés before, but the aftertaste was new. Maybe it was a clash with the mint she'd had earlier in the car. An anomaly, no doubt.

'These are wonderful photos,' Matti said, turning her attention back to the wall. 'Did you take them?'

'No, Felix did.'

'Really? That surprises me,' she said without thinking. 'I mean, I thought…' She scanned the photos again. 'You're not in a lot of them, so I just assumed you were the one behind the camera.'

'I'm like my son,' he said, as if her mistake had been perfectly natural. 'We enjoy observing rather than being observed.' His smile faded as his eyes moved from photo to photo. 'We both spend too much time at work. I don't know what you did to get him out of Copenhagen, but thank you for bringing him back to us.'

'Me? Coming here was very much Felix's idea.'

Jakob made a 'suit yourself' smile that said she hadn't persuaded him.

Dana joined them. 'Felix has a good eye, doesn't he?'

'Very much so,' Matti agreed. She considered his father's comment about Felix being an observer. It made sense. Felix managed the emergency centre as if he had two lenses. One on the big picture, another homing in on the smallest of details. Even if he was busy with a patient he had a sixth sense for knowing when the staff needed more support or if something had been unwittingly overlooked in a patient's care.

No wonder he'd balked when he'd been told he'd be working with Matti. Their one-night stand aside, she'd swept into his life like a hurricane, all bright-eyed and bushy-tailed, gunning to shake up his well-ordered world. Like a child, she thought, shaking a snow globe.

As she'd told Dr Larsen, he had an instinctive ability to create order from chaos. Emergency physicians had to be the calm in the eye of countless storms and Felix embodied that ethos. But something told her it was a different story when it came to his personal life. He wouldn't have tried to impose order on his wife but, she realised, he could impose it on himself, compartmentalising as much as he could in an effort to do the right thing.

'Where was this one taken?' Matti pointed at a large family photo taken in front of a quaint wooden beach house. The house was smaller and more rustic-looking than this one, fronted by a large covered outdoor porch that particularly appealed to her.

'Zealand,' he said. 'Felix's summer hideaway. My father's originally,' he explained. 'I passed it on to him when he married because the girls here weren't as keen as he was.'

'We like indoor plumbing, Father,' Dana said dryly. Then, to Matti, 'Felix is such a nerd, he was the only one of us willing to learn the local dialect.'

'Who's that?' Matti asked, pointing at a woman with dark hair.

'His ex-wife,' Jakob said.

Matti leaned in, curious. She saw a pretty twenty-something woman looking at Solveig, who was cuddling a baby. The wistful look in her eyes was almost haunting.

'Never really found her footing with us,' Jakob said.

She looked kind, with dark brown eyes that matched her hair, which she wore loose over her shoulders.

'I don't know why we keep that one up,' Dana said. 'She let Felix take all the blame for their divorce.'

Jakob excused himself, clearly not interested in ex-wife bashing. 'I'm going to top up my wine. Matti? Would you like some?'

She explained that Felix was getting her a drink and, despite herself, hoped his sister would continue. She wasn't disappointed.

'You know about their fertility issues, right?' Dana asked.

'Yes. It sounded very difficult.'

'For Felix, yes. And her. But she let him think it was all his fault.'

Matti frowned. 'He said it was unexplained fertility.'

'Exactly. But she was obsessed. Too much. Told him he wasn't eating enough walnuts, was riding his bicycle too much. Made him take every test imaginable. No saunas, baths, laptops, sitting, tight trousers.' She rolled her eyes. 'She even bought him a fan to, you know…' She waved her hand below her waist.

'Keep his testicles cool?'

'Yes, exactly. She couldn't see that she was piling so much pressure on him, of course they weren't going to get pregnant.' Dana shook her head and glared at the photo, then softened. 'She was a nice woman really, in a bad situation, but, as Felix's sister, I'll never forgive her for letting him shoulder the blame for their marriage ending.'

'He told me she wanted to make it work, that he was the one who withdrew.'

His sister shook her head. 'Nonsense. Felix is the type of man who wants the people he loves to be happy. He will do whatever it takes to make it so, even if it destroys him. She knew that about him and, even so, she let him fall on his sword. It's only now, in the past month, he's begun to come back to us. Something tells me it's you who's made that happen.'

Matti didn't feel right taking the credit, even as she rearranged the pieces of information Felix had given her with this new insight. In Felix's version of the same story, he was the one who had been the so-called bad guy. It made her wonder if he'd told himself this because he'd been so disappointed that he hadn't been able to give his wife what she wanted that he'd felt diminished as a man. That he wasn't worthy of her love. Her heart broke for him. She felt awful for ever thinking he was anything like her ex.

Matti pointed at another photo where, beneath a pile of children, she could just make out Felix's smile. It was actually one she'd never seen in real life.

'He'd make such a great father,' his sister said with a sigh. 'I wish he hadn't convinced himself this whole thing with his ex was a sign from above that he wasn't worthy.'

'What do you mean?'

'I mean—' Dana glanced across the room, checking that she could speak freely. 'After the divorce, Felix just withdrew from us. The kids mostly. He used to look after them all the time, but after his break-up it was like he didn't trust himself with them any more. Quick. Laugh like I've just told a really funny joke. He's coming.'

Matti did as she was instructed, but the laugh must've sounded weird because as she watched Felix approach, all she could think was, *I'd make babies with you. I think you'd be a great father.*

'Here's your drink, Matti. Sorry about the wait.' Felix held out a glass filled with a bubbly red liquid.

'Thanks.' She took the drink and beamed at him like someone who knew a very special secret. And, in a way, she supposed she did. Thanks to his sister, she saw him in an entirely new light now. He *was* kind to the core. Selfless. And he'd hidden that big heart of his behind a shield of cool aloofness to protect himself from being that vulnerable again. Maybe he feared he would never be 'enough' for someone.

You're enough, she thought. *You're more than enough.*

'What?' He drew back, nervous. 'Why are you looking at me like that?'

'I was just marvelling at what a good photographer you are,' she said.

Felix glanced at the photo she and Dana were standing in front of and quickly looked away. 'Cranberry and soda. Is that all right?'

'Perfect.' *Just like you.* She held it up. 'The mint sprig's a nice touch. Very festive. Thank you for making the effort.'

He smiled tentatively, bemused that she was looking at him like a love-struck teenager.

'That would be Solveig's doing. It wouldn't have occurred to Felix,' Dana cut in like a true older sister. Heralding her brother's merits one minute, disparaging them another. 'Enjoy it while you can. She puts everyone to work eventually.'

'Dana!' Solveig called from the kitchen. 'Come here. I need your help with the potatoes.'

Dana shot her a smile like, *See? Do I know my siblings or what?*

She knew more about Felix than Matti did, that was for sure.

A few minutes later they were called to the table, where Astrid's Advent wreath took pride of place. The youngest child was asked to light the candle, a tall creamy column with numbers running up the side to signify the countdown to Christmas.

Though Solveig and her husband sat at either end of the long wood-planked table, it was Jakob who invited everyone to join hands for grace. Matti bowed her head as he gave a simple but heartfelt prayer of thanks for the meal they were about to eat and the health they all enjoyed. As one, they said 'Amen', at which point the calm, centred moment of gratitude gave way to a lively exchange of plates and excited chatter.

'What's this one?' Matti asked Felix when he handed her yet another serving dish.

'Curried herring.'

'Oh, wow. That sounds interesting.' She dipped her head to smell the mix of spices, but the moment the scent hit her nose she wished she hadn't made such a show of enthusiasm. Knowing it would still be sitting on her plate at the end of the meal, she waited until Felix turned away to pass the serving plate to Astrid. Unlike Matti, Astrid inhaled the aromatic dish as if it was ambrosia and forked some onto her plate as the young girl next to her quizzed her about being a potter.

'Curried herring's not for everyone,' Felix said, glancing at her plate before offering her another tray. More herring. Pickled, she guessed as the light sting of vinegar hit her nostrils. Again, her stomach made it clear it wasn't interested.

Felix noticed. 'You don't need to try all the dishes. Just take what you like.'

She gave him a grateful smile. Her ex would've insisted she took some, that it would be rude not to.

'Thank you,' she said in a small voice, relieved to see the next platter was loaded with miniature open-faced sandwiches with a variety of toppings her stomach didn't object to.

The evening swept by in a happy blur, one conversation leapfrogging to the next until eventually it was time to make their excuses and head back to Copenhagen.

Astrid fell asleep almost instantly, tucked up beneath a blanket Karolin had insisted she take.

Felix was quiet but not withdrawn as they drove back. He'd put some soft music on the radio. Now that she understood him better, Matti wasn't fretting about what he might be thinking and enjoyed the quiet ride as much as the lively chatter they'd left behind.

It had been a lovely evening with a wonderful family. She said as much when Felix dropped them off, each with a bag of leftovers his sister had insisted they take.

Tucked in bed, she closed her eyes, trying to preserve the memories, unable to pinpoint the one thing that had literally unsettled her. Her stomach. She normally wasn't so fussy trying new foods. Nerves, she decided. Or hormones. Her period was due around now and sometimes she craved one thing and not another. Explanation enough to allow her to set it aside and drift off to sleep.

CHAPTER NINETEEN

Felix scanned the patient file he'd just been handed. Laceration to the neck. He headed straight in. 'Mr Hendriksen—' He kept his expression neutral, but his brain went into overdrive.

'Hey, Doc.' The man gave him a cheery wave despite the blood-soaked cloth he held pressed to the side of his neck. 'No need to be formal. Call me Lucky.'

Ice hockey players were a breed of their own.

'Lucky because that cloth you're holding isn't on your jugular vein.'

'Got it in one. Close, though. Cut-throat game,' he said. 'Or cut neck in this case.' He guffawed at his own joke.

Felix glanced at the chart again. Ullr Hendriksen. The name didn't ring any bells, but the fact he liked ice hockey meant his parents had named him well. As a teenager, Felix would've known whether his patient was on a professional team but, like so many things in the last few years, attending hockey matches had fallen by the wayside.

'Who won?' he asked as he pulled on a pair of gloves.

'Training match. No winners, but if I had to pick, my team.' Ullr gave him a gap-toothed grin—evidence this wasn't his first hockey injury.

'Anyone have a look at this at the rink?'

'Nah. It's just a scratch. One of the lads glued it up but...' He gave Felix a knowing wink. 'We had a birthday party to celebrate after and the old schnapps goggles made me run into a wall.'

'Schnapps goggles have a way of doing that,' Felix said dryly, getting a heady whiff of the herbs and spices that scented the strong alcoholic drink. 'I'm going to put the exam chair back a bit so I can see how lucky you were.'

He held a few pieces of gauze close by, then eased what he realised was a bar cloth off the injury. Whatever was underneath the beer and blood-soaked cloth would need a very thorough cleaning. He gave a huff of disbelief. The cut was millimetres—one or two—from the jugular vein. It was also deep and filthy.

'Well, Doc?' Ullr asked. 'What's the verdict?'

'You'll live.' As long as Felix made sure he didn't catch sepsis. He aimed a penlight at the wound. It didn't look pretty. 'How much wound glue did he use?'

'Small squirt,' Ullr said in his happy-go-lucky way. 'Why? Should've used more?'

The glob of skin glue was much larger than a squirt, but this was a stitches job. His friend had done the equivalent of tying a used toothpick to a compound fracture.

He pressed some clean gauze over the wound and asked Ullr to hold it while he taped it in place. He'd need a second pair of hands to properly irrigate it, check for any ancillary injuries to the surrounding tissue and properly stitch it together.

'I'm just going to fetch someone to help. I won't be a minute, but press this button if you feel faint or need help.'

'If you're getting a nurse, make sure you get a pretty one, yeah?' Ullr called after him. 'I don't want to be the only singleton at Christmas.'

'We're not a dating agency,' Felix intoned, darkly aware that he and this lunkhead shared the same fate. Single at Christmas. Again. He hadn't minded the last few years. This year, though? With all of the *hygge* research, coupled with Matti's enthusiasm, it already felt bleak.

He headed to the main desk, hoping one of their regular nurses, a six foot four ex-paratrooper called Lars, would be free, but he caught a glimpse of him disappearing into the lift wheeling someone to Surgery.

His next thought was Matti. She was pretty, obviously, but if Ullr thought he was in with a chance she'd shut it down sharpish. Kindly but clearly. The way she'd made it clear to him that all she wanted was friendship.

It had been a few days since they'd had dinner at his sister's and although she'd seemed to have a good time, since then he'd sensed a cooling. She was still bright and friendly at work, but when he'd suggested getting together to go see a gingerbread Copenhagen at an artisan baker's, something he was sure she'd love, she'd made her apologies. Same again last night when he'd asked her if she wanted to join him at a canalside café to watch the annual Santa Lucia kayak parade, a glittering, magical spectacle where dozens of boaters took to the canals wearing 'candle crowns', a compliment to the pedestrian version at Tivoli where young girls holding candles led the parade. Again, she'd made her excuses. To be fair, she literally lived on the canal and there was every chance she was watching it with Astrid. Or, he allowed the thought, packing up her things in preparation for Cambridge. Not that he had heard she'd got the job, but why else would she be avoiding him?

His mood lifted when he spied Matti at the registrar's desk, asking if there was anything she could help with.

'How do you feel about helping me stitch up a war wound?'

Her eyebrows rose, intrigued. 'What kind of war?'

'Ice hockey. Skate blade met a player's neck.'

She sucked in a breath. 'Crikey. Shouldn't they be in surgery?'

'Missed the jugular,' he explained as they headed to the exam room, stopping to collect a kidney tray full of saline. 'Nickname's Lucky. It's an apt moniker.'

'Still, though. That's cutting it close.' She threw him a glance. 'Ha-ha.'

'Yeah, I get it. Cutting it close. He had a mate glue it together before going out for drinks. There was a wall,' he deadpanned.

'Beer goggles?'

'Schnapps.'

She winced. Not only did alcohol act like a blood thinner, it was an ill-advised way to rehydrate after blood loss.

'Still bleeding?'

'Some. He used the barman's well-used beer towel to stem the flow.'

She made a comedy retch. At least that was what he thought it was.

'Right,' she said, rubbing her hands together. 'Time to put my needlework to the test.'

'Well done, Doc!' Ullr cheered when Matti came in the room. 'Just what I ordered.'

'A tray of saline syringes?' Matti asked.

'A curvy Christmas present,' Ullr said, fluttering his pale lashes at her. 'To help ease the pain.'

Matti shot Felix a *thanks for nothing* look. 'I'm afraid the only pain relief you'll be getting from me is an anaesthetic.'

Matti gave Felix an *Is this guy for real?* look, then set to work loading a tray with all of the necessary items they'd need to irrigate the wound. Felix prepared another for the suturing that would follow.

Ullr thought he was still in with a chance. 'Lady Doc, listen. My body's a temple. I don't want anaesthetic. Love is the only drug I need.'

'I don't think ice hockey injuries were considered when that saying came about.' Her tone was friendly but firm enough to make it clear. She wasn't interested.

They took his blood pressure, assured themselves the blood loss didn't warrant an infusion then took note of a few more stats and asked him about his allergies, penicillin in particular. He'd need antibiotics.

Ullr, undeterred, caught Matti by the wrist. 'Got yourself a boyfriend already, Lady Doc?'

'Hey!' It took every fibre of restraint Felix had not to grab Ullr by the collar and frogmarch him out of the hospital. He was a doctor, well within his rights to call out sexual harassment. And security. 'Let her go. Dr Meadows was clear. She's not interested.'

Ullr fuzzed his lips at him, made a show of letting go of her wrist, but was undeterred by Felix's reprimand. 'How 'bout you give me your phone? I'll put my number in it and you can give me a booty call whenever you like. I'm not sexist.'

'Clearly,' Matti said. Then, 'I'll pass, thanks. Dr Beck? I'm ready to irrigate when you are.'

Felix made sure he wasn't smirking when he turned around. 'Right then, Ullr. Let's see how you fare without the anaesthetic.'

About two seconds. Screamed like they were sawing his leg off.

Once they'd applied a topical anaesthetic and some local, they began.

It took longer than anticipated to irrigate the wound as the glue his teammate had used had not only failed to keep the skin sealed but had managed to attract a plenitude of debris. Once they'd checked for any signs of damage to his neurovascular and musculotendinous tissue, Felix cleared the small table they'd been using and brought over the suture kit.

'I want her to do it,' Ullr said, ever hopeful. 'And remember, no more anaesthetic. No pain no gain, am I right?'

She raised her eyebrows. 'I think we'll go with protocol on this one.'

'Honestly, Doc, I don't need—' He howled when Matti inserted a needle to give him some additional nerve blocker.

'Handled like a warrior,' she said cheerfully.

Ullr closed his eyes and lay back on the pillow. 'Do what you have to. Wake me when it's over.'

Matti loaded the needle holder with thread but then, to Felix's surprise, abruptly rose from the stool and asked him if he was all right on his own. She had a patient she needed to check.

Felix agreed but wasn't buying the excuse. Something else was up. She was a fastidious physician. Efficient, focused. It wasn't unknown for doctors to be distracted by something mid-flow and accidentally overlook a detail in a handover, but abruptly leave one patient for another? That wasn't like her.

He finished the sutures, then, realising Ullr had fallen into a post-celebration sleep, decided letting him sleep it off wouldn't be a bad thing.

He headed back to the main desk, stopping short when he caught a glimpse of a red-gold ponytail being flicked out from beneath a coat collar at the main doors.

'Was that Dr Meadows?'

Hannah, who was logging a new patient in to the system, nodded. 'She wasn't feeling well. Her shift was about to end, so she left.'

So she had told a fib. A small one, most likely for the patient's benefit. But why not tell him?

'Anything serious?'

'She didn't say.'

Normally, the doctors checked with him before leaving. It was strange Matti hadn't.

Hannah handed him a tablet and nodded at a teenager cradling his wrist. 'I assume you're free?'

'Of course,' he said distractedly, giving the exit another glance. No sign of Matti.

'Are we going somewhere or are you going to check me out here?' the teenager asked.

'C'mon,' he said, painfully aware of the weight in his voice. 'Follow me.'

'Oh… Dr Beck?' Hannah called.

'Yes?'

'I forgot. This letter came by courier for Dr Meadows. Do you mind keeping it safe for her?'

He glanced at the letterhead, instantly wishing he hadn't.

'Not in the slightest.' He took the letter and beckoned to the teenager. 'Let's take a look at that wrist, shall we?' If it was broken, it would heal. But if the letter he'd tucked into his pocket was what he thought it was, he wasn't entirely sure he would.

CHAPTER TWENTY

MATTI STARED AT the three tests she'd laid on the kitchen island, not knowing what to feel.

Numb. Scared. Confused. Those worked. She also felt like an idiot. And, for a fleeting moment, happy. But mostly she felt too overwhelmed to come up with one perfect description, other than *pregnant*.

She was a doctor and prided herself on being able to diagnose a pregnancy on symptoms alone and yet it had taken her far too long to put together her own symptoms and reach the same conclusion. She'd dismissed her recent fatigue as normal after the intense month she and Felix had been working before and after their paid jobs to put together the Holiday *Hygge* Fest. She'd written off her occasional swells of nausea and heightened sense of smell as her body's response to unfamiliar foods.

There was also the period she'd missed. She'd thought it had been due last week, but hers had never been regular so she hadn't thought twice about it. It took one of the nurses jokingly asking her if she was pregnant when she'd run out of the ice hockey guy's treatment room on the brink of throwing up after getting a whiff of schnapps, sweat and blood.

Given what she knew about Felix, pregnancy hadn't even occurred to her, but still. It wasn't uncommon for someone who'd failed to conceive with one partner to find success with another. Felix's ex-wife being a case in point. Now she had three little smiley faces staring up at her as a reminder that condoms weren't always a failsafe.

A knock on the door made her jump. Hopefully, it was Astrid with the photo album she'd wanted to share. She swept the tests into a drawer, not quite ready to share her own news. She answered the door and almost slammed it shut again.

It was Felix.

He held up a package and gave her a quizzical smile. 'I brought soup.'

'Oh?'

'Hannah said you weren't feeling well,' he said cautiously. 'It's chicken soup. A cure-all, according to my mother. I also got cheese soup for myself, but if you'd rather have that—'

'No.' She shook her head. She wasn't hungry. 'You have it.'

'The cheese or the chicken?' He looked perplexed. Which was fair. She hadn't invited him in, smiled or done anything a normal person would do if the father of the baby they'd just discovered they were expecting appeared out of the blue with some get well soup.

'I'm pregnant,' she blurted. His jaw dropped. Panicked, she made jazz hands and uttered a strangled, 'Surprise!'

He shot a look over each shoulder as if expecting a different surprise. There was not another surprise.

'By me?'

A cyclist rode by singing a Christmas carol, which made her think about the baby Jesus.

'Yes, by you. This wasn't an immaculate conception, Felix.'

When more revellers appeared, she realised this was a conversation they should be having inside.

She invited him in and after offering him a drink, which he refused, she pulled the tests out of the drawer and laid them on the coffee table in front of him. He was still wearing his coat and holding onto the bag of soup.

'Please say something.' *Something positive. Something that will make this less overwhelming.*

'Yes, of course. It's just—' He scrubbed his hand through his hair. 'My brain's gone all fuzzy.'

'Yours isn't the only one!' She laughed, but not because she was being funny.

He looked shell-shocked. As if part of him wanted to unleash the world's biggest smile and another part wanted to run for the hills.

Please say you're happy, she silently pleaded.

'I'm sorry, I know I'm not saying or doing whatever it is I'm meant to, but… I don't understand. You're pregnant with my child?'

Matti sucked in a breath. She knew he wasn't accusing her of sleeping around, but the question still hurt.

'That's what the tests say. Well, they don't specifically say it's yours, but you're the only one I've been with in actual years.'

They stared at one another until Matti couldn't stand the silence any more. She sat down in the chair opposite him. 'Look. I've only just found out myself. So, in terms of being shocked, we're on an even playing field here.'

He nodded. Touched each of the tests with the tip of his index finger.

'Oh, my God, Felix. You're killing me! Are you happy? Numb? Panicked? Please, please don't have this be the moment you retreat back into your shell.'

'I'm happy,' he said, blue eyes sheening over. He gave them a swipe. 'It's miraculous. Of course I'm happy, but…'

'But what?'

He rose, pulled a thick envelope out of his pocket and handed it to her. When her eyes lit on the familiar crest, she knew in an instant why he was reluctant to tell her what he was really feeling. He thought she had the job in Cambridge.

He'd been preparing himself to say goodbye to her, only to discover he was saying goodbye to her and the child he'd thought he'd never have.

'Felix, I'm sure this isn't an acceptance letter.'

'It's thick.'

'It's the modern world. They normally send emails or phone these days.'

Vividly aware of his eyes on her, she scanned the letter. She had the job. A dream job at a prestigious teaching hospital in a perfectly perfect university town.

'I got you a present,' he said, handing her a small bag. 'For congratulations.' He cleared his throat. 'Should've bought two.'

'Felix...' Matti began. This wasn't how she'd wanted to share the news of her pregnancy with him. It felt cruel. Like dangling a steak in front of a starving man then announcing it was for someone else. *Here's what you're not getting.* But did he really think she would take the job now?

'Open it,' he said softly.

She pulled out the snow globe and burst into tears. It was a miniature Cambridge college. In the centre of the green was a strawberry-blonde in a lab coat. She sobbed, 'You had a snow globe made for me.' It was the sweetest thing a man had ever done for her. Thoughtful. Specific. Selfless. Just like him.

He gave her a sad smile and, because he was him, a box of tissues. 'I thought the letter probably contained good news. It's never a thick letter if it's bad news.'

She wiped away some tears then picked up the snow globe, shook it, and as the glittery crystals fell over the tiny towers of the college chapel where she could, if she took the job, baptise her child, she felt torn in a way she'd never experienced. As if she were two people who had to merge into one to go forward. Which version of herself did she want to be?

'I don't know what to do,' she admitted. She couldn't decide without knowing what he thought. 'Tell me what you're thinking. Tell me what to do.'

He looked at her, those beautiful blue eyes of his looking every bit at sea as hers must be.

'Matti, I—' He shoved his hands through his hair and shook his head. 'I will do everything in my power to support whatever decision you make. I am so, so happy you are pregnant, but it isn't my place to tell you what I think you should do.'

'But—' She faltered. Why? What was his heart telling him? Did he love her? Want to stay in the friend zone? Or, a more painful thought surfaced, did he think she was lying about the child being his?

His sister's voice came to her.

'Felix is the type of man who wants the people he loves to be happy. And he will do whatever it takes to make it so, even if it destroys him.'

He knew what an amazing opportunity the job would be. A career changer. And he didn't want to stand in her way. But what was a job when the other option was having a child with the man she loved?

She held the snow globe to her chest as the thought crystallised. She loved him. She'd been keeping so many confused feelings at bay, but now that she'd allowed the thought she knew it was true. But if she told him and he didn't feel the same…it might break her. God, she wished he'd say something.

'I'm going to have the baby,' she announced with a certainty that surprised both of them. It sank in. She was going to have a baby.

She stared at Felix, searching his eyes, his face, his body, for any sort of sign that he thought this was a good thing.

His chin began to shake. 'Good.' A tear streaked down his cheek. 'I'm really… I'm blown away.' He blew out a huff of air as a few more tears slid down his face. He swiped them away. 'Thank you for telling me.'

'In what universe wouldn't I tell you?' she demanded.

He shook his head. 'You know what I mean.'

'No, Felix. I don't.' She was on the brink of saying it wasn't the kind of thing you kept a secret, but she had kept the fact she'd applied for a job in Cambridge to herself. A safety net, she'd told herself. A professional salve if her personal life blew up here which, to be fair, was happening. But also, she was keeping the fact she loved him to herself.

A memory of his sister saying something niggled at her mind. Something about Felix and fatherhood. She tried and failed to pin it down.

What she really wanted was to crawl into his lap and feel his arms around her. Match her heartbeat to his.

He needs to know if he can be a part of the child's life, Matti. You're torturing him. And then a new thought hit like a train.

He'd given her the snow globe *after* she'd told him she was pregnant. Meaning, he thought she should go to Cambridge because he didn't love her the way she loved him.

A swell of nausea rose in her throat. One that wasn't caused by her pregnancy.

The last time she'd believed a man was in love with her he'd rejected her when she'd been at her most vulnerable. She'd vowed never to let that happen again. And yet here she was, feeling more vulnerable than she had in hospital, putting her fate in someone else's hands. She willed him to say, *Stay. Please, my love, please stay. We'll raise our child together.*

But he didn't.

Tears blurred her vision. She angrily shook them away and lifted up the snow globe. 'Was this your way of saying goodbye?'

A flash of anguish creased his features. 'Matti, I—' He

stopped, regrouped. 'It was just something I thought you'd like. You're reading too much into it.'

'Am I?' she demanded, suddenly seeing red. 'Or is it that I'm "too much"?'

He looked at her, anguished. As if a thousand things he wanted to say to her were waging battle in his very cell structure. He wasn't denying it, though.

A hardness formed within her. Felix was right. She had a decision to make. It was her body. Her career. Her future. Whatever she decided would have the biggest impact on her and the child she was carrying. But it was *their* child.

He was a grown man. He could speak, put words together to help her make an informed decision. But instead he was putting it all on her.

'I think…' he began. 'I think it might be a good idea for each of us to digest this a bit. On our own.'

'You want to think about our baby on your own?' Her voice was shaking. Her whole body, actually. Every pore was filled with waves of emotion. Anger, disbelief, fear, heartache. All of the above.

'There's a lot to think about, Matti. Where you want to live. How you want to raise the child. Who you want to raise it with.'

She wanted to raise the baby with him! But for some reason, the words got stuck in her throat. She did, but only if he felt the same way. And that was something she refused to force out of him. He wanted time to think? Fine.

'Of course,' she said, not entirely amicably. 'You go think your thoughts and I'll think mine. Me and my snow globe.' She spat out the words and now that they hung between them, she regretted her tone. She was lashing out at him because she was scared. Which made her realise that if she was scared, he was too.

'I'm sorry. I didn't mean to sound awful. It's just so strange how two people who can handle life-and-death situations every day at work can't handle this.'

He gave her a long hard look, one she couldn't even begin to read. 'Whatever happens, we'll handle it. But not tonight, okay? Get some rest. Have some soup if you can. I promise it'll help settle your stomach.'

He rose and headed for the door. She stared at his back, willing him to turn around and tell her he loved her. That he was happier than he'd ever been. That they'd run off into the sunset and make a new snow globe with the three of them. When he opened the door, her heart began pounding so hard she could hardly see straight. Was this it?

She let out a little cry of relief when he turned back to her at the door, but when he spoke she felt more at sea than ever.

'I'm really happy for you, Matti. Truly. You deserve to make whatever choice will truly make you happy.'

Then he left, making it clear that the one thing he thought she didn't deserve was him.

CHAPTER TWENTY-ONE

FELIX DOUBLE-CHECKED THE address, then knocked on the door of the one house in Copenhagen where he'd never thought he'd be welcome. When his ex opened the door she ushered him in.

They didn't bother with small talk while she poured them both a coffee. He heard her children playing upstairs. Saw their art on the refrigerator. Their handmade decorations on the tree, twinkling away in the corner. A few presents tucked beneath it.

Ane joined him at the solid wood kitchen table which, like so many homes in Denmark, had an Advent wreath at the centre and a candle burnt down to the single digits.

'You look well,' he said, not sure whether to get straight to the point or give her a context for his sudden appearance. He'd rung her and asked if they could talk. She'd been surprised, of course, to hear from him. He'd assured her he wasn't asking in order to rehash their marriage or stir up her life; he just needed to know something and wanted to ask her in person.

'Thank you.' She took a sip of her coffee. 'If you don't mind me saying, you've looked better.'

He laughed. 'I've…um… I'm kind of going through it right now.'

Her gaze sharpened. 'Are you okay, Felix?'

'Yes and no,' he said, then, realising his answer could easily be misread, added, 'I'm not sick or anything; it's more of a problem here.' He pressed his hand against his chest.

'And you came to me?' She didn't hide her surprise.

It was a surprise to him too, but when he'd left Matti's heart in tatters, beating himself up for not telling her what he felt, he'd realised there was a question he'd never asked Ane that had been haunting him for years.

'Do you think I'd be a good father?' He searched her face as she reacted to the question. There was a lot to decipher. Surprise, confusion and then a softening.

'Are you kidding? Felix—' she reached across the table and gave his hand a squeeze '—I think you'd be a wonderful father. The way you were with your sister's children, changing nappies, rocking them to sleep, playing the same silly games over and over. That was half the reason I fell in love with you. I can't believe you had to ask.' She smiled at him as if he was being ridiculous, then, abruptly, it faded. 'Check that,' she said. 'I know why you asked.' She closed her eyes and gave them a rub.

When she looked at him again, he saw a version of her he wasn't familiar with. A more mature version, who didn't shy away from self-reflection. 'Felix, I owe you a long over-due apology.' She held up her hand so he wouldn't interrupt. 'When we were together, trying to conceive, I went a bit crazy. I think we both know I lived life like I was in a fairy tale. I had a great childhood, studied what I wanted in university, fell in love with a handsome doctor. I thought we'd fall pregnant as easily as women do in soap operas.' She rolled her eyes and gave an embarrassed laugh. 'I'm a bit horrified when I think of what I put you through. Demanding you do all of those kooky things. I was so focused on making sure we were ticking every single thing off a ridiculously long list, I didn't notice that what I was really doing was making you one of the items on the checklist, rather than enjoying what we had. I shut you out, Felix. And I'm so, so sorry for letting you think you were to blame for everything.'

'You didn't,' Felix said.

'I did,' she countered solidly. 'Believe me. I know I went to extremes to try and help us conceive. To this day, if I even smell a pineapple I run for the hills.'

He laughed. 'Good old bromelain. The enzyme that keeps on giving.'

They shared a smile.

She dropped her gaze for a moment then asked, 'Are you considering becoming a father?'

He nodded, unable to speak as the knot in his chest doubled in size. He wasn't just considering being a father, he was going to be one. And a husband, if Matti would have him.

He rode towards Matti's with the urgency of an organ donor courier. His heart, which he'd put on ice for far too long, was finally ready to take whatever life threw at him. He only hoped that when he reached Matti, she hadn't closed her heart to him.

The journey was almost comical in the number of obstacles it threw up. A tumble of merrymakers clutching one another as they left a bar. Couples so smitten they stepped into the road without looking. An elderly gentleman wearing a large fur hat standing in the bike line while his enormous dog sniffed a tree.

He'd been one of these people. So wrapped up in his own life he didn't notice the world around him. Ane, too. It was mind-boggling how two people supposedly living a shared life had actually been living two, very separate, realities. That wasn't what he wanted with Matti. He wanted a shared reality. A shared life. A child they raised together. A family.

He was in such a rush to get to her he made a hash of getting off his bike, stumbled, bashing his knee on the cobbled street, grazing his hands, his cheek. No matter. He was in love. He hobble-ran to her door, sounded the brass knocker set in the centre of a large holiday wreath.

No answer.

He tried again.

Nothing.

She had every right to ignore him of course. He'd done the one thing he knew would cut deep. He'd left her holding her heart out to him without giving any answers. He called out her name. Nothing. Screw it. He was going to go full *Cat on a Hot Tin Roof.*

'Matti!'

A window scraped open behind him. He whipped round. Astrid.

'She's here, Felix.' Judging by her expression, Matti had told her everything and he wasn't in her good books.

'Would it be all right to speak with her?' he asked.

'It depends,' Astrid said.

'I want to tell her I love her.'

A couple of women walking past sighed and said something about Romeo.

Astrid narrowed her gaze. Saying you loved someone clearly wasn't enough.

'I messed up,' he said. 'I shouldn't have left. But if she agrees to see me, I'll answer every question she has. Tell her anything she needs to know.'

Astrid disappeared. The seconds ticked past as if they were hours.

Astrid returned to the window. 'You have to wait a minute.'

'She'll see me?'

'She's getting the first aid kit.'

Felix frowned, confused, then put his hand to his cheek and saw that he was bleeding. He looked up at Astrid and caught her hiding a smile.

'I've been a bit of an idiot.' A sudden panic gripped him.

Heart in throat, he checked his pocket, heaving a sigh of relief that he hadn't broken what was inside.

Still no sign of Matti.

'She's coming, right?' he asked.

Astrid shushed him with a smile.

He felt as if his heart was going to explode.

'I love you, Matti Meadows,' he called out. 'I love you, I love you, I love you.'

She opened the door.

'I love you,' he said again, crossing to her. 'I love you.'

She narrowed her eyes, inspecting him. 'That cut needs to be cleaned. Come in.'

She turned and headed up the stairs. He followed, praying the fact she was letting him in meant she'd be open to accepting his apology.

'Sit there.' She pointed at a kitchen chair. Astrid had closed the window and was pouring him a cup of tea.

'I'll leave you two to talk,' she said, putting two mugs on the table, giving Matti's shoulder a gentle stroke before she left.

'Matti...' he began, flinching when she pressed a bit of gauze soaked in astringent to his cheek. 'I'm so sorry. I shouldn't have left the way I did. Ow!'

'Sit still,' she instructed sternly. 'You were saying?'

His heart pumped a ray of hope through his chest. 'My head went to every worst-case scenario when it should have been focusing on the good.'

'Your head?'

'My heart,' he corrected. 'I was scared. Scared I wasn't the man you deserve. I was an epic—' He scrambled to find the best word.

'*Røv banan?*' she suggested.

Ass banana was close.

'*Klaphat?*'

Big dumb idiot worked, too.

'*Vatnisse*,' he offered. 'As it's the holidays.'

A cowardly elf was an apt description, but a better word came to him.

'Selfish. I thought telling you the decision was yours was the selfless thing to do, but it wasn't.'

'No,' she agreed. 'It wasn't. Hold still.' She held up a plaster that had little elves on it. 'Fitting, don't you think?'

He laughed. 'It's perfect.' Just like her. He waited until she put the plaster on, then, as instructed, held out his hands for her to inspect. She wiped them free of debris with a level of care that, once again, felt like an infusion of hope.

'I want you to be happy,' he said.

'Even if that means moving to Cambridge?'

She hadn't said *alone*. And yes. He'd move to Cambridge.

'Even if it means moving to Timbuktu.'

She stood back and inspected him. 'Any other injuries?'

He stretched out his knee, gave it a rub, then pressed his hands to his heart. 'Here.'

She blinked a few times, chin quivering. 'I don't want to raise this baby on my own.'

He rose and thumbed a tear away from her cheek.

'I know. I don't want that either.' He wanted to kiss her, but he hadn't earned that right yet.

'What do you want, Felix?' Matti asked, more tears trickling down her cheeks. 'Honestly? What do you want?'

He pulled out another chair and gestured for her to sit. She did and, to his relief, didn't pull away when he took her hands in his.

'I want to love you, Mathilde Meadows. You and our child. I want to marry you. I want to make you laugh. I want to decorate Christmas cookies with you. Make paper snowflakes and real snow angels. I want to go sledging on Christmas morning. Embark on a voyage of discovery gathering every ounce of *hygge* we can.'

She hiccupped a laugh.

'I want all that and more,' he continued. 'If you'll have me. And if you don't—'

She pressed her fingers to his lips. 'I'll have you.'

Tears filled his eyes. 'I promise I won't ever leave you like that again. Give you cause to doubt my love. I'm not just saying this because of the baby,' he added, wanting to make sure she knew he had fallen in love with her weeks ago.

'Are you saying it because you actually think I really am Wonder Woman?' A watery smile teased at her lips.

'I'm saying it because you are a wonderful woman. One I would very much like to kiss, if you'll let me.'

She did, and as their lips met he felt a peace descend, a wholeness he had never known. The kisses were soft, gentle, loving. When they drew back, he remembered the gift.

'I have something for you.'

She gave him a teasing look. 'More soup?'

'Not quite.' He took the package out of his pocket and handed it to her.

She unwrapped the snow globe and this time he knew her tears were happy ones. Inside the tiny orb was a clutch of snow-covered trees, a man bent on one knee, holding a ring box open in front of a woman with red-gold hair.

'Yes,' she whispered, eyes gleaming. 'Yes.'

EPILOGUE

MATTI HAD IMAGINED their wedding day more times than she could count. But this, the real, actual day, was exceeding her dreams.

Not because it was opulent or at a chic city centre hotel or a soaring cathedral in the heart of an English market town, but because it was being celebrated with a boisterous, loving, completely wonderful group of friends and family who she adored. Not quite as much as she adored the man standing in front of the chapel's enormous Christmas tree, a smile on his face, hand outstretched, itching with the same anticipation to be together.

They held hands as they made their vows.

The celebrant hit the perfect tone, mixing humour with reminders that the promises they were making were not made solely for the two of them, but for everyone in the room, because their commitment to one another was also a promise not to isolate themselves, but to ensure they shared their love with everyone they cared for.

Matti felt a kick in her stomach and laid Felix's hand on it so he could feel. She looked like she'd swallowed a bowling ball. Not at all what she'd imagined she'd look like on her wedding day as a girl, but as Felix smiled at their second child's wriggling and she shot a smile to Astrid, who was holding their toddler, she felt more beautiful than she ever had. She'd learnt to see herself through Felix's eyes, as well as her loved ones'. Felix, too. Not to mention the large group of friends they'd made in the years since they'd begun their *hygge* challenge. This, she thought, this was the most *hygge* thing she'd ever done.

The first round of tears came as she shakily repeated her vows after the celebrant. The next when Felix did the same, the baby still wriggling away, as if she wished she could be with them. She gave her belly a rub.

You're here with us, little one. You're here. And we love you.

Once the vows were completed, Felix cupped her face in his hands and gave her a long, slow, delicious kiss, ignoring the playful catcalls from their friends.

'Thank you for sharing your life with me,' he whispered against her lips.

'Thank you for opening your heart to me.'

'I can't imagine what my life would've been like if I hadn't.'

'Luckily, you'll never know.' They savoured another delicious kiss.

Felix took their son in his arms and, holding hands, they headed back down the aisle beneath a cloud of silvery glitter. A family united. A family for evermore. The perfect snow globe moment.

* * * * *

If you enjoyed this story, check out these other great reads from Annie O'Neil

Snowbound Christmas with the Italian Doc
Christmas with the Single Dad Doc
In Bali with the Single Dad
New Year Kiss with His Cinderella

All available now!

MILLS & BOON®

Coming next month

FESTIVE REUNION WITH THE DOCTOR
Deanne Anders

Anna had changed in many ways since the last time he'd seen her.

There was a maturity in her emerald eyes and a confidence in her walk that even in medical school she'd lacked. But one thing hadn't changed. She still had a stubborn streak a mile long.

'Come on in,' he said, giving up. He'd might as well get this over with so that he could get back to his patient.

Walking around to his desk, he motioned her to join him.

'Whose X-ray is this?' Anna asked as she bent over him, her hair brushing against his shoulder, the fragrance hitting him hard.

Memories of their time together poured through him. He remembered the feel of her hair as he'd run his hands through it. He remembered the smell that had lingered on his pillow long after she had left him.

And he remembered the letter she'd left behind, the one that tore him apart until he'd wrapped his mind around the fact that what she'd done, though hurtful, had been the right thing for both of them.

Continue reading

FESTIVE REUNION WITH THE DOCTOR
Deanne Anders

Available next month
millsandboon.co.uk

afterglow BOOKS

Afterglow Books is a trend-led, trope-filled list of books with diverse, authentic and relatable characters, a wide array of voices and representations, plus real world trials and tribulations. Featuring all the tropes you could possibly want (think small-town settings, fake relationships, grumpy vs sunshine, enemies to lovers) and all with a generous dose of spice in every story.

♪ @millsandboonuk
⊙ @millsandboonuk
afterglowbooks.co.uk

#AfterglowBooks

For all the latest book news, exclusive content and giveaways scan the QR code below to sign up to the Afterglow newsletter:

SCAN ME

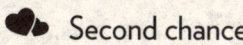
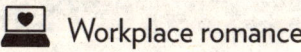
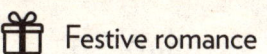

LET'S TALK
Romance

For exclusive extracts, competitions and special offers, find us online:

f MillsandBoon

X @MillsandBoon

◉ @MillsandBoonUK

♪ @MillsandBoonUK

Get in touch on 01413 063 232